# First Born Son

## BOOK 1 IN THE
## PHILIPPE DUVAL SERIES

## J MARY MASTERS

First published 2023 by PMA Books, A divn of Peter Masters &
Associates, ABN 72 172 119 877
Unit 111, 1 Halcyon Way, Bli Bli Qld 4560, Australia

 A catalogue record for this
book is available from the
National Library of Australia

ISBN 978-0-6458637-1-0

Cover design: J D Smith Design, UK
www.jdsmith-design.co.uk
Author photograph: Sheree McArthur
www.shereemcarthurphotography.com.au


www.pmabooks.com
Tel + (61) (0) 488 224 929
Email enquiries@pmabooks.com

# First Born Son

BOOK 1 IN THE
PHILIPPE DUVAL SERIES

## J MARY MASTERS

WWW.PMABOOKS.COM

# About the author

J Mary Masters (Judith) was born in Rockhampton, Queensland, Australia in the 1950s, the youngest of four children and raised on a cattle property. For more than twenty years, she was involved in the magazine publishing industry as a senior executive.

Having now given up full time magazine work, Judith is devoting her time to her writing career, with an emphasis on writing for women readers. Her stories feature a mix of town and country settings, drawing heavily on her early country life and also paying homage to her favourite city: Sydney.

She is a member of the Queensland Writers Centre (QWC) and the Australian Society of Authors (ASA). Judith has also completed a fiction writing course with noted literary agency Curtis Brown.

Judith now lives on Queensland's Sunshine Coast with her husband Peter.

Readers are invited to contact Judith through the following channels.

| | |
|---|---|
| Website | jmarymasters.com |
| Twitter | @judithmasters |
| Blog | jmarymasters.blog |
| Facebook | www.facebook.com/JudithMMasters |
| Email | jmarymasters1@gmail.com |

## *Belleville series*

BOOK 1 Julia's Story
BOOK 2 To Love, Honour and Betray
BOOK 3 Return to Prior Park
BOOK 4 Heirs and Successors  (2023)

## *Philippe Duval series*

BOOK 1 First Born Son  (2023)
BOOK 2 Price to Pay  (coming 2024)

# Acknowledgements & insights

Firstly, I would like to acknowledge the readers who have contacted me to say they enjoyed my Belleville series. It means a lot to an author to know someone is reading—and enjoying—their work. *Thank you.*

I describe *First Born Son* as a companion book to the latest Belleville book, *Heirs and Successors*. It covers a similar time frame to *Heirs and Successors*; however this book deals with the Julia Belleville/Philippe Duval relationship. I had to make the choice to publish a separate title to ensure that *Heirs and Successors* did not become a book too large, too complicated and too unwieldy to read.

Writers often say characters take on a life of their own, the writing being a mere conduit to getting their story on the page. As soon as I began exploring the early life of Philippe Duval, I knew it had to be more than a few chapters in the fourth Belleville novel.

Inevitably, there is some overlap between *Heirs and Successors* and *First Born Son*. And for readers meeting these characters for the first time, I hope I have provided enough information by way of background. You're invited to check out www.jmarymasters.com for more information.

I hope you enjoy the book. And if you do, please tell your friends.

Good reading.

*Judith M Masters writing as J Mary Masters*

# Key characters

| | |
|---|---|
| Dr Philippe Duval | Surgeon |
| Julia Duval (formerly Belleville/Fitzroy) | Philippe's wife |
| Pippa Duval | Julia & Philippe's daughter |

## AUSTRALIA

| | |
|---|---|
| Richard Belleville | Elder son of the family |
| Kate Belleville (formerly Lester) | Richard's second wife |
| William Belleville | Younger son of the family |
| Alice Belleville (formerly Fitzroy) | William's wife |
| Paul Belleville | Richard & Catherine's son |
| Anthony Belleville | Richard & Catherine's son |
| Susan Belleville | Richard & Kate's daughter |
| Marianne Belleville | William & Alice's daughter |
| James Fitzroy | Julia's former husband |
| John Fitzroy | James & Julia's son |

SYDNEY

| | |
|---|---|
| Dr Robert Clarke | Registrar/Surgeon |
| Patricia Clarke | His wife |
| Anita Clarke | Their daughter |
| David Clarke | Robert Clarke's brother |
| Deborah Clarke | His wife |
| Karen Clarke | Their daughter |
| Bianca Ferrari | Karen's business partner |
| Ian Dixon | Barrister |
| Angela Dixon | His wife |
| Lucy Dixon | Their daughter |
| Tim Lester | Kate Belleville's son |
| Nancy Lester | Kate Belleville's daughter |
| Kenneth Wright | Lawyer |
| Nicholas Gleeson | Lawyer |

## AMERICA

| | |
|---|---|
| Walter William Cox II | Patriarch |
| Walter William Cox III | Son |
| Barbara Cox | Wife |
| Walter William Cox IV | Son |
| Virginia Cox | Daughter |
| Clarence White | Butler |
| Frederick | Chauffeur |
| Mrs Anderson | Housekeeper |
| Howard Davis | Lawyer |

# PROLOGUE

*June 1968*

AS PHILIPPE DUVAL, EMINENT SURGEON, husband to Julia, father to Pippa, boarded the aeroplane that would take him back to the land of his birth, he had no inkling of what lay ahead of him, no foreknowledge of how his life was about to change forever. He had no way of knowing the journey, which began on a cold blustery winter's day in Sydney, would mark the end of the life he had known.

To him, the journey was simply a chance to revisit New York, the city of his younger days, while he helped his daughter fast track her medical career.

As he settled into his seat, he let his thoughts drift aimlessly across the full spectrum of his life so far, as if silently marking some invisible report card, but only he would know where he had marked himself as a failure.

On the whole, he was satisfied. Professionally, he was content. And personally? He enjoyed the companionship of his daughter. And their shared interest in medicine. Beyond that, his mind began to wander. His marriage? Not a failure certainly. But if he was honest he wouldn't count it as an unqualified success either. Had it come too late for them?

His mind drifted to the probable reason for his doubt. And then he rebuked himself silently. Even to think such thoughts was a disloyalty. He turned back to the medical journal that had previously failed to hold his attention.

Pippa sat quietly beside him, immersed in her own thoughts.

'I hope my mother's not lonely while we're away,' she said suddenly, aware they were both abandoning her.

'If she's lonely,' her father said with absolute assurance, 'she'll go up north to visit her family.'

Pippa nodded. Like her father, her thoughts had drifted to her mother. There had been times when she had wondered if her mother was truly happy with city life compared with her country upbringing.

Time and again the same questions came unbidden into Pippa's mind. What if she had never discovered me and my father? Would she have been happier and more contented continuing with her first marriage rather than marrying my father? Had the marriage come too late for them? She would have been alarmed to know the same thought had occurred to her father as he sat beside her.

With these half-formed thoughts, Pippa's mind turned to what lay ahead. Her father had gone to great lengths to secure the short hospital internship for her. She worried, given his reputation, they would have the same high expectations of her as a doctor. Even now she doubted she would ever be as committed to medicine as he had been. And still was.

And then she reminded herself there was another, even more pressing reason, for her to go to America and especially to New York. She had a desperate urge to fill in the blanks in her father's life, just as she had finally been able to fill in the blanks in her own early life.

Would she ever be able to fully forgive her mother for giving her up at birth? Just occasionally, her bitterness resurfaced until her rational mind prevailed. Her mother had been given no choice by her family. By her own mother, in fact. The shame of an illegitimate child was unendurable to the Belleville family of Prior Park.

But this time, she did not dwell on the past as she might have done. Instead she settled back in her seat and began to contemplate the future with a mixture of anxiety and excitement.

Beside her, her father seemed immersed in the latest medical journal yet after a few minutes, she noticed he had not turned a page at all.

'A good article?' she asked, nodding towards the magazine.

He smiled.

'Interesting,' he said, 'but I'm finding it hard to concentrate.'

She nodded and smiled, thinking she understood exactly what he meant.

He let his daughter go on assuming she knew what had caused his concentration to falter. She would have been alarmed to know the truth.

Even as he had attempted to return to his reading, Philippe's mind had drifted back to his final visitor on his last day at the hospital for some time. In the middle of writing up the final patient notes, his office door had opened unexpectedly. He could remember every little detail about his unexpected visitor. How her auburn hair cascaded delightfully over her shoulders. How her seductive smile lit up her perfect face.

He had avoided her for so long, but in the privacy of his office late that afternoon, he had weakened.

*Don't forget about me*, she had said as she put her arms around him. *I'm still here if you ever want me.*

*As if there was ever any doubt I still want her.* The idea was laughable, he thought. But since his marriage to Julia, he had avoided her. Deliberately. But that day, he had taken her in his arms and kissed her, tentatively at first, and then passionately.

He recalled her words exactly. *Will you go back to ignoring me when you get back?*

He had hurt her when he had walked away from her and married Julia. *No, I won't go back to ignoring you*, he had promised. *I've never stopped wanting you. Not for one moment.* By avoiding her, he had avoided facing the truth for years.

And then she had smiled and walked out of his office. And he had been left to consider how it was that one beautiful young woman had

3

the power to undermine everything he believed were the foundations on which he had built his life. Honesty. Integrity. Fidelity.

Yet he found himself beginning to contemplate the pleasure of seeing her on his return. And beyond that? He knew it would only take one small step on his part to become her lover again. The fact he thought himself capable of taking that step surprised him.

And then he banished those thoughts from his mind. He had finished with Karen Clarke years ago. She was part of his past. *I'm happily married,* he reminded himself, as if somehow by repeating the words silently, it would be rendered true. As if those few words could by themselves act as a protection against temptation.

But still he could not banish the image of her from his mind. Nor could he banish the memory of being her lover. And everything about the encounter continued to unsettle him.

# CHAPTER 1

*America*

EVER SINCE SHE HAD heard it, Pippa had not been satisfied with the brief unembellished story of her father's early life. She knew there had to be more. More to know. More to understand. But he was a man who did not like to live in the past. Why was it that he did not want to confront the past, she wondered? She went over and over the scant facts she already knew.

His mother was the daughter of a gardener to one of the wealthy families of Long Island. His father? Unknown, he had said at first, trying to throw her off the scent. But she had not believed him. Was his father perhaps a son of the household where his grandfather had worked? She had asked him outright and he had shrugged. *How can I know for sure*, he had replied? *There is no father listed on my birth certificate.*

*But your mother must have told you something?* She had persisted. *You can't have gone through your life with your mother and not been curious to know who your father was.*

He had sighed deeply, she remembered, and repeated what little he knew of his birth. She could see then it was a pain buried so deep he had expected never to confront it again. It was a story of disappointment. Of loss. Of the loss of someone he had never known. His

5

father. A void in his life that could never now be filled.

With that, he had handed her a photo. It was a copy of the precious photo he had given Pippa's mother Julia just before he left Australia as war raged throughout the Pacific. On the back it had the same important inscription. His mother's address.

It was faded but she knew the story of the photo, how it had been the means by which he had discovered her birth. She had asked if she could keep the photograph. He had nodded. And she had put it away carefully. And kept it for years, promising herself one day she would be able to find out more. She was sure it would be the key that would unlock the door of who her father really was. And who his father was.

And now, on a warm summer's day, she was about to set out on the journey that would take her from the crowded sidewalks of Manhattan to the historic port of Sag Harbor except this was no sightseeing trip. She was setting out to find the Sag Harbor address, now almost unreadable, that her father had written years before on the back of the old photo. Would it be possible that neighbours would remember her grandmother? Remember her father? In her more rational moments, she convinced herself she was on a foolish errand. But even as these doubts assailed her, she fought back against them. How can I not try? The voice in her head finally won.

Now, after weeks of non-stop work at the hospital, she was finally free for five whole days. Her father had lamented the clash with his attendance at a medical conference in Chicago but she had been secretly pleased. It left her free to do as she pleased.

By late morning, she had found her way to the historic harborside but it took her some time to find the small street on which her grandmother had lived. It was tucked away several streets back from the famous harbor but now as she stood in front of the house so clearly identifiable in the background of the photograph, she looked up uncertainly. Should she go up to the front door?

To her critical eye, the house looked unkempt and uncared for. The lawn was weeks overdue for mowing and the few shrubs in the front garden had been allowed to grow unchecked, their faded flowers left to wither on the stem. What had she expected? Not this, certainly. Something neater. She was dismayed. But she reminded herself this was not her grandmother's house. It hadn't been her grandmother's house for twenty years. Or more.

She pushed open the front gate and was about to head up the overgrown path towards the porch when she heard movement behind her.

'It's not available to rent,' a voice declared.

She stopped and turned, looking for the person who had spoken. She held her hand up to her eyes to help her see against the strong sunlight. The figure of a young man emerged from the haze of the sharp light. Within a few strides he was beside her and firmly pulling closed the gate she had pushed open.

'You should try down at the local real estate office,' he said, 'if you want a place to rent.'

She paused. Who was he? Did he own the place?

'Is this your place?' she asked.

'Not mine,' he said abruptly. 'It belongs to my grandfather, as do all the houses in this street.'

She looked around, noticing for the first time a line of similar small cottages, some much better kept than the house in front of her.

'That's a lot of houses to own,' Pippa said.

The young man shrugged.

'Maybe,' he said.

And then it was his turn to pause and look at her quizzically.

'You're not from round these parts, are you?'

Pippa shook her head, her long blonde hair cascading around her face.

'No. I'm Australian. My name is Pippa Duval.'

She wondered if the name might trigger a reaction but she was disappointed. He gave no sign of recognition.

'So, tell me, what's your interest in this house, Pippa Duval,' he asked, not having reciprocated with his own name.

Despite the pleasantries, she sensed an unmistakable air of arrogance in the young man so she hesitated. Was this the moment to blurt out the full story? Would that ultimately help her quest? Or hinder it? She had only moments to make up her mind.

'Someone I know used to live in this house,' she said, deciding to go carefully.

'Must have been a long time ago,' he said. 'It's been vacant since I was a small child.'

'Which accounts for the front garden being very overgrown, I suppose,' Pippa said, realising there was much more to the story of the house being vacant than an unkempt garden.

'My grandfather likes it that way,' he admitted. 'But we do send a gardener down every now and again to give it a tidy up.'

Pippa considered this small snippet of information for a few moments.

'The house must be special to him to keep it empty,' she said finally, hoping to prize more information from the young American.

'It is, apparently,' came the half-interested reply. 'But no one is quite sure why. We just speculate.'

'We just speculate?'

It seemed an odd thing to say.

'My father and I,' he explained.

The young man was more relaxed now. He lent against the gate, his arms folded casually across his chest. For the first time, Pippa was aware of him looking at her with greater interest. She moved a little to distance herself from him.

'By the way, you didn't tell me your name,' she said, looking at him intently.

'My apologies,' he said. 'Walter William Cox the fourth, at your service, ma'am.'

He made a mock bow in her direction.

'It's nice to meet you, Walter William Cox the fourth,' Pippa replied, executing a mock curtesy in his direction.

'Well, Pippa Duval,' he said, 'you haven't explained what a young Australian girl is doing trying to break into one of our houses.'

She frowned and shrugged her shoulders. What should she say? How much should she tell him? Could she trust him?

8

'It's a long story probably best not begun in the middle of the street,' she said finally. She was far from certain how much she should tell him.

'Then come home with me for lunch and you can tell me the long story,' he replied, with some semblance of gallantry.

Was he interested in her story or was this just a pick-up line, she wondered? He noticed her hesitation.

'Don't worry, you'll be safe. My mother will be there,' he said. 'And my sister. Not sure about my father. My car's just down the road.'

Was this a good idea, she wondered? It seemed like everything was happening too fast. He noticed her hesitation.

'Shall we?'

He motioned down the street towards his gleaming red Chevrolet Camaro.

'Thank you, I'd like that,' she said. 'Lead on.'

As they walked along the street together, she listened without interrupting to his commentary as he pointed out the workers cottages his grandfather owned naming each tenant as they passed slowly along the street until they reached his car. She wondered what his purpose had been visiting the street on a Saturday morning but whatever it was, he had not volunteered the information. Within minutes, he was deftly negotiating Sag Harbor's historic streets and heading in the direction of East Hampton.

Fifteen minutes later, Walter William Cox brought his car to a standstill in front of what was a modest home compared with its immediate neighbour but of pleasingly grand proportions when compared with most of the neighbourhood. To her left, Pippa could see a majestic house she judged to be the size of a small palace. Walter Cox followed her gaze.

'That's grandfather's house,' he explained. 'It will be father's one day soon and then mine, I expect,' without any real enthusiasm at the prospect.

'It takes the gardeners almost two weeks to trim the borders that stretch from the south lawn to the south gate, I've been told,' he added, somewhat unnecessarily.

Pippa turned back towards him. In her mind's eye, she believed she had already glimpsed the past, imagining her own father's grandfather hunched over the hedges, clippers in hand, snipping away until he was satisfied with his work.

'It looks like a palace,' she said, as much to cover her confusion as to pay a compliment.

He nodded and shrugged his shoulders as if to say, *it's just a house*.

'It's supposed to,' he said. 'It was built to impress.'

'Well, it certainly does that.'

Pippa had never seen a private home of such massive proportions.

'When my grandfather dies, I think my father may even demolish it and subdivide the land but my mother may have something to say about that,' he said, in a very matter of fact tone.

'Would that worry you? To see the family's heritage torn down?'

He shook his head.

'Not at all,' he said. 'It was a massive ego that built that house. It was never a happy home.'

'How do you know this?'

Pippa regretted the implicit challenge in her question almost as soon as she had uttered the words. It seemed such a personal question to put to a virtual stranger.

'Because that's what my father told me,' he replied as he climbed out of the driver's seat and walked to her side of the car to open the door.

'Will your mother be angry at an unexpected lunch guest?'

'Not at all,' he said. 'She's always encouraging me to bring girls home.

He grinned broadly and she laughed.

'She'll be surprised you've picked up an Australian girl,' she teased.

'She will be at that,' he said, as together they made their way to the front door which opened seamlessly as they approached.

He ushered Pippa into an immaculate house of deceptively stately proportions. She noticed the quality of the furniture and the exquisite pictures that graced the walls. But most of all, she noticed how her young host was warmly welcomed back to his home by the butler, who chided him gently for not forewarning them of his guest.

Minutes later, Pippa found herself being surveyed from head to toe by Barbara Cox, to whom Walter had introduced her just moments before. For the first time, she wished she had taken more care with her dress. She had not counted on being a lunch guest in such a grand home. Her first instinct was to apologise but the words were left unsaid. Instead, she found herself an object of much curiosity. Not much escaped the gaze of Walter Cox's mother.

'Walter says he found you breaking into one of our houses,' she said, without any hint of humour in her voice. 'You don't look like a housebreaker.'

Pippa was about to laugh but opted instead for a serious reply.

'He was mistaken, Mrs Cox,' she replied. 'I simply wanted to speak to whoever lived there. I didn't know at the time it was vacant.'

'So tell me,' she said, hardly waiting to hear Pippa's explanation, 'what brings you to America? You're a long way from home.'

It was like an interrogation from a headmistress, Pippa thought. If you get an answer wrong, you'll find yourself in detention after school.

'I have a short internship at St John's hospital in Manhattan,' she replied.

She thought the simplest and shortest explanation was the best option.

'For a nurse? That's unusual, surely,' Barbara Cox replied.

'I'm Dr Pippa Duval, Mrs Cox,' she explained patiently. 'I'm planning to specialise in paediatrics. My father arranged it.'

Walter Cox, sensing the rising tension, chose that moment to intervene in the conversation.

'Pippa knows someone who lived in the cottage that Grandfather hasn't let out for years', he said. 'She says she has a long story to tell us.'

'Then we must hear it, Walter,' Barbara Cox said, her stiletto heels making a hollow sound as she led the way into the dining room where the table was laid for a lunch Pippa had assumed would be a casual family affair but which turned out to be something quite different.

As she entered the room, Barbara Cox motioned to the butler to lay another place. His white gloved hands obeyed the command swiftly even as the message of an additional guest was being conveyed to the kitchen.

'My mother doesn't like casual dining, even at lunch,' Walter whispered in her ear.

Behind them, the sound of more footsteps alerted Pippa to the arrival of another person.

'Ah, I see you've brought home a stray, brother dear.'

'Now, Virginia, be nice,' her mother commanded. 'This is Pippa Duval. Your brother has invited her to lunch. She's a doctor.'

'Just what my brother needs,' she retorted.

Was that look of distain more than just sibling rivalry, Pippa wondered?

'A psychiatrist I hope?' she added, looking hopefully in Pippa's direction, who shook her head.

'I'm sorry to disappoint you on that score,' she replied levelly. 'I'm going to specialise in paediatric medicine.'

'Sounds fascinating,' she replied.

Having failed to score a point, she sunk into a sullen silence.

'Is Father coming for lunch?'

Walter Cox had completely ignored his sister's catty remarks, leaving Pippa to believe he was totally unmoved by her juvenile outburst.

'I think so,' his mother responded, consulting a diamond encrusted timepiece encircling her slim wrist, 'so we will wait a few minutes for him.'

Barbara Cox indicated a place at the table for her unexpected guest and Walter, remembering the manners his mother had drummed into him, pulled back the chair for her to sit down.

'Thank you,' she said.

She nodded to Virginia who sat opposite but was greeted in return with only the merest hint of civility. Glasses of iced water appeared as if from nowhere.

'Now we must hear your story, Pippa,' Barbara Cox said. 'Why were you so interested in the old cottage that no one has lived in for years?'

There was no hint of foreknowledge in Barbara Cox's question, nothing beyond polite curiosity, as if the question was the merest commonplace and Pippa's story would be nothing more than a diverting topic of conversation for a lunch table devoid of more interesting company.

'I don't quite know where to begin,' Pippa replied, hesitating.

Was this quite the right place and the right time to launch into her story?

'Why don't you begin at the beginning, young lady,' a voice behind her demanded.

She half turned in her seat towards the direction of the newcomer. As her eyes focused on Walter William Cox the third, her face went pale. There was much about him that was different but not so very different that she could not recognise a man who must be very closely related to her father.

In shock, she blurted out the very first words that came to her mind.

'You look just like my father!'


'Well, Dr Duval,' Walter said, as they headed west from East Hampton. 'You gave us all something to chew on.'

Pippa smiled. He at least had not been hostile towards her. Her departure from the house had been outwardly very civil but beneath the forced smiles she had detected a frostiness she could not fail to notice.

'I'm sorry it turned out the way it did,' she said apologetically. 'It wasn't my intention to blurt out what I did but when I saw your father, it was an automatic response. It just came out.'

He laughed.

'It did, didn't it! But it explains a lot.'

Pippa was beginning to relive, with considerable embarrassment, the very awkward lunch following her outburst. But Walter's response intrigued her.

'What do you mean: it explains a lot?'

He risked a sideways glance even as he urged the car's powerful engine to a faster and faster speed.

'Remember I said the big house was never a happy place,' he reminded her. 'Now we know why. My grandfather was forced to marry someone the family approved of, rather than the woman he loved. My grandmother must have known that. She died years ago, a sad unhappy woman as I remember.'

'But your grandfather is still alive, isn't he?'

'Yes, he is. But he's not well. And he and my father don't get along.'

'Why is that do you think?'

Pippa was curious. She and her father had their differences but she loved him dearly. And then she remembered her adoptive father. He had been a cold, disappointed man who had spared her very little time or love.

'It's funny you know,' he replied. 'My father always said he felt like a second son. Now it appears as if he was right. He was a second son.'

'But your father seems very reluctant to want to take this any further,' Pippa said. 'He did not ask me to bring my father on a visit.'

To her, it was simple. She compared it with her own story. When it became known her mother Julia had given birth to her out of wed-lock, she had been accepted without question into the Belleville family, regardless of the short-lived scandal that ensued. Why could the Cox family not do the same? It was a question that nagged at her.

She waited for Walter to respond. She looked at him. It seemed as if he was weighing up the options. Loyalty to his family. Or honesty. In the end, he chose to be honest with her.

'My father will be worried that your father will want to make a claim on Grandfather's estate,' he said finally. 'Prestige and wealth are important to my father, to my mother and to my sister. They couldn't abide a scandal in the family. They might get dropped from the guest lists that count.'

Could people really be swayed by such considerations, Pippa wondered? Were they really so shallow as to care about a bit of gossip? But Walter hadn't included himself. He hadn't said prestige and wealth are important to us.

'But not to you, Walter? Are you different from your family?'

'I like to think so,' he said, 'but no one has ever really put that to

14

the test. I've had a dream life. I've been allowed to get away with practically anything. Failing college exams. Wrecking a motor launch. Writing off my first car. No consequences.'

He shrugged.

'I never have to work if I don't want to. I could just live the life of a playboy.'

She considered this new information. Behind his words, there was a hint of melancholy as if, already, his life was robbed of any true meaning.

'And your parents would be happy with that?'

'Not happy, exactly, but accepting, for a while anyway. I can get away with it while I'm in my twenties.'

'And after that?'

'It will be time for my father to step down from his various boards and for me to take his place. And keep the family coffers growing.'

'And become the father of Walter William Cox the fifth, I suppose,' Pippa added, understanding now the life that had been prescribed for Walter, whether he liked it or not.

He laughed, but it was not a happy sound.

'You get the picture completely,' he said, as he concentrated on negotiating the inevitable traffic snarl through the streets of lower Manhattan.

'But you haven't told me what your father will think of what happened today?'

She had hoped he wouldn't ask that question. She was also hoping that her father had not decided to skip the last session of the conference and come back to New York early.

'I don't know, to be honest,' she replied. 'He's always been very circumspect about what he told us about his early life with his mother. He's talked about the Army and medical school readily enough. But he's busy too.'

'A surgeon, you said?'

'Yes, a very good one.'

She was proud of the respect he commanded in his profession.

'Yet he left it all behind in New York to move to Sydney when he found you?'

15

She was aware that part of her story had sounded incredible, yet she had insisted it was true. She could see how they doubted that a man keen to reach the top of the medical profession would willingly leave the one place that would help him achieve his career prospects only to bury himself in a country half a world away. But in the end, they believed her.

'Did he have help with the college fees, do you think?'

This question, too, had occurred to Pippa and not for the first time. Had there been some money to support his studies he had not known about, she wondered?

'I don't know,' was her honest answer. 'I doubt he knows for sure. All I do know for sure is that he never met his father. Never knew who he was. His mother wouldn't confirm his suspicions.'

'So you said,' Walter reminded her.

It occurred to her then that Walter thought her father might have wanted her to seek out his unknown family.

'He doesn't know I had this in mind,' she explained, not wanting any doubt to remain. 'He's in Chicago at a medical conference, although he may have decided to come home today.'

'He might be there when I drop you off at your apartment?'

'He might be,' she said, sorry now she had mentioned the possibility. Any encounter was likely to be extremely awkward and require a lot of explanation.

'Don't worry, just say I'm a hospital buddy. My name will be meaningless probably. Just introduce me as Walter.'

'You're curious to get a look at him, aren't you?'

'Well, he could, after all, be my uncle, and you could be my cousin. Reason enough to be curious.'

She smiled and relaxed. She felt she could trust him.

'And what will you tell the rest of your family if you do meet him?'

'Depends,' he said. 'But if I'm convinced your story is true it may be my grandfather I want to talk to.'

'Would that be wise?'

'Oh, he and I get along well. It's just my father he locks horns with. My grandfather thinks I'm a young man in his own image.'

'And are you?'

'In some ways I think I am, but before you ask, I haven't got any young women pregnant and tucked them away in one of the family's rental houses.'

'Well, that's a relief,' Pippa said, joining in his banter. 'I'm not sure your mother would take such news well.'

For just a moment, Pippa imagined the scene and she could see he was visualising it too.

'Wouldn't be pretty, would it?'

And they both laughed as he edged the big Chevrolet into a convenient parking space just a few yards from the apartment block.

It was now late afternoon. It had been a long and emotional day and Pippa was tired.

'Thank you for driving me home,' she said as she climbed out of the car. 'You saved me many hours on a crowded train. It was very good of you.'

'It was the least I could do,' he said, 'after the grilling my family gave you.'

She was about to walk away but he stopped her.

'Here's my phone number,' he said. 'We can't just leave it there.'

'You're right,' she said, as she took the slip of paper from him and then searched in her bag for a pen to reciprocate the gesture.

'Here's my number too,' she said quickly.

It was Walter who noticed the yellow cab pull up in front of the apartment building a matter of twenty yards away. Pippa, facing Walter, had not seen her father paying off the cab and then notice his daughter standing a short distance away on the sidewalk. He was beside her in a few quick strides having first handed his bag to the concierge.

Pippa greeted her father with a loving hug. She was pleased to see him back so she did not have to spend another night alone in their apartment but she hoped fervently that Walter would stick to the story they had concocted.

'And who's this?' Philippe asked, extending his hand towards Walter.

'Walter Cox, a hospital buddy,' Pippa said, praying that Walter would play along.

17

'A doctor too, Walter?' Philippe assumed, shaking his hand while eyeing him keenly. 'What's your specialty?'

Pippa held her breath. What was he going to say?

'Psychiatry, sir,' he said, without hesitation.

'That's a good field, Walter,' Philippe said. 'Mental illness is still much under acknowledged and under researched.'

Walter nodded his head slightly, as if in agreement.

'I won't keep you, sir,' he said, his impeccable manners impressing Philippe. 'I think Pippa looks tired.'

'She does indeed,' Philippe agreed as he linked arms with his daughter and turned in the direction of their apartment building. 'We'll see you another time perhaps.'

As father and daughter walked away together, Pippa risked a quick backward glance.

In one small insignificant gesture, Walter acknowledged their kinship. He gave her a thumbs up and, pointing towards Philippe, mouthed the words: *he is my uncle* before turning back towards his car.

# CHAPTER 2

SUNDAY DAWNED FINE OVER New York city. Philippe sat alone in the small kitchen of his apartment, relishing the quiet of the early morning and his first cup of coffee of the day. It had been only a few weeks since he left Sydney and returned to the city he had left ten years earlier.

Yet in the course of those few weeks, he had begun to realise there were aspects of his former life in New York he still missed. It was not a constant yearning for the life he no longer had. Rather it was a sense that one part of his life had ended irrevocably. He knew he could now never return to New York permanently. He had faced that fact some time ago, knowing he could never ask Julia to live in New York. There were times he thought she had failed to settle fully into their life in Sydney. Without any friends or family in New York, he knew she would find the city a lonely and depressing place. And Pippa? He could not imagine her becoming a permanent New Yorker, despite her excitement at being offered a short internship.

'A penny for your thoughts.'

Pippa's sleepy voice startled him momentarily. He greeted her with a smile.

'That would be overpaying for them,' he said, reverting naturally to his parental role. 'Did you sleep well? You looked very tired yesterday.'

She pulled a chair out and sat opposite him. He poured her a cup of coffee and watched as she ladled several heaped teaspoons of sugar into the cup.

'Needing a sugar hit?' he said, indicating the copious amount she had added to her coffee.

She laughed, suddenly aware she had added far more sugar than she intended.

'I forgot what I was doing.'

'Not distracted by a certain young doctor, by any chance?'

Her face reddened slightly but not for the reasons her father imagined.

'It's not what you think, actually,' she said, choosing her words carefully.

He shrugged his shoulders.

'I wasn't actually thinking anything but he seemed like a decent young fellow.'

She nodded. Was this the time to launch into a full explanation of what she had discovered during her trip to Long Island? She sipped her over-sweet coffee absentmindedly while avoiding her father's direct gaze.

'Why don't we go out for breakfast?' her father said suddenly. 'There's a great diner down near Battery Point where I used to go years ago. I've been told it's still there. You can tell me all about what you got up to yesterday. Something interesting I suspect.'

She put her coffee cup down. It was like he was taking control of the situation for her. Without even knowing anything. Or does he know something? No, she decided, he can't possibly know where I was. But doubts crept in. Could he?

But then he always surprised her. She had learnt over the years that nothing much escaped him. He noticed every slight change in mood.

*I bet he's like that with his patients*, she had said more than once to her mother. *I bet they can never put anything over him.* And she remembered how they'd both agreed that was the way he was and laughed together. It seemed endearing somehow. As if he was an omnipresent figure in her life, not watching her every move exactly, but alert to any unhappiness or disappointment she was feeling, as if it was his job to make her world right.

The Sunday traffic was light so it wasn't long before father and daughter were sitting opposite one another at the diner studying the bewildering array of breakfast dishes on offer.

'The décor hasn't changed at all,' Philippe said, looking around him at the pale grey Formica tabletops and the chrome chairs with padded vinyl seats. 'I used to come here quite a lot.'

There was just a hint of wistfulness in his voice.

'Another life, wasn't it?' Pippa said, understanding his mood and the reason for it. 'Would you come back here to live if you could?'

To Pippa, it seemed like the right question to ask. She hoped it would give her the opportunity to talk about his early life.

'I don't think so,' he said, after a moment's reflection. 'I think sometimes it's easy to be wistful about the past. There were times when I was very lonely here. I worked all the time then.'

'But you did get married,' Pippa reminded him.

He grimaced, as if the memory was an embarrassment. Pippa knew the marriage had been very short lived.

'Let's not talk about that,' he said. 'It wasn't a happy period in my life. It should never have happened.'

'Perhaps it was a natural response to losing your mother,' Pippa ventured.

He shrugged his shoulders.

'Who knows, perhaps it was,' he conceded. 'I did not expect my mother to die when she did. I blame myself. I was so preoccupied I missed the signs. And she hated me fussing about her health.'

Pippa closed her eyes briefly and took a deep breath. Now or never, she told herself. As she opened her eyes, she looked directly at her father.

'Did you know her cottage has been vacant since she died?'

There. She had said it. She had started the story.

Philippe looked up quickly from the plate of eggs that had just been placed in front of him.

'Sorry, what did you say?' as if he could possibly have misheard her.

'I went out to Sag Harbor yesterday,' she said, watching his reaction carefully.

'And you visited the cottage where my mother lived?'

She nodded her head slightly.

'But you said it's been vacant since my mother died more than twenty years ago. Did one of the neighbours tell you that?'

She could see he was trying to visualise the street. To him, it was the most likely explanation.

'No, it wasn't one of the neighbours.'

'Who then?'

He was suddenly very anxious to know. He began to realise there was so much she hadn't yet told him.

'Does the name Walter William Cox mean anything to you?'

She was testing his memory. But more than that, she was testing his version of his early life from which she'd always believed he'd omitted the most important details.

'I don't think so ...'

He had started to deny any knowledge of his father's family but then he saw the look in her eyes and he stopped.

'Tell me what you think you know, Pippa.'

He was not angry with her exactly but she had wrong footed him and he did not enjoy the feeling. It was as if he had been found out in a lie by his own daughter. But she was not going to let him off so easily.

'It's not speculation,' she insisted. 'I believe it's the truth about your mother and who your father is.'

For Philippe, the whole conversation was careering out of control. Why had she done this by herself? And then he realised and began to quietly berate himself. She had been abandoned herself and sent to an orphanage when she was born. Now she knows the full facts about her own birth, she wants me to have the same certainty.

He relaxed then. He was a man of fifty-three. And she was his daughter. She, more than anyone else, had the right to know about his parents, who after all were her grandparents. He reached across the table and took her hand.

'It's alright,' he said reassuringly. 'I'm not angry with you. Let's eat our food and you can tell me the whole story from beginning to end. It sounds as if you had an interesting day yesterday.'

'Let's walk down to Battery Point,' Philippe said, as he counted out the money for the restaurant bill. 'That was quite a lot of information to take in over breakfast.'

She laughed.

'It was rather, wasn't it?'

'So you think I should be Walter William Cox the third,' he said, testing out the name as if it really did belong to him.

'Actually, that's what the current Walter William Cox the third is afraid of.'

He threw his head back and laughed then, attracting a few curious stares from among the Sunday crowd heading for the Staten Island ferry.

'What! He's worried I'm going to make a claim on some mausoleum of a house in East Hampton. I remember seeing it once or twice. It's just a vulgar expression of some wealthy man's massive ego. It deserves to be pulled down.'

Was this the moment to tell him his father was still alive? She could not quite bring herself to tell him this last vital piece of information. She was still trying to judge just how well he was reacting to everything she had told him.

'You haven't told me what you remember from your childhood? Do you think your father ever came around to visit?'

They were standing now looking out over the vast grey expanse of the Hudson River. Pippa's long blonde hair floated in the breeze that lifted off the water.

'Not that I remember,' he said, 'but he may have done. I remember there was a photo of a man in his late twenties, taken possibly sometime after I was born but before I have a reliable memory of anything. I wasn't in the photo though but I would be fairly sure it was taken at our cottage.'

Pippa considered this new information for a moment.

'It seems he was rushed into a suitable marriage. Walter's father is maybe only two years younger than you. If he visited your mother, it would not have been often, I suspect. Too much risk of gossip.'

After years of burying the facts about his early life, it had suddenly become easier for him to speak of it. He could not account for his change in attitude. Was it a measure of how much he cared about his daughter and how much the knowledge of his early life meant to her? Perhaps. And perhaps, a small part of me wants to know, he thought. Has always wanted to know.

He considered more carefully what Pippa had said. The man he supposed to be his half-brother was only two years younger than he was. Pippa was right. It meant his father had been pushed into a suitable marriage very quickly by his overbearing family.

'Well, my mother did say, when I pushed her to tell me more, that my father was too weak to go against his family. He obviously buckled to their demands and married a girl of their choice.'

Pippa nodded, suddenly aware of how important their conversation had become to both of them. He needs to know what I know, she thought. All of it. She pushed on.

'According to Walter, the marriage did not go well. His grand-mother was a sad disappointed woman who died well before her time.'

For Philippe, it was as if the long-forgotten pieces of an old unfin-ished jigsaw were slowly being fitted into place after years of lying discarded on a table. Yet it was Pippa's next question that began to peel back the forgotten layers of his life.

'Did you ever wonder how your mother afforded your college fees?' she asked. She had long been curious as to how his mother had found the money to send him to the best medical school.

He thought for a moment. Where was this heading? But he knew. Of course, he knew. He sighed deeply. It hurt him to admit his own failings.

'I accepted her story that she had saved for years in a college fund,' he shrugged, aware of how naive he must now appear to have been.

'From a cleaner's wage? Really? Are you sure?'

For the first time in his life, he was forced to confront his own self-ishness. Was he simply guilty of living the self-centred life that was the special preserve of the young? Or something more? Why had he not pressed his mother on it? Was it because he hadn't wanted to know the truth? Had an unseen benefactor funded his education without his knowledge, as Pippa suggested? These were now questions without answers.

'You're right,' he admitted. 'I should have asked more questions but I was consumed by college and getting ahead in my profession. It was all my mother asked of me. That I should make her proud.'

Pippa put a comforting arm through his. She had not meant to upset him.

'I'm sure she was proud of you,' she said. 'I suspect she never asked for help for herself, only for you, except for the rent which was never raised on her cottage in all the years she lived there.'

She noticed a tear run down his cheek. She guessed uncomfortable memories had come flooding back into his mind.

'So, what you're saying is he wouldn't marry her but he nagged his father into keeping her rent low to assuage his guilt.'

'Possibly,' Pippa said although she knew there would never been any proof. 'And then, by the time you were going to college, his father had passed away and he was in sole charge of the Cox family wealth. Easy then to divert some money for your college tuition.'

They had talked for some time, she posing the questions, he answering as best he could until the breeze, now stronger, forced them to move back from the water's edge. As they began to move away, she hesitated. She had not yet put the question she most wanted to ask: *do you want to go out to East Hampton and meet them.*

But he pre-empted her.

'What's next from all this?' he asked as he turned towards her. 'There's another chapter to come, isn't there?'

Pippa smiled encouragingly and nodded.

'Yes, you're right. There's another chapter to come. There has to be another chapter.'

She handed him the slip of paper on which Walter Cox had written his phone number. For one brief moment, she thought he was going to screw it into a ball and throw it away. Instead, he handed it back to her.

'Why don't you give him a call and the three of us can meet. He will know how best to approach his family or if we should do so at all.'

She nodded and pocketed the slip of paper.

'But before I do that,' she said, placing her hand on his arm, 'there is one more thing I need to tell you.'

Before she could say anything further, he knew instinctively what was coming.

'My father is still alive, isn't he? That's what you're about to tell me.'

She nodded, relieved he had worked it out for himself.

'He is.'

'I haven't met him though,' she added hastily, suddenly concerned he thought she might have omitted to mention he had been at lunch with the rest of the family.

He stood very still for a few moments, his mind clearly trying to absorb the news that his father, the man who had only ever been a shadowy unknown figure in his life, was alive, was flesh and blood. Shock and disbelief fought an unequal battle over his reaction to this sudden news.

'All the while we've been talking, I had assumed he had died,' he said, his voice suddenly so quiet Pippa struggled to hear him. 'But then you never said he had died, only that his wife had died.'

Pippa lent in towards him, understanding only too well his mixed emotions at the news. She had experienced that very same emotion herself, finding out her beloved adoptive mother who had died so tragically was not her real mother and then later finding her real mother, yet always grieving for the woman who had brought her up as if she was her real mother.

'Does that change anything?' she asked, tentatively.

He smiled as he turned to face her.

26

'You mean does it make me want to get on the first plane back to Sydney and resume my life as if none of this has happened?'

For the first time, she could not find the right words to reassure him.

'I promise I won't do that,' he said finally. 'This is important to you. I can see that. And it's strange. It has made me curious too. Let's see where it takes us.'

They linked arms and together turned to walk in the direction of the street to hail a cab for the ride back to their mid-town apartment.

It was late afternoon. The apartment was bathed in the soft light of the sun's last rays. Soft jazz echoed through the rooms as a soothing backdrop to the end of the day. From his favourite armchair, Philippe watched his daughter and smiled at the seriousness with which she had begun to tackle a recipe she had clipped from the Sunday newspaper. Up until this point, he had prepared most of their meals except on the days their housekeeper left dinner already cooked for them or they chose to walk to one of his favourite restaurants nearby.

The insistent sound of the ringing telephone cut through this scene of peaceful domesticity. Philippe answered, half expecting to hear his wife's distant voice, but he was greeted instead by an unfamiliar distinctly American accent.

'It's Walter William Cox here,' the caller said, with the assurance his name would be instantly recognised. 'I assume that's Philippe Duval.'

For the first time in his life, Philippe was startled into momentary speechlessness. Pippa, her cooking temporarily abandoned, had come to stand alongside her father, expecting the call to be from the younger Walter Cox.

'Are you there, Duval?'

For Philippe, hearing the voice with its sense of easy superiority brought back long forgotten memories of every slight he had ever suffered for being born out of wedlock, of being talked about as the bastard son of a whore. He had suffered these slights and borne the scars unseen, while every fibre of his being wanted desperately to expose their hypocrisy. He was tempted to hang up. Instead, he finally spoke, his voice calm and measured.

'Yes, it's Doctor Duval speaking.'

He waited for a response.

'I'll get straight to the point,' the voice boomed. 'Your daughter came uninvited to my house yesterday and told some fanciful story about you without a shred of evidence to back it up. So don't think your gold-digging slag of a daughter will ever be welcome in my house again. And if you go around repeating that outrageous story about my father being your father, my lawyers will come down on you like a ton of bricks.'

Philippe's first response was one of shock until anger flared beyond his ability to control it.

'How dare you! How dare you say that about my daughter,' he yelled. 'As I understand it, she came to your house at the invitation of your son. And if you don't like what she had to say, that's too bad. Because it is all true. Do you hear that? It is all true. Whatever you say, whatever you want to deny, the facts are that my mother was your father's one true love. And I was the product of that love.'

He paused for breath. He could not remember a time when he had been so angry. He had said more and revealed more than he had ever intended. The voice at the other end of the telephone spluttered and stammered.

'Bloody nonsense. It's all bloody nonsense,' he screamed, his words almost unintelligible. 'My mother was a saint and my father loved her. He wouldn't have touched a woman like your mother. A cleaning lady! He wouldn't have even noticed her let alone fucked her.'

Walter William Cox spat the words down the telephone line. Philippe instinctively wiped his cheek as if the vile spittle might have somehow reached him.

'How dare you say such a foul thing about my mother,' Philippe yelled back. 'She lived her entire life paying the price for loving a man who would not marry her because he valued wealth and prestige above her.'

He banged the phone down aware that he might otherwise say something he would later regret. He sat for some minutes trying to regain his composure before he spoke again.

'Well, that was one very angry man,' he said as he looked across at Pippa. 'I take it you heard most of that?'

She nodded, not knowing exactly what to say. She had never expected such a reaction. Where did this leave them? She was sorry her father had been subjected to such a torrent of abuse.

'I'm sorry,' she said finally. 'I should never have gone behind your back to find out about your father. I just thought of it as a big adventure. It seemed so harmless. We don't want their money. We just want to know the truth.'

Philippe nodded.

'You and I know that,' he said, 'but it does make me wonder if he thinks I'm after their money. It has to be more than that, surely?'

And then Pippa remembered.

'There could be more to it. Walter said his father always felt like the second son. Could that be it?'

Philippe shook his head, knowing that speculation was useless. He saw now his most important task was to reassure his daughter it had not been her fault. How could she have foreseen such an outburst?

'Now you know what sort of people they are,' he said. 'You'll know now why I despise them and their sort. I think you understand why I was so desperate to get away and make something of myself.'

He paused. There was more to say.

'I think you understand now why I moved heaven and earth to find you and make a life with you, my dear child,' he said. 'I knew what it was like not to be wanted by my father. I was never ever going to repeat that mistake.'

She was crying now, tears cascading down her cheeks as she came to sit on the arm of his chair.

'I understand everything now,' she said quietly. 'And thank you for not abandoning me.'

With that she headed back to the kitchen to rescue the chicken that gave every appearance of being over-cooked as Philippe sank back into his armchair, unnerved by the call but more determined than ever to finally meet his father.

# CHAPTER 3

WALTER COX PEERED THROUGH the open doorway of his father's study. He saw that his father was facing away from the door, looking out across the manicured lawns and neatly trimmed hedges of the immaculately kept garden. Walter paused and then moved forward quietly to stand just inside the door.

Then he saw what he was looking for. The crumpled piece of paper on which Pippa Duval had scribbled her phone number. He knew then that his father had searched for it. Searched his jacket, turned the pockets inside out until he found it, because he had deliberately and carefully hidden it deep within a small pocket.

It was then he caught the last few words his father shouted down the phone.

He froze momentarily at the fury of his father's words, at the unbridled anger he overheard. Should he turn and walk away, pretending he hadn't heard the awful slur his father had just uttered? But that would be cowardly.

Instead, he strode into the room and took the receiver from his father and hung up the phone. He reached across and snatched the small piece of paper from his father's desk.

'Even by your standards,' he said, anger distorting his voice, 'that was a low act. Who were you talking to? Not Pippa I hope?'

Walter William Cox sneered contemptuously at his only son as if there was nothing about him that gave him any cause for paternal pride.

'No, I was talking to her bastard father if you must know,' he said, his anger unmistakeable. 'They're just a pair of gold diggers and I'll see them off. You'll thank me for it one day.'

Walter let out a hollow mirthless laugh.

'I don't think so, old man,' he said. 'You're way off the mark with this. Pippa's father is one of the finest surgeons in his field. Admired, respected, sought after. He doesn't want your money. He doesn't need it. You, on the other hand ...'

He paused, searching for the right words.

'... But you, you're mean. You're hated by everyone who owes you their living and tolerated by your peers because you buy their respect. Do you hear me? You have to buy their friendship.'

His father opened his mouth to speak and then shut it again. What had he done to deserve such a son? He was shaking now, with an anger the like of which he had never felt before.

'You!' he yelled. 'What have you ever done? You've never done a tap of work in your worthless shallow life.'

Not for the first time he wanted to strike out at his son. He imagined smashing the handsome face, upsetting the easy-going laid back charm he so despised.

Walter looked at his father and shook his head from side to side, sadness etched into his features. He had tried hard, very hard, not to despise his father. In this, he had failed.

'What you actually mean is I've never done a tap of the sort of work you do, which is fucking worthless. That's what's worthless. Not what I do.'

He stood his ground, no longer intimidated by his father's contempt. No longer censoring his own words. No longer pretending ...

'So, big man, what do you do that's so much more worthwhile than what I do?'

He looked at his father then, really looked at him for the first time and saw the ridicule for what it was. The fear in his father's eyes that he could no longer control his son.

'You don't know anything about me,' Walter said. 'You have no idea what motivates me. What I care about.'

His father looked bewildered. What was there to know about his worthless son who had never taken the slightest interest in the family's extensive business empire?

'I do the repairs and maintenance for your tenants that you are too mean, too tight fisted and too miserable to attend to,' he said, watching carefully for his father's reaction.

His father laughed but it was not a pretty sound.

'You don't have any of those skills,' he shouted. 'Do you expect me to believe that rubbish? You couldn't drive a nail.'

'That's where you're wrong, old man,' he said. 'Remember old Dave who you sacked for taking a ten-minute breather on a job last year?'

'Barely.'

'Well, old Dave now works with me to teach me the skills I need to do the repairs on the houses.'

'And I suppose old Dave does this out of the goodness of his heart?'

'No, old Dave does it because he's back on the payroll, courtesy of my grandfather. And he's allowed to work at his own pace now. You didn't know, did you? Too busy with important things to notice.'

His father stood motionless, his anger threatening to explode.

'Get out of my sight,' his father growled.

Before Walter could react, he watched in horror as his father bent to pick up a small bronze sculpture of a winged angel from his desk. Without warning he threw it with all his might at his son.

Walter ducked, the heavy marble base of the statue glancing off the top of his head and shattering the glass door of the bookshelf immediately behind him.

'That went well, old man,' he remarked casually.

'Get out,' his father yelled. 'Get out before I kill you.'

Walter retreated through the open doorway just as his mother and the household staff came running into the room to be greeted by a pile of shattered glass.

Barbara Cox looked at her husband, her contempt barely concealed.

She stood in front of him, shaking with anger at what he had just done.

'I have done everything for you, Walter William Cox,' she said, her words deliberate and precise. 'I have been the wife you wanted, the mother you wanted for your children. But this?'

She gestured helplessly at the wreckage of the bookcase.

'This time, you have gone too far.'

There were no conciliatory words, no reassurances coming from him. His rage was not yet spent.

'As if I fucking care,' he yelled at his wife. 'As if I fucking care.'

He could match her contempt easily. He found with very little effort he could hate her as much as he hated his son.

Walter tentatively explored the top of his head. He was sitting in the kitchen being fussed over by Molly, the family's long-suffering house-keeper.

'Don't fuss, Molly,' he said, more than once. 'I don't think it got me more than a glancing blow.'

She dabbed at the top of his head where a small streak of blood had dried in his hair.

'What's got your old man so stirred up today?' she asked, without really expecting an answer.

'You won't want to know, Molly,' he replied gently. 'Nothing to do with you.'

'Wouldn't happen to be something to do with that old cottage in Sag Harbor your grandpa has never let out again?'

'Where did you get that idea from, Molly?' he asked.

Had someone been gossiping, he wondered. Had family conversations been overheard? He was well aware Molly knew everyone. And everything. Everyone and everything connected with his family, that is.

'I'm not going to say anything more,' she said, her voice suddenly quieter, as if she was in possession of secret information she could not share. She tapped the side of her nose.

He laughed at the gesture.

'Gossip won't help anyone just at the moment,' he said, knowing that he was powerless to stop her.

But she was suddenly serious for a moment.

'No, you're right,' she said. 'It won't help anyone. Except your grandfather that is. You should go and talk to him now.'

He looked at her and she nodded as if to say someone needs to tell him what's going on.

'I will, Molly,' he said, hoisting himself out of the chair.

'Now, go now,' she said as she guided him towards the back door. 'Servants talk. It's better he hears everything from you rather than half a story and most of it wrong from someone else.'

He laughed and hugged her briefly. She had looked out for him ever since he was a baby and he loved her for it.


Walter was well aware that Clarence, his grandfather's butler, expected him to visit the house via the front door but he routinely dispensed with this nicety preferring instead to enter via the kitchen. 'You are not a tradesman,' Clarence had sniffed on more than one occasion. 'You are family. Family should always enter via the front door.'

How many times had Clarence said that to him over the years? And he had invariably replied, my grandfather is not a lord, Clarence, nor a duke. And this is not England. We don't care about such things.

'Then why have a butler,' he had always replied, to which there was no satisfactory answer.

But Clarence was much more than a butler.

As his grandfather's health had declined, Walter knew Clarence acted as a necessary go-between keeping the unwanted world outside at bay. He deftly turned away unwelcome visitors and had been known to stand guard at the threshold of his employer's suite of rooms like a rottweiler protecting his master.

Being a Sunday afternoon, Walter was sure he would find Clarence in his own private sitting room indulging in his favourite activity of listening to the radio and reading a book. He looked up as he heard Walter approach.

'Ah, young sir,' he said, closing the book in which he had been engrossed moments before. 'What can I do for you? Crept in via the back entrance again, did we?'

Walter laughed.

'Of course, I did, Clarence,' he said. 'You don't imagine you're ever going to change that habit after all this time, do you?'

Clarence sighed. He had lost that battle long ago.

'How is my grandfather this afternoon?'

Clarence consulted his watch.

'He's probably awake now from his afternoon nap. He's been in pretty good form of late even though the doctor says his heart isn't strong. Do you want to go up and see him?'

Only Walter was allowed such a liberty. Other visitors would be met with far less enthusiasm. *How long did they want to visit? What was their purpose? Couldn't it wait until tomorrow as Mr Cox had a bad night last night?* And so on. They were the strategies he used to keep unwelcome visitors away from his employer, the people Walter William Cox the second no longer wanted to be bothered with. But his grandson was an exception.

'Thanks, Clarence,' Walter called back over his shoulder as he headed in the direction of the main stairwell.

'Good to see you, boy,' his grandfather said, raising a hand in greeting.

The voice coming from the day bed in the dimly lit room was stronger than Walter had expected.

'Open the curtains and let some light in, for heaven's sake.'

Walter moved to the large windows that afforded a wonderful view of the whole estate and pushed back the heavy curtains. Late afternoon light flooded the room.

'How are you Grandfather? Clarence says you've been pretty well lately.'

A sound emerged, not quite a snort. Was it a snigger? Walter couldn't tell except that he knew it was his grandfather's way of discrediting his butler's opinion of his health.

'Nonsense,' he said. 'What would he know? I have good days and bad days, that's all I can tell you, and that father of yours never comes anywhere near me now. He's desperate you know to be in charge of everything. Can't blame him really. When he does come, it's only to see if I'm still alive and then he goes away disappointed.'

He eyed his grandson critically.

'What's wrong with your head? Was it a girl? Did she hit you over the head because you got too friendly?'

Walter laughed. It was a possible explanation, he thought. But, no, he had to tell his grandfather the truth.

'My father threw that awful bronze sculpture at me,' he said. 'Fortunately, I ducked otherwise they might have been putting me in the coffin before you.'

'Stupid fellow, what did he do that for? Did you write off another car? Or a boat? Did he find out what you'd been doing with old Dave? He wouldn't like it knowing we went behind his back like that.'

His grandfather chuckled at the idea. Putting a spoke in his son's ambitious wheel, as he often said, was one of the few pleasures left in his life. That and his memories.

Walter sat down opposite the old man, who was now sitting upright and keen to chat. How best to start the story? Where to start? And then he decided there was only one way.

'Does the name Philippe Duval mean anything to you, Grandfather?'

Walter watched carefully for any sign of recognition, even a flicker of acknowledgement but he saw nothing in the old man's face. Not at first. Then he was sure he saw the merest hint of a smile before he spoke the words of denial.

'I don't think so, boy,' he said dismissively.

He already knows, Walter thought. The old bastard. He already knows everything. Or thinks he does. But how? Walter shook his head.

'You can't fool me, old man, you can't fool me.'

His grandfather laughed in a way he had not laughed in a very long time.

'You're smarter than your father that's for sure. By some considerable margin I would think.'

Walter inclined his head, acknowledging the compliment, assuming that's what it was.

'You know all about Philippe Duval, don't you?'

'Yes,' he said, without elaboration. 'Of course, I do. I made it my business to know.'

'And you kept his mother in one of your cottages at a peppercorn rent for all those years.'

He nodded.

'But not in the way you think,' he added quickly. 'Ella Duval was not my mistress. We were young lovers, yes, but she would have nothing more to do with me when she discovered she was pregnant and I couldn't marry her.'

'Couldn't. Wouldn't.' Walter shrugged. 'A fine distinction.'

'I was young, stupid, and easily bullied by my father. He was not a nice man. Just like your father. Marrying the right girl from the right family was everything to him.'

'And so that's what you did,' Walter said, 'and no one was happy.'

'You're right. No one was happy. My poor wife, your grandmother, was madly in love with someone else. I was in love with someone else. And yet we were tied together in a marriage neither of us wanted.'

It seemed so stupid, Walter thought. And it condemned three people to a lifetime of misery. Or at least a lifetime of regret.

'You must be proud though of what your first son has achieved despite the circumstances in which he was brought up?'

Walter was testing him. Did he really know as much about Philippe Duval as he claimed?

'I am,' he said simply. 'My father had died by the time he was ready to go to college so there was no difficulty for me to fund his education. It was the best investment I ever made. I'm proud of him.'

Walter knew for certain it was something his grandfather had never said about his own father.

'And he did the right thing too when he had the chance. He made the right choice just as I made the wrong choice.'

Walter was unsure of what he meant. What choice had Philippe

Duval made that could be compared with his own grandfather's moral failure?

'I don't follow,' Walter admitted.

His grandfather smiled. Walter had thought he was about to deliver startling revelations to his grandfather. As it turned out, the exact opposite occurred.

'When Philippe found out his Australian girlfriend had given birth to his child during the war, he did what he could to find her. He wasn't successful the first time, I believe, but when Pippa's adoptive parents died and she found out about him and wrote to him, he headed to Australia immediately. That was around ten years ago.'

Walter had heard Pippa's much briefer version of how her father had reunited with her, but he shook his head disbelievingly, wondering how his grandfather knew so much.

'How can you possibly know all this? You can't,' he said. 'It's just not possible.'

How could it be that his grandfather had never shared this information with anyone in the family. He asked the question again.

'How can you possibly know all this about Philippe Duval?'

'You've still got a lot to learn, boy,' his grandfather said. 'Money talks. I bribed his housekeeper. Handsomely. That's how I found out about the letter Pippa wrote him.'

He paused for breath, enjoying the shock he could clearly see on his grandson's face.

'And then, later, some worried father in Sydney got a private eye to investigate his background over here. When this stranger started asking questions around Sag Harbor, I knew within minutes. I had Clarence track him down and check him out. It was very enlightening. Clarence has a gift for interrogation.'

'So he was interested in some woman other than Pippa's mother?'

It was the only conclusion Walter could reach.

'Apparently. In any case I don't think her father liked what he found out,' he said simply. 'Thought Philippe might be a gold digger I expect. Not to mention the unsavoury antecedents we invented in his family tree.'

Again, Walter was struggling to take in all that his grandfather was telling him. The revelations had left him incredulous.

'You astound me,' he said finally. 'Not one word of this ever reached my family. Not one word.'

His grandfather nodded and smiled, secretly pleased at how successful he had been in keeping all this to himself. Well, to himself and Clarence.

'And I would have preferred it had stayed that way,' he said.

'Why for goodness' sake? Philippe is my uncle, which makes Pippa my cousin.'

His grandfather suddenly became more serious.

'You still don't get it, do you?' his grandfather replied, this time with a sharp urgent note to his voice. 'It's not you I'm worried about. It's your father. He was always a jealous, mean child. Your father would be likely to think Philippe's after the Cox money.'

Walter shook his head.

'I've met Philippe, briefly,' he said. 'And from what Pippa has told me, I'd say he would simply not be interested in the wealth this family has accumulated. Besides, he has no claim on it.'

His grandfather smiled briefly. He hesitated.

'You're right, boy,' his grandfather replied. 'Philippe is far more interested in his career and in his own family.'

'But I suspect a part of him must have wanted to know his father,' Walter said. And then he looked directly at his grandfather. 'And I think a part of you would like to know him too before it's too late.'

The old man smiled. Walter was unsure if the smile signalled agreement or regret.

'Here's Clarence with a beer for us,' he said, suddenly perking up at the prospect of a drink.

Walter accepted the cold beer. He certainly needed something.

'Clarence, I've told Walter all about Philippe Duval,' he said, with a conspiratorial grin.

Clarence nodded, knowing full well that Walter could be trusted. 'I heard about yesterday's lunch, young sir,' he said. 'I heard also your father is, shall we say, a little put out by this development.'

Walter laughed heartily.

'You, Clarence, are the master of understatement,' he replied. 'He nearly killed me an hour ago. Well, he threw that ghastly sculpture at my head. It was just as well my reflexes were quick.'

It was Clarence's turn to smile.

'It shattered the glass in the bookcases, I assume. I just saw the glazier drive up to the house not five minutes ago.'

'Well, the bookcases can be repaired, but I'm not sure about the rest of it, to be honest,' Walter said, knowing he could speak freely.

'And Dr Duval?' Clarence asked. 'Do you think he will want to meet his father?'

Walter smiled. Here was Clarence doing what he does best. Mediating.

'I think there is a very good chance Dr Duval and his daughter would very much like to call, if they were invited,' he said. 'The only issue will be getting my father out of the way.'

'Oh, that can be easily arranged,' Clarence said.

Walter's grandfather chuckled.

'Not permanently, you understand Clarence, just out of the way doing something he thinks is vitally important, for a few hours at least.'

'I think you've forgotten, sir, he'll be at Shinnecock Hills later this week for a corporate golf tournament. Cox Industries is a major sponsor.'

'Brilliant, Clarence, that's ideal.'

He looked at Walter.

'It's up to you now, Walter,' his grandfather said. It was clear the old man, despite everything, wanted desperately to meet his elder son. His first born son.

'Well, my father made a right fool of himself on the telephone earlier,' he explained. 'He insulted Philippe with words I simply couldn't repeat.'

He saw the look of disappointment in his grandfather's eyes.

'But I'll do my best to persuade them to come to lunch.'

'Good boy.'

His grandfather nodded and upended his glass to drain the rest of the beer.

'I'm depending on you now,' he said. 'Don't let me down.'

With that, Clarence began to clear the empty glasses and gestured to Walter it was time to leave his grandfather in peace.

# CHAPTER 4

WALTER KNEW IT WOULD take some persuasion to convince Philippe to accept the invitation to lunch with his grandfather. More than he had anticipated, in fact.

He had called hoping to reach Pippa but instead he found himself talking to Philippe. He was uncertain what kind of reception he would receive. He was painfully aware of the abuse Philippe had endured from his father. He cleared his throat and began to speak with an uncharacteristic formality.

'Dr Duval, it's Walter Cox here. You'll remember I brought Pippa home the other day.'

He waited for Philippe to acknowledge him, half expecting to hear the click of the line being cut dead.

'Yes, I remember,' Philippe replied evenly. 'What can I do for you?'

Walter paused and took a deep breath.

'Sir, my grandfather has asked me to call and let you know he would like to meet you and Pippa. He has asked me to invite you to lunch on Wednesday if that is convenient.'

Philippe listened politely but hesitated with his reply. Did he really need to get involved with this family after all these years? After all, his mother had managed to distance herself from them. Why should he be any different?

'Are you sure that's a good idea, Walter' Philippe replied. 'Your father was very blunt on the phone to me yesterday. There was no mistaking his views on the matter. He threatened me, in fact. I have to say I did not like being threatened in that way. He insulted my mother. He insulted me. He insulted my daughter. I don't plan to expose myself or my family to such insults again.'

He waited for Walter to respond. Did Walter know about his father's phone call? He wasn't sure. He was certainly in no mood for olive branches.

'I'm sorry my father spoke to you in that way, sir,' Walter said, aware that his apology was barely adequate. 'I heard the tail end of his conversation with you. I can only apologise. My grandfather was furious when he found out.'

He hesitated. What more could he say to make amends?

'Besides, my father will not be involved in this visit,' he added, hoping that his father's absence would be enough to reassure Philippe.

After a long pause, Walter was relieved to hear Philippe accept the invitation.

'Very well,' Philippe said. 'What time would we be expected? And what is the address?'

But Walter was one step ahead of him.

'My grandfather's chauffeur Frederick will call for you and Pippa at around ten thirty, Dr Duval,' he said. 'He'll be driving a Mercedes-Benz saloon. A grey Mercedes.'

'That's very kind of you, Walter,' Philippe said, 'but there is no need to send a car for us.'

'I think it's the least we can do, Dr Duval,' he said, not giving Philippe any further opportunity to protest. 'I look forward to seeing you and Pippa on Wednesday. I know my grandfather will be pleased.'

With that, the line went dead, leaving Philippe in a state of considerable anxiety. Where is this going to lead, he wondered? How does a man in his fifties meet his father for the very first time?

There had been nothing in his life to date that had prepared him for the possibility. But if he turned down this opportunity, he worried he would regret it for the rest of his life.

It was a perfect late summer day, with just a hint of freshness in the air. The big grey Mercedes came to a stately halt in front of Eastbury Hall.

'Wow, this place is huge,' Pippa whispered to her father, as they alighted from the car and were afforded their first close up view of the house.

Philippe paused. He too was overwhelmed by its size and grandeur.

'You're right, it's huge. I hardly remember it to be honest. I'd only ever seen it from outside the fence when I was a child,' he said, searching far back into the memories of his early childhood.

'I think your father must employ a lot of gardeners,' Pippa observed as she looked around her at the immaculately groomed lawns and shrubs. 'Of course, that's what your mother's father was employed to do.'

She already knew that part of his story but she had hoped by bringing it up, there might be other forgotten pieces of his history that would fall into place.

'Sadly, I barely remember him. He died when I was eight years old.'

To Philippe, his grandfather seemed like a shadowy figure, someone who was spoken about only very occasionally. Could that have been because of the shame his mother felt, he wondered? Or was his premature death the culmination of a deprived life, the early loss of his wife and the disappointment of his daughter's situation? He would never know now. He suddenly felt an uncontrollable wave of regret at how much he had never understood about his childhood.

As Philippe and Pippa mounted the front steps the massive front door opened silently and a stately figure, quite in tune with the house, appeared before them.

'How do you do, Dr Duval, Miss Duval,' he said. 'My name is Clarence, Mr Cox's butler. Welcome to Eastbury Hall. Mr Cox senior will be down shortly. Shall we go in.'

Philippe and Pippa followed Clarence into the grand entrance and then into a formal drawing room which Philippe thought was probably more appropriate to an English stately home than the home of a nouveau riche American.

'Is Walter Cox joining us?' Philippe asked. 'The youngest Walter Cox that is?'

Clarence smiled and acknowledged the distinction.

'He is, Dr Duval,' he replied. 'No doubt he will bound through the back door any moment.'

Philippe risked a sideways glance at Pippa who was trying her best not to laugh at the absurdity of the formal greeting from the butler.

'It's a stunning place,' Philippe whispered to his daughter, who nodded while trying hard not to stare open mouthed at the ornate luxury that surrounded them on every side.

'Mr Cox enjoys a martini before lunch when he is entertaining,' Clarence said, motioning to the sideboard where four glasses were laid out in readiness.

'That would be very welcome, Clarence,' Philippe replied politely.

He had rarely drunk martinis and he doubted Pippa had ever tasted one but it seemed to be expected. Martinis were the accepted pre-lunch drink so therefore they would drink martinis as if it was something they did every day.

Father and daughter were invited to sit on a beautifully upholstered sofa but just as he was about to sit down, Philippe was immediately attracted by two impressive portraits. He was sure of the artist but nonetheless he searched for the telltale signature of John Singer Sargent.

'They are fine portraits, are they not? Only the best for my father and mother. Your grandparents.'

Philippe was momentarily startled. He had been so absorbed in the paintings he had not heard Walter William Cox approach. For the first time in his life, he turned to face his father.

But he could think of nothing to say. Nothing that was going to bridge fifty-three years of disappointment. Nothing that was going to wipe away the hurt and anger at how his mother had been treated.

'You don't really look like your mother, do you?'

'I don't know, to be honest, who I look like,' Philippe said, but even within a few moments of meeting his father, he could see the resemblance with himself.

Leaning heavily on his gold topped cane, Walter William Cox extended his hand towards Philippe, who hesitated. What would shaking his hand mean? Would this one simple act be expected to wash away everything from the past.

But he took his father's hand anyway, the handshake a little firmer than he expected.

'We should have done this a long time ago, Philippe,' he said, his head slightly bowed in apology. 'But you did not pursue the connection as I thought you might have.'

'What reason would I have had to *pursue the connection*, as you put it?'

'Curiosity, perhaps?'

'But I did not know for certain who my father was.'

'Your mother never told you?'

Philippe shook his head. The years were falling away. His memories were suddenly as fresh as if they happened yesterday.

'She would not confirm your identity,' he said.

'But surely on your birth certificate?'

Again, he shook his head.

'Father unknown it says.'

'But I told her she could name me,' the older man said. 'I always assumed she had.'

He thought for a few moments.

'I suppose she was worried her father might lose his job if she named me as the father of her child.'

*It can all be discussed politely now*, Philippe wanted to say. *Now that it no longer matters.* But he remembered the years of struggle for her. The years of shame. The whispers behind the hands as he walked with his mother.

'You could have done more for her,' Philippe said.

There would never be another opportunity for him to challenge his father's actions. Out of the corner of his eye, he could see Pippa was transfixed by the ebb and flow of the conversation.

'She wouldn't take anything from me for herself,' he said, with genuine sadness, 'except the cottage at a low rent.'

'For herself you say?'

'Oh, yes, she would take nothing, but for you, she struck a bargain. She knew you were clever.'

Philippe was silent. He knew what was coming.

'I was pleased you excelled at medical school,' the old man said. 'It cost me a lot of money but it was money well spent.'

'I did not know. Thank you.'

The old man shrugged.

'Of course, you didn't know,' he said. 'She swore me to secrecy. I owed her that much. But I know she was proud of you. I was too in my own way.'

For Philippe the past was suddenly falling into place as it had never done before.

They had been standing facing one another but now Clarence was gently urging the old man to sit in his favourite chair. His martini had been placed on a table within easy reach.

'I hope you like a martini, Philippe,' he said, as he sipped his drink carefully, savouring every mouthful. 'I have few indulgences left to me now.'

And then he turned his head and noticed Pippa for the first time.

'Well, my dear, you started a chain of events you didn't foresee I'm sure,' he said, not unkindly.

'I did, sir,' she said. 'It was well intentioned. But perhaps ...'

Her voice trailed off. She was yet to be convinced that her intervention would work out for the best. She sipped her drink cautiously trying not to grimace at the unfamiliar taste.

'How is everyone today? Sorry I'm late, but not too late for a martini, I hope, Clarence.'

Walter Cox patted his grandfather's shoulder and then went forward to shake Philippe's hand.

'I'm so pleased you came, sir,' he said. 'I think my grandfather would have been disappointed not to finally meet you.'

Philippe struggled for words. What could he say? It was an honour. No, it was not an honour because his father had not been honourable.

Clarence handed the drink to the latecomer, admonishing him at the same time for his tardiness. His eyes then alighted on Philippe's empty glass. He looks like a man in need of a lift was Clarence's immediate thought. Without asking, he took the glass and quickly refilled it. Philippe smiled his thanks.

'This has been a day of revelations, Walter,' Philippe said finally. 'I still don't understand though, why your own father should be so upset and annoyed at me. I have no interest in anything to do with the Cox estate, not for me nor for my daughter.'

There he had said it. Was that what they wanted to hear, he wondered? Would that satisfy them? He felt he had to say more.

'We have a very comfortable life in Sydney,' he added. 'And Pippa's mother is a considerable heiress in her own right. We don't need money.'

It was the elder Walter Cox who answered, his eyes alight with what Philippe would remember later as mischief.

'He's jealous.'

'Of me?'

Philippe was incredulous.

'He doesn't even know me unless you told him about me?'

The old man shrugged.

'Might have done,' the old man admitted.

For a few moments, complete silence descended on the room. Who would be first to speak? Philippe was beginning to feel as if the very foundations of his life were being chipped away, piece by piece. He noticed the shocked look on Walter's face.

'When, Grandfather?' he asked, the lightness gone from his voice. 'When did you tell my father?'

The old man gestured as if to say what does it matter but he saw the look in his grandson's eyes and faltered.

'Oh, if you must know, he annoyed me one day when he was about your age, throwing his weight around as if he owned everything. I told him then to watch out because I could easily recognise my first born son and I might appoint my first born to be in charge of everything when I died.'

'So, for half his life, my father has nursed this grudge against you? And worried that you might fulfil your threat.'

The old man shrugged but there was no hint of any real contrition.

'I guess so,' he conceded reluctantly. 'But look here. He and I just never got on well. I never took to him. He never took to me. As far as he's concerned, the only thing I can do for him now is die.'

Pippa had been sitting quietly taking everything in. She felt she now understood the extreme reaction of Walter's father to her story.

'It's no surprise your father reacted the way he did, Walter, after what I said over lunch.'

He smiled at her.

'I had no idea I was leading you into a nest of vipers, Pippa,' he said. 'I'm so sorry.'

But his grandfather was unrepentant.

'I would have loved to have been there, young lady,' he said. 'It would have been great entertainment to have watched my son squirm.'

Standing quietly in the background, Clarence watched and listened. Among those gathered, he wondered what was to be gained by the airing of the family's deepest secrets. Would there be a day when they would look back with regret at how everything had been managed? He worried that all pretence at constraint was gone. But outwardly, he betrayed none of this concern. With his usual formality, he announced lunch was served and ushered the group into the dining room.

One course followed another. Philippe was grateful the food was light and the servings small.

'You have a fine cook, sir,' he said, trying to steer the conversation onto neutral ground.

The old man grunted.

'It's the only time I get decent food,' he complained, 'when I have people to lunch. The rest of the time they feed me invalid food.'

He pulled a face, much as a naughty child might, except that no one was quite in the mood to cajole him.

'And your wine cellar is something to be admired, I suspect,' Philippe said, holding his glass of vintage chablis up to the light.

He could see the old man was secretly pleased at the compliment.

'Well, it's no good having a fine house and then serving rubbish wine at the table,' he said. 'Clarence sees to the cellar. He has a good nose.'

Clarence, who had been hovering to refill their glasses, inclined his head slightly at the rare compliment but said nothing.

It was then the air of quiet calm around the lunch table was rudely shattered by an angry, bellowing voice that came out of nowhere.

'Well, what have we here? What the devil is he doing here?'

Walter William Cox the third, his face an unhealthy shade of red, pointed across the table at Philippe.

'It's all very cosy, isn't it! Hatching a plan behind my back I don't doubt.'

The old man shook his head.

'What do you mean, hatching a plan? You were always a stupid boy, given to hysterics.'

Philippe was shocked. The hatred between the pair was on full display. How do you repair such a broken relationship, he wondered, unless someone was prepared to back down? He looked to Walter. He too was open-mouthed at the savagery of the words being uttered but he was the first to stand and go towards his father, his voice soothing.

'Let's talk about this another time, Father,' he said as he walked the few paces to intercept his father. 'It's not what you think.'

He turned towards his son.

'Of course, it's what I think it is and you're mixed up in it too.'

He almost spat the words in his son's direction.

'I know what it is. A nice little tête-à-tête behind my back, hoping I wouldn't find out.'

'It's nothing of the sort,' the old man said, losing patience with his son's outburst. 'I suppose that sneak of a daughter of yours telephoned you?'

He did not get a reply but he knew he was right. She had always sided with her father in their disagreements. But he was tired of it all. Tired of the arguments. He wanted peace and quiet.

'You were always stupid, I'm afraid,' the old man said, without any attempt at conciliation. 'I've no patience with you. Just get out of my house and leave me in peace.'

His son, enraged by the latest insult, snatched up a ceremonial dagger that had lain, unnoticed, on a nearby table. He lunged forward, catching everyone but Clarence by surprise. The dagger clattered harmlessly to the floor as Clarence disarmed him in one easy fluid movement.

'You don't want to be doing that, sir,' he said calmly, while all the time maintaining a vice-like grip on Walter William Cox whose anger and rage shimmered through his body like a volcanic eruption.

The old man reached out for his wine glass, apparently unperturbed by what had just occurred.

'Top up the wine glasses, Walter,' the old man said, 'while Clarence escorts your father out.'

Through all the commotion, Philippe and Pippa had remained silent, knowing if they intervened, the whole scene might escalate beyond control.

It was Philippe who first noticed Clarence struggling to keep Walter William Cox upright, as if he had become a dead weight. Pippa had seen it too and simultaneously they rushed to help, just as he collapsed on the floor, despite Clarence's efforts to hold him upright.

Philippe knew the telltale signs well. Abnormal breathing. Glassy eyes. A weak pulse. He looked at his daughter and mouthed the word *stroke* and she nodded.

'Call for an ambulance,' he yelled. 'I think he's had a stroke.'

'I will do that at once, Dr Duval,' Clarence replied, his voice calm and reassuring.

Philippe could hear Clarence demanding an ambulance be despatched immediately. After a few moments, he returned to see what more he could do.

'Do they have far to come?' Philippe asked. 'We need to get him to hospital urgently.'

'Not very far,' Clarence replied. 'They're just about a mile outside the estate boundary.'

Even as he spoke, they could all hear the distant wail of the siren.

'Do you think he'll be OK?' Pippa whispered to her father as she knelt alongside the patient, who had been placed in the recovery position. Philippe continued to check his vital signs concerned he had lapsed so quickly into semi consciousness.

'I hope so, Pippa,' he said, more than anything to reassure her. 'At a guess I would say he's had untreated hypertension for some years as well as a lifestyle that didn't help. I think today's events pushed him over the edge.'

The words had been meant for Pippa but Walter, coming alongside them, caught their meaning.

'Do you think he'll make it, Dr Duval?'

Philippe hesitated. He did not want to offer false hope of a full recovery.

'He has a chance if we can get him to hospital quickly,' Philippe said, trying to be reassuring. 'You should let your mother know.'

Then he looked around, surveying the room critically. Clarence had replaced the ornamental dagger on the table where it had lain untouched for years. Philippe looked up and issued a quiet warning.

'Walter, there's no point in telling your mother the details of what happened here,' he said. 'Or anyone else for that matter.'

There was now nothing in the room to suggest any altercation had taken place. Clarence had quietly seen to that. Everything was in place, just as it should be.

Walter nodded. He was shaken but not insensible to the implications of what had occurred.

'I agree,' he said, and he looked at Clarence, who nodded slightly as if to signal his agreement.

'It's possible your grandfather's behaviour can be explained by his advancing years,' Philippe said in a low voice, hoping Walter would understand what he was really saying without his having to spell it out. Philippe thought it highly likely Walter's grandfather was in the first stages of senility. Above all, he did not want this to be Walter's lasting memory of his father, a bitter man angry enough to want to kill his own father.

'I think your grandfather finally goaded your father so much that he could no longer stand it,' he said quietly. 'I think he reached the point today where he could not walk away.'

Walter nodded, grateful for Philippe's good sense and perspective.

'I believe you're right,' he said. 'Their arguments seem to have become much more bitter in recent years.'

Through it all, the eldest Walter Cox had remained sitting at the table, an impassive observer of his son's collapse, seemingly disconnected from the scene taking place in front him. Finally, he spoke.

'What are you two whispering about? Is he dead?'

Philippe moved across the room and pulled a chair out from the table to sit alongside the old man, leaving Pippa to manage the patient. There was little they could do for him.

'He's semi-conscious,' he said, ignoring the jibe. 'I think he's had a stroke. His only chance is if we can get him to hospital quickly.'

Even as Philippe spoke, Clarence was ushering in two ambulancemen who had taken the precaution of bringing a stretcher with them. Philippe watched as the two men lifted the almost lifeless body of Walter William Cox onto the stretcher and headed for the door.

# CHAPTER 5

BARBARA COX, ALERTED by the ambulance siren, was unprepared for what she saw as she passed the prostrate body of her husband as it emerged from the big house. She had fully expected to see the elder Walter Cox's lifeless body. Instead, she saw what she assumed was the dead body of her husband. Behind her, her daughter Virginia let out a cry of anguish.

'It's my fault,' she wailed. 'It's all my fault.'

'What's your fault?' her brother demanded, as he followed the ambulancemen down the front steps.

But he was barely interested in her reply and paid it no attention. He turned instead to his mother.

'I will go with him in the ambulance,' he said quickly. 'He's had a stroke. He's in a bad way.'

And with that he quickly climbed into the back of the ambulance before the doors were shut with a heavy bang.

Philippe looked up as the newcomers entered the dining room.

'Can someone please tell me what's gone on here?' Barbara Cox demanded. 'What's happened to my husband?'

'And who are you?' she asked, turning to face Philippe.

Philippe took a few paces forward to introduce himself but he never got a chance to speak.

'Meet your brother-in-law Dr Philippe Duval, Barbara,' the old man chuckled. He had dreamt of this moment. He liked his daughter-in-law even less than he liked his son.

'How do you do, Mrs Cox,' Philippe said, acknowledging the introduction politely. 'I think you've met my daughter Pippa?'

He was greeted with a look of absolute distain.

'Aah, the gold diggers,' she said, with a rudeness that shocked Philippe into momentary silence.

With some effort, the elder Walter Cox rose to his feet. Using the table to support himself, he waved his walking stick in Barbara Cox's direction. There was no mistaking the threat he intended to convey.

'If,' he said loudly and deliberately, 'if I ever hear those words from your lips again, I will cut my son, and therefore you and your sniv-elling daughter, out of my will. You will not get a penny. Do you hear me? Not a penny.'

He coughed deeply. It had taken almost all his remaining energy to utter those few words. But he could see they had struck home.

The colour drained from Barbara Cox's face but she remained defi-ant. She wanted to say *you're a stupid old fool and you're getting more senile by the day* but she was wary. What if her husband died? She would need to stay on good terms with her father-in-law just in case the worst happened. But still, she could not bring herself to back down. She began one last feeble defence of her outburst.

'Why else would they be coming around here if it's not for your money?' she asked querulously, her voice in danger of becoming a high pitched whine.

In her mind, there was no other possible explanation. Her imagi-nation did not extend further than the desire for wealth and prestige. Nothing else had ever been so important to her. She, Barbara Cox, had put up with a marriage to a man she had come to despise for only one reason. His money. There was no other motivation she could understand or accept. And she was not going to be denied what she felt she had earned by a senile old man.

It was Philippe who answered. He was losing patience with having to explain his complete lack of interest in his father's wealth but he did so again in the conciliatory voice he reserved for his most difficult patients.

'I have no interest in the Cox wealth, Mrs Cox,' he said. 'Nor does my daughter. We are happy with our lives in Sydney. My daughter was simply curious to find out about my side of the family. She knows her mother's family very well. But her story, like mine, began with being born out of wedlock.'

She shrugged her shoulders, unconvinced by his declaration but feeling somehow she was being made to look a fool except she didn't quite understand how or why. She turned to her father-in-law.

'Tell me what happened here,' she demanded. 'Why was my husband being carried out on a stretcher?'

The old man laughed. It was not a pleasant sound.

'I thought you might think I'd done you a favour, Barbara. Didn't you threaten to divorce him just a day or so ago? I wouldn't have blamed you. He's not a nice man.'

Philippe sighed deeply. Why was he insisting on stirring up further trouble? Hadn't there been enough upset already?

'Mrs Cox,' Philippe said quietly. 'I think you'll find your husband has had a stroke. He was upset seeing me here but he had absolutely no reason to be concerned. It proved too much for him and he collapsed.'

She could see Philippe was sincere. Despite her rudeness to him, he had responded with the air of the calm medical professional he prided himself in being.

'A stroke you say. So suddenly? Without warning?'

Philippe nodded, pleased she had now calmed down and was listening to him.

'It gave all the appearance of a stroke,' he replied. 'And yes, they can happen very unexpectedly. Your husband probably needed to be taking blood pressure medication, I would think. Do you know if he was prescribed anything by his doctor?'

She smiled bleakly then.

'He had pills, Dr Duval,' she said, using his name for the first time, 'but he didn't take them all the time. I did try to tell him that he was meant to take them regularly but he just ignored me, I'm afraid.'

Her revelation came as no surprise to Philippe. In his experience, it was difficult to get men of a certain age to acknowledge their mortality. A simple thing like trying to get male patients to take preventative medication regularly was high on his list of frustrations.

'That's a pity, Mrs Cox,' he said, soothingly. 'But it's no good worrying about what's past. Let's hope and pray the hospital can help him pull through.'

It seemed to Philippe she was on the verge of apologising to him but instead she turned back towards her father-in-law.

'I'll go to the hospital now,' she said, suddenly adopting the role of grieving wife. 'I will let you know how he gets on.'

Philippe held his breath. I hope he says something appropriate, he thought.

The old man simply nodded, clearly worn out by the events of the day.

I think he's overplayed his hand this time, Philippe thought. How will he ever repair the rift in his family? For a moment, Philippe stood looking at the shell of the man his father had become and wishing that he had known him in his younger days. Was this the outcome of bitter years of regret, he wondered? Marrying the wrong woman? Not being able to love the child she gave him. All the time wishing for something that could never be.

With Clarence's help, the old man started to leave the room but he paused. He fumbled in the pocket of his jacket.

'Here, you should have this, Philippe,' he said.

Philippe reached out and took from his hand a small black and white photo. Unlike the one his mother had kept, this photo showed a young man holding a small boy in his arms. Philippe was transfixed. It was the photo he had hoped to find among his mother's possessions.

'I've had it for fifty years,' his father said, his sadness in what might have been unmistakable. 'You should have it now.'

'Thank you. I appreciate it.'

'As ye sow, so shall ye reap.'

Philippe had to lean closer to him to hear the whispered words.

'It is entirely my fault I am reaping a barren harvest from my life's

57

work,' he said. 'Mourning the loss of your mother and you, I couldn't find any room in my heart for Walter. Is it any wonder he turned out the way he did? Ignored by his father and smothered by his mother. Not a good beginning for a child.'

Philippe was silent. What could he say? At times growing up, he had been bitter not to have a father. He remembered how he had been bullied and abused by other children.

'Let's hope it's not too late for you to make amends,' Philippe said, offering what hope he thought might be reasonable.

But the old man shook his head sadly.

'I think we both know it's all gone too far,' he said. 'But I have faith in young Walter.'

Philippe noticed a slight brightening of his mood at this prospect.

'He seems a sensible young man,' Philippe ventured, hoping he had not misread the signs.

'He is indeed,' he said, smiling. 'I don't think he can be pushed into doing something he doesn't want to do. He's made an art form of avoiding his father's demand that he should join Cox Industries and learn everything about the company.'

'Perhaps he sees a different future for himself?'

Philippe had sensed an ambivalence about the future already mapped out for Walter in the short time he had known him.

The old man hesitated. To admit such a possibility was to admit the end of the industrial empire he, and his father before him, had built from nothing. But he already knew that was likely. What did it matter? What was there to show for it but the great house too big for comfortable living and massive wealth that couldn't buy the three things he now most wanted: good health, a contented family and time.

He shrugged.

'Unless you want to give up your doctoring and become a company man?'

It had been said in jest but Philippe's father looked closely at him to gauge his reaction. Philippe caught Pippa's eye. He could see instantly the conflicting emotions of alarm and amusement in her face.

'Definitely not,' he replied, 'but thanks for the offer. Pippa and I will go back to Sydney and resume our lives. We'll see this little episode as an adventure that we'll store away in our memory banks for those lazy summer Sundays when we have the leisure to think of it all again.'

The old man nodded. Philippe was surprised he did not look disappointed. I guess he already knew what my answer would be, he mused.

'You made the choice for us more than fifty years ago. It can't be changed now on a whim,' Philippe added, to make sure his father understood the issue was beyond doubt.

'You're right of course,' he said, as if he agreed. 'But I want you to feel you can visit at any time. You should bring your wife to see me.'

'We'll see,' Philippe said, wondering how that would be possible.

'This one visit has meant a lot to me. You have turned into a fine man, Philippe. I'm proud to know you are my son, even if I never acknowledged it openly until now.'

He began then to cough violently again and this time Clarence put his arm around the old man.

'I think it's time I got him up to his room, Dr Duval,' he said quietly. 'Frederick already has the car at the front of the house to take you home.'

'Thank you, Clarence. I would appreciate you letting me know how everyone gets on. Young Walter has our number.'

As they headed down the steps to the waiting car, father and daughter paused to take a final look back at the great house. For both, it would be a day they would never forget.

Pippa tried hard to immerse herself in her work but Philippe could see she was distracted. For nearly a week, there had been no news of Philippe's half-brother Walter William Cox. Despite her father's reassurance, she continued to feel as if she was responsible for his collapse.

Philippe hoped, against everything his experience had taught him, he would recover, worried that Pippa would blame herself if the worst happened. More than once, Philippe had tried to reassure his daughter that the stroke was inevitable. It could have happened at any time, he told her repeatedly.

Still, he too was anxious for news so he was pleased when a call came through from Walter. He was in New York for the day and would call in to see them to tell them the latest news of his father.

It was late afternoon when Philippe greeted him at the door. Of all the Cox family, he liked and trusted Walter.

'I think you might be surprised to know that my father has made something of a recovery,' Walter said. 'His physician says that whatever spontaneous recovery occurs in the next couple of weeks will probably be the limit of his recovery, which is quite good considering. He can speak but there is some paralysis in his left side. I think they hope that some specialist therapy will help.'

Philippe listened to this report in silence, understanding every aspect of what Walter was saying and then feeling a wave of relief that Walter's father had survived the stroke.

'That's encouraging news, Walter,' he replied, as he ushered him into the living room. 'Pippa has just arrived home from a long shift at the hospital. She'll be delighted at that news.'

Pippa, fresh from the shower and a quick change of clothes, greeted Walter with a smile.

'That's great news, Walter,' she said, taking up the chair opposite him, having first poured herself a glass of white wine. The men, she noticed, were already halfway through their first drinks.

'But it's not all good tidings I bring,' Walter said, his voice suddenly sombre. 'I came to tell you that my grandfather died last night. In his sleep. It wasn't unexpected.'

Philippe bowed his head slightly. He was unsure how he felt at the news. Just days ago, he had finally met his father for the first time, but had it all come too late? Had he been better off with no knowledge of his father, except through the faded image of a young man in an old black and white photograph? Now he must deal with the lasting image of an old man broken by years of bitterness. But Philippe spoke the words expected of him.

'Thank you for coming to tell me, Walter,' he said. 'It's very good of you to deliver the news in person.'

'It was no trouble, Dr Duval,' he said. 'It was strange. After meeting you, I got the feeling my grandfather seemed to feel he had fulfilled his one last ambition and there was nothing more for him. Clarence said he was content at the last.'

If Philippe was surprised by this revelation, he did not show it. Perhaps it was true for both of them, their meeting had concluded an unfinished chapter in each of their lives. Regret for what might have been served no purpose now.

'You might find yourself having to shoulder more responsibility now, Walter,' Pippa said. 'Your life as a playboy might be at an end.'

'Pippa, that's not a very appropriate thing to say,' her father said, in a rare rebuke.

But Walter laughed, knowing exactly what she was referring to.

'Pippa's right, Dr Duval,' he said, defending her. 'It may well be time for me to take on more responsibility.'

Philippe smiled. He began to wonder how Walter would face the responsibilities of managing a large enterprise if his father could no longer perform that task.

'In fact, I've been with the lawyers today,' he said. 'They are allowing me to manage my parents' affairs for the time being. They were not very forthcoming about my grandfather's estate although they did tell me there were some last minute changes to his will which he signed off yesterday. They said there will be no public revelations until after his funeral.'

Philippe looked up in alarm.

'I hope those last minute changes don't involve me, Walter,' he said sharply. 'Please tell me they don't involve me.'

Walter shrugged his broad shoulders.

'I don't know what changes he made, to be honest,' Walter replied, 'only that he made some changes. It might have been to do with my father's stroke. He may have thought my father would not be able to continue as head of the company.'

But he was only speculating. He repeated what the lawyers had told him.

'Apparently my grandfather left strict instructions there was to be a reading of his will after his funeral and nothing was to be revealed before then.'

'Something of an old-fashioned approach don't you think?

'Positively Gothic, if you want my opinion,' Walter said.

Philippe smiled at this description. Walter's right. There had been something Gothic about my father.

'I got the sense he liked to manipulate things. Perhaps he couldn't resist doing so one last time from the grave.'

'You're showing him too much respect, Dr Duval. What you mean is he enjoyed manipulating people.'

Philippe nodded slightly. He guessed from his own limited experience that Walter was right. He knew his grandfather too well.

'If you don't mind me asking, Walter, what was he like as a younger man?'

The young man paused to finish his beer considering how best to answer the question.

'He was indulgent of his grandchildren but even so we were just a little bit afraid of him when we were very young. He was always busy. He was a charming host when he wanted to be and a brutal business tycoon when he wanted to be. A loving grandfather when he felt like it and an acerbic father when he felt like it. My father was no match for him unfortunately. Not as charming a host nor as ruthless a business-man. I think my grandfather came to despise my father for his per-ceived failings, never realising that the failure was his. I think it's fair to say he—and he alone—created the tormented wreck my father has become.'

It was a long speech to which Philippe listened intently. Even on such brief acquaintance, he had guessed much of what Walter was now telling him.

'Walter, was your father well enough to be told the news of his father's death?'

It was Pippa who asked, not yet sure just how well Walter's father had recovered. Would the news aid his recovery, she wondered, or hinder it?

'Yes, he's been told,' he replied. 'He nodded and mumbled a few words that we struggled to understand. But it was clear he knew what we were talking about.'

'I must go,' he said, with a quick glance at his watch. 'The traffic is going to be pretty thick at this time of day. My mother is expecting me for a late dinner.'

Both Pippa and Philippe walked to the door with Walter, thanking him for taking the time to call in to see them.

'One more thing.'

Walter paused, not quite knowing how to phrase the invitation he had promised his grandfather he would deliver.

'I have to tell you, Dr Duval, that my grandfather left a special request that you and Pippa attend his funeral.'

'Do you think that's wise, Walter?'

Memories of his ill-fated visit to meet his father were still fresh in Philippe's mind. He doubted his presence would be welcomed by other members of the family.

Walter paused then, trying to think how best to say what needed to be said.

'Just let me say,' he replied, 'before you say no, that certain family members have been warned. In their usual oblique fashion, the lawyers have said that anyone who protests at your presence could face consequences. But they did not specify what they meant by consequences.'

Philippe did not respond immediately. It had been his natural reaction to say *no, he would not attend*. But none of the anger and disappointment he felt was of Walter's doing and it suddenly seemed unfair to burden him with his anger. But still he wrestled with how to respond. Did he really need to be dragged further into the Cox family and everything that entailed? He made no promises.

'Let us know the details, Walter, and we'll see. I can't promise anything.'

With that, Walter had to be content. He knew though that it had been his grandfather's last wish and he would try his best to ensure Philippe and his daughter attended the funeral.

# CHAPTER 6

IN THE END, PHILIPPE had given in to Walter's repeated urging to attend the funeral of his grandfather set down for the following Monday. As he and Pippa shuffled into the grey stone church behind a growing crowd of mourners, Philippe wondered why he had never been inside the church as a child. But even as he was wondering why, he could already supply the answer.

This is where the Cox family had worshipped, married, been baptised and buried for generations. He knew then nothing would have induced his mother to cross its threshold. To the Cox family, church going, like everything else, was a matter of reinforcing their privilege and status. In reality, their attendance at church was nothing more than a breathtaking display of their hypocrisy, which was so deeply embedded there was no chance they would recognise it. Despite his misgivings, it was hard not to admire his surroundings.

'Beautiful church,' Philippe whispered to Pippa, as they both gazed upwards at the impressive, vaulted ceiling. 'I imagine it could be a replica of an English church.'

'It is, Dr Duval. It's a replica of All Saints' Church in Maidstone in England which is where a lot of East Hampton's settlers came from in the early days.'

Both Philippe and Pippa turned to greet Clarence, who was directly behind them.

'It's good to see a familiar face, Clarence,' Philippe said, shaking his hand warmly. 'I am sorry we meet again on such a sad occasion. I believe you worked for my late fath… for your late employer for many years.'

He stumbled over the word. He had never said *my father* or very rarely throughout his entire life. It seemed very strange to be doing so now. He could not quite form the word. It was so foreign to him. He found he could not say it, not publicly. Not within earshot of at least fifty people. There was no way to bridge the chasm of more than fifty years. But Clarence understood exactly.

'It is a very sad day for me, Dr Duval,' he said. 'I admit he was a difficult man at times, especially in the later years, but he was loyal. I started work on the estate before the war. I'd had a spot of bother with the law and he was the only one who would give me a chance. I never ever forgot that.'

As they spoke, they had moved along with the crowd. Philippe was looking for a place to sit where he and Pippa could blend with the crowd who had come to pay their respects. But Clarence motioned them towards the front of the church. Philippe shook his head.

'I don't think that's a good idea, Clarence,' he protested. 'The last thing I want to do is draw attention to myself.'

But Clarence was insistent.

'Almost his last words to me were to make sure you attended his funeral. And he is to sit in the family pews. He said that to me more than once. I promised it would happen.'

Philippe sighed and looked at Pippa. What could they do? It would be unseemly to argue with Clarence in the middle of the church with hundreds of people filing in.

'Be prepared for some curious stares,' he said quietly to Pippa, as Clarence led the way to their allocated places, immediately behind the front row where Walter, his father, mother and sister would be expected to sit.

Philippe was relieved when Clarence sat down alongside them.

'Is Walter's father up to coming, Clarence, do you know?'

Philippe had not heard anything more of the patient since Walter's visit the previous week.

'I believe so, Dr Duval,' he replied, 'although people will be shocked to see him in a wheelchair. Most will know that he's had a stroke of course. It's hard to keep something like that quiet.'

'I think he's fortunate if he's able to get out and about in a wheelchair so soon, to be honest.'

Philippe had held out little hope for his half-brother's recovery. Certainly, he did not expect a full recovery but he had kept that well-informed opinion to himself.

'I haven't seen him myself,' Clarence said with his customary wariness, 'but I'm told he is doing quite well considering.'

Philippe did not want to probe too deeply. He knew the extent of recovery from a stroke varied from one patient to the next and depended on many factors. With the best treatment and the best rehabilitation facilities, he hoped Walter's father would recover much of his physical ability over time but he wondered if the level of his recovery would see him well enough to return to his old job as head of the family company with all its stresses and demands. Somehow, he doubted it.

Suddenly, the hubbub of conversation ceased, signalling a beginning of the service. He looked around as Barbara Cox and her daughter Virginia, both dressed head to toe in customary black, walked slowly down the aisle to take their seats in the front row. Behind them, Walter walked slowly pushing his father in a wheelchair. Philippe noticed how his half-brother turned his head to acknowledge one or two people but he did not speak.

The younger Walter inclined his head towards them and whispered a greeting over the top of his father's head, which was enough to make his father turn around. For just a few moments, they stared at one another. Philippe wanted to reach out to him, to say something meaningful, but he held back. What was the point? He did not want to risk provoking a scene. In front of him, the other family members stared straight ahead. He noticed Walter put a comforting hand on his father's shoulder before carefully positioning the wheelchair alongside the first pew.

With that, the rector began the service and Philippe was left to pursue his own thoughts.

Against his expectation, Philippe was relieved that very few people seemed to express any interest in his presence at the funeral service. He said as much to Clarence as they walked out together.

'I think they think you're a lawyer, Dr Duval,' he murmured, as he greeted one or two people he knew well.

'That will do very nicely as cover, Clarence,' he replied. 'I'm sure I can do a reasonable imitation of a lawyer, if called upon.'

'Speaking of lawyers, I believe you will be called upon to attend the reading of the will this afternoon.'

'Me? Are you sure Clarence? What possible interest could his will be to me?'

Clarence paused, unsure what to say.

'Do you know something I should know, Clarence?' he demanded. 'If you do, tell me now. I don't like surprises.'

But Clarence shook his head and repeated what he had heard the week before from Walter.

'No one knows for sure what's in his will, except the lawyers, and they will only reveal everything at the reading of the will after the funeral.'

'And who is meant to be at the reading? Do you know that?'

'Oh, yes, I know that much.'

He counted the attendees off on his fingers as if he was making certain he did not miss anyone.

'Walter. His father and his mother and his sister of course. You and your daughter. And me. Seven in all.'

'And you have no idea what is contained in the will? No hint?'

Clarence shook his head.

'He could be a very devious man at times. He enjoyed his little games. This could well be the last of his little games in fact. All I know is he made some changes and he was pleased he had done so. But he took the secrets to the grave. That is, until we hear from the lawyers this afternoon.'

They had walked out into the sunshine. Philippe noticed how small groups of people milled around, chatting, laughing, as if attending a funeral was just another event on their busy social calendars. He was not tempted in the least to meet any of them. The chatter paused momentarily as the sleek black hearse, bearing its burden of the dead man, moved slowly away.

'The family are going to the cemetery for the interment,' Clarence explained as they watched the hearse move at its glacial pace down the driveway followed by the mourning car. 'Do you want to go?'

Philippe shook his head. It was the thing he least wanted to do.

'That's far too intimate a setting for Pippa and me,' he replied quietly. 'Let his real family have some privacy to say their final good-byes. After all, I barely knew him. Our presence would be an unwelcome distraction.'

Clarence nodded.

'I think that's very wise, Dr Duval.'

And then he followed Clarence's gaze towards a group of three men headed in their direction.

'Lawyers,' Clarence whispered.

Philippe nodded. Clarence had hardly needed to tell him. Everything about their demeanour revealed their connection with the elder Walter Cox. The most senior of the men held out his hand towards Philippe who took it cautiously.

'My sincere condolences at the loss of your father, Dr Duval,' the man said with rigid formality. 'I'm sorry we haven't met before today. My name is Howard Davis. I'm head of the legal team looking after Mr Cox's affairs.'

Why does that not surprise me, Philippe thought. He tested the idea in his mind. A team of legal people. No doubt an expensive team of legal people. The closest he had come to such an arrangement were the trustees Julia met with every month or so. But they were not exclusively engaged in managing Julia's financial interests. This team standing before him was very much engaged with their single wealthy client. And obviously anxious to make sure such arrangements continued.

'Mr Davis, thank you for your condolences but you must know I hardly knew my father at all,' Philippe replied. He felt he was being drawn further and further into a situation over which he had no control.

Howard Davis smiled.

'I'm aware of that, Dr Duval,' he said, inclining his head slightly. 'It was a matter of deep regret for my client until very recently.'

Philippe tried hard to hide his surprise. He had never imagined he had been the subject of discussion between the father he had never known and his lawyer. It both alarmed and perturbed him.

'I assume this is your daughter Pippa?' Howard Davis said, turning towards her and extending his hand politely. 'It's good to meet you too Dr Duval.'

How does he know so much about us, Pippa wanted to say? And why does he know so much about us? But she caught her father's warning look and instead simply returned the greeting.

'Are you heading to the big house now, Dr Duval?' Davis said, turning back to Philippe but actually looking to Clarence for the answer.

'We were just going to head back there, Mr Davis,' Clarence said, having been on the periphery of the group and watching, with great interest, the interchange between Philippe and his employer's principal lawyer.

There was no condescension, no haughtiness that Clarence could detect from the lawyer, which surprised him. If anything, he had seen a willingness to please. He wants to be onside with Dr Duval, he thought. The lawyer wants very much to be onside with Philippe Duval, the unacknowledged bastard son. In Clarence's world, that meant only one thing. Dr Philippe Duval was about to become very important in the eyes of the Cox family's legal team. If he, Clarence, was right then the Cox family was in for a nasty surprise.

'That's good, Clarence,' Howard Davis said simply.

He turned back to Philippe.

'Dr Duval, this is neither the time nor the place for further discussions. We will see you this afternoon once the funeral reception has finished.'

Philippe inclined his head, half in acknowledgement and half in relief that the conversation was not going to be continued in the middle of the funeral crowd. It had left him unsettled. What had his father done? Why were lawyers seeking him out in the middle of the funeral from which he had hoped to drift away unnoticed?

'You look pale. And worried,' Pippa said quietly. 'Why do you think your father's lawyers thought it necessary to come and introduce themselves?'

By now they were standing alongside the chauffeur-driven Mercedes and Clarence was opening the back door for them.

'I have my own car parked over in the parking lot, Clarence,' Philippe said, suddenly confused as to why he was ushering them to the chauffeured car.

'If you give me your keys, Dr Duval, and tell me what model I'm looking for, I will drive your car to the big house. Frederick will drive you and your daughter.'

It was more a command than an invitation.

'I don't think it's necessary for us to be driven,' Philippe said. 'I'm sure I can find my way there if that's what you're worried about.'

But Clarence shook his head from side to side.

'My late employer insisted that you be treated as one of the family, for the world to see. Make sure they arrive at the house with Frederick driving them he said to me. And so, I'm fulfilling his final instructions, Dr Duval.'

He held the door open for Philippe while Frederick had quickly walked around the back of the vehicle to open the other passenger door for Pippa.

At every turn, Philippe felt himself being outmanoeuvred. He grimaced across at Pippa who smiled reassuringly at him.

'Relax,' she said. 'It's just a car. A few more hours and the day will be over.'

But he was still very tense.

'A few more hours of this and I might be heading straight for the airport,' he said, with a wry smile.

'The trappings of wealth have not seduced you then?' she asked, smiling, knowing the answer before he could even reply.

He shook his head.

'I have everything I need,' he said simply. 'I have you and your mother. I have a great job at a great hospital. I live in a wonderful city. I could not live like this.'

He waved his hands at the expensive houses lining the road, all needing to be tended by poorly paid, poorly educated people who regarded themselves as fortunate to have the jobs. But he did not forget how easily he might have been one of them except for the college fees that had been paid on his behalf. How would he have fared without that help, he wondered? Would his fierce intelligence have been enough to overcome the obstacles of his birth? He knew it would have been difficult. Was he in danger of becoming a hypocrite, he wondered?

Within minutes, the Mercedes was making slow progress up the driveway of Eastbury Hall, a bevy of cars following at a respectful distance before peeling off to a designated parking area. As the Mercedes came to a halt, Frederick emerged from the car quickly to prevent Philippe opening his own door. A young gardener had been designated to open Pippa's door.

The household staff were lined up down the stairs as if awaiting inspection. By Philippe's quick count, there were at least twenty people uttering words of welcome and awkward condolences. To him, it was a surreal charade but he acknowledged the muttered words with a nod of his head each time. Pippa, unsure what to say, simply followed her father's lead.

They were both relieved to see Clarence at the top of the stairs. He ushered them into the room where they had first met the eldest Walter William Cox. It seemed like a lifetime ago.

'Would you and your daughter like to stand here, Dr Duval,' Clarence said, pointing to a spot in the wide doorway.

He saw Philippe's look of enquiry bordering on confusion.

'To greet the guests in place of the rest of the family who will be back from the interment very shortly,' he explained patiently.

'Outmanoeuvred again,' he said in a low voice to Pippa, as

Clarence began to introduce the mourners, each of whom, struggling to hide their surprise, muttered the acceptable platitudes of condolence before moving on in search of a glass of champagne.

Without any explanation, Clarence, as he introduced each person, said simply: 'I would like you to meet Mr Cox's elder son, Dr Philippe Duval, and his daughter, and therefore Mr Cox's grand-daughter, Dr Pippa Duval.'

As one name followed another in an endless procession, Philippe and Pippa both watched fascinated as the struggle for good manners over burning curiosity played out silently in each person's mind.

'Thank God for politeness,' he said after fifteen minutes or more of introduction and banal condolences. 'I never knew good manners were so important.'

Pippa laughed quietly.

'But they're all itching to know the story,' she said, 'and here come the rest of the family.'

Philippe followed the direction of her gaze. It was Walter who raised his hand in a friendly salute.

'It's good to see you taking your rightful place, Dr Duval,' he said quietly as he came up to them.

Philippe acknowledged Walter's sentiment with a slight nod of his head.

'I doubt your father or mother will see it that way, Walter,' Philippe cautioned. 'And remember it is not a situation of my making. I would not have chosen to usurp your father's position. How is he, by the way?'

Philippe was sure the long day would be tiring for a man who should still be regarded as a patient.

'He's not too bad all things considered,' Walter said. 'He would like to speak with you.'

'Now? Is that a good idea?'

Walter nodded.

'There'll be no fireworks,' he said, his voice low for fear of being overheard. 'He wants a public reconciliation. He wants everyone to see that he accepts you as part of the family.'

Walter was about to say as *head of the family* but he thought better of it.

Philippe nodded thoughtfully. He understood how this was all to be played out. It's a pantomime for public consumption in which he is to have a starring role. The thought of it made him squirm inwardly. How had it all come to this? How had he found himself in this position? But he voiced none of these concerns to Walter.

'To quell gossip, I suppose?'

He looked at Walter, who nodded slightly.

'Partly,' Walter replied. 'But I think he realises how living life in bitterness is a waste of a life. Let me take you over to him.'

He turned to Pippa.

'Do you mind if we just exclude you for the moment?'

She nodded. She too was anxious that there be no more bad blood between her father and his half-brother. She watched as Walter guided Philippe towards his father, his wheelchair having been abandoned in favour of an armchair from which he could not rise under his own strength but at least it did not give him the appearance of being an invalid, which he hated.

Philippe pulled up a chair close to him. He was practised at such things. He slipped easily into professional mode, almost treating his half-brother as a patient. He knew exactly how to speak to patients whose recovery was not yet complete.

He held out his hand. Walter senior hesitated and then grasped Philippe's hand. There was little strength in his grip.

'How do you feel, Walter?' Philippe asked. It was the first time he had addressed his half-brother by name.

'Not too bad considering,' he muttered, his voice weak, his speech slightly slurred.

'You seem to have made a very good recovery all things considered,' Philippe offered.

'So they tell me, Philippe,' he said, his despair and irritation obvious to even the most casual observer.

'You'll have to be patient, I'm afraid. There may be a long road ahead with rehabilitation. But it is worth it if you can stick to the program. I've seen remarkable results in situations much worse than your own.'

This was a small white lie but he justified it to himself. He knew an optimistic patient responded much better to treatment.

'Thanks for your encouragement,' he said. 'I'll remember that. Walter's been very good helping me.'

He glanced up at his son who was hovering behind his chair.

'You've every right to be proud of your son,' Philippe said, happy to be on safe common ground. 'He's a credit to you.'

'Just as no doubt your daughter is a credit to you.'

Philippe smiled. How quickly their conversation had turned to exchanging commonplace pleasantries about their children. Gone was the swaggering arrogance of a man who previously commanded all he surveyed. In his place, Philippe saw a man defeated by his own hubris. A man who had not realised he'd had nothing to fear from his unacknowledged older brother until it no longer mattered.

Philippe stood up then and extended his hand to his half-brother's wife who, along with her daughter Virginia, formed a half circle alongside her husband's chair. She plays the solicitous wife well, Philippe thought, as their hands met for the briefest of moments.

Barbara Cox had looked on silently during the brotherly exchange, observing the meeting with quiet contempt, her white hot anger exceeded only by her self pity at being saddled with an invalid husband. Beside her, her daughter Virginia gave Philippe the briefest of nods and a small smile of acknowledgement that froze instantly on her lips.

'Your husband has had a very serious medical episode, Mrs Cox,' Philippe said with all the diplomacy he could muster. 'He's still very much in the first stages of recovery as I'm sure you know. He'll need plenty of time to recover. No stress.'

Philippe paused. He was beginning to sound like their physician, so he said nothing more.

'Thanks for the advice, Dr Duval,' she said, through tight, angry lips.

Her husband spoke too, his voice briefly stronger and more forceful.

'After what the old man has probably done with his will, I expect I'll have time on my hands.'

Philippe simply shrugged his shoulders. He did not want to enter into such a discussion.

'No doubt you'll find out in due course,' he said. 'I hope for everyone's sake he hasn't left behind any surprises.'

But it was clear to him his half-brother was unconvinced.

'Oh, I think he has, Philippe,' he retorted, his old belligerence returning briefly. 'I think he's loaded both barrels and fired them. You were lucky you missed knowing him, until the very end. He was an old bastard you know. Lucky you to grow up without a father. I bet he's skipped me and put my son in charge of everything. It's the sort of thing he'd do with relish.'

He started to cough then, his breath coming in heaving gasps.

'It would be better if your husband didn't upset himself,' he said, turning towards Barbara Cox and repeating his earlier warning. 'It won't help his recovery.'

She responded with icy politeness.

'Thank you for your professional opinion, Dr Duval,' she said. 'We'll be sure to take note of it.'

With a nod to the younger Walter, Philippe turned to go in search of Pippa among the crowd that had managed to turn a funeral reception into a cocktail party. He had done what had been asked of him. There were no more olive branches he would willingly extend to his half-brother or his family. He could not easily forget, nor forgive, the insults he and Pippa had endured.

One or two people eyed him curiously as he passed. Not for the first time, he wished Julia had been with him, that they could have attended the funeral as a family. Deep in thought he did not immediately see Howard Davis approach him until he was directly in front of him.

'Dr Duval,' he said, as Philippe stopped at the mention of his name. 'Could we meet in say fifteen minutes?'

Philippe consulted his watch. He had expected the reading of the will to follow the end of the funeral reception, which he suspected would only end when the champagne ended. Were the whole proceedings to be brought to a sudden end, he wondered?

'Of course, Mr Davis,' he replied. 'Are the other parties being gathered together for this meeting?'

'You mean for the reading of the will?'

'Yes. Of course.'

'Not yet, Dr Duval,' he said, deferentially. 'We must speak with you first. In Mr Cox's study would be best. Clarence will show you the way.'

Philippe nodded. *Why just me*, he wanted to ask. None of this was making any sense as he began looking for Pippa in the crowd.

# CHAPTER 7

CLARENCE HELD OPEN the door to what had always been the late Walter Cox's inner sanctum, a room others had entered only by invitation, and then only rarely. As Philippe entered, he noticed the dark wood panelling with floor to ceiling bookcases, each filled with carefully curated volumes. He wondered if any of the books had ever been read. A large highly polished desk dominated one corner of the room. He could see at a glance that it, at least, had been well used.

In the middle of the room, visitor armchairs were clustered around a low coffee table. It was to one of these chairs that Clarence directed Philippe. The legal team headed by Howard Davis was already awaiting his arrival.

'Coffee, Dr Duval?'

Clarence began the ritual of pouring coffee, each man in turn muttering his thanks. It was clear to Philippe that nothing would be said until Clarence had completed the task. As he left the room, he closed the door quietly. Philippe fully expected he would take up a position outside the door to deter unwanted visitors.

Inside, Howard Davis sipped his coffee as if he was deciding how best to begin. His colleagues sitting nearby remained silent. After some moments, he cleared his voice.

'Dr Duval,' he began, 'you may wonder why we are here meeting with you.'

'You're right, Mr Davis, I have no idea why I've been asked to meet you but I have a feeling you are about to tell me.'

'Indeed,' he replied simply, opening his substantial briefcase and pulling out a file of papers that reminded Philippe of a medical file for a seriously ill patient with multiple health problems.

With practised fingers, Howard Davis began to unravel the legal ribbon which had kept the bulky file together.

'I have been instructed by the late Mr Cox,' he intoned, 'to advise you that you are his principal heir, Dr Duval, and that you are henceforth to be regarded as head of the Cox family. We thought it prudent to discuss this with you before the family gathers for the reading of the will.'

'What! You can't be serious!'

The exclamation of shock was involuntary. Philippe had turned pale. *This was ridiculous. Why would a father he had never known do such a thing?* Unanswered question after question flitted through his mind.

'Mr Davis, I don't understand what you are saying. I barely knew my father. I met him only a matter of a few weeks ago. Why would he do such a thing?'

The lawyer was calm. He had foreseen Philippe's response.

'Let me reassure you, Dr Duval. You may have barely known your father but, believe me, your father knew you. At least he knew what you were doing, what you were achieving. He knew how you lived your life. He hoped you would come to see him when he heard you were in New York again. Fortunately, your daughter set the wheels in motion, so to speak.'

Philippe found none of this information easy to understand or accept. Had he been spied upon for years by his own father? It sounded very much like it.

'Why didn't my father reach out to me if he knew so much about me?'

It was an obvious question. He wondered though if the lawyers would know anything at all about his father's motivations.

'I don't know for sure, Dr Duval,' Howard Davis replied cautiously, 'but I can make an educated guess. I think he was worried his other son might react very badly if it became known he had initiated the contact with you. Their relationship, I'm sorry to say, soured over the last few years.'

Philippe was silent, not knowing what to say, trying to take in the enormity of what he had been told and how it might affect his life. He had not wanted this. He had hoped to walk away, and maybe, in a year or two, bring Julia for a visit. But this news. What would it mean for him? For Pippa?

'Tell me,' Philippe demanded, 'was it a recent change to name me as his major beneficiary?'

'No, sir, it was not.' the lawyer replied. 'This part of his will has remained unchanged for at least eight years.'

This was a new shock to Philippe who had already heard the gossip of late changes to his father's will. He assumed this is what the change had been.

'Eight years you say. That's around the time I went to Australia to be with Pippa. And then I met up with her mother again and we later married.'

Was that the reason, he wondered? He shook his head. It seemed unlikely.

'I have been your late father's lawyer for around twenty years, Dr Duval. I know there were many regrets he had but it was the regret he felt at not marrying your mother and ensuring you were his legitimate son that troubled him the most. He decided to make amends posthumously in the only way he could. I think you reaching out to your own illegitimate daughter was something he really approved of. He believed you had proved yourself to be a better man than he was. I believe he saw you as a man of great strength of character. He admired you. He spoke about you often when there was just the two of us.'

Philippe got up and walked towards one of the large windows, staring out at the view across the vast estate. Did he own all this now? What could he possibly do with it? He shook his head at the irony of it all. He pictured himself, a barefoot boy running past the front gate trying to spot his grandfather working in the garden. And then waving madly when he spotted him. And his mother pulling him away quickly for fear they would be seen.

He turned back from the window.

'You say I am his principal beneficiary, Mr Davis, which I still find hard to believe. Did he leave any instructions for me? Any indication of how he wanted me to proceed? Isn't it likely his will may be contested by other interested parties?'

The lawyer, who had up until this point remained seated, stood up and walked towards him.

'You have no need to worry, Dr Duval,' he replied confidently. 'There'll be some huffing and puffing, I've no doubt, but the will is watertight. Its provisions are quite complex and generous to the other members of the family. Now that you have had time to digest the news, you may want to read this.'

He held out an envelope to Philippe. It was addressed by hand. He was immediately reminded of the letter he had written Pippa twenty years before. It was as if history was repeating itself, except that this time the writer was reaching out to him from the grave. He opened it slowly and turned back to use the light from the window to read the words his father had written.

*Dear Philippe,*

*By the time you read this I will be in my grave. I hope we have had the chance to meet.*

*I have followed your life and your career with great interest. I'm sorry if you think that was spying on you, but I had to know how things turned out for you. I had to know if you needed my help. But to your credit you did not, apart from the college fees, and I'm pleased, proud even, to know you made good use of that opportunity.*

*It is to my eternal regret that I did not marry your mother. I was so easily influenced in those days when I was young. I loved her and I went on loving her, but she would take nothing from me after I refused to marry her, except that is, to pay for your college. It was little enough.*

*My second son and his family will be adequately provided for. The lawyers will explain the ins and outs of the family trusts etc. I could never get on with him but he hasn't done a bad job with the company. Young Walter won't want to go into the business so it could be time to dispose of it. Howard Davis will advise you about it. It would be prudent to keep him and his team on. He knows everything about the financial affairs.*

*My son Walter has often talked about demolishing this house. I think he thought such an idea would shock me but I think he's right. It belongs in the past, an absurd example of one man's unrestrained ego.*

*The lawyers will go through all the bequests. Everyone who has been of service to me is provided for as have the rest of the family, including your daughter.*

*I don't know how you will feel about becoming a rich man. I discovered, too late, that money and position meant nothing against living a life of regret.*

*I did little enough for you in life. This is my gift to you with my death. Use it wisely.*

*Your father*
*Walter William Cox II*

Through the silence in the room, he could hear the ticking of the mantle clock. What should his next move be? He breathed deeply. He had not sought this. He had not wanted it. All he could see ahead was conflict. He turned back towards Howard Davis who seemed to be waiting for him to say something, anything at all.

'Will you send for the youngest Walter Cox please,' he said.

Davis nodded towards his most junior colleague who immediately rose from his chair and headed towards the door. Philippe could see the whispered conversation taking place through the half opened door. He assumed Clarence had been sent in search of Walter.

'I assume you want to acquaint young Mr Cox with the terms of the will before this afternoon's formal reading?'

Philippe nodded.

'I think it would be a good idea, don't you?'

'You want him to act as peacemaker with his father I assume?'

82

Philippe nodded.

'Assuming a peacemaker is required, then, yes, I do. I don't intend Walter and Barbara Cox to be disadvantaged by this turn of events. They would have spent years imagining the day when they would control everything. Can you imagine the humiliation for them when it is known Walter is not the main beneficiary?'

'I can, Dr Duval, but it is the fact they coveted the wealth so openly that led my client to make the will he has. He does not want them to be poor. But he did not admire them. Not as he admired you.'

'But there were late changes to his will, were there not?'

Howard Davis inclined his head.

'You are well informed. After his son's medical episode, he realised his son might not recover sufficiently to resume his job as president of Cox Industries. There is a very able vice president. His name is Kenneth Harper. You may have even met him today. Your father left instructions to recommend you approve his promotion to president. We will set up a meeting for you to interview him in the next few days. I can also tell you that he made extra provision for Barbara Cox on the proviso that she continues to live with her husband and provide support to him. If she were to leave him, she would lose that extra provision which is paid annually and receive a much-reduced settlement.'

Philippe couldn't help but smile to himself. His father had thought of everything. He had understood his son and his social climbing wife completely. Philippe's wry smile did not go unnoticed.

'I see you approve, Dr Duval,' he said.

'Well, let's just say I understand his motivations.'

The lawyer continued.

'It wasn't only the provision for Barbara Cox that was amended. He was more generous to Clarence. And while it wasn't part of his will, he did set in motion a process to seek offers for Cox Industries.

'The whole company?'

'The entire company. Of which you are now the sole shareholder, Dr Duval. We will await your instructions in due course.'

Before Philippe could ask further questions, the door opened to admit the youngest Walter William Cox. He looked first at the lawyers and then at Philippe, who beckoned him into the room.

'Walter, the lawyers have just delivered some surprising news. I want you to hear it so when the formal reading of the will takes place, you at least among your family will be prepared for what's coming.'

Walter smiled and nodded. Seeing Philippe with the lawyers, he hardly needed to be told what was coming. He had known his grandfather very well. Too well perhaps.

'Let me guess, Dr Duval,' he said without a hint a rancour. 'My grandfather has made you his principal heir. Am I right?'

Philippe nodded. Walter then threw back his head and laughed.

'The old bastard. My father and mother will be livid. But I assume they will not be paupers, turned out of their home?'

His tone then turned serious. Surely his grandfather had not disinherited his family completely. Philippe was quick to reassure him.

'No, Walter, they will not be paupers and they will not be turned out of their home,' Philippe said quickly. 'But you should read this. It confirms that your grandfather's decision regarding his will is not a recent capricious act to spite your father.'

Walter took the letter and scanned it quickly. He nodded as he read it and began to understand what lay behind the decision.

'Now you understand, Mr Cox, that your grandfather's decision to make Dr Duval his main beneficiary was an idea of long standing.'

Howard Davis was anxious the young man understood.

'It was a will he made around eight years ago,' he explained. 'It was not a will he made because of what has occurred in the past few weeks. I think you really need to stress this to your family.'

Walter heard the lawyer out in silence. He felt he had to know just how well his father had been provided for.

'If I'm to act as peacemaker,' he said, 'you'll need to tell me some more details. What does my father get?'

He was listening intently. Despite their differences he felt almost as if he was betraying his father. He wondered if, in time to come, he might have to choose sides. He hoped not.

'By any measure your parents will be people of substantial means.'

Howard Davis reached for his bulky legal file. He did not want to risk giving Walter incomplete information.

'Your parents' house was surveyed out of the main estate onto a separate land title recently which your father will inherit outright. He will receive a substantial cash sum, a share portfolio and ongoing income from the family trust. There is separate provision for your mother. And for your sister too. I assure you they will all be able to go on living the life they always have.'

'That's if he recovers well enough,' Walter said, aware that a full recovery from his stroke was now unlikely. 'He certainly won't be able to go back to work for some time, if at all. Are you aware of that?'

'I am, Mr Cox,' he replied. 'I am familiar with the senior executives at Cox Industries too. There is a very competent vice president. I expect he should be stepping up to the top job immediately, but that will depend on Dr Duval.'

The lawyer turned to Philippe who was only now beginning to understand the enormity of the legacy that had been thrust upon him.

'Mr Davis, I have some knowledge of how hospitals should be run but absolutely no knowledge of how industrial companies should be run. I will act on your advice in this matter.'

The lawyer inclined his head.

'We should meet tomorrow, if that is convenient, and we can discuss the most pressing issues.'

'Welcome to the corporate world, Dr Duval,' Walter said, with just the hint of a grin. He had feared his grandfather might pass over his own father to make a will in his favour. His sense of relief was palpable.

Philippe caught his eye and smiled in return.

'You look relieved, Walter, if I may say so.'

'I am, Dr Duval. For one awful moment I thought he might have named me as the principal heir. I'm relieved he didn't. As to my father's situation, being relieved of the responsibility might turn out to be the best thing for him.'

Philippe shrugged his shoulders. It was hard to imagine his half-brother taking such a point of view but he saw no point in arguing with Walter.

'I hope we can get him to see it that way, Walter. For his own sake, any upset is only likely to set back his recovery.'

Howard Davis began to gather his bulky legal file. He had said all that needed to be said until the formal reading of the will.

'Dr Duval, shall we reconvene in an hour with everyone present?'

They all looked towards Philippe, who nodded his agreement.

'The sooner we do this the better,' he said. 'There is absolutely no point in delaying reading the will. It's better for everyone to know exactly how things stand as soon as possible.'

With that, Philippe headed out in search of Pippa. She too would need to be told before the formalities began.

Exactly an hour later, seven people, two of whom harboured their own barely concealed expectations, sat in a random group in front of Howard Davis who, for the first time in his life, sat in the upright chair normally occupied by his late client.

Once again, he unbundled the large legal file. Philippe wondered idly what else was in the file that Howard Davis guarded so carefully. Trust agreements perhaps? Original deeds? Most certainly the original of his father's will. But the lawyer guarded it as if he was guarding a priceless object. Was he worried that if it left his side, documents might go missing or be tampered with?

'Ladies and gentlemen,' the lawyer began, his voice calm and authoritative, 'thank you for coming. I am here to read the last will and testament of Walter William Cox the second. You are here because of your significant interest in this matter as a beneficiary.'

Philippe noticed Barbara Cox shift a little in her seat. She's impatient for the lawyer to get to the real matter in hand, he thought. She's probably longed for this day. She doesn't yet know her expectations are about to come crumbling down around her. But he checked himself at such uncharitable thoughts. He did not really know the woman at all. Beside her, her daughter Virginia sat rigidly upright, her face expressionless, as if it was all a tedious waste of her time.

At the back of the room, Clarence White sat uncomfortably. He had been grateful for the faith Walter Cox had shown in him. And he had repaid that trust and faith with loyalty. But he couldn't help but wonder what lay ahead for him. For more than twenty years he had run the big house to suit his employer. He didn't trust the next Walter William Cox. He expected to be rendered homeless within days. And yet, here he was, invited to the reading of the will with the relatives. For entirely different reasons from Barbara Cox, he shifted uneasily in his chair. He had no expectations so there could be no prospect of disappointment.

'I will deal with some minor bequests first,' the lawyer said evenly.

'Each staff member of my household is to receive two thousand dollars for each complete year of service, but there is extra provision for Clarence White.'

The lawyer nodded in his direction.

'Clarence White has been a loyal and trusted employee and friend to me for more than twenty years,' the lawyer read. 'In recognition of this service, I also leave Clarence White the ten workers' cottages in Sag Harbor. They are his to do with as he pleases.'

Clarence gasped. He had no idea what the cottages were worth, but he had never dared to dream of owning his own home.

There was an audible gasp too from Barbara Cox which she quickly stifled. Compared with the bulk of her late father-in-law's fortune, the Sag Harbor cottages were a trivial bequest and nothing more than an irritant with constant complaints from tenants who demanded money be spent on repairs. Clarence was welcome to them, she decided quickly.

Howard Davis continued.

'To each of my three grandchildren—Walter William Cox, Virginia Barbara Cox and Pippa Ann Duval—I leave one million dollars each in cash.'

Again, audible gasps broke the silence in the room.

Pippa looked at her father and whispered.

'What am I going to do with a million dollars?'

Barbara Cox turned to her daughter, whose face contorted in anger. 'What's he doing leaving money to that girl?'

She spat out the words, her contempt on full display. Mother and daughter thought as one. They shared their outrage in whispered undertones until Howard Davis cleared his throat and began to speak again.

'Now I come to the disposition of the main part of Walter William Cox's estate,' he said.

There was a collective intake of breath that was almost tangible. The only sound to be heard was the sound of crackling paper as Howard Davis turned the page on the precious document he was holding.

'I am now going to read the words as they were dictated to me by the late Walter William Cox the Second,' he said, trying hard to suppress the unexpected emotion beginning to creep into his voice.

'In making this will, it is my intention to make amends for the injustice one person has suffered at my hands: my first born son Philippe Duval.'

The lawyer paused a moment and looked around. What is to come hasn't dawned on Walter or Barbara Cox yet, he thought. He pressed on and began to read again.

'I want everyone with an interest in my will to understand that I acknowledge Philippe Duval as my son. As my *first born son* that is. It is to my eternal shame that I did not marry his mother and thus make him my legitimate son. But I now redress that injustice.'

Again, the lawyer paused and looked briefly at the small group of people whose attention was entirely focused on him.

'Firstly, to my second son Walter William Cox I leave the house in which he and his wife reside, a cash settlement, a share portfolio and lifetime income from the family trust and to his wife Barbara Cox, I leave a cash settlement with certain provisions, which are stipulated herein.'

Howard Davis paused again, breathed deeply and began to read the final words that would smash the hopes and dreams of Barbara Cox and her husband.

'I leave my entire estate, less the bequests outlined previously, and less the provision for my second son Walter William Cox and his wife Barbara Cox, to my first son Philippe Duval. To be clear, Philippe Duval inherits my entire shareholding in Cox Industries. He inherits this house and all its contents. And he inherits the residue of my estate. He also has the primary decision-making role in the personal investment portfolios and the family trust. Philippe Duval is now head of the Cox family. Those are my wishes and I expect my wishes to be followed.'

Barbara Cox was first to her feet, yelling and screeching at Howard Davis.

'We'll contest this,' she wailed, her voice full of bile and fury. 'This is outrageous. After all Walter has done for the company. To be treated like this by his father. It's not fair.'

She looked around her for support. Her daughter was on her feet too. Beside her, her husband shook his head.

'Sit down, Barbara,' he said, his voice surprisingly strong. 'For God's sake, sit down. Don't make a spectacle of yourself. Screaming like a fishwife is not going to help.'

But her outrage only grew. *What sort of a man are you*, she wanted to say to her husband. *You just sit there and let this interloper steal your entitlement from under your very nose.* She looked around, wild-eyed, her anger and humiliation so intense she was momentarily robbed of the power of speech.

Philippe was about to speak but the lawyer caught his eye and shook his head slightly.

'Let me handle this, Dr Duval,' he said quietly, almost inaudibly.

But young Walter, who had been sitting apart from his family, intervened first, moving quickly to stand in front of his parents. His mother turned to face him, her anger now directed at her son.

'You knew about this, didn't you,' she snapped, 'and you didn't tell us. What sort of son are you? Creeping around behind our backs with your grandfather. You probably put the idea in his head just to spite us.'

But he was calm. He knew her moods too well to fall into the trap of trying to reason with her. Instead, he turned towards his father and held out his hand to help him to his feet. He knew not to let go of him. The paralysis of his father's left side was somewhat improved but not so much that he could stand unaided.

'Let's talk about this calmly,' Walter said to his father, who nodded as if in agreement.

'What's to talk about, son? I may have had a stroke but I can understand what the lawyers are telling me. My father passed me over in favour of his bastard son. What else do I need to know? Fifty years of trying to please him meant nothing in the end.'

He sighed, seemingly already resigned to his diminished status.

This is what a man looks like when he's beaten, Walter thought. He couldn't help but feel sorry for him. Defeated by a father he tried so hard to please who in return never really cared for him. Never cared enough. Never appreciated his efforts. But Walter could not blame Philippe. He knew Philippe had neither sought to usurp his father nor had he wanted what had now been thrust upon him. Perhaps later he would be able to convince his father of that. He doubted he would ever convince his mother. Or his sister.

Philippe signalled to Clarence who came to help Walter with his father.

'We'll talk later,' Philippe said, as he watched Walter guide his father out of the room.

Walter nodded and motioned to his mother and sister.

'Let's all go home,' he said. 'Father has had a trying day.'

Barbara Cox could not even summon the barest courtesy towards Philippe and Pippa. Stony faced, her indignation barely contained, she stormed past them in the wake of her husband and son. Her daughter paused briefly to glare at them but said nothing for there was nothing to say. It was as if it had just dawned on her that every expectation the family had nursed for years lay shattered like broken glass at their feet. And now there was no remedy except to hate the man who had brought this about. And hate him she would. Until her dying day. Or his.

# CHAPTER 8

AS THE LAST LIGHT of the day faded, Philippe sat quietly in his favourite chair. Absentmindedly, he sipped the glass of bourbon Pippa had placed by his side, hardly tasting the liquor.

Clarence had insisted Frederick drive them back to Manhattan and Philippe had finally been persuaded by Clarence's whispered aside that Frederick would feel slighted if it appeared the new master did not trust his driving. And so it was that the two of them arrived back at the mid-town apartment they shared to very different circumstances from which they had left it.

They had remained silent during the trip, remarking only on the banal and the ordinary. Were chauffeurs discreet, Philippe wondered? He had no experience to guide him so he had cautioned Pippa to be quiet during the drive.

Now, in the privacy of their home, he sat quietly, pondering what lay ahead of him and wondering how it was going to change their lives. And if it did change his life and that of his family, would it be for the better?

Pippa sat opposite her father, waiting patiently for him to break the silence. It had been a momentous day. What would it all mean for them as a family? Would he want to abandon his life in Sydney in favour of Long Island?

'What are you thinking about?' she asked finally, her impatience to discuss what had occurred getting the better of her.

He smiled, took a large sip of bourbon and noticed, for the first time, that the ice had almost completely melted.

'I need a top up,' he said, handing her the glass. 'I need something to soothe my rattled nerves.'

Pippa got up to refill his glass and poured more white wine into her own glass. She handed him the fresh drink.

'What happens next?' she asked. 'You've just become a very wealthy man, by all accounts. How does that change things?'

He held up his hand to stop her there. And then he laughed quietly.

'My darling girl, do you honestly think I have all the answers to those questions? I've only known about this for a few hours.'

Pippa shrugged.

'I thought you might have had an inkling of what was going to happen.'

But he shook his head vigorously.

'I didn't read anything into any of the events of the past week or so, to be honest. I thought at most he might leave me the Sag Harbor cottage I grew up in with my mother, if he was going to leave me anything at all. I had no expectations at all, except perhaps to bring your mother for a visit in a year or two. I think young Walter would have always been welcoming.'

'And now? Perhaps you should tell Mother first,' Pippa said. 'She's going to be surprised.'

And then she laughed.

'She always thought she was the wealthy one. She's going to be in for a surprise when she finds out your inheritance dwarfs hers.'

They laughed together then. He and Julia had rarely discussed money and he had never asked her about the Dalrymple trust fund she had inherited from her mother. She had been content to live in the house he had first bought in Sydney before they married. It was his income that paid the household bills. Her money had been mostly spent on her designer fashion indulgences and her trips up north to visit her son and to visit her extended family. He had never regarded her as extravagant.

He was suddenly serious again.

'I don't need this, Pippa. We have a good life in Sydney. Great wealth can be a burden as well as a blessing.'

She nodded. And she understood too that being left his father's wealth now could never compensate for the shame of being brought up as a fatherless child.

'Perhaps I shouldn't have got in touch with them. I should have left well alone.'

Philippe shook his head.

'It would have made no difference. I didn't really have the chance to tell you that my father made this will eight years ago, according to the lawyers. He seemed to know everything about my life. He must have had private detective agencies spying on me, as improbable as it seems.'

'Well, I'm relieved if you want to know the truth. I was beginning to feel that I had meddled where I shouldn't have and now your life is upended as a result.'

She finished the remains of her wine and then headed to the kitchen. She opened the refrigerator and then looked hopefully at her father.

'An omelette? Or is that now too simple a supper for a rich man?'

He laughed.

'An omelette will be fine,' he said, as his thoughts immediately turned back to what lay ahead of him.

He knew the coming week would be filled with meetings with lawyers. He was not cheered by the prospect. For the first time in his life, he felt seriously out of his depth. He checked his watch.

'I think I should call your mother,' he said, as if seeking confirmation.

'Of course, you should.'

He picked up the phone and dialled the international exchange. After some minutes he heard Julia's voice echoing down the long distance line. He took a deep breath. He hadn't thought about how he would deliver the unlikely news that he had inherited a fortune from his American father. He paused.

'I have some news to tell you,' he said.

He paused again. Pippa saw he was struggling to put into words what had occurred that day. She grabbed the phone from him. She could hear the alarm in her mother's voice as she said hello.

'What's wrong?' Julia demanded. 'What's going on?'

Pippa laughed then.

'Nothing serious, nothing to worry about except Dad has just inherited a fortune from his father.'

It was Julia's turn to become speechless at the other end of the phone.

'What do you mean inherited a fortune?'

'Just that,' Pippa said, 'but perhaps I had better start from the beginning.'

Julia listened in silence as Pippa told her what had occurred in the past few weeks.

'Until this happened today, we were keeping it to tell you when we got home.'

She then handed the phone back to her father.

'I'm sorry, I just didn't know where to begin to tell you how all this happened.'

Just as her daughter had done, she immediately understood his mixed feelings. Slighted as a child, how could he rejoice in this grand gesture from the father he had never known while he was growing up?

'Would you like me to come over and be with you?'

His mood brightened immediately.

'Yes please,' he replied. 'When do you think you can get a flight?'

'I'll try for tomorrow,' she said.

As he hung up the phone, he turned towards Pippa.

'Thanks for helping out,' he said. 'I had no idea how to tell her. She's going to come to New York.'

She smiled, pleased at her mother's sudden decision.

'I could see you were struggling to tell her. Now come and help me with the omelettes,' she said, pleased to see her father relaxed and smiling again.

An hour or so later, Dr Robert Clarke hung up the phone and sat staring into space for a full minute. He wondered later what coincidence had brought his brother David to his door that very minute.

'You look as if you've just discovered someone stole your lunch money,' he said, as he eased his large frame into the best of the visitors' chairs in his brother's office.

'Worse,' he replied, as he lost the short internal struggle to keep Philippe's news to himself.

'Bad news about a patient?'

To David Clarke, it was the most likely explanation for his brother's despondent mood.

Robert shook his head.

'No, nothing like that. That call I just took was from Philippe.'

'He's in New York, isn't he?'

'He is but he was meant to be coming home in about ten days' time. He's just called to ask for indefinite leave.'

David Clarke shrugged.

'So, there are other doctors. Hire someone else. Let him stay in New York. Good place for him as far as I'm concerned.'

Robert eyed his brother keenly.

'Has he been seeing Karen again? You still seem very hostile towards him.'

David Clarke shook his head.

'I don't know about now,' he admitted, 'but his history with her makes me wary. She's never got over him. Still has his photo by her bed in her apartment. Won't look at other men, even though I've introduced her to every eligible young man of my acquaintance. Almost too late now for her to give me a grandchild.'

Was this the time to tell his brother she had miscarried a child to Philippe? He let the moment slide.

'I think you'll be sorry you didn't promote the match when you hear what Philippe just told me. He's inherited the bulk of his father's wealth. A large industrial company in America plus a large mansion on Long Island. He didn't put a figure on it but I think it's many millions of dollars we're talking about.'

Robert sat back in his chair, watching, with some satisfaction, as his brother took in the news.

'But he was a bastard in the biblical sense as I understood it?'

'Yes, he was, but remember, every bastard has a father. And this father decided in his final years he had wronged his first born son. He made amends big time.'

It was David Clarke's turn to look stunned.

'Millions you say?'

'Millions and millions of dollars.'

Robert emphasised the words, enjoying his brother's discomfiture. It was a rare situation. He almost never got the better of his older brother.

'Do you think I should tell Karen?'

'Up to you,' Robert said, 'but it is confidential information. It would be better if it's kept to a small number of people.'

This caused David Clarke to laugh heartily. It was not a pleasant sound.

'You think this news can be kept quiet?'

'It can, providing you don't spread it around the boardroom. I assume you are here for the Foundation meeting?'

David Clarke looked at his watch and stood up.

'You'll have to tell the hospital board if he's not coming back.'

'I know that. But not today. Nothing is settled. If you must tell Karen, then tell her, but please ask her not to spread it around. Philippe wouldn't want that.'

As David Clarke headed out the door, he muttered something that sounded like agreement or was he simply cursing himself for having insulted Philippe, making it abundantly clear he would never approve of him as a son-in-law? Robert Clarke couldn't tell.

In the end, he picked up the telephone to call his niece. They had always been close. Somehow, he knew it would be better for her to hear this news from him rather than from her father.

It was only a matter of days later that the household staff assembled on the steps of Eastbury Hall to welcome officially the new master and mistress of the house.

Frederick, his uniform freshly cleaned and pressed and his shoes shined with all the vigour he could muster, was quick to open the car door for Julia. Philippe had stopped her just in time from opening the door herself.

Frederick will want to do it, he had whispered. She nodded and waited for the chauffeur to walk to her side of the car. She thanked him as she climbed out as gracefully as she could.

Philippe noticed Clarence coming forward to greet them and steered Julia in his direction.

'Your daughter not with you, Dr Duval?' he asked.

Philippe shook his head.

'Not today, Clarence, she's at work at the hospital. She must fulfil her obligations there. I've brought my wife Julia with me.'

Clarence nodded and welcomed her and then motioned them towards the assembled staff.

I hope they don't curtsey, thought Julia. We're not royalty.

She acknowledged the introductions. Housekeeper, cook, maids, gardeners, a maintenance man and others whose jobs she couldn't remember. She turned then to look up at the house. It was vast.

'It's a very commanding house,' she said politely.

She did not say *beautiful* because beautiful was quite the wrong word. Philippe had forewarned her. It should be pulled down but people depend on it for their jobs. Everyone who works there is very anxious about their future.

She paused, turning around once again, to look particularly for the other family's house, which stood close by.

'I assume that's the house your half-brother has inherited?'

She had said it quietly to Philippe and he simply nodded. Already his father's lawyers were being bombarded with accusations and threats of lawsuits from his half-brother, none of which was unexpected. And none of which were expected to succeed.

She said nothing more as the two of them followed Clarence into the house to begin a tour of the grand mansion that left them stunned by its opulence but with a growing sense of unease at having to take their places as its owners.

Beyond the garden, on the other side of the hastily erected fence that now divided the two properties, hidden within the shadows of a large oak tree, one solitary figure noted their arrival.

Barbara Cox, her anger unabated by the short passage of time, watched the scene unfold before her eyes. It took all her self-control not to scream *Get out of my house. Get the hell out of my house* as her anger turned to tears of self-pity and pooled into a lake of visceral resentment of the man who had usurped her husband.

Barbara Cox would have felt vindicated had she known Philippe felt no sense of being at ease or at home in the grand mansion. After the tour of the house, he and Julia sat together in the upstairs sitting room from which all evidence of its recent occupant had been erased. A tray of coffee appeared as if by magic.

'Are you OK to stay here for a few days?' Philippe asked. 'I do have some things to deal with.'

Julia nodded but before she could speak further, the door opened again, this time to admit Clarence and the housekeeper Mrs Anderson to deal with the most pressing domestic matter: what would madam like for meals during the next week?

Julia smiled to herself. She at least had the advantage of having seen her mother deal with these matters at Prior Park and later she had done the same at Mayfield Downs during her first marriage. But an Australian country kitchen was likely to be a far different proposition from a grand household in America.

With a deft touch, she invited the housekeeper to convey her best wishes to the cook and to pass on her hope that their meals would be light and made with fresh produce. Perhaps lobster one evening? And, please, no fried food, she had said. Philippe smiled and congratulated her on her diplomacy.

Almost as soon as she had dealt with that small domestic crisis, others came begging for decisions: what flowers would madam like cut for the house from the cutting garden? The carpets were due for spring cleaning: what day would it suit madam to have this disruption in the house? And the window cleaners were due this week: what time would it suit madam for them to start their work? And the head gardener is keen to show her around the gardens. Could madam spare some time this afternoon? Or tomorrow morning?

'It is a very long time since a woman was in the house,' Philippe said, when they were finally alone again. 'Everyone is so keen to impress you.'

She laughed.

'I feel like the second Mrs de Winter when she first arrives at Manderley although I don't think Mrs Anderson would be any match for Mrs Danvers. I hope they aren't disappointed.'

Philippe looked puzzled.

'Rebecca. Daphne du Maurier's novel,' she explained. 'Your reading needs to be broadened beyond medical texts, I think.'

He laughed then. She was right. He had very little time to read for leisure. And then a voice interrupted.

'I can assure you they won't be disappointed, Mrs Duval.'

Philippe, on hearing the voice, turned towards the door and smiled broadly.

'Walter,' he said, 'it's very good to see you. Come in and have a coffee. It's good of you to risk a foray into enemy territory,' before making the necessary introduction to Julia.

Walter chuckled and then grew serious for a moment.

'You know it's not my view of how things have unfolded, Dr Duval,' he said, before turning his attention to Julia.

'I'm very pleased to meet you, Mrs Duval,' he said. 'If I may say so, Pippa looks just like you. You could so easily be mistaken for sisters.'

She smiled with just a hint of pleasure at his obvious flattery.

'Please call me Julia,' she said. 'And if you go on calling my husband Dr Duval, he'll think he's about to operate on you.'

Walter laughed as he sat down opposite Julia.

'I've been told Australians don't stand on ceremony,' he said, his easy boyish charm putting her at ease instantly. 'It's so refreshing.'

Without warning, the door opened to admit Clarence with a fresh pot of coffee and an apology for the intrusion, which Philippe waved away.

'Walter is always welcome as is the rest of his family,' Philippe said. 'Any time.'

'Thank you, Philippe,' Walter said. 'That means a lot to me. I've come in and out of this house just as I wanted from the time I could walk.'

'Your visit is timely,' Philippe said, ignoring his thanks, 'but first, how is your father? And your mother?'

'My father's health is pretty good, all things considered. He's happy, if only he would admit it, not to have the burden of work and the responsibility of the estate. If only my mother would recognise that they have the best of both worlds. They are wealthy but with no responsibility for managing that wealth. They can just live a pleasant life, especially when my father is out and about again.'

Philippe was about to speak but Julia pre-empted him.

'And you, Walter, how do you feel about what has happened?'

He was thoughtful for a moment. How to answer such a question simply and honestly? Does it help them for me to say the depth of my parents' anger seems to know no limit, he wondered. And that I understand and sympathise with them. For nearly fifty years, my father had expected to be the principal heir to his father's wealth. For their sake, I have to be honest.

'My parents are angry. I am angry,' he admitted, emphasising each word he spoke, 'but I am angry mostly with my grandfather who lacked the courage to tell my father what he had done. Or perhaps he enjoyed the prospect of the chaos he would leave behind. I don't know for sure.'

He paused. There was a heavy silence in the room.

'I'll be honest because that's what you want me to be,' he continued. 'My parents are angry with you, Philippe. Angry that you even exist. Angry that my grandfather preferred you over my father. My father sees it as the ultimate slap in the face and he's right to see it like that, in my opinion. He worked hard to build the business further and he did that successfully. Yet there is not one recognition of that from his father. It's a bitter pill for him to swallow.'

Philippe sat very still as he listened to Walter. Once again, it was

Julia who spoke.

'But, Walter, you said your father would be happy not to have the burden of it all.'

'I think it's possible to be angry about what my grandfather did but still feel that my father is better off without the worry of it all. But that's me being practical,' he said.

Philippe had listened carefully to what Walter had said. He was desperate to distinguish between Walter's need to publicly display his loyalty to his parents and his personal acceptance of what had occurred. How much could he involve Walter? Was it unfair to ask him to be the peacemaker and risk upsetting his parents further? But he could see no other way. There was no one else.

'It's going to take a while to get all the legalities sorted out, Walter,' he said. 'It will only take longer and cost a whole lot more money if your father challenges the will. It could drag on for years. Is that really going to benefit him in the end? I'd like to get matters settled as quickly as possible. I think you can help me there.'

He looked across at Walter to gauge his reaction.

'I'd like to help,' he said finally. 'I really would like to help. But I don't want to have to pick sides. If you can think of a way that will help us all reconcile, then I will do it.'

'What if you attend all the meetings with the lawyers with me,' Philippe said. 'You can then report back to your family what is happening.'

'If you like,' he replied, 'but it's not my preferred way to spend the day.'

'Nor mine if it comes to that,' Philippe said.

Already a plan was forming in his mind to involve Walter in the business matters. But he refrained from saying so. Time enough for him to have to face the prospect.

'When is the meeting you want me to attend?' Walter asked.

'Tomorrow morning, here at the house at ten o'clock,' Philippe replied. 'I'll spare you the tedium of this afternoon's session.'

'Good, because I have plans for this afternoon,' he said, his mood now more relaxed. 'May I borrow your wife?'

Walter turned towards Julia.

'It's a beautiful day. Let me show you Long Island,' he said.

She turned towards Philippe for reassurance before accepting. Philippe nodded and smiled at Julia.

'That sounds like an offer my wife can't refuse.'

Julia brightened at the prospect. With Philippe locked in meetings, she faced a lonely afternoon.

'Thank you, Walter,' she said. 'That would be delightful.'

'I'll come back and collect you at two,' he said, before heading out the door.

It did not occur to him to wonder how he might accomplish the outing without alerting his mother, who watched the comings and goings at the big house intently.

# CHAPTER 9

IT WAS THE ROAR of the Camaro's powerful engine that heralded Walter's arrival to keep his date with Julia. He brought the car to a spectacular stop on the gravel driveway, showering small stones in all directions.

At the front door, Clarence rolled his eyes but said nothing as Walter raised a hand in greeting. Julia walked quickly down the front steps. It was only Clarence who noticed the head gardener, who had been clipping the topiary nearest the driveway, looking despairingly at the deep tyre tracks. He yelled for one of his garden labourers to get a rake and a fresh barrow load of gravel.

'It's what we're paid for, boy,' he said, as the young lad complained. It would soon look pristine again.

Walter was oblivious to all this. His car was his pride and joy. He held the door open for Julia who murmured her thanks.

'Nice car,' she said, guessing a comment was expected.

'Thanks,' he said. 'I wrote the first one off unfortunately.'

Seeing her alarm, he was quick to reassure her.

'I've since had driving lessons from one of the top Indy Car drivers,' he said. 'Father insisted. I know how to drive properly now.'

She smiled, somewhat reassured.

'I'm pleased to hear it,' she replied, choosing all the same to buckle herself in with the seatbelt.

'Very wise,' he nodded, and followed her lead, before simultaneously letting out the clutch and tramping the accelerator, forcing his passenger back into her seat as the massive engine responded.

Before long they were heading east on the Montauk Highway with Walter pointing out landmarks, almost shouting to make himself heard over the noise of the engine.

'It's a beautiful area,' Julia said, as she caught glimpses of massive houses nestled within walled estates and the charming shingle houses of the early European settlers. 'I really appreciate your taking the time to show me around.'

In what seemed like no time at all, they were approaching the furthermost easterly point of the island.

'That's Montauk Point Lighthouse up ahead,' Walter said, as he eased back on the accelerator. 'This whole area was taken over by the US Navy in World War II to protect New York shipping lanes.'

He brought the car to a standstill and they climbed out to view the scene.

The tall white painted tower rose majestically into the sky, sending out its warning light to nearby shipping. Around them, the wind was beginning to rise from a turbulent sea.

Julia looked around her seeking evidence of the navy's former occupation of the area but she could see nothing at all. It's just like it is around Prior Park, she thought, there's no evidence of the army camps there now either.

'You're fortunate there was no war on the US mainland,' she said suddenly.

'But that didn't mean we weren't involved,' he replied, 'but of course you know that. That's when you met Philippe, wasn't it? When American troops were stationed in Australia.'

'You're well informed,' she countered, 'but yes, you're right, that's when I met Philippe. And your father? Was he in the forces?'

She desperately wanted to change the subject away from her early relationship with Philippe. She had no desire to relive the pain and humiliation of their separation and Pippa's birth. And everything that followed from it.

He laughed mirthlessly then.

'People like my father don't go to war,' he said. 'They hide behind their occupations. And their wealth. Did you have family who fought for Australia?'

She nodded, remembering the years of worry.

'My brother Richard, the elder one, joined the RAAF—Royal Australian Air Force—and then served in England in Bomber Command. He was lucky to survive.'

'Now there's something I would enjoy doing,' he admitted unexpectedly. 'Flying. I'd love to learn to fly.'

She grimaced at the recent memory of her nephew's narrow escape from death.

'My nephew Paul, Richard's son, was mad keen on flying. He still is as far as I know but it almost cost him his life earlier this year. He crashed in the outback. An Aboriginal stockman found him. Otherwise, he'd be dead.'

'Wow,' he said, 'you certainly live dangerously Down Under. Being a speed freak is the most dangerous thing I do.'

But even as they stood contemplating the war that had been, there was another war going on too. Vietnam. She wondered if he might find himself drafted to fight for his country.

'You've obviously avoided the draft here? You'd be about the right age to be called up I imagine?'

He frowned. It had been a source of a disagreement with his father.

'I thought I should do my duty but my father insisted I apply for a college exemption, which I did. But I didn't tell him I went for the medical anyway. They wouldn't pass me because of a shoulder injury I got playing football in high school. It's painful at times.'

'A bit of luck perhaps?'

He shrugged. He didn't want to be seen as a shirker but he had been relieved to have a legitimate reason for not joining.

The breeze had stiffened considerably and Julia began to shiver, her light dress no match for the sudden drop in temperature.

'Oh, I'm sorry,' he said, taking off his jacket to put around her shoulders. 'It's getting chilly here. There's a bar I know nearby. Why don't we head there for a drink?'

She nodded, thankful for the suggestion.

Minutes later, he was guiding her to a table in the Montauk bar of which he was clearly a frequent customer. A small glowing lamp decorated each low wooden table. Artistic photographs of fishermen and marine life hung along the walls. A well-stocked bar ran along the entire back wall of the room which smelled, not unpleasantly, of tobacco and the sea.

'Walter, what brings you here at this time of day?' the barman yelled, his hearty baritone reverberating through the room.

Walter returned the greeting with a cheery wave as he walked towards the bar.

'A drink, Barney,' Walter replied. 'What else brings me to a bar?'

'With a new date I see?' Barney said, barely looking up from pulling a beer.

'Not a new date, Barney,' Walter corrected him. 'With my aunt, Barney, with my aunt. A little respect, man, if you don't mind.'

The beer in Barney's hand overflowed spectacularly into the spill tray as he looked up, momentarily distracted by Walter's words.

'Ah,' he said, as he reapplied his attention to the important task of pulling a beer, 'so the aunt must be Dr Duval's wife, I presume?'

Barney smiled then, his face glowing with the warm satisfaction of having turned the tables on his young customer.

'News travels fast, Barney,' Walter replied, his words non-committal, his voice deliberately even.

'News does indeed travel fast, my friend,' he said, as he pushed a glass of beer across the bar towards Walter. 'How's your old man? Fit to murder someone I bet.'

Walter laughed then. Barney, inveterate gossip that he was, had clearly pieced together the snippets of information he had heard and drawn exactly the right conclusion.

'He would be, Barney, if that someone wasn't already dead.'

The barman laughed heartily. And then he was serious for a moment.

'My old man, for what it's worth, said he was delighted Ella Duval's boy finally got what he deserved. He knew her you know. My old man knew Ella Duval and he remembered the boy. He thought it was a crying shame that young boy had to grow up never knowing his father, while everyone else knew who his father was. And Ella Duval too proud to take much help.'

Walter didn't quite know what to make of this latest information. There was so much he didn't know about his own family. So much that others seemed to know.

'No one ever told me, Barney,' he said finally. 'No one ever told me my father had a brother.'

He repeated himself, this time with greater emphasis.

'No one ever told me, Barney. You know I really wish someone had told me.'

Barney lowered his voice. He sensed Walter's simmering anger and his frustration. He had to say something to help.

'I guess by the time you came along the gossip had died down. The Duval boy had gone off to college and then into the army. There was no reason to talk about it anymore. The last time anyone saw him was when he came back for his mother's funeral not long after the war ended. More than twenty years ago I reckon.'

At that moment, Walter understood how much more there was to the story of his family and his uncle in particular. There was so much more he hadn't even thought about. He watched in silence as Barney loaded up his infamous cocktail shaker with a scoop of ice before adding a bewildering array of liquor to produce a drink Walter could not recognise but he hoped Julia would enjoy.

'My special for your special guest,' Barney said as he set the tall glass with its lavish garnishes alongside Walter's beer.

'Thanks, Barney,' he said as he picked up the drinks. 'If my father finds out I've been consorting with the enemy, I'll cop both barrels.'

'He won't hear it from me, Walter,' Barney said. 'He was never one of my regulars anyway. And I hear he can't get about much now.'

'That's true. Not since his stroke. But he's recovering. Getting a bit better every day.'

It was a small lie that helped Walter cling to the hope his father would one day fully recover. Drinks in hand, he turned back towards the table where Julia was waiting.

And then, out of the corner of his eye, he noticed a small group of young people crowding through the narrow doorway. He groaned inwardly. It was too late to avoid his sister Virginia. She saw him at the very moment he noticed her.

'Brother dear,' she said with exaggerated emphasis for the benefit of her friends. 'Fancy meeting you here. I hope we're not crashing your date.'

Behind the bar, Barney stood stock still for a few seconds, before wiping his hands and walking from behind the bar.

'Miss Cox, how wonderful to see you,' he gushed, in a vain effort to divert her attention from her brother. 'I have just the table for you and your friends. Why don't you follow me?'

But it was too late. Virginia's eyes had followed the direction her brother was headed. Her eyes narrowed.

'So, what's this, brother dear,' she sneered. 'Consorting with the enemy. Making sure you're in the good books? Hoping they might give you a few crumbs from their very rich table? The table that actually belongs to your own father. Or do you just fancy older women now?'

He stood his ground then. Behind his sister, he could see the stunned looks of her friends. No one was speaking lest they miss something vital they could later embellish in the retelling. A public showdown between brother and sister would fuel the gossips for weeks.

'Your rudeness knows no bounds, Virginia,' he said patiently. 'If you had any manners at all, I would be happy to introduce you to your aunt, Julia Duval. But since you don't ...'

She threw her head back, her forced hollow laughter echoing throughout the bar.

'You make me sick,' she shrieked.

Before he could stop her, she grabbed the cocktail from the tray he was holding. In what seemed like one movement, she moved a few yards to her right and emptied the contents of the glass over Julia who could do nothing to avoid the drenching.

'You vile bitch,' Walter yelled as his sister turned and signalled to her friends to follow her out of the bar.

Shocked into momentary silence, all Julia could do was stand up and attempt to brush the sticky liquid from her clothes.

'I'm so sorry,' Walter stuttered. 'I'm so sorry.'

She waved away his offer of help. Barney has already bustled over with fresh towels which she used as best she could to dry her dress.

'Well, I can't say it was a pleasure to meet your sister, Walter. Does she do that kind of thing often?'

She turned to Barney who continued to fuss over her.

'I'll have to take a rain check on that cocktail, I'm afraid. Next time.'

He smiled and breathed a sigh of relief she was not storming out of his bar in anger.

'If I apologise a hundred times, it will never be enough. I am so, so sorry,' Walter said, his anger beginning to trump his embarrassment. He was already rehearsing what he would say to his sister. It would mark a new low point in their already fractured relationship.

'Let's get you home,' he said, as he guided Julia out of the bar.

Philippe is going to be livid, he thought. He will not take kindly to his wife being attacked and humiliated like this.

It was in that moment too that Julia saw the task that lay ahead of her husband in trying to bring about a reconciliation with Walter's family. In Walter's sister, she had glimpsed an anger that ran so deep it might never be appeased.

Philippe, hearing the unmistakable roar of Walter's car on the driveway, had walked to the front door to greet Julia. He was surprised to see her clutching her sodden skirt, trying unsuccessfully to hide the wet ruined fabric from curious eyes.

'What happened?' Philippe asked innocently. 'Someone got clumsy with a drink?'

She shook her head.

'I'll tell you later,' she murmured as she headed upstairs to her room, nodding slightly in the direction of Clarence. But Philippe was not so easily put off. He could see she was upset so he followed her. As he closed the door behind them, he put his arm around her shoulders.

'Tell me what happened?' as they both surveyed the ruined dress.

'Walter's sister,' she sighed, and then proceeded to recount in detail the scene that had unfolded in the Montauk bar.

Philippe found himself apologising as if it was somehow his fault.

'I'm so sorry. I should never have put you in that position. I had no idea they would stoop to such a level.'

'You weren't to know that would happen. It's sad but Walter really despises his sister. He thinks she has the worst traits of their parents.'

She had gleaned that much on the drive home.

'That's what comes with being brought up with too much privilege,' Philippe said.

'Perhaps,' she replied, in half agreement, 'but I was brought up in privilege too. I hope I don't treat people like that. And, unlike Walter, I love both my brothers dearly. Even William after what he did in keeping us apart.'

He had never heard her speak about her brothers in such a fashion. They had hardly ever spoken of William's role in separating him from Julia. It seemed suddenly incongruous to be speaking about it now. But it was clear to him she was comparing the warmth of her own family with that of the Cox family.

'I'm pleased you didn't continue to bear a grudge against William,' he said finally. 'He was a very young man and under your mother's influence at the time. There have been times when I've sensed his embarrassment at his own behaviour but he never says anything. Not to me, anyway.'

She smiled, remembering her brother's half-formed apology at their mother's graveside.

'He tried to apologise to me you know,' she said, remembering. 'I could see he was sincere. And he was ashamed of what he had done. I couldn't bear the thought of a rift in the family. We had to move on. What had been done couldn't be undone.'

To Julia, it all seemed so long ago. Another lifetime.

'The Cox family could certainly learn a lesson from you,' he said quietly.

He sat for a few moments thinking over the events of the afternoon.

'I'll leave you to change,' he said suddenly and with that he was gone.

Downstairs, Philippe motioned to Clarence.

'Come with me. I might need support.'

Clarence nodded. He did not need an explanation. He had seen the state of Julia's dress and Walter's mix of anger and embarrassment when he had helped her out of his car. He knew something had happened.

Together, the two men strode purposefully across the lawn and thrust aside the half-finished fence between the two properties.

Walter's fury had barely abated by the time he arrived home. His mother set aside the magazine she had been reading on hearing the front door slam. His father, sensing his son's mood, struggled to his feet unaided before grabbing for the walking stick he was determined to discard. But not just yet.

'What's up, Walter?' he demanded. 'Slamming doors and storming in here like that.'

But it was his mother's question that stopped him in his tracks.

'What have you been doing Walter? Where have you been? Marching in here like some village lout.'

Her voice was cool, unemotional, disdainful.

She knows, Walter thought. She knows what I've been doing. She's trying to get me to believe she didn't know. But she does know. She was spying on the big house when I left with Julia. She wants me to spell it out, thought Walter.

'You know where I've been, Mother,' he said, trying to match her cool detachment.

'Do I?'

'Yes, you do,' he retorted. 'You've been spying on the comings and goings of the big house. I've seen you. I saw you today.'

He watched her reaction closely. Was there a tiny crack in her façade?

'And why shouldn't I?' she snapped.

He could think of a hundred reasons.

'Because it makes you look ridiculous.'

He had lashed out in anger at her pettiness. At her meanness. At that moment, he felt nothing but contempt for her. And then he saw, in her eyes, a bitterness he had never noticed before. Had it all meant so much to her to be mistress of the big house, to be able to laud it over her friends?

She turned her back on her son and rounded on her husband.

'This is all your fault,' she yelled, as she looked him up and down with a contempt she did not try to hide. 'What sort of a man are you? Say something. Or are you just going to let me be insulted by my own son?'

Throughout her marriage, her respect for her husband had slowly but surely ebbed away until she had been left only with the consolation of being able to say *my husband is president of Cox Industries which he will inherit from his father one day*, a company everyone knew, a rags to riches story in a mere three generations. It meant something. And by association it had given her a position in society. The price: her public loyalty to a man she had come to detest. The ultimate payoff: the grandest house of which she would eventually become mistress. She had talked about it endlessly to her friends. She had described the changes she would make. She had consulted designers. She had never entertained the notion it should be demolished. And now she had been humiliated.

'What were you doing, Walter?'

His father shuffled slowly towards him, his every step painful to watch, but he waved away Walter's offer of help.

Walter shrugged. There was no reason to dissemble.

'Clarence told me Dr Duval was bringing his wife Julia for a visit. I thought I would be neighbourly.'

He waved his stick at his son.

'You know I've got lawyers working on a challenge,' he said.

'And how far have they got?'

His father shrugged.

'It all takes time, boy,' he conceded.

'Do you think a challenge is wise?'

He saw a flicker of the old arrogance in his father's sneering reply.

'So you think I should just give up and accept that the legacy I expected to inherit for the best part of fifty years has now been left to some interloper? Where's your loyalty, Walter? What sort of a son are you?'

But Walter wouldn't be drawn into a discussion of loyalty.

'It isn't about loyalty,' he pleaded. 'Please don't make this about loyalty. It's about dealing with the situation as it is. Do you honestly think my grandfather would have signed a will that wasn't watertight? If you think that, you didn't know him very well.'

But his father was not listening.

'He wasn't infallible, Walter, despite what you think. He made mistakes.'

'You're right. He made mistakes but he owned up to his biggest mistake. Not marrying Philippe's mother and making him legitimate.'

'And you think that makes everything all right do you? Even though it disadvantages your own father?'

This was too much for Walter.

'For God's sake,' he shouted. 'Look around you.'

His arm swept a wide semi-circle, indicating the expensively furnished living room.

'You're not exactly poor. You've been left this beautiful home. You have money. You have income more than enough for your needs. You might have even been glad to be able to take it easy and concentrate on recovering your health. But, no, it's only ever been about the money, hasn't it? Your life has only ever been about money. Talk about me disappointing you. You disappoint me.'

The only sound that pierced the silence following his outburst was the ticking of the hallway clock. Had it grown louder all of a sudden as if it was a ticking timebomb?

'So that's how it's to be, Walter?' his father sighed. 'You've chosen sides it seems.'

His father struggled back to his armchair, spent by the effort of arguing. Walter watched as he struggled to settle himself in his chair. He didn't want to leave it like this.

'I wanted to tell you Philippe has invited me to sit in on the meetings with the lawyers. I'm going to do that. I think it's in everyone's interests.'

Then he turned back towards his mother who had been listening intently.

'And would you please tell that daughter of yours to refrain from throwing drinks over Julia Duval. It's very unseemly to see Virginia act like a common bar room hussy.'

He could not bring himself to call her *my sister*.

'She must have been provoked. What did you say to her?'

He knew his mother would jump immediately to Virginia's defence.

'Let's be clear on this. She was not provoked.'

He thought for a moment. Was it merely coincidence that had brought his sister to the same bar? He stared at his mother.

"Not unless you provoked her?'

'How could I? I wasn't there.'

'So it was a mere coincidence she ended up in the same bar as me? You didn't suggest she follow me by any chance? Pick up a few friends on the way as cover?'

She turned pale but fought back. Her outrage grew even more because of the truth of his accusation.

'As if I would do such a thing,' she snorted.

'You would do such a thing,' he replied. 'Sadly, you would.'

He looked first at his father and then at his mother.

'This stops today,' he said. 'You will not embarrass me any further. I will make sure your interests are protected. But I will not have you harass Philippe and his family. He is a good man. He did not ask for this but he is doing his best to be fair to everyone. If you cannot accept this, I will move out today so what's it to be?'

'No one is going to do that to my wife and not apologise,' Philippe declared, as he and Clarence neared his half-brother's house.

'Virginia?'

Philippe nodded, confirming Clarence's suspicions.

'Yes, Virginia decided to empty a drink all over my wife and humiliate her in public. My wife has nothing to do with all this.'

When they reached the house, Philippe did not bother to knock. The door was unlocked. Without waiting, the two of them walked through the entrance hall. Clarence pointed to the living room and as they approached, they both heard Walter's voice issuing what sounded like an ultimatum. With Clarence behind him, Philippe strode into the room as all eyes turned towards him.

'Walter's right.'

Philippe's angry voice surprised them.

'This stops today. Do you hear me? I will not have my wife assaulted. I will not have my reputation trashed.'

He looked from one to the other. From Walter Cox to Barbara Cox.

'So, what's it to be? Do you want all-out war? Because if you do, I'll give you all-out war. And make no mistake, I will win.'

He was shaking, his anger bubbling to the surface as if it had been contained for far too long. A childhood of snubs and behind-the-hand whispering had left their mark. He had hated their privilege. He had hated their smugness. He thought he had left it all behind. But now all the old feelings came surging back. He was no longer Dr Philippe Duval, eminent surgeon, but Philippe Duval, the poor kid in the hand-me-down clothes and worn out shoes. It had been years since those images had surfaced in his mind. He knew he would never be that again but the early experiences had scarred him.

His half-brother struggled to his feet. He could meet anger with anger. Challenge with counter challenge.

'You're very certain of everything now, aren't you?' he retorted. 'Suddenly master of all you survey leaving us with the crumbs. What makes you so certain you will win? My lawyers think I have a good claim to overturn it all.'

Philippe stood his ground. It was time for some truth telling.

'Your lawyers simply want to earn a big fat fee from you. That is all.'

He hesitated. *Will I tell him what makes me so certain?* Philippe was unsure. *Is this the right time?* He waited for his half-brother to speak but it was young Walter who spoke first.

'Just accept it, Father,' Walter urged. 'Take it easy. Recover your health. Enjoy your life.'

The elder Walter Cox looked at his son and then pointed accusingly at Philippe.

'If he tells me why he thinks he will win against my challenge. There's something he's not telling us. I know it.'

All eyes were on Philippe. There was no other alternative. They had to know. There is something absurd about me fighting to keep this inheritance that I never wanted, he thought. But if I don't end this, I'll be in lawyer meetings for years to come. He took a deep breath.

'I did not know it until this afternoon but my father ...'

He paused. How do I say this, he wondered? He took another deep breath.

'My father went to the trouble of a formal adoption. He adopted me as his son when I was a young man. I assume my mother agreed to it but she never told me. If your lawyers are relying on my illegitimacy in their challenge, then they will fail.'

He waited for the full impact of his words to be digested. And understood. But did they understand what it meant? He decided to spell it out.

'This means I am his son *by the letter of the law*. And he has done what countless men before him have done. He has left the bulk of his estate to his eldest son.'

His half-brother sank back into a chair, his shoulders slumped, his body seemingly drained of the little energy he had been able to summon. Barbara Cox then began to speak.

'You think that ...'

But she was cut short. He husband half turned towards her. His voice was weak but his words were clear.

'For goodness' sake, woman, don't you see. It's over. That old bastard has outsmarted us at every turn.'

But Philippe was not finished. He turned towards Barbara Cox, who glared back at him with eyes filled with hatred. He dispensed with any pleasantries.

'When your daughter gets home, I expect her to come to my house and apologise to my wife. My wife is not accustomed to people who behave like she did.'

Barbara Cox nodded slightly. Another humiliation. She did not trust her own voice to reply.

'I'll make sure Virginia comes over, Philippe,' Walter said quickly, desperately wanting to make amends.

Philippe nodded and smiled at him.

'Good. Thank you, Walter. And don't forget I'll expect to see you on Monday so you can get across all the details with the lawyers.'

He had said what he came to say. He turned then.

'Let's go, Clarence,' he said. 'Julia will be wondering where I've got to.'

Together, the two men walked out into the late afternoon sunshine.

'Your father would have been proud of you,' Clarence ventured.

Philippe smiled.

'I never thought to revisit this part of my life, Clarence,' he said quietly. 'In all the years since my mother died, I've been back only once. That was to show Julia the cottage I lived in as a child when we came over for our honeymoon.'

'Did you ever feel something was missing from your life, severing connections with your childhood as you did?'

Philippe shook his head.

'Not once my mother died. The only family I ever knew was my mother and her father. There was nothing to keep bringing me back.'

'And now?'

'I have mixed emotions to be honest, Clarence,' he said, 'but I've been given a responsibility that I can't walk away from. It's not in my nature.'

'You know, I think your father must have known that,' Clarence replied thoughtfully.

Philippe smiled. Did he admire his father, a man he had known only such a short time before his death?

'Well, he knew what mischief he was leaving behind him that's for sure,' Philippe conceded. 'My half-brother is right on one point. He was an old bastard in many respects. But let's see if we can tidy up the mess he left behind and all begin to act like civilised human beings.'

'Now that would be a pleasant change,' Clarence said, chuckling to himself as memories of the arguments he had witnessed began to surface. 'A very pleasant change indeed.'

As they approached the house, Philippe put a reassuring hand on Clarence's arm.

'There must be a good bottle of wine in that cellar you so jealously guard,' he said.

Clarence nodded, his mind already beginning to run through the catalogue of wines he knew by heart for something suitable.

'Leave it to me, Dr Duval,' he said, as he headed in the direction of the cellar.

# CHAPTER 10

PHILIPPE HARDLY NOTICED Clarence move quietly around the table to refill his coffee cup and remove the plate he had pushed to one side.

He was sitting back in his chair relaxing. It was Saturday. No lawyer meetings. And Pippa would be with them for lunch. He had let Julia sleep on. She was still not quite adjusted to the change in time zones so he waved away Clarence's suggestion of taking breakfast to her room.

'Let her sleep,' he had said. 'She can have breakfast when she comes downstairs.'

For Philippe it was a rare pleasure to have a quiet moment to read a newspaper, especially The New York Times. There wasn't much he now missed from his old life but the famous newspaper was one of them. He glanced through each of its fifty-eight pages with a half-remembered familiarity.

He lingered over the reports of the Vietnam War. Hadn't we seen enough of war? What was to be gained from bombing North Vietnam? He wondered how many times the newspaper had published a list of young men from the New York area who had been killed in action. He read the four names with a sense of despair. Another generation giving up their youth. For what? A war in which America really had no legitimate role. Wasn't it simply a country trying to throw off the yoke of colonial rule? But mostly he kept these opinions to himself.

He flipped through the early pages, most of which were filled with advertising. He recognised the business names. Macys. Saks Fifth Avenue. B. Altman & Co. Should I surprise Julia with a mink coat, he wondered, as he lingered over one of the advertisements? But he thought better of it. Far better for her to choose a coat for herself if she wanted one. But he couldn't help imagining Karen's delight at such a gift. Hard to hide, he thought, so he immediately dismissed the idea. But a small piece of expensive jewellery? Entirely possible. The thought lingered in his mind for some minutes. Why does she continue to invade my mind in quiet moments, he wondered? But he already knew the answer to that question.

And then he brought his thoughts back to the present. He glanced at the baseball scores. It's like old times, he mused. The New York Mets lost to the Phillies. And then he read with distaste the injuries to a heavyweight boxer who had won an important bout at Madison Square Garden. He wondered what long term effects he would suffer. He skipped over the editorial with its focus on the political issues of the day. For the first time, he read the business pages with more than casual interest. Days of meetings with lawyers and with the senior executives of Cox Industries had left him slightly bewildered but nonetheless determined to understand the intricacies of the businesses he had unexpectedly inherited.

He looked towards Clarence, whose guidance and advice he had come to rely on, just as his father had done.

'Clarence, do you think I should have Kenneth Harper and his wife to lunch? Or dinner?'

He had no need to explain to Clarence that Kenneth Harper was now president of Cox Industries.

'Very appropriate if I may say so, Dr Duval,' he said. 'It was not unusual for Mr Cox to entertain his executives and their wives. Until he became too ill, that is. And then I believe the younger Mr Cox and his wife would often host them.'

Philippe thought for a moment.

'I don't think we would involve Mr and Mrs Cox,' he said, 'but young Walter would be welcome.'

Clarence smiled approvingly. Beneath the polite and urbane exterior, he glimpsed in Philippe the steeliness of a Cox. There was no sign of any misguided attempt to assuage his half-brother's feelings.

'Shall I telephone them?' Clarence asked.

'Is that how it's done?'

'It is, sir,' he said firmly, privately alarmed that Philippe would think of doing the inviting himself.

Philippe nodded. He did not want to upset long standing social niceties.

'And is Frederick collecting Pippa this morning?'

Again, Clarence nodded, remembering how he had exerted pressure on Philippe to send Frederick instead of having Pippa catch the train. What were chauffeurs for if it wasn't to drive members of the family, he had been forced to say. Frederick will be in fear of his job. And in the end Philippe had acquiesced.

'He would be well on his way now,' Clarence replied.

He had won another small but important victory. Slowly but surely, he was teaching Philippe how to live like a rich man, even if Philippe still struggled with the notion of his sudden, unaccustomed wealth.

At that point, the ringing of the telephone interrupted the quietness of the dining room. Philippe could hear a muffled conversation that for him aroused no interest. Compared with a career spent responding to the urgent demands of being a doctor on call, a telephone call now was only of minor interest. He was pleased to have Clarence to filter this part of his life. If he did not choose to speak to someone, he simply shook his head.

He folded the newspaper and glanced up as Clarence returned to the room. One look at his face was enough for Philippe. This had been no ordinary phone call. His normally impassive face was grave.

'That was young Walter,' he said. 'Bad news I'm afraid.'

'Is it his father?'

Philippe was guessing but it was the most likely reason for them to receive bad news. Clarence nodded slowly.

'Yes. His father is dead. Walter found him this morning when he went to wake him.'

There was no other way to break the news to Philippe.

'How? Did he say? A heart attack I suppose.'

He wanted to say *should I go over?* But he thought better of it. Walter would have called him if there had been anything he could have done.

'Walter thinks he probably had a heart attack during the night,' Clarence said. 'The doctor came immediately but it was too late. He had been dead for some hours, apparently. Unfortunately, he'd refused to have a night nurse stay with him.'

Philippe nodded. It was an all too familiar scenario. His half-brother had been a man who had ignored his doctor's advice for years and then suffered a debilitating stroke as a consequence. And even after his stroke, he had continued to ignore medical advice. Philippe had seen the whisky decanter his half-brother had kept close at hand. It was never full and untouched.

'And I will be blamed, Clarence' he said, voicing his thoughts. 'They will blame me. Certainly, his wife and his daughter will blame me.'

Clarence had foreseen Philippe's response.

'It's possible they will blame you publicly,' Clarence ventured, 'but after everything settles down, I think Barbara Cox will enjoy her life much more as a wealthy widow than as a wife tethered to an invalid husband she despised. And her daughter Virginia will take her lead from her mother, mark my words.'

Philippe did not quite know how to respond to Clarence's candid assessment.

'I'm sure you understand, Dr Duval, that I would never say such a thing except to you in private.'

Philippe stifled an inappropriate smile. There was something slightly pompous about Clarence, he thought, but he knows his value to the household too. And to me in particular. And he is most likely right.

'Did you ask young Walter to come across and see us as soon as he could?'

He wanted to see Walter but the gulf between the two households made it difficult.

'As soon as the undertakers have been, he will come across,' he said. Philippe nodded.

'It will hardly be the weekend for entertaining, Clarence,' he said. 'Anything of that nature must wait until after the funeral.'

Clarence murmured his agreement. He had not needed to be told.

Was this the consequence of all those bitter years, Philippe wondered? In his half-brother he had seen bitterness, resentment, anger and fury. He had never seen happiness, contentment, pleasure and joy. Was my existence really at the heart of everything that he had perceived had gone wrong with his life? With his relationship with his father? Had he wanted it all too much? Had he been desperate to be loved and admired by his father only to find out his father had loved and admired another son? A son he didn't know except through second-hand reports.

Philippe shook his head. It was all becoming too much. What could he do to make amends? Nothing. It was all too late. It was beyond his power now.

Walter William Cox the third had breathed his last breath in the early hours of the morning, almost certainly succumbing to a heart attack, according to his doctor, who spoke in a hushed voice to his son.

It had been Walter's regular duty to rouse his father and help him out of bed each morning in preparation for the daily visit of a male nurse to help him shower and dress.

Walter had expected nothing to be different about the routine on this particular day. It was the eerie silence in the room that had first alerted him.

If his father was still asleep, he expected to hear the rhythmic sound of his breathing. If he was already awake, he expected some form of greeting, depending on his mood, even if it was to berate him for being late. But he had heard neither.

With a rising sense of alarm, he had leant forward and touched his father, at first gently, and then with more vigour. He felt beneath the bedclothes then to check for a pulse but the arm he touched was already cold and lifeless. He knew instinctively then his father was beyond help despite his urgent plea moments later when he telephoned the doctor to come quickly.

After a cursory examination of his patient, the doctor had needed no words to confirm what Walter already knew to be fact. His father was dead.

*I must speak with your mother*, the doctor had said, nodding in Walter's direction. *Of course*, he remembered replying. *She may need something to calm her*. The doctor nodded. *It will be a great shock*, they had both agreed.

But Walter did not join the doctor. He could not, at that moment, face his mother. Instead, he sat alone in the room. A sheet had been respectfully drawn up over his father's lifeless face.

How had it come to this, he wondered? He fingered the near empty bottle of tablets he had picked up from the bedside table. Something, some instinct, had made him tidy away the tablets that had spilt from the overturned bottle before the doctor had arrived. He stared at the bottle intently. Surely, yesterday, it was nearly full. And now, less than a half remained. Or was his mind playing tricks on him. He couldn't be sure.

He could not bring himself to think the unthinkable. Instead, he placed the bottle back on the bedside table. He would never know if his father had reached for the tablets during the night as the pain of his heart attack had grown intense. Or had he accidently, or otherwise, taken too many. He shook his head from side to side. Whatever had happened would not change the facts now. His father was dead. And the doctor was satisfied at the cause of his death. There would be no autopsy, he had said quietly. *We don't want to upset your mother unnecessarily.*

But the idea plagued him and would go on plaguing him: had his father reached out and taken too many tablets in the darkness of the night? And if he had, was it simply an accident? Or was it something else?

He wept then, not for the man he had lost but for the man his father might have been had he not been twisted and tormented by his own father.

In that bleak moment, he gave thanks for Philippe. In him, he had seen all the qualities one might admire in a man. In a father. But if not in a father, then in an uncle. As head of the family. Without Philippe, he knew he would have been thrust unwillingly into such a role. The thought of it made him shudder involuntarily.

Days later, Philippe, with Julia and Pippa by his side, was being driven in the second of the mourning cars as they made their way in slow procession to the very church where, only weeks before, his father had been farewelled.

'This must all seem very strange for you,' he whispered to Julia.

She smiled briefly.

'It does,' she said. 'Mourning someone I have never met. Someone who loathed you. Being nice to a family who loathe you.'

He shook his head slightly.

'I don't think young Walter feels like that. In fact, I'm sure he doesn't.'

Julia slipped her hand through his arm.

'I didn't mean him. He's very charming. A very genuine young man.'

Philippe smiled.

'He is, isn't he? And to think Pippa tried to hoodwink me by telling me he was a trainee doctor when I met him.'

They all laughed then. Pippa had taken the repeated teasing about this incident in good stead once she had explained it had been too complicated to tell the real story of who he was.

Julia smoothed out the skirt of her new black dress bought especially for the occasion. Her blonde hair was mostly hidden by a very smart black hat with a small face veil.

'I hope I don't have to wear this again any time soon.'

Philippe gave her an appraising look. He could see she was dressed in the height of fashion but it was her natural unadorned beauty he really admired. In idle moments, his mind would drift back to the war years remembering how she had been when he had first met her, an unsophisticated country girl on the cusp of womanhood.

'You look beautiful as you always do,' he reassured her.

She was used to his compliments but she was secretly pleased all the same. Above all, she did not want to give people a reason to gossip about her. It was important to her she appeared appropriately attired.

'I was so relieved Mrs Anderson, your housekeeper, came to my rescue. There was nothing among the clothes I had brought with me that would have served the purpose. And Pippa needed a dress and hat too. She couldn't wear what she had worn to her grandfather's funeral.'

Philippe refrained from uttering a small exclamation of surprise at his wife's admission she had nothing to wear. He knew from experience his wife never travelled with less than three suitcases. But he let the comment go unsaid.

'And it was so easy. Mrs Anderson made the appointment for us. There was a range of outfits already laid out for us. And how could I buy just one dress after everyone was so nice? Once we had decided on the funeral outfits, it seemed a shame to waste the opportunity.'

This time he smiled broadly and laughed quietly to himself.

'And the bill for all this is on its way to me, I take it?'

It was her turn to smile broadly. Pippa was laughing too. Her mother had not been the only one to indulge herself.

'Oh, yes, Mrs Anderson gave them directions. *Send the bill to the big house*, she said. *It will be seen to promptly*. And we were bowed out of the shop, shamelessly leaving your hapless chauffeur to struggle with the parcels. I could get used to this life. I have no idea how much it all cost. I didn't look at any of the price tickets. Mrs Anderson assured me that would be regarded as vulgar. And we don't want people gossiping about your vulgar Australian wife, do we?'

In the privacy of the mourning car, the three of them laughed together at the absurdity of the life into which they had been unexpectedly thrust.

In the mourning car ahead of them, the stony silence of the three chief mourners was broken only by Virginia's occasional sobs and her mother's opinion, voiced at intervals, that Philippe Duval could have shown them some consideration and stayed away from the funeral of the brother he had usurped.

'Hypocrisy, that's what it is,' she said repeatedly, as if she had just discovered the word and enjoyed the sound of it spoken out loud.

Walter, shaking his head, said nothing until he had heard the word one too many times.

'It is not hypocrisy, Mother,' he said quietly. 'I don't agree with you there. It would have caused enormous gossip if he had chosen to ignore his brother's funeral. Don't you see that?'

But his mother would not be placated.

'All my friends are on my side,' she declared. 'They will snub him.'

Walter shrugged his shoulders. He wanted to say *and you think this will worry Philippe? I can tell you now it will not.* But he did not. He could see the stubbornness in the set of his mother's face and in the lack of kindness in her eyes. She will take this resentment to her grave, he thought forlornly. It will blight her life, just as it blighted my father's. But she can't see it. This is how she will live on. In bitterness. In regret. In hatred. Hating a man I so admire. A family I admire. Where have we gone wrong, he wondered?

As their mourning car came to a halt outside the church, he looked up momentarily at a darkening sky that promised imminent rain. The mood of the weather suits the mood of the day, he thought, as he handed his mother out of the car and she took his arm. He would play his part today but he would not be a party to his mother's visceral resentment.

He decided then and there he wanted instead to be part of Philippe and Julia's family. To get to know Pippa better. He was suddenly buoyed by the prospect.

Barely twenty-four hours after the funeral, it was no surprise to Philippe to be asked to agree to an urgent meeting with the lawyers who seemed otherwise to work at a glacial pace.

Once again Howard Davis opened with formal condolences to both Philippe and Walter, who had responded reluctantly to the summons from Philippe.

'We had not mentioned this before,' Howard Davis said apologetically, as if he should have foreseen the death of Philippe's half-brother, 'but this tragic event has changed certain aspects of my late client's will.'

He paused then and looked up, before looking back down at the thick file of papers he had spread out before him.

'What has changed, Mr Davis?' Philippe asked, although he already had an inkling.

'My late client, realising the potential seriousness of his son's medical condition, stipulated that if his son died within thirty days of his own death, then the bequests to him specifically should not stand, to avoid a double set of death duties.'

Philippe heard Walter's quick intake of breath. He knew immediately he was concerned for his mother.

'What happens to those bequests, Mr Davis?' Philippe asked. 'Can you be specific.'

'Yes, of course, Dr Duval,' Howard Davis replied, scanning a document Philippe had not seen before.

'The house is left to Barbara Cox for her use during her lifetime. At her death, it will be jointly owned by her children.'

That seems satisfactory, thought Philippe. It means she can't sell the property but in all other respects, it is her home.

'Barbara Cox will receive the cash settlement she was otherwise set to receive, plus the cash settlement that was intended for her husband. She will also receive the ongoing income from the family trust that would otherwise have gone to her husband. The share portfolio, however, reverts to you, Dr Duval.'

It was Walter who asked the obvious question.

'Will my mother be able to live the life she is used to with that income, Mr Davis?'

'Of course, Mr Cox,' he replied. 'The income will be substantial. I'd be surprised if her expenses would exceed her income. And if the cash she receives is invested, there will be more income from that source.'

He thought for a moment.

'It would be good if we could explain it to her, Mr Cox, perhaps with you in attendance. I doubt Dr Duval's presence would be welcome.'

Walter smiled.

'No, Philippe's presence would not be welcome, Mr Davis,' he agreed. 'And if my mother should decide to tell her friends that she has in turn inherited everything my father inherited, then neither you nor I will say anything to contradict her.'

For the first time Walter could remember, Howard Davis smiled and nodded.

'Of course,' he said, as he gathered his papers together, 'but I hope she will see why this provision was made. It was in everyone's interests.'

But Walter would not be drawn. He was unwilling to predict his mother's reaction to what he was sure she would see as another slight. She would be wealthy but not in the way she had dreamt of. He worried it would be small consolation to a woman who had already decided she and her family had been treated with gross unfairness.

# CHAPTER 11

CURIOUS EYES PEERED OUT from behind faded curtains and broken shutters as Philippe, Clarence and Walter walked slowly down the Sag Harbor street Philippe had once called home until they reached the familiar front gate. Philippe pushed it open and held out his hand to Walter for the key to the front door. He was pleased to see the gardeners had been and the place was tidy.

The other two men hung back as Philippe went from room to room, dismayed at the deterioration twenty years of emptiness had wrought. There was now nothing to remind him of his mother or of his childhood. It was just an empty shell of a house, not a home. It no longer stirred the memories as it once had done.

'Would you like to keep the ownership of this house, Dr Duval?' Clarence asked.

Philippe knew it was a genuine offer but he shook his head.

'No, Clarence, thank you' he replied quietly. 'I think it is best to close that chapter of my life. It will be yours along with the others when everything is settled.'

'Thank you. I had no idea this legacy would be coming my way. I'm very grateful for it.'

Philippe then turned to Walter.

'I don't think we should be handing these houses over to Clarence in a state of disrepair,' he said. 'Can I rely on you to get a team of tradesmen together to bring them up to a proper state of repair?'

Walter smiled and nodded.

'Of course, you can rely on me,' he said. 'I will see to it on Monday. The tenants will be relieved.'

He would, for once, be able to deliver good news to the tenants, many of whom were still employed by Cox Industries. He had been the one to hear their complaints and in turn he had battled constantly with his father for money to do proper repairs instead of the makeshift patch jobs his father thought would suffice. At times, in frustration, he had turned to his grandfather to plead for money for repairs. He had not known how it had occurred but the cottages had become his responsibility, almost by default.

Looking along the street at the ten timber cottages with their traditional open porches and pretty front fences, Clarence felt an immense gratitude for the legacy Walter William Cox had bestowed on him.

'You'll be wanting to retire to the easy life now, Clarence,' Philippe said, with a wry smile. He knew there would certainly be enough income for Clarence's needs from the rental income. But Clarence shook his head.

'Not while there is a big house to manage, Dr Duval,' he said.

Fearing that he had been presumptuous, he quickly added, 'Well, not while you still need me to manage it, I should say.'

Philippe, noticing the hint of uncertainty in Clarence's voice, was anxious to reassure him.

'Don't worry, Clarence, there'll always be work for you while you want it.'

Philippe looked at his watch. It was nearly five o'clock.

'Let's go and have a drink together. There must be a bar close by. I've got something I'd like to tell you both about my plans for the future.'

'I think we'll be safe,' Walter said, remembering what had happened to Julia. 'I don't think my sister comes Sag Harbor way very often.'

The incident still rankled with Philippe. No apology had ever been forthcoming, overtaken, as it was, by the tragic events that followed.

Clarence hesitated. Was it quite seemly for him to be socialising in public with his employer? Philippe noticed the hesitation and understood the reason for it, which he quickly dismissed.

'Clarence, it's OK. I've adopted Australian ways,' he said. 'Come and have a drink with us.'

He patted Clarence on the back to reassure him.

'Australians don't care so much about class distinctions. I think it's a good way to be.'

Walter agreed wholeheartedly.

'I think it's a good way to be too,' he declared. 'My mother spends her life preoccupied with climbing the social ladder and worrying about what other people think. It's a waste of time and energy. It's pointless.'

In Philippe and his family, Walter had glimpsed another world, a more relaxed approach to life, a greater warmth.

And now for the first time he felt a sense of excitement about the future, about his future and an optimism that something good would finally emerge from the massive wealth his grandfather and his father before him had built. And from the tragedy that had befallen his own family.

Walter had steered them to what he considered to be the best of the numerous bars operating in Sag Harbor. Here too Walter received a cheery greeting from the barman who knew, without being told, exactly who Walter's companions were. As he approached the bar, the barman nodded in Philippe's direction.

'The new owner of Cox Industries, I presume?'

'Yeah, that's Dr Duval,' he replied, following the barman's gaze.

'He's my uncle,' Walter added, with some emphasis. He wanted to be sure there was no misunderstanding.

'Sorry to hear about your dad,' the barman said, changing tack. 'It must have been a tough time for you.'

'It was,' Walter replied without elaboration. 'Now what we need are some drinks. Beers for me and Clarence. Your best bourbon on the rocks for my uncle.'

The barman nodded and began to get the drinks. There was clearly no more gossip to be gleaned from his young customer. But still he paused for a moment or two amazed at the easy camaraderie he witnessed among the three men.

He was old enough to remember the young barefoot Philippe Duval trailing behind his mother, too shy to say very much but eyeing the world with a wisdom beyond his years. He shook his head at the memory. Now, forty years or so later, he was among the richest men on Long Island, all because his father righted a dreadful wrong. But he had made his own way in the world anyway, the gossips said, to become a top surgeon. Life was full of surprises, he muttered, but no one saw this coming.

Largely unaware of the barman's interest in him, Philippe thanked him courteously as he placed the generous drink in front of him. He sipped cautiously, savouring the familiar sweet aroma of the dark liquid. Both Clarence and Walter waited for him to break the silence.

'I have something to say,' Philippe began quietly, suddenly aware the barman was busy wiping already clean tables nearby. 'Something important. And it involves both of you.'

And then he paused, catching Walter's eye and pointing to the barman. Walter's command was less polite than Philippe might have wished.

'Give us some space, Joe,' Walter said loudly. 'Private business to discuss.'

The barman blustered and then walked back to his usual spot behind the bar and out of earshot. Walter turned back to Philippe.

'I think he got the message. We don't want to be adding anything new to his vast store of gossip.'

Clarence nodded his approval.

'Good move, Walter. There's already enough gossip about the family.' He was going to say and not all of it complimentary but then he thought better of it.

Philippe shrugged his shoulders. Local gossip was to be expected and he barely gave it a second thought, except for Walter's sake. And with that he began to lay out his plans.

'As I am the only shareholder of Cox Industries, I have decided to accept a takeover bid for the company. In its entirety.'

Walter let out an audible sigh of relief.

'Thank goodness for that,' he said. 'For one moment I thought you were going to involve me in running the company in your absence. I would have had to say I had no appetite for it. Nor aptitude either if it comes to that.'

Philippe smiled broadly then. He had already known that about Walter.

'Don't worry, Walter, I never imagined you in that role. But I do have something in mind that I think will be more to your taste. That is, apart from travelling the world chasing an endless summer.'

Walter was about to protest there was more to his life than the pursuit of pleasure but he thought better of it. It was no doubt how others viewed his life up to this point.

'If I may be permitted to ask, Dr Duval, is this the buyer your father had begun to negotiate with?'

'It is, Clarence. It is the best thing to do. I have no desire to run an industrial company, neither does Walter.'

'And if I may be permitted to ask another question which you may think impertinent: are they willing to pay the asking price?'

Clarence had been unable to contain his curiosity on this point. He had been the only other person, apart from the lawyers, privy to the earlier negotiations.

Philippe smiled slightly. He hadn't planned to make it public but then he could think of no reason not to reveal the price to Clarence and Walter.

'All this is in absolute confidence of course,' he said, looking from one to the other. 'The buyer, a large private company with complementary interests, is willing to pay the asking price, which is upwards of three hundred million. That's being worked out by the lawyers now. There are always adjustments and write downs of plant and other things to be considered, I'm told. But the final figure will be substantial, although I won't receive it in one payment. It will probably be three payments spread over three years.'

Walter let out a low whistle. It was by some measure considerably more than he had estimated the company was worth.

'And then you're going to spend your remaining days in the lap of luxury in the south of France or somewhere suitably glamorous.'

Clarence would never have dared suggest such a thing. It was Walter who was beginning to imagine Philippe's life as a super wealthy jet-setter.

A picture of such a life formed briefly in Philippe's mind. He shook his head.

'You know very well I would be bored in a week and within two, I'd be on the staff of the local hospital. Within six months, having revived my rusty French, I'd have a band of eager medical students following me around the hospital and within twelve I would be delivering papers at medical conferences throughout Europe. The only difference would be the quality of the hotel room I could afford.'

They laughed together at the absurdity of the idle life Walter had imagined for Philippe. He signalled then to the barman and another round of drinks appeared as if by magic.

'So if you're not going to retire to a life of luxury, what are you going to do with all that money?'

'Oh, I have plans, Walter, and this is where you come in.'

'Me? Are you sure?'

'Oh, yes, I'm sure,' Philippe said. 'This will keep you out of mischief.'

'And what exactly is it that will keep me out of mischief?'

'With half of the proceeds, I propose to establish a charitable foundation. I've been inspired by what Andrew Carnegie did although my interests will be different.'

Clarence noticed the bewildered look on Walter's face.

'Andrew Carnegie was a Scotsman who emigrated to America at the age of twelve with his parents whose cottage industry had been wiped out by industrialisation. He made a fortune in the steel industry and then proceeded to give away most of it by the time he died. His great achievement was to help establish around three thousand public libraries.'

'Thanks for the history lesson, Clarence,' Walter said, somewhat chastened by his lack of knowledge. 'It seems I should spend more time reading than messing about with cars and boats.'

'Well, you'll have less time for messing about with cars and boats, if I have my way, Walter. I want you to help out with the foundation but I also want you to be my understudy in managing the family's wealth. I'll need you to help me with the investment decisions and eventually, you'll be able to act in my absence.'

Walter looked up, surprised. His father had never considered him worthy of his trust.

'And the work of the foundation?'

'Its focus will be on supporting medical research programs. Pippa may also be involved if she chooses to be. I would ask your sister too to be involved but she may not be inclined.'

Walter pulled a face at this last suggestion. He knew Philippe was trying to be scrupulously fair.

'Let's leave my sister out of it for now,' he suggested. 'If she expresses a genuine interest, then you can think about it then. When we set it up, I will let her know the option is there.'

Philippe was satisfied to leave it at that. He turned to Clarence.

'I've had a rethink on the big house. I think it's an opportunity to keep a large tract of land under-developed. I think we should use part of the house as the headquarters for the foundation and open the garden to the public. I'm sure you could take care of that for me.'

'What an excellent idea, Dr Duval,' he beamed, his eyes lighting up at the prospect of having some control over what would happen in the future. Philippe was pleased at his enthusiasm.

'We could open with a picnic on the lawns for the local people one Saturday, probably in the spring. It would attract hundreds of people.'

'Good idea, Clarence. We have around six months or so to put all this in place. I plan for the foundation to pay for the upkeep of the house and gardens so it will be free for people to come and enjoy the gardens.'

They both looked at him with a new level of respect. He had

known what exclusion meant. No one was going to be excluded now. None of the local children would now be excluded by the big wrought iron gates that separated the wealthy owners from those who could only ever dream of owning such a house.

After several minutes of intense discussion, Philippe stood up.

'I think we've made enough progress today,' he said. 'The next thing for you to do, Walter, is to inform your mother and your sister of my plans. I would tell them myself, but it may be better coming from you.'

Clarence nodded to himself. In every respect, Philippe had proved himself to be superior to his half-brother. He was determined to be fair, despite the insults laid at his door. The old man had been right. Here is a man of absolute integrity and honesty. Ella Duval would have been so proud of him.

Julia and Pippa were waiting patiently in the dining room for Philippe. He was uncharacteristically late for dinner which had been set at seven o'clock.

'What's he up to?' Julia asked her daughter.

'All I know is he went with Walter and Clarence to inspect the Sag Harbor cottages this afternoon.'

Pippa had spent the afternoon with her head buried in medical textbooks, oblivious to everything else going on around her.

It was Clarence who provided the answer as he began to serve the wine.

'Dr Duval is on the telephone, madam,' he said.

Julia nodded her thanks. Clarence's formality would have pleased my mother, she thought, but it seems out of step with modern life now.

'Sorry, I'm here now.'

They turned to see Philippe striding towards the table. He turned to Julia.

'I was talking to Robert Clarke,' he explained. 'He rang while I was out.'

'Of course. And I imagine his first question was: are you coming back to your old job? And if so, when?'

'You're absolutely right,' Philippe replied. 'Those were his exact words. Robert doesn't do a big line in small talk although I think he was itching to ask me one or two other pertinent questions.'

'Like how much money you've inherited.'

Julia looked at her daughter.

'Really, Pippa, I don't think that's quite the thing to say to your father.'

But she laughed.

'Why not? We'd all love to know.'

Philippe laughed then.

'My darling girl, you are incorrigible. When it's all settled, I will tell you but I can tell you I'm accepting a bid for Cox Industries that is above the three hundred million dollar mark.'

Julia glanced quickly at Clarence. Was it quite appropriate to speak so freely in front of him?

'Oh, don't worry,' he said, noticing Julia's concern. 'Clarence knows everything there is to know pretty much.'

'And what will you do with three hundred million dollars? Retire to a life of leisure? Is that what you told Dr Clarke?'

'No, that's not what I told Dr Clarke, my dear girl. I told him to expect me back in a couple of weeks. Your mother and I discussed the option of living here in America but Australia is her home. It's your home. It's home to me too now. And I believe I still have something to offer the medical profession.'

He turned his attention then to the over-sized lobster on his plate.

'And did you discuss your plans with Walter? Is he keen to be involved?'

Julia had seen Walter's agreement to Philippe's plans as pivotal to their being able to return to Sydney.

'I did,' he replied, 'and he's very excited by them. And Clarence here is going to take care of the house and the opening up of the gardens.'

'What's all this?' Pippa asked, realising she had been left out of the discussions.

'I'm going to set up a foundation which has the aim of funding medical research.'

He paused to take a long sip from his wine glass.

'The foundation will be housed here, in this house, and the grounds will be made available to the public as a public park. Entrance will be free.'

'With all the money?' Pippa asked. It seemed to her to be a very generous thing to do.

'No. With half of the sale proceeds of Cox Industries. Like other foundations, we'll try to interest others in contributing based on our philanthropic interests.'

She thought about this for a while.

'So where does Walter fit into this scheme?'

'He's going be the deputy chairman,' Philippe said. 'He'll have the authority to make decisions if I'm unavailable.'

'And what about me?'

'If you think that would interest you.'

Pippa mulled it over in her mind.

'We could have an Australian branch,' she suggested. 'And I could run the Australian office.'

Philippe did not respond immediately. Was she thinking she would give her medical studies away altogether, he wondered?

'Let's talk about it. I didn't mean for you to abandon your medical career just yet. You at least need to finish your internship.'

She nodded. That much was obvious.

'And what would we call this foundation?' she asked. Like Walter, she was excited by the idea.

He smiled. There was only one choice of name.

'It will be the Ella Duval Foundation,' he said. 'Let's drink to its success.'

The three of them clinked glasses. Behind them, Clarence smiled broadly for the first time in many months.

# CHAPTER 12

*Australia*

JULIA LEANED BACK in her chair and surveyed the crowd around the lunch table. She sighed deeply at the sheer pleasure of being back at Prior Park after such a whirlwind trip to America. This is what a loving family feels like, she mused. We care about each other. And everyone is here, except Anthony. She wondered how he coped being away from the family with his mother in England. The warmth of her family's welcome had seemed so real she felt she could almost touch it.

William, the younger of her two brothers, sat in his usual place at the end of the table, his back to the double doors that led to the wide verandah. Philippe had been placed on his left. William doesn't want to miss a chance to grill you, she had said quietly to Philippe who had only smiled at her warning. He had known exactly what was coming at the family lunch.

The younger generation had ranged themselves on one side of the table. Her niece Marianne and Pippa, deep in conversation, looked as close as sisters. And her nephew Paul and son John, closer than cousins, kept up an equally lively conversation.

She smiled, relieved that John's early wariness of Philippe had been replaced by a benign acceptance. And the younger of her two nieces Susan had loudly reminded everyone she had turned eight the day

140

before. Her mother Kate had gently chided her for wanting to be the centre of attention. Being the youngest, she was indulged beyond what was good for her, according to her father, Julia's brother Richard, who, as it transpired, indulged her the most.

But Susan was not destined to be the centre of attention on this occasion. This time it was Philippe to whom the questions came thick and fast, all of which he answered good naturedly, although his first act had been to check on Paul, whose recovery from a near fatal plane crash he had overseen earlier in the year.

As Julia had prophesied, it was William who was keen to probe the story deeper. It clearly puzzled him. How does a man suddenly become the beneficiary of his father's multi million dollar estate when he had never ever had a relationship with his father? It seemed so improbable to William.

'Did you have any idea your father had tracked your career? No inkling?' he asked, as Philippe finished telling the full story. Up until that point, they had only heard snippets from Julia.

Philippe shook his head. He had asked himself the same question. He had tried to remember any unusual incidents across the years that might have given him a clue to his having been followed or spied upon. But he could think of nothing.

'None at all. And I never entertained the thought of tracking him down. Not after the way he had treated my mother. In fact, I didn't even know for sure who my father was, although I had guessed.'

William thought about this but still it seemed so implausible.

'So it was Pippa's chance meeting with the grandson that set everything in motion for you to finally meet your father?'

'It was,' Philippe said, 'but that wasn't the catalyst for making me his principal heir. According to the lawyers, my father had already made me his main beneficiary years before we met.'

The hubbub of conversation had died down as dishes of vegetables were passed around from hand to hand and the meal became the full focus of everyone's attention. It was Kate who broke the silence.

'And what now for you, Philippe? My sources tell me Robert Clarke was worried he'd lose your talents.'

She had no need to tell Philippe his monumental change in fortune had been—and still was—the major topic of conversation among their mutual friends in Sydney. He laughed, amused at how nicely she had prodded him to confirm his future plans.

'Young Walter Cox has suggested I might spend the rest of my days in the south of France leading the life of an idle rich man. I couldn't imagine it myself. I said I'd be bored in a week and on the staff of the local hospital within two weeks.'

'But you could have stayed in New York and worked there?' she persisted.

'I thought about it but there are other people to consider.'

He nodded in Julia's direction who was busy at that moment helping Alice find space on the table for yet more platters of food.

'Do you think she would survive a New York winter? And Pippa? I wouldn't want her to turn out like Virginia Cox.'

Pippa looked up at the mention of her name and laughed.

'I could probably do a passable impression of a spoiled rich bitch if I put my mind to it,' she pouted. 'And I so miss having the chauffeur on call.'

At which point everyone laughed.

'You couldn't pull it off for more than ten minutes,' Paul declared flatly, 'and you're certainly not going to get away with that behaviour here.'

'But seriously, will all this change your career plans, Pippa?' Kate asked, wondering how becoming quite well off herself through the legacy from her grandfather might change her ambitions.

She looked at her father. How disappointed would he be if I didn't pursue my medical career, she wondered? She opted for a diplomatic answer.

'I have to take up where I left off when I went to New York,' she replied. 'I have another six months or more to get to the next point in my career. Then we'll see. There may be an option to be involved in the foundation we're setting up.'

'That sounds so interesting,' Kate said, 'but won't that be based in New York?'

She shrugged.

'There's no reason why there couldn't be an office in Sydney,' she said, looking towards her father, 'even with the main foundation headquartered on Long Island.'

Kate said nothing more. She could see she was treading on delicate ground. Pippa's got it all worked out, she thought, apart from convincing her father about her change in career.

Alice, who was accustomed to hosting large family lunches, pushed her chair back from the table and motioned to her daughter Marianne to start collecting the empty plates in preparation for the arrival of dessert.

Paul too jumped up. He had been told so many times by his father to help his aunt that he did it automatically now, nudging his cousin to help. A simple nod from Philippe had Pippa on her feet too so the task was quickly done.

Julia and Kate got up to help too but were waved away.

'I think I've got enough helpers,' Alice said with a smile, 'willing or otherwise. The pudding will be out directly.'

Julia followed Alice anyway, chatting amiably about her shopping trips to the many fashionable stores on Long Island. It's like old times, thought Alice, when we used to devour the women's magazines together to see all the latest fashions. Who could possibly have seen what lay ahead for Julia? My own life has been much more predictable, thank heavens. I would have lacked the courage to face what she has faced.

Behind them, Kate had remained at the table along with Philippe. She moved along the empty seats to sit next to him.

'You've certainly had an exciting time,' she said.

'Exciting is one way to describe it, Kate,' he said, as he sipped his glass of excellent burgundy appreciatively. He had brought several bottles with him from the cases he had shipped home from the vast cellar at Eastbury Hall.

'I see you travel with your own wine now,' she said, nodding in the direction of the half empty bottle.

He laughed.

'Call it an indulgence, Kate,' he said. 'Will you have some more?'

She held out her empty glass for him to refill.

'Why not,' she said. 'I can relax today.'

'Do you miss your Sydney friends?' he asked suddenly.

For her, marrying Richard had meant a change from being mistress of the beautiful Southern Highlands home at Berrima Park which her son Tim had inherited to Richard's home in Springfield.

'Sometimes, but I go back quite often. I'm like Julia in reverse. I've still got Tim and Nancy to think about.'

Knowing that Nancy was the same age as Pippa and Tim the same age as Paul, Philippe doubted that either of her children now needed quite so much supervision from their mother.

'And Angela?'

He knew Angela Dixon had always been her particular friend.

'Oh, yes, Angela's always happy to see me,' she admitted, without embarrassment. And then she wondered, does Philippe know she covered for me when my affair with Richard began? But that was no longer a dangerous secret for her. But what about Philippe, she wondered? There were still murmurings.

'Have you caught up on all the news yet from Robert Clarke?' she asked, testing the waters.

'Not all of it,' Philippe admitted. 'He was in a rush when I spoke to him a couple of days ago. He was due at a meeting of the hospital board.'

She nodded. She could well imagine Robert Clarke's impatience for matters with Philippe to be settled. She knew he was not a man who indulged in idle chatter.

'He'll be wanting you to start back at the hospital as soon as possible, I imagine.'

It was more a statement than a question. He smiled.

'Yes, I'm due back next week.'

She nodded. Her information had been good.

'Angela told me you were due back at the hospital. She'd been talking to Patricia Clarke of course. You've been a topic of some interest, I must say.'

Again, he smiled.

'I expected that, although I did tell Robert to keep it to himself. But I knew he would tell his wife, and once he did that, well, what can I say?'

She laughed then.

'You didn't seriously expect your big news to remain secret, did you?'

He shook his head ruefully. She paused for a few moments then. Should I tell him the other piece of news? The news about Karen? The wine had given her a boldness she might not have otherwise possessed. She pressed on.

'By the way, did he tell you the news about Karen?' she asked quietly.

It was a name he had not heard in some time.

'No, what news would that be?' he asked cautiously.

'Angela told me she was involved in a serious car accident earlier this week. Not her fault apparently. A truck ran a red light.'

He tried and failed to keep the alarm out of his voice.

'Is she alright, do you know?'

'I believe so, pretty bruised and battered. She's still in hospital I think.'

He nodded. There was no outward display of concern.

'Thanks for telling me. I'm sure Robert will fill me in when I see him next week.'

He paused and smiled at her. He wondered idly how much Richard had told her. Not everything, he hoped.

'And thanks for being discreet,' he added.

She knew what he meant and smiled. She had seen his eyes light up involuntarily for just a moment at the mention of Karen's name.

Richard, about to sit down at the table, had overheard the exchange and tackled Kate as she slipped back into her assigned seat.

'I heard what you said to Philippe. You told him about Karen. Did you really need to tell him that piece of news here, today?'

'I was discreet about it,' she replied. 'Anyway, they were friends. He should know about it.'

Richard shrugged.

'They were more than friends,' he said. 'And if she was just a normal friend, you wouldn't have been whispering that news to him.'

'Well, there's no point in bringing Julia into the conversation, is there?'

'No, I guess not,' he agreed, but still he felt that sense of unease at the mention of Karen's name.

He knew the reason. What others had only guessed at and gossiped about he knew for sure. He had known how deeply involved Philippe had been with her. And how deeply she had loved Philippe. And probably continued to love him.

He looked up as his sister Julia placed a large bowl of trifle on the table. Surely, it's all in the past, he thought. She looks happy. He looks happy. Pippa seems happy. I should stop jumping at old shadows. The past is the past. Let's hope it stays there.

Julia's brother would have been disappointed had he known a visit to Karen's hospital room had become Philippe's first priority on his return to Sydney.

It was late morning on his first day back when he opened the door to Karen's room cautiously, not wanting to disturb her unnecessarily. He looked first to the sleeping figure in the narrow hospital bed and then to the many large bunches of spring flowers that filled the available space in the room. She stirred then and opened her eyes. Her hair lay in an auburn tangle across the pillow. She smiled and admonished him gently.

'You should have told me you were coming ...'

She gestured helplessly as he sat down on the edge of her bed. He was suddenly uncertain what to say or how she would feel about him visiting her.

'How are you? I heard about your accident from Kate and then from your uncle just now. How are you feeling? Robert said you copped quite a battering.'

His tone became all professional then, trying to assess the extent of her injuries without appearing to do so.

'I've had a headache forever but it's not as bad today,' she said, trying to make light of what had happened.

'And a badly sprained wrist as you can see,' holding up her left arm that was now encased in a heavy bandage.

He smiled reassuringly and spoke encouragingly.

'That will mend pretty quickly and the bruising will disappear after a few weeks.'

If he was alarmed by her bruised and battered appearance, he tried not to show it. He knew it was mostly superficial and she would heal. He knew too how much worse the accident might have been. Her uncle's words echoed in his mind. *She's lucky she wasn't killed. Car's a terrible mess. Complete write off.*

'I see Bianca's been keeping you in the loop by the look of things,' he said, nodding towards the swatch of fabric samples and the small stack of the latest fashion magazines on her bedside table.

She half turned her head with some effort.

'Yes, we're having to make decisions for next winter's collection,' she explained.

'Your business is going well, I hear,' he said chattily.

She nodded. He noticed her small grimace of pain as she tried to sit upright. He bent over her to help her.

'It is going well,' she said, with just a hint of pride in her voice, 'despite my father's misgivings.'

'Surely he's convinced by now you and Bianca know what you're doing?'

He wondered what more she had to do to earn her father's approval.

'Sometimes I think he is,' she said. 'It's just such a woman's world that he can't see how or why it works as a business.'

He laughed quietly to himself. He was going to say if her father had seen Julia's spending spree in the dress shops of Long Island and New York, he'd have changed his mind about the fashion business. But he hesitated. It's probably not something she wants to hear, he thought. Not right now, anyway.

'Something's amused you?'

147

He shook his head slowly.

'Not really. Just thinking how hard it is for some men to change.'

She was quiet then for a few moments. He knew what was coming. She was just trying to think how best to frame the question.

'Uncle Robert told me he's surprised you came back. Is it all true?' she asked, her eyes suddenly watching him intently. 'Is it true you inherited a fortune?'

He laughed quietly. He had known to expect the question but he couldn't resist teasing her a little.

'Do you think you should be listening to gossip like that?'

'Well, I wouldn't call it gossip. Not coming from Uncle Robert. He doesn't usually gossip as you know.'

He smiled broadly then and patted her uninjured hand.

'I shouldn't tease you like that. I know you're dying to know everything.'

She pulled a face. It was almost a pout, but not quite. I remember that look, he thought. A look that said *you can't deny me.*

'Tell me everything,' she demanded. 'I want to hear the whole story.'

He was pleased to see a little of her old spirit returning. And with that he began to relate an abridged version of the events that had culminated in his unexpected wealth and the tragic events that had accompanied it.

'And after all that, you're coming back here to work in the hospital? Not taking a world tour or planning to live the life of an idle rich man?'

He nodded.

'I think I'm more valuable as a surgeon than as an idle rich man. Besides, with too much time on my hands, I'd only get into trouble.'

She tried to laugh but the effort hurt her bruised ribs. He looked at her tenderly. He could not resist the temptation to reach across and stroke her bruised cheek. It was a small gesture of comfort and concern.

She smiled. He leant forward to kiss her on the cheek.

'I promised I wouldn't ignore you anymore when I came back,' he said quietly. 'I haven't forgotten but you must focus on recovering from your injuries.'

He reached over and placed a small jewel box on her bedside table.

'Open it later,' he said, as he lifted the fingers of her uninjured hand to his lips. 'You'll know I was thinking of you while I was away.'

He could recall their infrequent meetings since he married Julia. Each time they met, the same sweet memories had come flooding back. She only had to smile at him in a certain way and he would feel the old familiar longings. He had done his best to avoid her. But not anymore.

'Don't tire my patient out.'

The command came from the doorway as Robert Clarke strode into the room. He had taken in the tender scene with a sense of dismay. *Why couldn't Philippe leave her alone? Perhaps I should have encouraged him to stay in New York after all.* Philippe stood up quickly and turned to leave.

'I'll leave you in Robert's capable hands,' he said by way of farewell.

As he brushed past his colleague, he could not mistake the warning look nor could he misunderstand the whispered aside: *leave her alone, Philippe. She's doing just fine without you around.*

Philippe said nothing. He knew the advice was well meant but he resented it just the same.

*I do not need you to tell me how to behave*, he wanted to say, *Karen is my friend* but he took a deep breath and stayed silent. There was nothing to be gained by responding. Nothing at all.

Later, as Robert Clarke finished his routine checks of his patient, he glanced around the room. There were more flowers, he was sure. And what was that on her bedside table? A jewellery box. He was sure it hadn't been there earlier in the day. So he's bringing her expensive presents now.

And then he saw the look of happiness in her eyes. It's all going to start up again, he thought, shaking his head from side to side as he left her room. I hope he's discreet. His wife will be devastated if she ever finds out.

# CHAPTER 13

IT WAS UNSEASONABLY HOT for late spring in Sydney. Pippa, relishing the prospect of a week away from her hospital routine, sat perusing the latest letter from her cousin Marianne.

'What news from Marianne?' her mother asked.

Pippa folded the letter quickly for fear her mother would ask to read it.

'Usual stuff. It's already very hot up there. Her father and Uncle Richard are eyeing off another property to add to the Belleville holdings. Her father is going to look at it next week.'

'Whereabouts is it? Where's this new property?'

'Somewhere remote. On the way to St George, I think.'

Julia laughed.

'Everywhere beyond Sydney is remote to you, Pippa. And the other letter?'

Doesn't anything escape her, Pippa wondered?

'From Walter. He thinks we should have planned to go across for Christmas. He says a white Christmas in New York is a wonder to behold.'

She looked at her mother with a mixture of hope and expectation.

'Well, that's not happening this year. I don't think Dr Clarke would be too happy if your father took more time off. Anyway, he's been talking regularly with Walter and Clarence. And the lawyers too. He'll probably want to go over early next year to check out the work on the big house and the gardens. The lawyers say some matters are piling up that only he can deal with.'

Pippa hesitated. Her mother seemed distracted. Had she imagined it or had there been a growing tension in the house since their return from America?

She watched as her mother carefully watered each of the potted plants that had begun to wilt in the morning sun.

'I'm off to have lunch today with Nancy Lester, Anita Clarke and Lucy Dixon. A girls catch up. It's been too long.'

Julia brightened, pleased that Pippa was maintaining the friendships forged in her schooldays.

'What's Nancy up to these days? Still running the house at Berrima Park for her brother?'

Pippa nodded. She had been slightly disappointed that her good friend had not pursued her own career.

'I think she does a lot for him. He was very young when he inherited everything from his father and then their mother married Uncle Richard. And had Susan of course.'

Julia let the water pour unchecked from the watering can until the excess water began to pool around her feet.

'Damn,' she said, setting down the watering can.

Pippa couldn't help but notice her mother's reaction. But why? She shrugged. She didn't know the details but she knew her uncle and Kate Lester had begun an affair before Kate was widowed. Bestowing the Belleville name on Susan had confirmed everyone's suspicions. But that's all in the past, she mused. Well in the past.

'You look as if you've been reminded of something you'd rather not remember.'

'My darling girl, don't be absurd,' Julia said, unconvincingly.

But even as she spoke the words a scene replayed in her mind. Karen Clarke, smirking, hiding a delicious secret. Angela Dixon being forced to break the news to her that her own brother was the father of Kate Lester's baby. Susan, now eight years old, the innocent at the centre of the scandal.

Pippa didn't press her mother for an answer. If there was something troubling her, she knew her mother would have to deal with it in her own way.

'Anita is doing well,' she said, changing the subject. 'I saw Dr Clarke the other day. He was beaming when I asked after her. Having a daughter follow in his footsteps is more than he expected, I think. He asked how I was getting on.'

'What did you say?'

'I smiled and said I was getting on very well. And changed the subject.'

'And are you getting on very well?'

'Depends on how you define getting on very well.'

But Julia wasn't going to be side-tracked.

'Your father is worried you're going to give up medicine.'

'Maybe.'

She looked up at her mother to gauge her reaction.

Julia paused. Well-meaning people had interfered in her life. She wasn't going to make the same mistake with her daughter.

'It's your life, Pippa. You must do what you want. Your circum-stances have changed quite a bit. I assume this means you're serious about working for the foundation when it's finally established?'

She smiled and nodded.

'I am. It sounds very worthwhile. I think I've almost convinced Dad to set up an office in Sydney so we can do some Australian projects. I really think I can achieve a lot more that way.'

Julia made no further comment. In the end, she expected Pippa would get her own way.

'By the way, don't forget I'm catching a plane at one o'clock. I'll be back in a few days.'

Prior Park, the place to which my mother regularly escapes, she thought.

'Say *hello* to everyone up there for me,' Pippa yelled as she disap-peared inside to change.

Why is it that anything connected with Karen Clarke still has the power to unsettle me? Julia shook her head and cursed the latest gossip and half heard conversations that, taken together, had successfully robbed her of her peace of mind.

'Great location, Pippa. Sorry I'm late. Traffic.'

Nancy Lester greeted each of her friends in turn.

'Relax. No one's working today, Nancy.'

Pippa set down her half-finished glass of champagne and reached for the bottle to fill a glass for Nancy.

'Wow. Champagne. Are we celebrating? What are we celebrating?'

Pippa laughed.

'Friendship. We haven't been together since I got back from the States.'

Anita Clarke laughed too.

'You mean we haven't been together since you discovered you have a very wealthy father and are not too badly off yourself.'

Lucy Dixon affected mock outrage on her friend's behalf.

'Anita! That's a bit much. Perhaps Pippa doesn't want to talk about it. It's a private matter.'

Anita laughed and shook her head, her long dark brown hair floating free in the breeze.

'Of course, Pippa wants to talk about it. I would if I'd suddenly discovered my father was extremely wealthy.'

They all looked expectantly at Pippa who was enjoying being the centre of attention. It hadn't always been the case. When the truth about her birth had been discovered, she had been shunned at school except by Lucy, Anita and Nancy. She would always be grateful for their friendship. She remembered how much it had mattered.

She began her story, skipping only one or two details. At the end, those around her fell silent. Lucy, who had followed her father into the law, was first to start firing questions.

'There would have been a challenge to the will by the half-brother surely?'

'Oh, he would have done so but he was persuaded not to when he found out my father had actually been officially adopted by his natural father.'

This puzzled Lucy.

'Surely your father knew this?'

Pippa shook her head.

'His mother told him nothing. Didn't even put his father's name on the birth certificate. I think she was so disappointed he wouldn't marry her.'

'But she let him pay the college fees for your father to attend medical school?'

It was Anita's turn to probe the story.

'That's right. My father was completely unaware of it at the time.'

'And then your father's half-brother died? That was convenient. He doesn't sound like a nice man.'

Nancy thought Anita had overstepped the mark, speaking in such a way. She rebuked Anita in her own calm way.

'That's not a very nice thing to say. It's not nice to speak ill of the dead.'

But Pippa laughed. The death of her father's half-brother had been unfortunate but they certainly had not mourned his passing.

'It's true, though. My father tried to get him to see sense but he flatly refused. Called my father a lot of names I can't repeat.'

Champagne glasses were being refilled. Their meals, which had been growing cold as they listened intently to Pippa's story, became the focus of their attention.

It was only Anita, facing towards the restaurant reception, who noticed Pippa's father with her cousin Karen. At that very moment, Philippe looked in her direction and saw the group of four young women. He turned quickly and was gone.

*Did I just imagine that?* She looked up again in time to see a distinctive silver Mercedes-Benz heading away from the restaurant. *I've seen that car before in a designated parking space at the hospital. I know exactly who it belongs to.*

'You look worried about something, Anita?'

'It's nothing, Pippa, nothing at all. Just thinking about a patient and whether I'd left all the instructions I needed to.'

Pippa smiled. She understood those concerns. Anita smiled too, relieved that her friend believed the lie.

'And how has your mother coped with it all?'

Anita was suddenly curious. She remembered the snippets of gos-sip about Philippe before he married Pippa's mother. Mostly conver-sations hastily cut short between her parents as soon as they became aware of her presence. But it was enough to confirm her suspicions.

She hadn't thought about it all until very recently. All it had taken was a seemingly innocent remark spoken casually by a colleague. *Dr Duval is taking a lot of interest in your cousin's recovery. I thought your father was looking after her?* She had feigned disinterest. Even so she couldn't fail to notice the slight knowing smile that accompanied the remark. *They're friends. They move in the same circles,* she had replied, cutting the conversation short.

'Well, I'm not sure what my mother thinks of it all, to be honest, but she had a massive spending spree in the shops of Long Island and Manhattan. The bills got forwarded to my father. The news of who she was seemed to precede our arrival everywhere we went.'

Pippa warmed to her subject, adopting her version of an American accent.

'Ah, Mrs Duval, so wonderful to see you here. And your beautiful daughter too. How can we help you today? Would you care for a glass of champagne while we show you our latest collection? We have just the thing for you. This cocktail dress would look *wonderful* on you. It is trimmed with gold leaf which makes it a little out of the ordinary. It will look *absolutely divine* on you. And don't worry about your car. Of course, your chauffeur is perfectly fine parking in front of our shop. Not a worry in the world.'

They all giggled at the scene Pippa described.

'Did she buy the cocktail dress? I'm guessing gold leaf trimming meant outrageously expensive?'

Lucy asked the question to which they all wanted to know the answer.

'Of course, she did. How could she refuse such flattery?'

Then Pippa laughed remembering her father receiving the bills. She dropped her voice an octave to mimic his reaction.

'Well, I inherited millions of dollars but at this rate my wife will have spent it in a year.'

They all laughed together at Pippa's description of her mother's spending spree.

'Anyway, she had fun over there but it hasn't changed her life really. Nor mine for that matter. In fact, she left today to visit her family up north. And to see my half-brother, John.'

'So she's away for a few days?'

Pippa nodded in Anita's direction as she sat back for her plate to be removed.

'Just a few days. She thinks we can probably manage for a few days without her.'

She laughed and her friends joined in but she did not notice how quickly the laughter died on Anita's lips as her thoughts turned to what she had just witnessed.

*Well, it looks like your father can certainly manage for a few days without your mother. There could be a perfectly innocent explanation for what I saw earlier. Except I doubt it.*

Instead, she reached for her champagne glass. For Pippa's sake, she must not let anything spoil the lunch. It felt so cosy, so friendly, just the four of them.

It was a perfect day with the sun glistening off the harbour. A gentle breeze rising from the water to quell the worst of the early afternoon heat. This was life at its best.

'Will our lives ever get better than this?'

Anita looked around her and at her friends.

'My mother thinks it will when I have a husband.'

They all rolled their eyes in sympathy with Lucy.

'Some nice barrister, I suppose, with his career path firmly set on becoming a Queen's Counsel and triumphing in important cases?'

'I think you've got it exactly, Anita,' Pippa said. 'Just as I imagine your mother has put your father on the alert for a brilliant young surgeon. He's probably interviewing candidates already.'

Anita rolled her eyes and let out an audible sigh. *Pippa's probably closer to the truth than she knows.*

'And what about you Nancy? You can't go on keeping house for your brother forever. There must be some nice young grazier on the lookout for a wife?'

The girl blushed, uncomfortable that the attention had become focused on her. She was conscious of her own apparent lack of ambition as she looked around the table. Lucy shining in law; Anita and Pippa taking medicine in their stride. It made her feel inadequate. How could she compete?

It was Pippa who noticed the slight redness in her freckled cheeks at being teased but it was Lucy who offered a hint.

'Now a certain young pilot is back in the air things might change.'

This was news to Pippa. To Anita too, who, unlike Pippa, did not immediately make the connection.

'Pilot? When did you meet a pilot?

But it was Pippa who provided the answer.

'Of course, my cousin Paul Belleville. Tim's friend. I had no idea. My cousin Marianne and I exchange letters but she must have been under strict instructions not to say anything.'

'But isn't your mother married to Paul's father?'

Anita was beginning to piece it all together.

Nancy nodded, praying that the conversation would soon move on. It was all something of an embarrassment to her. And to Paul too.

Lucy, sorry now for having broken her friend's confidence, was keen to move the conversation along.

'And you, Pippa? By the sound of it a certain young American has left quite an impression on you?'

It was Pippa's turn to blush.

'Don't be ridiculous,' she said.

But she could see immediately that no one believed her. Not in the slightest.

Philippe glanced around nervously as the waiter led the way to a table in the far corner of the restaurant. This time, he did a quick scan of the tables before sighing with relief. *No one here we know. Thank goodness.*

He glanced at his companion. She had laughed like a naughty schoolgirl at being forced to retreat from their first destination at Watsons Bay. He had been annoyed with her. Annoyed with himself too. This time he insisted on a table in the far corner of the restaurant.

After a few minutes, Karen looked up from the menu and smiled at him. He returned her smile but shook his head slightly.

'You know I should not be here. Not with you. Not in this way. Not just the two of us.'

He put his menu down and looked across the table at her. Did he really need to explain his nervousness? *What if they were seen? How hard would this be to explain away?* She threw back her head and laughed quietly.

'How very ungallant you've become, Philippe. After all, we're just friends having lunch. If you felt like that, why did you invite me?'

He grimaced. She was right. His words had been clumsy and ill-mannered.

'You know what I mean,' he said, looking directly at her. 'You know exactly what I mean.'

He noticed then how some of the scars and bruising from her recent accident were still visible on her face and neck, despite her makeup.

She's still recovering, he reminded himself. *I should be kinder to her. But kind is dangerous. Kind can be misinterpreted.* But so can frequent hospital visits, he thought. It had been so easy to visit her. And then she had come to look forward to his visits. It was too late when he realised that he, too, had begun to look forward to seeing her. Without realising it, she had become part of his life again. And he had become part of hers.

But he guessed she was angry with him still. He knew she had a right to be.

'You've ignored me, pretended I didn't exist for the past eight years,' she said finally. 'It was as if I had meant nothing to you. And now, I'm not sure what's changed?'

He looked at her closely. She was still as beautiful as he remembered. Why does she bewitch me like this? He loved the way her long auburn hair cascaded over her shoulders. He remembered her face on the pillow next to his. He remembered their love making as if it was yesterday. And now, as he looked at her, he felt the same familiar longings buried deep within him.

And then he knew, as if he had not already known, why he had spent the past eight years avoiding her.

He knew he couldn't trust himself around her. And now? He felt as if he was standing on thin ice that was beginning to crack beneath his feet. He knew he should turn and walk away. But he could not.

'I'm sorry,' he said. 'I'm sorry for hurting you. You must know you meant a lot to me. You mean a lot to me.'

His tone was gentler now. More caring. But most of all careful. He knew he was treading on forbidden ground. Yet he felt he had to explain.

'But I was committed elsewhere. I had to keep my word. I couldn't trust myself around you. And I hoped you would find someone else. I really believed you would find someone else.'

She smiled. For once he's telling the truth, she thought. She noticed he deliberately avoided any mention of Julia's name.

'And now? Are you still committed elsewhere?'

She closed the menu and set it down on the table. Suddenly the atmosphere between them became tense.

'You know I'm still committed elsewhere.'

She shrugged her shoulders as if to say *do I know that for sure?*

'You know that I'm committed to my marriage,' he said, this time with more emphasis. 'Nothing's changed.'

She noticed his wedding ring glistening in the dim light. She reached out and touched it.

'Well, that's what you say. This tells the world you're committed elsewhere,' she said, tapping lightly on the plain gold band. 'But sometimes outward signs can be meaningless. Lives can change.'

He pulled his hand away.

She sat back and eyed his reaction. Is he trying to convince me? Or himself?

'Let's order,' he said abruptly as the waiter appeared beside their table. 'And let's enjoy our time together.'

As the waiter walked away, he tried again. He hadn't expected her to challenge him in quite this way. Were they really going to revisit everything from the past?

'Believe me, I never meant to hurt you. I want us to be friends. You mean a lot to me. Your friendship means a lot to me. I told you before I went away I didn't want to go on avoiding you.'

She smiled then and raised her glass.

'To our future friendship then.'

'To our future friendship,' he replied as he raised his glass towards her.

'Please don't be angry with me about the past,' he said. 'You know there is much I regret but how can I regret being with you? Despite everything, I don't regret meeting you. I could never do that. I only wish my circumstances had been different.'

She nodded. She did not trust herself to speak. In those few moments, she began to fall in love with him all over again. But in a new way too.

This time, she had no illusions. However much or however little he was offering her, she would take it.

# CHAPTER 14

IT WAS LATE AFTERNOON. The sun would very soon dip below the western horizon. Anita was finally heading home from the lunch that had extended well into the afternoon. With no immediate plans for the evening and knowing her parents would be out, she chose the longer route home, a route that would take her, with a minor detour, past her cousin Karen's apartment at Rose Bay.

What am I doing spying like this? I shouldn't be doing this.

She ignored the voice in her head and slowed her Mini to negotiate the turn from the main road into the quiet suburban street where Karen lived. She drove past the elegant art deco apartment block to the end of the street and executed a perfect U-turn. It was only then she noticed a distinctive silver car slowing to park in front of the block.

Panicking, she quickly eased the Mini into a tight park on the opposite side of the street some distance away. Close enough to see. Not close enough to be noticed. She silenced the engine and waited.

She watched as Philippe got out and walked to the other side of the car. She saw him extend his hand to Karen and together they walked to the side entrance of the building, his arm lightly draped around her waist.

I shouldn't be spying on them. This is wrong. She began to berate herself. But she could not look away. She watched transfixed as

Philippe hesitated for a few moments and then he drew Karen into an embrace and kissed her.

Anita felt her face redden with embarrassment at what she was seeing. She looked away. *I can't watch this. I can't watch this betrayal.*

After a few moments, she looked back. They remained standing very close together their arms around each other as if nothing else mattered at that moment.

*Please don't go in.* She voiced the words out loud as if they could hear her. *Please don't go in. Send him away, Karen. He doesn't belong to you.*

She wanted to run over to them. To tell them to stop. *I can't watch this anymore.* She started the engine and quietly eased the Mini out of the parking spot. She turned the car around and headed up the street away from them.

In the rear vision mirror, she spotted Philippe heading back towards his car. She heaved an audible sigh of relief. Thank goodness. But she had seen too much. She was angry. For Pippa. For Pippa's mother Julia.

And yet she could tell no one. How could she explain how she had seen them? She prayed no one would never find out. That he would come to his senses.

And Karen? She knew her cousin too well. She knew they had once been lovers. And she knew Karen would have him back. On any terms.

Upstairs at the front window of her apartment that overlooked the street, Karen watched Philippe drive away. She could still feel the warmth of his embrace. She touched her fingers to her lips. Why do I suddenly feel so elated, she wondered? I don't think he's ever going to leave Julia.

And yet away from prying eyes, in the fading light of the day, he had reached out to embrace her, at first tentatively, and then passionately. And without hesitation or regret, she had responded.

And then he had left her, with barely a word. As if he did not trust himself to speak. As if staying a moment longer would be his undoing.

She turned away from the window and walked to her bedroom. For more than eight years, his photograph had remained a fixture at her bedside. She picked it up and examined it closely. He hasn't changed, she thought. A little greyer at the temples maybe. She put the photograph back in its place. I know what he'll be feeling now. Guilt. He'll feel as guilty as he ever has about me.

She smiled then and stretched out on her bed. For her, there was no guilt, only the pleasure of being with him. And anticipation. Of what? She was unsure. He had made no promises and she had expected none. But she was sure, at some time in the future, she would see him again.

David and Robert Clarke walked together, both shrugging on their dinner jackets at the last minute. David Clarke had co-opted his younger brother and his wife to make up the numbers at a business dinner he was hosting at Rose Bay.

As they neared the restaurant where their respective wives were waiting, David put his hand on his brother's arm and nodded in the direction of a familiar car parked close by.

'What's he doing in this part of town?'

The Clarke dealership had sold the distinctive silver Mercedes to the newly rich American, as David Clarke was inclined to describe him now, rarely using Philippe's name.

His brother stopped and looked in the direction he'd indicated.

'Was he on call at the hospital today?'

Robert shook his head.

'Not really. Unless an emergency came in that needed him in particular. Or one of his patients took a turn for the worse.'

And then he remembered.

'His wife was going off to visit her northern relatives today. She had a plane to catch around lunchtime, I think. And Pippa and Anita and their other girlfriends were meeting up for lunch.'

'So left to his own devices this afternoon, he ends up in the same suburb where my daughter lives.'

Robert let out a deep-throated chortle.

'That's drawing a long bow, isn't it? He might just fancy the area.'
David Clarke was unconvinced.

'I believe he visited Karen quite a few times when she was in hospital.
I assumed you knew.'

His brother shrugged. Philippe was a valued colleague. It put him
in a difficult situation.

'Just after he got back, I came upon him in her room. I did try to
warn him off. He didn't take kindly to my interference but I only
ever ran into him there on one other occasion. But I did ask the nurs-
ing staff how often he visited.'

This was all news to David Clarke.

'And what was their answer?'

Robert hesitated. He shook his head. Why am I having this conversation with my brother, he wondered? I don't need this.

'Let me guess. They told you he came practically every day to see
her.'

His brother turned and gestured helplessly as if to say *what could
I do about it?*

'And you didn't think to tell me about it?'

'For heaven's sake, I'm not his keeper,' Robert mumbled. 'He's free
to visit patients if he wants to. She didn't tell me to tell him not to
visit. Besides she's old enough to know her own mind.'

'Yeah, but it's me that has to clean up the mess when he abandons
her.'

Robert stopped abruptly and put his hand on his brother's arm.

'What do you mean? Clean up the mess? What mess?'

'Forget it, Robert. Forget I said that.'

'Oh, no, brother, you're not going to get away with that. You
meant something specific. What did you mean? *Clean up the mess.*
What mess?'

David Clarke turned to look at his brother. It was all in the past.
Well in the past. But he had not forgotten. He had not forgotten how
devastated his daughter had been.

'You remember she went away suddenly just before he got married.
March as I remember.'

'Yes, I remember. There was a lot of gossip at the time although I only heard snippets for obvious reasons.'

'What if I told you that gossip was true. My daughter was pregnant. She was carrying that man's child.'

It was a shock for Robert Clarke to hear this so many years later. How did I not know this, he wondered? He started to do the obvious calculations. She was back by late October. No sign of a baby.

'But she didn't have the baby, did she?'

David Clarke shook his head.

'No, she had a miscarriage in April in London.'

Robert nodded, relieved in his own way that his niece had not chosen another option.

'Makes sense. In the first trimester it's not uncommon for a woman to miscarry. Did Philippe ever come to know?'

Again, David Clarke shook his head.

'No, she was determined he would never know. And then of course there was no need to tell him. She never told her mother either. I don't think she could face the prospect of Deborah's recriminations at the time.'

'And you funded her quick departure to England?'

'I did. What else was I going to do?'

'And now? Do you think he's revived his interest in her?'

'Think about it Robert, what man is unaffected by inheriting a massive fortune. In my opinion, he always had a hint of arrogance about him. Now I hear he's going to play the philanthropist and set up a charitable foundation. He'll have every research institution in Australia flattering him and wanting him to take a seat on their board. It would go to any man's head. Maybe he's got a bit bored with his pretty but provincial wife. My daughter has turned the heads of many men. But I think if he renewed his interest, he'd find a warm welcome back in her bed.'

Such a crude assessment left Robert Clarke speechless for some moments. He did not recognise in Philippe the man his brother was describing. He knew Philippe to be a caring doctor, too caring at times. Always concerned for his patients and their families, for overworked junior staff. The best men in our profession all have a hint of arrogance, he wanted to say. More than a hint of arrogance sometimes. But it's professional pride. We must ooze confidence. It reassures our patients and it helps us deal with incompetent junior doctors who want to argue with us.

'You're wrong about him, brother. You're not describing the man I know. Forget his sudden wealth. So he drives a better car now and will probably buy his wife diamonds for Christmas. I don't see much evidence that it's changed him beyond a few expensive indulgences.'

It was Robert who was first to notice Philippe walking back towards his car. At that short distance, he could not fail to see them. Robert called his name and raised his hand in greeting. Philippe knew he could not avoid the encounter. He walked towards them.

'You're a fair way from home, Philippe,' Robert said with forced cheerfulness. 'Planning on a harbourside acquisition perhaps?'

Philippe laughed.

'Perhaps. It's a beautiful harbour. I often come down this way. Over the years, I've taken lots of photographs of this area. It's very tempting to consider living right on the harbour.'

'And your new car? Performing well, is it?'

It was an obvious conversation starter for David Clarke.

'It is going very well thanks. Now Pippa wants a new car of course. Not satisfied anymore with her little Mini just like Anita's.'

'You'd do well to think about a Mercedes for her. I really think the car saved my daughter's life.'

'It's a big car. Could she handle it? She's only young. Not a very experienced driver.'

'We could organise advanced driving lessons, as we did for Karen.'

Philippe was about to say advanced driving lessons hadn't helped Karen avoid her accident but he was desperate to avoid mentioning her name.

Robert laughed inwardly. Despite everything, his brother never missed an opportunity to do business.

'I'll think about it,' Philippe replied politely, anxious to get away. He looked across towards the restaurant. 'I think you are keeping your wives waiting. That's not a good thing in my experience.'

Both men looked around and grimaced.

'You're right. We'd better go.'

'See you on Monday, Philippe.'

The two brothers turned and walked away.

'Did you smell that fragrance, Robert? I caught just a hint of it as the breeze came through.'

His brother shook his head, puzzled.

'What fragrance? What are you talking about?'

'I'm talking about a perfume called *Justine*. It's Karen's favourite. She wears it all the time.'

'You're deluded, brother. You reckon you could smell Karen's perfume on him?'

'Absolutely. No doubt. I know where's he spent his afternoon and it isn't looking at real estate or taking photographs of the harbour, I can tell you that now. He's been with Karen.'

Robert shook his head in disbelief. His brother was jumping at shadows. He was becoming paranoid.

'You're imagining things. That's just complete nonsense. Philippe is absolutely devoted to his work and to his family.'

'We'll see. Time will tell who's right. He's not the saint you think he is.'

'We'll agree to disagree,' Robert muttered. But he knew his brother had a point. Philippe had certainly messed with Karen's life. Was he about to do so again? For all our sakes, I hope not, he thought.

He smiled and greeted the women, offering his arm to his wife Patricia, who began to ask what had kept them so long.

He shrugged.

'Just some business talk,' he said. 'Just some boring business talk. Let's go and have a good dinner at my brother's expense.'

She smiled.

'That sounds like a good idea.'

'I was beginning to wonder if you'd got lost.'

Pippa greeted her father warmly as he came through the door. He threw his car keys onto the hall table and hugged his daughter briefly.

'How was lunch? Was it a good catch up?'

'It was great,' she said. 'First piece of gossip. Nancy is keen on Paul.'

He looked at her trying to make sense of that statement. She rolled her eyes. He must be preoccupied, Pippa thought, otherwise he would know who I'm talking about.

'My cousin Paul. He visits them occasionally. He's Tim's friend. Nancy's brother. Well, now he's fully recovered he's visiting them again.'

Philippe nodded.

'I realise who you meant but Nancy's mother is married to Paul's father. How will that work?'

'No law against it. They're not blood related. It will be a bit awkward for a while I guess if they get together.'

'Does Richard know about this? Or Kate?'

Pippa shook her head vigorously.

'No, of course not and you're not to tell them either.'

He laughed quietly. More secrets.

'And Anita and Lucy? How are they getting on?'

'Very well but no boyfriends they would own up to at any rate. Lucy's mother is pretty keen to act as matchmaker and we suspect Dr Clarke is casting his eye over the young doctors for a suitable candidate for Anita. I think he'll have a hard time getting Anita to fall in with his matchmaking plans.'

Of all her friends, it was Anita who Philippe knew the best. Their paths crossed in the hospital corridors from time to time. Once or twice, she had come to him for professional advice rather than seek out her father.

'I agree with you. I think Anita has a mind of her own. She has a terrific aptitude for medicine. If she sticks at it, she'll have her father's position one day. It would be a shame to waste that talent.'

'You mean by marrying and having babies?'

'Well, it's tough for women to do motherhood and a career at the same time,' he said diplomatically.

'That will change soon,' Pippa said with a gesture more eloquent than her words.

He decided not to pursue a discussion that threatened to become another opportunity for his daughter to berate him as old fashioned and out of touch, which he would loudly protest he wasn't. He wanted women to have equality of career opportunities. It was the family practicalities that he saw as the difficulty.

'I hope you didn't drive your car in that condition?'

It was pretty clear to him she had drunk too much.

She shook her head.

'No, my car's still out at Watsons Bay. I got a taxi home. Lucy offered to drop me but I decided it was too far out of her way and Nancy was following her home to stay with her.'

He was relieved.

'Don't worry I'll drive you out there tomorrow to collect your car.'

'Thanks. That would be great. And what did you do this afternoon? Anything interesting.'

She flung herself untidily onto a lounge chair.

'I took some photos. I had a look around a few harbourside suburbs. I wondered if we might move to a harbourside house.'

He surprised himself. The lies came easily. Is this how it starts, he wondered? What will my excuses be if I start spending time with Karen?

The very idea of his casual acceptance of such deception shocked him. But does it shock me enough not to do it, he wondered?

He walked around the house turning on some lights. He was surprised it had changed so little in the years since his marriage.

Wedding photos had been added. Pippa's graduation photos. A group photo from Prior Park. Some books Julia had chosen were added to his bookshelves. New curtains had replaced his original choice. A new sofa had been added. But little else had changed. She had seemed content with his choices. Until now, he had never stopped to ask himself if she was happy. Truly happy. Although he had sometimes wondered if she was happier at Prior Park than in Sydney.

And me? Am I truly happy? He paused in the act of opening a bottle of red wine.

'Do you want me to do that? You look very preoccupied? What's up?'

He shook his head.

'Nothing. I'm fine. It's a tough cork, that's all.'

Eventually, the cork gave a satisfying pop and he poured the deep red liquid into a glass. He held up a second glass and Pippa nodded.

'Just a small glass thanks,' she said. 'Will it mix with champagne?'

He laughed. It brought back memories of his own youth. He couldn't be a hypocrite though. Not about this. But he did give her the standard warning.

'Well, if you've got a headache in the morning, you won't get any sympathy from me.'

He sat down in his favourite chair. For once, there was no jazz music. His thoughts were distraction enough. He closed his eyes. Pippa began to speak but he could not have recalled what she said.

Instead, his thoughts drifted back to the afternoon. To Karen. To the pleasure of her company. To the pleasure of being with her. And to the anticipation of seeing her again.

It was as if sometime that afternoon he had abandoned all pretence. As if everything he believed about himself, about his fundamental honesty, had crumbled to dust. One woman had undermined all that. Spectacularly.

# CHAPTER 15

AN INTENSE STORM HAD finally cleared the sultry atmosphere that had hung over the city for days. A sharp southerly change followed quickly, lowering the temperature to bring immediate relief with a blast of cooler air and a stiff breeze.

It was late afternoon and Philippe sat in the growing darkness, trying to recover from the stress of the day. He had performed two particularly demanding operations, both with successful outcomes. Having the house to himself was a relief. He knew Pippa would be on night duty all week, the inevitable lot of young doctors.

He sipped a glass of wine and immersed himself in the luxury of being free of obligations. His favourite jazz record played softly in the background.

Inevitably his mind drifted back to his lunch with Karen. He remembered how she had accused him of ignoring her for years, of pretending she didn't exist. It had hurt him to be reminded how much he had hurt her. He had never meant to. And now?

He closed his eyes. He suddenly felt desolate at the prospect of walking away from her again. For him his attraction to her was much more than an uncomfortable truth. It had upended everything he understood about himself and his basic honesty.

And Julia? He did not want his marriage to fail. Could he separate the two parts of his life? How many men have negotiated this minefield, he wondered idly? He put his glass of wine down on the coffee table and reached over and dialled Karen's number. She sounded breathless when she answered.

'Sorry, I've just got in from my yoga class.'

'And how was yoga class?' he asked.

'Oh, it was fine,' she said airily. 'It's a great way to relax.'

He paused.

'I wanted to apologise for leaving so abruptly on Saturday.'

He could hear her breathing heavily on the other end of the line. She had obviously run up the stairs to pick up the phone.

'You did leave rather suddenly, didn't you?'

She wasn't going to let him off lightly.

'I'm sorry. Yes, I did. I couldn't ...'

He was struggling to find the right words. She knew exactly what he wanted to say. He didn't have to spell it out.

'Are you by yourself this evening?' she asked.

'Yes, I am. Pippa is on night duty.'

She knew Julia would still be away.

'Why don't you come over. Bianca is coming over. She's going to cook. There'll be enough for three. She can be our chaperone.'

He laughed then and relaxed.

'Do we need a chaperone?'

'You tell me.'

He laughed quietly. He knew she was forcing him to accept responsibility for their relationship. She was a free woman. He was not a free man. If he wanted to resume their relationship, she did not want him to blame her if his conscience troubled him. He knew it would be his problem. Not hers.

'Won't Bianca be surprised if I'm there?'

'No, she won't. She understands. She knows all my secrets.'

'I'll see you soon then,' he said and hung up.

'It's a while since we last met, Philippe,' Bianca said as she kissed him on both cheeks in the European way.

Philippe looked at her closely. Still the same elegant immaculately dressed woman. *She's not surprised to see me here but there's a hint of censure in her dark eyes.*

Karen handed her friend a glass of wine and as she did he heard Bianca whisper *è ancora innamorato di te?*

He noticed Karen laugh and shrug her shoulders. Even I cannot answer that question, he thought. Do I still love her? Or was she asking if I still loved my wife? His limited Italian was not up to the task of interpreting. He offered to help as Bianca took charge of the kitchen but she waved him away.

'There's not much to do. Karen's already done so much.'

He noticed how quickly and efficiently she moved around the small kitchen. She reached for a pan to make her famous pasta sauce. The pot of water was already coming to the boil for the pasta.

'Karen's told me about your recent good fortune,' she said as she expertly fed spaghetti into the pot.

He looked at Karen. He wondered how much the story had been embellished. She came to stand alongside him. He felt her free hand touch his arm. He couldn't resist her closeness. He slipped his arm around her waist. Bianca's keen eyes missed none of these small intimate gestures.

'It was all an enormous surprise to me, Bianca. I never knew my father. I was never sure of his name even. It was my daughter Pippa who began to delve into it all.'

Bianca already knew that part.

'And then he died and he left you a very wealthy man.'

To Bianca, this was the crux of the matter. Philippe had gone from being the child of a poor unmarried mother who had struggled to raise him to the heir to an industrial fortune. How does that change a man, she wondered? Does he suddenly feel he can have whatever he wants? She turned to glance at him. She could see he was more relaxed than she expected him to be. He knows I can be trusted, she thought. He hasn't tried to keep Karen at arm's length. He isn't concerned about me seeing them together like this. Something has changed him. *He's less cautious.*

'I didn't want his money,' Phillipe said, 'but it came to me anyway.

173

My father was making amends for refusing to marry my mother. And sadly, he really hated my half-brother. Really despised him. It was awful to see.'

Bianca shrugged. She knew families, Italian families, where bitter feuds had carried over for generations.

'And this money you didn't want? Would you ever think about investing some of it in a small fashion enterprise?'

'Bianca! For heaven's sake.' Karen laughed. She hadn't expected Bianca to talk about the financial struggles in their business.

He laughed too to cover his surprise.

'Karen told me everything was going well.'

Bianca gestured extravagantly as only an Italian could.

'It is going well but clients take too long to pay. We're undercapitalized. We have a loan but we missed the September payment. And now he's put the interest rate up. I don't see how we'll make that up and the December payment.'

He looked at Karen for confirmation.

'I invested some capital from my trust account but my father set it up so I can't touch the principal investments. He told us to borrow money just like every other business. I don't want to go to him for a bail out.'

*Should he help them?* He turned the question over in his mind. There could only really be one answer.

'How much do you need?' he asked. 'To free yourself of the loan and to have some spare capital?'

He'd become used to talking business now, something that had once been so foreign to him. Bianca looked across at Karen.

'Philippe, it's very generous of you but I don't want you to feel ...'

But Bianca cut her short. Why not let him be generous? It will salve his conscience she whispered to her friend. She mentioned a figure that, to Karen, seemed outrageous. To Philippe, it seemed inconsequential compared with the figures he'd been dealing with.

'That's fine. My local lawyers will handle it.'

He scribbled out their details on Karen's telephone notepad.

'I'll call them tomorrow then you must send over the loan details.

It can all be settled in a few days.'

'Thank you, Philippe. You are truly a wonderful friend.' Bianca saluted him.

'One more thing,' he cautioned. 'No one must ever know. Too many difficult explanations. It's a gift. You never have to repay it. The money will come straight from one of my American accounts.'

And with that, Bianca knew he was buying her silence. And Karen? He was buying her gratitude. They did not speak of it again.

Instead, the three of them sat down together at Karen's small dining table, eating pasta, drinking wine together, laughing and enjoying each other's company. It helped the tensions of the day ebb away for all of them.

And for Philippe, there was no more restraint. Karen sat beside him, touching him affectionately, he responding as her lover would.

*Just don't hurt her again, Philippe,* Bianca wanted to say. *She's more fragile than you think. She's been through more heartache because of you than you will ever know.*

Afterwards, as they stood together at the door and watched Bianca head down the stairs, Karen turned towards him.

'You didn't need to bail us out, Philippe,' she said. 'We would have managed. I had no idea she was going to ask you for money. I'm so sorry if it put you in an awkward position.'

But he smiled and reached out for her, wanting immediately to calm her fears he had felt manipulated.

'What's money for if it's not to help a friend out? It's the least I can do for you. No strings attached, my darling,' he said gently. 'We'll never mention it again.'

He had never used such endearments towards her before. He bent his head and kissed her.

For her it was a moment of pure happiness. She knew then he would not walk away from her.

'The chaperone's gone home,' she teased. 'Aren't you supposed to go too?'

'Only if you want me to go,' he said. 'But I want to stay. I've missed being with you. I very much want to stay, my darling. I want to make love to you. Now. Tonight.'

There was no hint of reluctance in his embrace. No hint of restraint in the way he caressed her body. No hint of caution.

She turned, a small smile of triumph on her lips, and led the way into her bedroom.

Philippe stopped briefly to admire his surroundings as he walked slowly through the finest shopping arcade in Sydney. He looked up to the glass roof three storeys above him. It was all wonderfully Victorian with its cast iron balustrades and timber framed shopfronts.

It was unusual for him to have free time during the workday. It was a rare luxury. He was grateful for it. It had given him time to reflect on the events of the previous evening. He had reluctantly left Karen's bed in the early hours of the morning. He remembered an unsettling eeriness about stepping out into the dark quiet street. Had it simply stirred a memory of earlier times? And what of future times? It was no longer, for him, a question of *if* but *when* he would be with Karen again. Yet he did not want his marriage to fail. He clung to the hope that Julia would never find out.

He walked on aimlessly until he stopped in front of a window display where exquisite gems sparkled invitingly back at him. Isn't this what rich men buy their wives for Christmas, he mused? Especially rich men with guilty consciences?

He examined the window display more closely. His eye was drawn to a stunning blue sapphire and diamond necklace with matching earrings.

With a speed Philippe could only admire, a sales assistant, smartly dressed in a dark suit, was by his side extolling the virtues of the expensive sapphire and diamond piece.

'It's an impressive sapphire and diamond piece, sir,' Claude Green gushed, his sales patter well practised and smoothly delivered. 'It's set in yellow gold with wonderful drop earrings to match. I'm sure your wife would be delighted with it.'

To Philippe, the sales pitch was nothing more than a confusing mix of diamond carats and design points that he did not fully understand.

'Would you care to take a closer look at it, sir?' he said, guiding Philippe towards the entrance of the shop.

'Yes, of course,' Philippe replied, allowing himself to be manoeuvred into the inner sanctum.

As he entered, a small, dapper man bustled forward to greet him.

'Dr Duval, it is so wonderful to see you here. Levi Cowen at your service. You are *very welcome*. Come and sit and let us take care of you. Perhaps there is something you already have your eye on?'

Philippe tried desperately to recall the name but it meant nothing to him.

'Have we met before Mr Cowen?' Philippe enquired politely. 'If so, I apologise that I don't seem to have a clear memory of it.'

The jeweller smiled.

'Just in passing, Dr Duval. Just in passing. At your hospital's charity ball last year.'

He dismissed Philippe's concern with a wave of his hand.

'Such a crush. It's hard to remember everyone one meets.'

He probably wouldn't remember me, Philippe thought, except for my substantial change in fortunes. As hard as he had tried to keep the story of his inheritance out of the newspapers, somehow it had leaked.

'No doubt you are looking for that special gift for your delightful wife. And perhaps something for your very engaging daughter too?'

Philippe smiled at the silver-tongued patter. He supposed such flattery would be Levi Cowen's stock in trade.

After a few minutes' consideration, he had settled on the purchases he would make. For Pippa, his choice had been a simple but elegant diamond and gold chain pendant. For Julia, the sapphire and diamond set he had initially selected. He wrote the name of his accountants on a notepad. He knew the store would want payment first.

'Please send your account here, Mr Cowen.'

Levi Cowen nodded and thanked him.

'It's a pleasure doing business with you, Dr Duval.'

Philippe smiled and turned to leave. And then he noticed an unusual piece. A stunning diamond and platinum pendant with a stylised K at its centre. He pointed to it.

'That's a beautiful piece.'

The jeweller took it up tenderly, as if it was fragile.

'One of our spectacular custom pieces,' he said, stroking the piece lovingly. 'Unfortunately, the client's wife decided she didn't like it. He bought her something else of course but we were disappointed. We had our top designer work on this piece. It's very modern. Platinum setting. Thirty-four marquise diamonds.'

Philippe closed his eyes briefly. *There is one person I know on whom this will look stunning.*

'I'll take it,' Philippe said before he could change his mind.

He knew he had made the jeweller's day. The piece had obviously sat unsold for months.

'Does your daughter have the initial K perhaps?'

Levi Cowen could not remember if he had been told the daughter's name. *Perhaps he will keep one piece for her birthday.*

Then he noticed Philippe's slight shake of the head and wary look. He was practised at reading the subtle unspoken cues from his clients. He inclined his head as if to say *no more personal questions.*

'Please deliver the first two pieces to me at St Vincent's.'

The jeweller nodded. 'And the third piece?'

'By hand to this address please. It must not be left on a doorstep.'

He wrote down Karen's name and address.

'Of course, Dr Duval.'

He wanted to say *we are not in the habit of leaving exquisite jewellery on a doorstep for any common thief to pick up.* But he did not.

'Is there a greeting with that package, Dr Duval?'

He handed Philippe a blank card with the shop's insignia and address.

What could he say that was safe? He could think of nothing. No words that would not be incriminating. Instead, he wrote a banal greeting.

*K Merry Christmas P xxx*

'Thank you for your help,' he said as he walked to the door. 'And your discretion.'

He knew he did not need to spell it out as the proprietor smiled his most charming smile and bowed Philippe out of the shop before heading back to his office. Nothing else cheered Levi Cowen to quite the same extent as a successful and profitable sale.

In such a benevolent mood, he did not remonstrate with the small group of assistants who remained gossiping together at the extravagant purchases of their most recent customer.

Among them, Claude Green, who had been given the responsibility of packaging the gifts, looked at the handwritten card and accompanying address which Levi Cowen had handed to him.

'Do you know the lucky lady whose getting that fabulous diamond and platinum pendant?'

It was a younger, bolder member of staff who asked the question to which they all wanted to know the answer. Claude Green looked again at the name and the address. He nodded.

'Yes, I know who she is,' he said. 'I certainly know who she is.'

But he had taken the precaution of covering the address so prying eyes could not read it. Only he and Levi Cowen would ever know the destination of the third package. He would deliver it personally.

'His mistress, I suppose.'

He turned on the young girl Betty.

'We do not say that word here, Betty. You should know better. Mr Cowen will have you straight out the door if he hears you.'

She laughed.

'But it's true, isn't it? Otherwise, why the secrecy? I hope she likes it. I'll be looking through the social pages to see if I can spot who's wearing it.'

'Don't do that, Betty,' he said with a serious note in his voice. 'Or at least if you do see a lady wearing it, keep it to yourself. We don't gossip about our clients.'

Betty looked at him, her brown eyes agog with mischief. He knows who she is. And he knows she's very likely to have her photograph in the social pages. And I bet she's beautiful too, a thought that depressed Betty for a full minute as she fingered her own mouse-brown curls and then smoothed her skirt over her ample hips.

'You can't pick them, Mr Green, can you?'

It was one of the older assistants who had listened thoughtfully to his colleague's efforts to curb Betty's interest in the mysterious recipient of the third package.

'No, Albert, you can't. You certainly can't.'

His voice was tinged with disappointment because he knew exactly what Albert meant. He recalled the good things he had heard about Dr Duval. About his outstanding work as a surgeon and how much the hospital staff admired him. But he turns out to be just like other wealthy men, he mused. A bit bored with his wife, he turns to another woman. And then he does what they all do. He buys her expensive gifts. But to salve his conscience, he makes sure the most expensive gift is reserved for his wife.

One by one the staff drifted back to their work, each feeling just a little more keenly the deep resentment of working every day among the flawless diamonds and precious gems they would never themselves be able to afford.

# CHAPTER 16

'YOU LOOK RELAXED after your trip up north,' Philippe said, admiring his wife across the table as he perused the menu of the small exclusive restaurant he had chosen for their reunion dinner.

Julia looked around her. The restaurant was housed in a converted convict-built cottage, its beautiful old brickwork left exposed, the large fireplaces filled with ornamental pots of native flowers. On a balmy summer evening, they had chosen to sit in the courtyard. We could be in Tuscany, she thought. And Philippe had thought of everything, instructing the sommelier to decant a bottle of Penfolds Grange Hermitage in advance of their arrival.

'What do you think?' Philippe asked, as he held his own glass up to the light. 'It's said to be the best wine Australia produces. I asked them to decant a bottle in advance of our arrival.'

'It's very good,' she said, unsure what else to say. 'Do you think it would pass Clarence's high standards to be included in the cellar at Eastbury Hall?'

He smiled at that prospect.

'I think I might surprise Clarence and order a case for us and a case for the cellar there. It's about time Clarence found out he's not the final arbiter of everything that goes on in that house.'

He sipped the wine appreciatively.

'I imagine you went riding every day at Prior Park.'

181

She nodded, the memory of one particular ride bringing a faint flush of colour to her cheeks. She was grateful for the soft lighting.

'I did,' she said. 'My mare was almost back to riding fitness by the time I left. She hadn't been ridden much in recent months.'

'And how was the wedding? Your son was groomsman, wasn't he? I guess that's why he wanted you to delay your return home so you could see him in action. No doubt you'll tell me he was the star.'

She had been prepared for his questions. She answered casually.

'He was,' she said. 'And yes, I thought he was the star. I'm sure he'll break a few hearts before he's much older.'

He laughed. He knew her son looked like his father James. There was nothing of her blonde good looks in the boy, unlike with Pippa who favoured her mother.

'I guess his father was at the wedding too. I hope your ex-husband didn't make a scene when he saw you.'

He was remembering the scene, years before, when he and Julia had met unexpectedly in a hotel restaurant. It seemed like a lifetime ago. He would never forget James Fitzroy's visceral anger. Preoccupied with his own thoughts, he did not notice the small tremor of nervousness that Julia failed to suppress.

She opened her mouth to speak, to say something, anything to change the course of the conversation but she was saved by the timely intervention of the waiter who began to rattle off the specials for the day.

'I think the wine dictates the food,' Philippe said, forgetting she had not answered the question. 'Filet Mignon perhaps. They are renowned for it here.'

She nodded, hardly trusting herself to speak. She reached for her wine glass, leaving Philippe to order for them both.

He looked across at her. She was wearing the gold trimmed cocktail frock she had bought in New York. Her blonde hair was swept up into a classic chignon. It makes her look more sophisticated, he thought. And more beautiful. He reached into the pocket of his jacket then.

'I have something for you, my darling,' he said.

He surprised himself at the ease with which he used the same endearment he had used with Karen. His voice sounded apologetic.

'I know I've been very distracted these past few months. Too many things to think about. Too many demands on my time. I thought you deserved an early Christmas present.'

He slid the slim box across the table. She picked it up and began to fumble with the catch. It took several moments for the lid to open. He was rewarded by the look of delight on her face. The sapphire and diamond necklace and earrings sparkled in the candlelight.

'Oh, that's so beautiful, Philippe,' she said, overcome with a mixture of emotions. 'You have such exquisite taste. You're too generous.'

She reached across the table to kiss him. It felt like their first proper kiss in months.

'It's a pleasure, my darling,' he said. 'I'm so pleased you like it.'

She had reacted to the gift exactly how he hoped she would.

'But where will I wear it?' Julia asked, concerned that it would forever lay in the jeweller's box unworn.

Instinctively she understood how wearing such an expensive piece of jewellery might simply make the other women in their social circle even less friendly towards her. She feared it might be seen as flaunting her husband's wealth. But he had known that too.

'I am sure you will find somewhere to wear it. You should take it with you to New York next time. Clarence tells me the invitations are piling up.'

She laughed.

'Well, you realise I will have to have a whole new wardrobe if that's the case. I can't possibly wear what I bought there months ago.'

She was teasing him and he knew it. He laughed.

'I'll forewarn the stores, shall I?'

She laughed too. Philippe reached across the table to her and raised her fingers to his lips.

'You look really beautiful tonight. The time away by yourself has been good for you.'

She smiled. How was it possible to feel more guilt than I do right at this moment, she wondered? She remembered with a sense of shame how easily she had discarded her marriage vows. How readily she had succumbed to her first husband's advances. All because of a few words of malicious gossip about Philippe and Karen Clarke. And yet Philippe had been thinking about her, buying exquisite jewellery for her. She felt more than ashamed.

And Philippe's thoughts? She did not know he too was feeling a guilt he had never known before. And just as her thoughts had drifted elsewhere, his thoughts had drifted to Karen. It was as if thinking about her could conjure her up in the flesh.

He looked up as the maître d'hôtel welcomed a large group to the restaurant. He saw Karen just as she saw him. With a slight smile in his direction, he watched transfixed as her hand drifted to the deep neckline of her dress to rest on the stunning diamond and platinum pendant that had been delivered to her so secretively. He remembered how she had thanked him. And later, how she had lain contentedly in his arms.

He was grateful for Bianca who saw him too, smiled faintly, and quickly steered Karen and the rest of their party to a table in the far corner of the restaurant.

He turned back towards Julia worried that she had noticed Karen. But he breathed an inaudible sigh of relief. There was nothing to suggest Julia had noticed her.

In the far corner of the restaurant, Bianca turned to whisper to Karen.

'Doesn't he know this restaurant is a regular haunt for the rag trade?'

But Karen wasn't listening. Her eyes were still on Philippe. And on his wife.

'She looks very beautiful with her hair up,' Karen said. 'The dress is fantastic. New York, I bet. It must have cost Philippe a fortune.'

She could not quite quell the surge of jealously that came from nowhere. She understood then what it felt like to be the other woman in his life.

'Remember, he's married. He doesn't belong to you.'

I wonder how many times I've issued that warning to her, Bianca wondered.

'Oh, but that's where you're wrong, Bianca. He does belong to me. He just won't acknowledge it. Not yet. He has always belonged to me. And he can't walk away from me. Not again.'

Bianca shook her head. Philippe had surprised her with the ease with which he had slipped back into Karen's life. She had not expected that.

And the wedding ring on his finger? It no longer seemed to inhibit him. Not for the first time was she left wondering what had changed him. What had made a normally cautious man more reckless. More willing to take risks. More willing to betray his wife. As if he no longer feared the consequences. But his behaviour tonight gave the lie to that idea.

She looked around at Karen then. There was only one answer. Philippe could not resist her. She knew he had deliberately avoided her friend for years yet as soon as they began to meet regularly again, he had fallen under her spell. Had the prospect of losing her in the accident changed everything for him?

And now? Will he really give up his wife for Karen? Not if his behaviour with her this evening is any indication. Unless he has not yet faced up to the truth of where his heart lies.

Bianca shrugged. He'll probably just be like other men and expect to go on having them both.

The late afternoon sun created a patchwork of light in the living room. Philippe stood in front of the sideboard perusing the Christmas cards displayed three deep on the polished surface.

He wondered idly who all these friends were wishing them *Merry Christmas*. He joked with Pippa that the number of cards seemed to have grown threefold from the previous year.

She had simply laughed and suggested a wealthy man attracts friends he didn't know he had. He thought sadly she was right. He had left the task of opening the cards to Julia. Now, with them all neatly displayed, one caught his eye.

He read the greeting. It was from John, with a very warm greeting for his mother and Pippa. His name at least had been included.

He was about to put the card down when he noticed a photograph that had been placed behind the card. Almost hidden, it seemed. He picked it up.

It was a photograph of a horse. He assumed it was a recent acquisition that John had made and he wanted to show his mother. He was about to set the photograph back where he had found it until he glanced at the back.

'Firegleam. A pretty bay filly,' the inscription read.

It was the next line that caught his attention.

*'J Merry Christmas J xxx'*

It's the exact same inscription he had written on the card to Karen. Except J was for Julia. But was J for John? It's not the way a son would write Christmas greetings to his mother. And the other alternative? He could not bring himself to think it.

And then he remembered. She had never answered the question he had asked about her ex-husband James. Had he made a scene at the wedding? She had never said. In fact, she had never mentioned him. But something about her had been different since that trip. At times he remembered she had seemed nervous. Anxious. Preoccupied. Almost as if she was mirroring his own feelings.

He put the photograph back and picked up the glass of wine he had been drinking. It unsettled him. It seemed so trivial, so unimportant. But was it? Was she hiding something? If so, what exactly? He knew if he was being honest with himself something of the spark had gone out of their marriage. Was it his fault? Probably. There had been profound changes in his life.

For the first time, he began to understand how he had changed. He had never expected to be a wealthy man. And now?

It was as if a new life was opening up for him. One he hadn't planned for. But it was one that came with exciting opportunities and new possibilities. He had discovered a side to his personality he had never known existed. A little more ruthless perhaps. A little more self-interested.

And then, in the midst of it all, an old loyalty had reignited. Unexpectedly. Compellingly. Spectacularly. How could he explain it? He couldn't.

How could he explain the ease with which he had succumbed to her charms again? He couldn't explain that either. Except that somewhere, somehow, he had changed and guilt had become an emotion he could disregard when he chose. And regret? It was something for another day.

# CHAPTER 17

THE PARTY WAS ALREADY in full swing at Robert Clarke's Christmas Eve gathering by the time Julia and Philippe arrived. For once, Pippa was with them too, having managed to get a week off by swapping rosters.

As he helped Julia out of the car, Philippe quickly glanced up and down the street for the one car he hoped he would not see. But it was there, parked further up the street. He was suddenly nervous. An inappropriate gesture. An intercepted smile. Any small thing could betray their closeness. But it had been impossible to refuse his colleague's invitation. He hoped the crush of people would be such that he could avoid Karen.

She had called him at his office the day after their near meeting at the restaurant, teasing him and asking him if he had noticed her new boyfriend among her group the previous evening. At first, he had feigned indifference to the news. But he was not indifferent. And they both knew it.

He had not thought anything more about their conversation until he walked into Robert Clarke's house with his wife on his arm. Barely inside the door, he caught sight of Karen across the room. He stopped abruptly almost causing Julia to stumble. He had been quite unprepared for the sight that greeted him.

She looked stunning, the platinum and diamond pendant he had given her nestled into the neckline of her long low-cut dress, her auburn hair curling beautifully about her almost bare shoulders. And then he noticed her partner slip his arm around her waist and lean in to kiss her lightly on her cheek.

Across the room, David Clarke completely tuned out from the babble of conversation immediately around him. He had been waiting for this moment. Anticipating it even. Anticipating the moment Philippe Duval walked into the room to see his daughter Karen with another man.

Robert Clarke too had been anticipating the event but with dread. As he watched Philippe walk in, the task of pouring a glass of wine for one of his guests was completely forgotten until wine began to overflow onto the floor.

Anita too had been anticipating the moment. Like her father and uncle, she saw and understood the flash of dismay and then anger in Philippe's eyes. He's on the verge of betraying himself, she thought. He looks as though he's about to go up to Karen and claim her. She had never seen a man so quickly and completely overwhelmed by jealousy.

Patricia Clarke, ever the complete hostess, saw it all too and glided towards the new arrivals. *Wherever and whenever this affair explodes into the open as surely it must, it's not going to be at my Christmas Eve drinks party*, she had whispered urgently to her husband.

'Julia, it's lovely to see you,' she said, 'and what a delightful dress. I so envy you being able to shop in New York.'

She turned to Philippe.

'I'm so pleased you could come. There are some drinks circulating and Robert was just pouring some wine he thinks is just right for drinking. I think it's been hidden in his cellar for years. And Pippa, how lovely you look tonight. Next time I hope you and Anita will have boyfriends on your arms.'

It was perhaps not quite the thing to say but it sounded so artless no one would have considered it had a more profound meaning.

Pippa laughed.

'Some hope, Mrs Clarke,' she said politely. 'No time for boyfriends at the moment for either of us.'

She spotted Anita then and walked across the room to join her.

Patricia breathed a quiet sigh of relief. Philippe had taken the hint and walked over to the bar to join Robert. She was able to steer Julia on to the open terrace that adjoined the living room to a small group including Angela Dixon, who greeted her warmly.

'You look as though you're making a bit of a hash of opening that wine, Robert,' Philippe said. 'Can I help?'

'I think the cork has become a bit brittle to be honest,' he replied, thankful for the relief of commonplace conversation.

From over Philippe's shoulder another voice volunteered help too. Philippe turned to greet the newcomer.

Robert, his hand poised at the point of reinserting the corkscrew, almost dropped one of the most treasured vintages in his cellar.

Nicholas Gleeson took the bottle from his host's hands and began to extract the partly decayed cork expertly but carefully, which gave Robert Clarke sufficient time to recover his power of speech.

'I don't think you've met my colleague, Dr Philippe Duval. Philippe, this is Nicholas Gleeson, an eminent lawyer I'm reliably informed.'

He paused in the act of wrestling the cork from the bottle and shook hands with Philippe.

'It's good to meet you, Dr Duval,' he said. 'I've heard a lot about you.'

Philippe inclined his head, his good manners sorely tested by the encounter.

'Well, I'm sorry I can't return the compliment,' Philippe said, with an unmistakeable iciness in his voice.

Gleeson smiled.

'Fully understandable,' he said. 'I wouldn't expect my name to mean anything to you. But I've just returned to Sydney from a couple of years in the Melbourne office of the local firm who handle your affairs in conjunction with your New York lawyers.'

It occurred to Philippe for one appalling moment Nicholas Gleeson might be privy to all his dealings. He might know everything about me. The thought horrified him. Philippe decided to test the extent of Gleeson's knowledge.

'You're not part of the team I deal with. Or has something happened without me being consulted?'

He could see the consternation in Philippe's eyes. He recognised a man with secrets when he saw one. But he was quick to reassure him. The firm would not want to lose such an important client. The firm's appeal to Sydney's wealthy had grown exponentially since it became known Philippe Duval had chosen the firm for his local work.

'No, I work in quite a different area of law. I do some criminal work. Commercial work. I was simply given a general briefing on returning from the Melbourne office about the new clients the firm had taken on. Very general, I assure you.'

He handed the opened bottle of wine to Robert.

'I've taken over doing the work for David Clarke. His long-term lawyer retired recently. And I met his daughter Karen a few weeks back when she came in to sign some documents.'

Philippe nodded. It was news to him that David Clarke was a client of the firm but it explained how Karen had met him. He wondered then how appropriate it was for a senior partner to date the daughter of a client. He knew he could finish Nicholas Gleeson's career by merely suggesting impropriety. He had quickly learned the lessons that had helped his father prosper. Strike first. Fight for what you want. Take the tough decisions others wouldn't.

'Our paths almost crossed the other night by the way. I noticed you and your wife dining at The Coachman. I was there with Karen and a group of others. She told me who you were. I was in half a mind to introduce myself then but it seemed rude to interrupt such an intimate tête-à-tête with your wife.'

Is he trying to wrong foot me, Philippe wondered? He did not trust the half smile that seemed to say *I know more about you than you think.*

Philippe turned to Robert who had made no attempt to decant the wine. He was an unwitting witness to the exchange. My brother is going to grill me about it, he thought. He could see his brother across the room. He's missing nothing, Robert thought. *Nothing.*

'Robert, you need to decant that wine. Unless you plan to stand there all night holding the bottle and not sharing it with your guests.'

'Well said, Dr Duval.'

Nicholas Gleeson had not been invited to call him Philippe. He accepted a glass of burgundy from his host and then turned to leave. He felt perhaps he had already said too much.

He wondered then about Philippe Duval. He was not a stupid man. Far from it. But he was certainly an arrogant man. How could he not know his lawyers' office was agog with gossip of his investment in Karen Clarke's fashion business? As a gift, for heaven's sake. There were too many support staff doing boring paperwork for it not to be gossiped about.

And the associated accounting firm that paid his bills? How could an accounts clerk be expected not to gossip about the expensive jewellery Duval had bought? After all the accounts clerk's best friend was the managing partner's secretary.

He had overheard it all laid out in detail. A sapphire and diamond set for his wife. A beautiful diamond and gold pendant for his daughter. And a third piece. For his mistress perhaps? The exquisite diamond and platinum pendant with the initial K picked out in diamonds. The invoices had been accompanied by photographs.

He had asked to see the photographs, using some simple excuse to explain his interest. And thus, he was able to recognise the piece Karen had worn at the restaurant. And again tonight. Both times he had commented on how stunning it looked on her. She had smiled and acknowledged the compliment. Nothing more. But she looked quietly radiant. A woman in love, he thought. Just not with him. He did not blame Philippe Duval for falling under her spell. But he resented him all the same. He might otherwise have had a chance.

He moved effortlessly through the crowd greeting the handful of people he knew. And then a thought occurred to him. What about Duval's pretty wife? He had noticed her when they arrived. A very attractive woman, quite different from Karen. He decided then he wanted to meet her. He looked around and saw a familiar face. Ian Dixon. Of course. He had noticed their hostess guide Julia Duval to that group. She clearly knew them.

He had not met Ian Dixon since his recent return from Melbourne but they had worked cases together in the past. He walked over to greet him and the inevitable introductions followed.

'Mrs Duval, it's delightful to meet you. Your husband is a client of our firm.'

He was testing the waters. Did she know that?

She shook hands with him.

'Please call me Julia,' she said, smiling politely.

Her blue grey eyes held his for just a moment longer than necessary, he thought. Does she know she's being made a fool of by her two-timing husband, he wondered? But there's no obvious sign she knows anything about it.

'Philippe hasn't mentioned your name,' she said conversationally.

'No, we'd not met before this evening. I'm not part of the team that looks after his interests. One of my major clients is David Clarke, Karen's father.'

He looked closely at her. Was that a flicker of annoyance on her face? And did he hear a quick intake of breath from Angela Dixon? So, her friends know but there's a conspiracy of silence around her. To protect her. And her daughter. I wonder how long that will hold.

It was Ian Dixon who broke the stalemate in the conversation.

'How was Melbourne by the way? I hear your star rose quite quickly there. I was wondering what brought you back to Sydney?'

'It was an opportunity too good to pass up. Retirements of some senior partners. Finally, I could get back to Sydney in a senior role,' he said. 'Melbourne's great but I've always preferred Sydney. Besides, Melbourne wasn't big enough for me and my ex-wife.'

'I heard about the divorce on the grapevine,' Ian said, 'which leaves you looking around for the next Mrs Gleeson I guess.'

Ian hadn't quite intended to infer that perhaps Nicholas Gleeson had his eyes on Karen as the next Mrs Gleeson but that was exactly how the comment was interpreted. All eyes turned towards Karen who was chatting animatedly with her cousin Anita. Pippa too was part of the group.

He shrugged.

'If you're thinking about Karen Clarke, I think you'll find she's already spoken for. But who knows? Maybe she'll change her mind.'

It was Julia who broke the strained silence.

'I didn't know she was serious about anyone. I must be out of touch with the latest gossip.'

He saw Ian Dixon's very slight shake of the head and a warning look that said, *we know what you know but it's not your place to say it.*

'Oh, you didn't hear that from me. It's just gossip probably but there were no names mentioned. I think she enjoys playing hard to get. But I enjoy being included in her group of friends. It makes a nice change to socialise with a group where I'm the only lawyer.'

He looked at Julia appraisingly. She was wearing the sapphire and diamond drop earrings. She had clearly thought the necklace would be too much for a drinks party, he thought. She looks gorgeous with her blond hair swept up.

'And you Julia, I wouldn't take you for a lawyer?'

She laughed and shook her head.

'No, I'm not a lawyer but I seem to spend a fair amount of time with them, one way or the other.'

'Involved in the estate matters with Philippe?'

He couldn't resist the question. He couldn't see why she would be involved. Did she have need of a lawyer apart from her husband? Was she already sounding out divorce options?

'No, nothing to do with Philippe,' she said. 'My mother left me a trust fund of some substance. I meet with my trustees usually once a month. It will come as no surprise to you that the trustees are lawyers. And then there's investment advisers of course.'

He reached into the inside pocket of his jacket then and withdrew a business card.

'If you ever find yourself in need of extra advice, for whatever reason, I'd be happy to help.'

She looked at the card and then tucked it into her purse. He wondered if one day she might be looking for someone to handle her divorce. Family law wasn't his specialty but he would make an exception for her, especially if it meant parting Philippe Duval from some of his fortune.

He went one step further.

'We should have coffee one day soon,' he said. 'It's always good to have a second opinion about the advice you're getting.'

She smiled then.

'That's very kind of you, Nicholas. Perhaps I'll take you up on that sometime.'

Was that a polite brush off, he wondered, or a subtle invitation from a woman being neglected by her husband? He couldn't decide. She intrigued him.

From the country, he'd been told when being briefed on the firm's new clients. But privileged. Rich family. Pippa, their daughter, had been a teenager when they finally married. He wondered how the first husband had greeted the revelation. Not well, it seemed. Took her straight to the divorce court and retained custody of their son.

And then she linked up with her first love and hoped for a happy ending. But he had heard Karen whisper to her friend Bianca a matter of days ago that Philippe belonged to her. Always had. And where would that leave Julia? In need of a shoulder to cry on. Her cool beauty challenged him. And then he felt a subtle pressure on his arm. Ian Dixon drew him to one side.

'I see where this is going, Nicholas,' he said in a low voice. 'A warning. We protect Julia and her daughter. There are things she doesn't need to know if you get my meaning.'

He laughed quietly.

'Are you serious? Are you seriously telling me she won't find out about the way her husband's carrying on?'

Ian shrugged.

'No one knows that for sure, unless you know more than we do. More than you should know, given client confidentiality.'

'Don't worry, Ian, I'm not about to betray any professional confidences. But you might ask yourself who has enough money to buy a woman an exquisite diamond and platinum pendant with her initial picked out in perfectly matched diamonds. He's hardly being discreet, is he?'

Ian sighed. He'd seen it all before. It was like a rerun of an old movie. Except this time, no one knew exactly what the ending would be. And he felt sorry for Julia. Except that he had been surprised to learn the gossip was not only about Philippe this time. He had heard only Angela's side of a recent telephone conversation with her friend Kate but he managed to fill in the missing bits and Angela had not denied it.

He had thought then a disappointed woman might well be a soft target for a man who hated her second husband. And only one man fitted that bill. Her first husband. The father of her son. What do they say about revenge, he mused? And then he remembered. *It was a dish best served cold.* He had shaken his head at this latest news. He couldn't help but think that, like her brother Richard, her life was anything but straightforward.

He cautioned Nicholas Gleeson again.

'If you meddle, this could backfire on you disastrously. Don't say I didn't warn you. He's wealthy now. Which means he's powerful.'

His warning, though, had the opposite effect on Nicholas Gleeson. He speculated on how easy it might be to turn a coffee date into early evening drinks. He knew he had been used to make Duval jealous. It was time the tables were turned.

He was starting to warm to the idea of romancing Philippe Duval's wife. He found he could easily imagine her blonde hair loosened and spread out on the pillow next to him. It was an enticing prospect. He had suffered a rare rejection with Karen but now he understood why. What sweet revenge it would be on his rival to seduce his wife, to have her come willingly to his bed. Even now he was anticipating the enjoyment. And the victory it would deliver him. A plan started to form. It would be easy enough for him to find out her husband's movements, especially if he headed to New York without her.

He noticed then her glass was empty. He took it from her hand and headed towards his host. Robert Clarke refilled the glass and then watched with interest as Nicholas Gleeson manoeuvred himself alongside Julia.

'Thank you, Nicholas,' she said, looking around. 'I have no idea where my husband has disappeared to.'

He smiled.

'I'm happy to take care of you in his absence,' he said, his charm offensive beginning.

Across the room, David Clarke was looking around too for Philippe. And for Karen. He walked across and tackled his brother, whose bottles of vintage wine were being rapidly reduced to a stack of empties.

'Well, that was interesting,' he said quietly. 'I thought we were about to see fireworks. But have those two slipped off somewhere? I bloody hope not.'

'Are you sure about what's going on?' Robert asked. 'It's all just speculation on your part.'

But his brother shook his head.

'He's poured money into Karen's business. As a gift. My accountant confirmed it to me.'

Robert Clarke let out a long sigh.

'I'm disappointed I must say.' He liked Philippe. He admired him as a surgeon. And as a colleague. But he was left with a sense of bitter disappointment at his colleague's personal life. 'I wonder how all this will play out?'

And then they both looked across at Nicholas Gleeson standing alongside Julia, the two of them laughing together as if they were old friends.

'Are you thinking what I'm thinking, Robert?'

'What would that be, David?'

'That his wife might think another man taking an interest in her might bring her errant husband to his senses.'

'Maybe. But would she be so devious? Patricia's always thought the pity of it all is how much in love with Philippe she still is.'

David Clarke considered this for a moment and nodded.

'You know her brother Richard wasn't particularly keen on the marriage. He always felt it was a relationship that was better left in the past, particularly when he came to know about Duval's interest in Karen.'

Robert Clarke regarded his brother's opinion with some cynicism.

'Yet you were dead against him marrying Karen, as I remember. Warned him off.'

'I know, Robert,' he said finally. 'Don't remind me. I admit I was wrong. And I don't care he's suddenly become extremely wealthy. I realise I really messed with my daughter's happiness. I thought she'd move on to someone else. But she never has.'

It was such a change of tone from his brother that Robert Clarke couldn't believe his ears. His brother had never been a man to admit mistakes. To be contrite.

'And now?'

'I'm not interfering but as sorry as I would be for his wife, I hope he divorces her and marries my daughter.'

At that very time, away from prying eyes in the darkness of the garden, Philippe, his anger barely contained, confronted Karen.

'You enjoyed making me jealous, didn't you?'

He had a tight grip on her arms as if he wanted to shake her.

'Tell me, are you sleeping with him? Have these past months just been a diversion for you?'

'My darling Philippe, what a lot of questions.'

She was alarmed at how serious he had become. She had just meant to make him jealous. She hadn't meant to make him doubt her sincerity. Besides, she never asked him if he still made love to his wife.

'Well?'

'Of course, I'm not sleeping with him,' she retorted, alarmed at his intensity. 'I'm surprised you feel you even need to ask me that question.'

And then she smiled at him and put her arms around his neck. For a few moments he felt the thrill of her body pressed against his. He realised how close he had come to making their relationship public by his actions. And in the process publicly humiliating his wife. Yet part of him was still annoyed with her. She knew by the way he held her, by the angry passion of his kiss.

'We must go back inside,' he said finally, 'but not together.'

'Not until you apologise for doubting me.'

He smiled then. He had never been able to stay angry with her.

'I apologise for thinking the worst of you,' he said. 'Jealousy does strange things to a man.'

She stood back from him. She wanted to see if his apology was genuine. As she stood there, he reached out and began to trace the outline of the pendant he had given her with his fingers.

'It looks beautiful on you,' he said.

On a warm summer evening, it was still cool to the touch. Then his hand drifted beneath the flimsy fabric of her dress. He began to caress her breast with the lightest of touches. And then he stopped abruptly.

'You can't go back in completely dishevelled,' he said quietly, 'but if I go on doing this, you will be. I won't be able to stop myself.'

She laughed. He knew she would not have stopped him.

'Then you will need to see me again soon. Very soon. In private,' she teased.

'Very soon,' he said. 'My wife and daughter are going down to Bowral for a few days after Christmas. I'm on call so I can't go. We can spend some time together then. And I have another surprise for you.'

He kissed her lightly on the cheek and turned to walk back inside the house but she held his hand and drew him back. She wanted to be sure he had forgiven her.

'I didn't think you would react the way you did when you saw me with another man,' she admitted.

He smiled at her.

'Well, now you know,' he said. 'You're mine. I'm not sharing you with anyone.'

She smiled to herself and let go of his arm. She had achieved exactly what she had set out to do.

And the next step? For her to be able to say to him *you're mine and I'm not sharing you with anyone.* She was impatient for that day.

# CHAPTER 18

IT WAS MID-AFTERNOON on a glorious summer day by the time Pippa and Julia turned into the driveway of Berrima Park. They were the last to arrive. It was to be something of a family reunion only this time not at Prior Park. For the first time anyone could remember, Prior Park would be devoid of all its owners.

But the occasion had demanded it. To the surprise of almost everyone, Paul Belleville had proposed to Nancy Lester on her birthday a few weeks earlier. Pippa of course had known. Marianne had known too. He had prevailed upon his mother to give him the engagement ring she had received from his father. His father's long time friend John Bertram, a Qantas pilot, had been entrusted with the role of courier. And it had fitted Nancy perfectly. A family dinner had been hastily arranged at Berrima Park to celebrate their engagement.

'I'm sorry your father couldn't come down with us,' Julia said.

'Oh, he's coming, don't worry,' Pippa assured her. 'He's coming tomorrow afternoon in time for the dinner. We discussed it and I managed to get Dr Clarke to step up in his place.'

Julia smiled then. She was pleased he was making the effort. He had told her that morning he was having to go back to New York in mid January, despite his reluctance to travel in the northern winter. He had not invited her to go with him. A quick business trip, he had said.

She had tried hard to hide her disappointment at being excluded. And just at the point where she had hoped their marriage was going to get back on track with his beautiful gift of expensive jewellery. Yet nothing much had changed despite his admission that he had been neglecting her.

She had always expected to be excluded from his professional life. But now she felt excluded from most of his life as he grappled with the myriad legal issues of inheriting a complex legacy, with more and more people laying claim to his available time.

And on the pretext of not disturbing her when he dealt with late night phone calls, he often chose to sleep in their spare room. Just occasionally, he became the warm and loving husband he had once been. Yet he often seemed distracted, as if his thoughts were elsewhere.

And there were other things she tried to ignore. The conversations that shut down suddenly as she approached. The sideways looks at him when they were out. The whispered asides. The knowing glances.

And James? She had tried hard not to think about him but that didn't always work. As she lay in bed alone at night, she remembered the pleasure she had taken in being with him.

Was it the illicit pleasure that had rendered his lovemaking more enjoyable than during their years as husband and wife, she wondered? Or had she never really given their marriage a chance as she mourned the loss of Philippe and their daughter? She didn't know for sure but the strong sexual attraction she felt for him had surprised her. She shook her head slightly to rid herself of the memory of his intimate caresses, of the memory of the desire he had aroused in her.

But it was Pippa's excited voice that finally cut through her thoughts. She smiled. She knew Pippa always looked forward to seeing her family.

'I believe everyone's here already,' Pippa said as they approached the end of the driveway. 'Aunt Alice, Uncle William and Marianne arrived yesterday. John is here too. He travelled with them. Uncle Richard should have arrived this morning too. Kate and Susan actually spent Christmas here so Kate could prepare for the dinner. Anthony will be the only one missing. And Paul's mother of course. Paul told me Anthony is coming for a long stay in their summer break, so maybe they'll have a winter wedding while he is here.'

As the magnificent house came into view, Julia felt a familiar twinge of sadness at seeing it again for the first time in years. She had been an occasional visitor when Kate and Richard visited since their marriage. The house always reminded her of what they had lost at Prior Park.

'What did you think of my new car?' she asked her mother as she brought her new MG B to a halt in a hail of gravel, ignoring the fact that the stone chips would mar the gleaming red paintwork.

Julia laughed.

'I think your father overindulges you if you must know.'

'What else is he going to do with his only child?' she replied cheekily as she stepped out of the car to the admiring glances of her cousins and half-brother who clustered enviously around the new sports car.

She kissed each of them in turn and reserved a special hug for her friend Nancy before grasping her left hand to admire the diamond ring she now wore so proudly.

It was Richard who extended his hand to help his sister out of the low set car.

'Good trip was it?' he asked laughingly as he hugged her and pointed to the car.

'Hair raising,' she said with a smile. 'Her father indulges her shamelessly.'

'Well, I hope he indulges you shamelessly too,' Richard said, expecting nothing less of a man whose wealth now dwarfed their own.

She shrugged. It was not the answer he had been hoping for, so he said nothing more.

Her son John heard the exchange too as he came across to greet his mother. He was always delighted to see her and more so without her husband. She hugged him fondly, suddenly aware of how tall he had grown. He seemed to tower over her.

'My father sends his love,' he whispered. 'He's looking forward to your next visit. Did you see the surprise he has for you? She's stabled at Prior Park now. Being schooled ready for her lady rider.'

He smiled then, a secret knowing smile, as he saw the flush of colour on her cheeks and a look of guilt flash across her eyes. He knew for certain then he was right. They had spent the night together. And he had noticed how his father's mood had improved dramatically since her visit. Her photo had reappeared in his bedroom.

'What did your uncles say about that arrangement?'

She could imagine William's look of surprise.

'Not much, to be honest. Uncle Richard simply raised his eyebrows. *Nice filly*, he said, *but she'll never be a stock horse*. Uncle William muttered something like *it's a gift for our sister*. He didn't say from whom.'

'She looks beautiful but your father shouldn't have done that.'

'It was a peace offering,' he said quietly. 'A token of his love.'

She shook her head, the warning look clear in her expression.

'Philippe is coming down tomorrow. I think he may have seen the photo. If he tackles you about it, please don't tell him your father bought the horse. He doesn't know ...'

He smiled conspiratorially and interrupted her.

'My dear mother, don't worry. Your secrets are safe with me. If he asks, I'll tell him it was a gift from me.'

He would not be the source of embarrassment for her. And he was sure his uncles wouldn't be either. He fervently hoped her marriage would unravel without his help. Or his father's.

He picked up his mother's cases and followed her into the house where Kate was presiding over the tea tray, as if she was once again mistress of the house.

If Julia had known exactly where her husband was and what he was doing as she and her daughter arrived at Berrima Park, she would have quickly realised the concern she harboured about the state of her marriage was fully justified.

Karen had been expecting him. She had spent some time at her living room window that afternoon looking out for his car before she saw it turn slowly into her street.

Within minutes, she was welcoming Philippe who noticed how the silky fabric of her dress left nothing to the imagination. He hoped it was just for his benefit. It was barely decent. He took a sip from the glass of wine she had given him.

'You have the ability to drive a man crazy,' he said as he sat down beside her. He was remembering their encounter of a few days ago. It had been their first real disagreement. And it had been his fault.

She shrugged and smiled, her eyes alight with mischief.

'Of course, it was your fault.'

She leant over and kissed him. He could feel her body through her thin dress.

'That is how you drive me crazy,' he said, setting down his glass of wine.

He eased the dress off her shoulders and reached for the zipper at the back which yielded easily. He began to caress her. He loved her uninhibited response. He loved how her desire for him matched his desire for her. She aroused him as no other woman had ever done.

But there was more to it than that. Much more. If he had known what the gossips had said, he would have agreed with them. *She only has to smile at me to have me back by her side.*

Later, as she lay alongside him, he stroked her hair that streamed out over the pillow next to him. They were both spent from the intensity of their lovemaking.

'I told you I had another surprise for you.'

She rolled over on her side to face him.

'Something nice, I hope?'

He smiled.

'What about a trip to New York for you and Bianca? You've always wanted to get into the New York market. I'll take care of all the expenses.'

She sat up then, as excited as a small child who had been promised a special treat, her nakedness distracting him. He reached out to stroke her bare breasts. She did not try to stop him. She enjoyed the softness of his touch on her skin.

'For the February fashion shows?' she asked. 'That would be wonderful.'

He nodded.

'If you can manage it by then. I'm going over very soon. In mid January.'

'And tomorrow night? Will you come to Bianca's with me? We can discuss it then.'

But he shook his head.

'Sorry, but duty calls. Julia's nephew Paul is getting engaged. There's a family dinner down at Bowral. Pippa has convinced me I have to go. She got your uncle to cover for me so I can't get out of it.'

She was disappointed but she understood.

'And your wife will be back home when?'

'Not sure, but probably the next day. Or the day after. And I'll be busy at the hospital probably. It may be hard to see you before I go to New York but I will try. Clarence will be in touch with you from New York to organise the trip for you.'

He kissed the top of her shoulder as she turned her back to him and nestled into the crook of his arm.

'Do you think she knows about us?' she asked suddenly.

He shook his head.

'I don't think so. I hope not. Not yet.'

'Not yet?'

He shrugged.

'I don't want to make promises about the future. Not yet. What if you get tired of me after a few months?'

She shook her head.

'I always thought it would be you getting tired of me.'

It was his turn to shake his head.

'If you knew the number of times I thought about you in the years I spent ignoring you, you would know the answer to that.'

'And yet you were able to ignore me almost completely,' she said. The memory of it still hurt her.

He took her hand then and put her fingers to his lips.

'It was the hardest thing I ever did,' he said. 'Seeing you from time to time was torture, believe me. Several times I was on the brink of saying I wanted to see you again. But then I remembered you had gone overseas to get away from me, from seeing me marry someone else. I didn't know how you felt about me. And then you came to my office the last day before I left for New York. I knew how you felt about me then.'

He noticed then a single tear slide down her cheek. She had wrapped the sheet around her as if she needed protection.

'Is it something I said? Look at me,' he said softly.

She shook her head again. There would never be a better time to tell him her big secret. If there was a chance for them to be together in the future, she felt he had to know.

'I have something to tell you about me going overseas before you got married,' she said thoughtfully. She paused for a moment, wondering how to say it but there was no easy way.

'I didn't tell you I was pregnant when I went.' There, she had said it, finally, after all these years. 'I didn't want to force you to give up on marrying Julia.'

He was shocked. He had never guessed. But she had never had the baby. Should he ask? There were two possibilities. He stayed silent, hoping she would tell him.

'I had a miscarriage a month after I left.'

He cradled her in his arms then, understanding for the first time what she had been through because of him. He had been more concerned with himself, with keeping their relationship from Julia than worrying about her. For one awful moment, he had suspected she might have taken the unthinkable option to end her pregnancy.

'I'm so sorry,' he said. 'I had no idea. No idea at all. After that, I'm surprised you didn't hate me.'

'No, I didn't hate you,' she said. 'I would have been delighted to have had a child with you, married to you or not.'

She had chosen her words carefully as if it was all permanently in the past. For his part, he realised, by falling in love with her and then turning his back on her, he had denied her the opportunity to try for another child with her vow never to marry anyone else.

206

'I'm pleased you told me.' he said. 'Very pleased. I should have been there for you and I wasn't. I'm sorry for that.'

He couldn't help but hear the echoes of the apology he had made to Julia too.

'I hope this doesn't change anything between us,' she said, suddenly alarmed that he might begin to view their relationship through the prism of the past.

'No, it doesn't change anything for me. It makes me admire you all the more. You went through all that by yourself.'

She nodded, remembering the dark lonely times.

He understood for the first time how much she had suffered because of him. She had paid a higher price for being in love with him than he had ever imagined. But he was still left wondering how he was ever going to leave his marriage. How do I destroy the fairytale ending to my wartime romance with Julia without her hating me? And without my daughter hating me? He had no answers yet to those questions. Except in recent days, he had begun to wonder if Julia herself was looking to end their marriage. There were some small signs he had yet to understand. Meaningless perhaps. But taken together, what did they mean? He wasn't sure but he wondered if the next day might bring some answers. Given the opportunity, he thought he might test a theory with her brother Richard.

It was well into the evening at Berrima Park. The engagement cake had been cut, the young couple had been cheered and the champagne bottles emptied at an alarming rate. The table which had sported the best tableware and highly polished silverware was now an untidy mass of used plates and discarded wine glasses.

Extra household staff had been brought in to relieve Kate of most of the workload of hosting the dinner for her daughter's engagement. A chef and his kitchen staff had been hired from one of the local restaurants that closed for a Christmas break to prepare the meal, which had turned out to be simple but excellent.

Kate was happy to turn her back on the mess and let others do the cleaning up, except for the serving of the engagement cake. Richard had whispered to her to keep Julia occupied while he had a word with Philippe, so Kate had enlisted Julia to help her.

Everyone else had drifted out to the verandah to enjoy the warm summer evening, some to drink coffee, others to refill their glasses with more wine or post dinner spirits.

It was the opportunity Richard had been waiting for. He tapped Philippe on the shoulder and inclined his head towards the garden.

'Have you got a moment for a private chat?'

Philippe guessed what was coming as he followed Richard into the darkness of the garden. He would have avoided the encounter had he not wanted to put his own questions to Richard.

'I've been hearing disturbing reports about your behaviour, Philippe,' Richard said, in a low voice. He was struggling to find the right words.

'Really. And what reports would they be, Richard?' he shot back.

He wasn't going to make it easy for him.

'That you've rekindled your affair with Karen,' Richard said bluntly, deciding then that there was no point in being subtle.

He shrugged.

'What business is it of yours?'

But he knew what the answer would be.

'Because you are married to my sister,' he snapped. 'She deserves better treatment from her husband.'

But Philippe's irritation at the line of questioning had quickly tipped over into anger. He had stomached his brother-in-law's interference in the past. But he had reached his limit with Richard's arrogant superiority.

'I thank you not to interfere in my private life,' he said. 'I don't appreciate it.'

He hadn't quite expected such angry words, just the usual ticking off. He wondered how Richard knew. He seemed so confident of his information. Someone had been gossiping but he was at a loss to know who. Certainly not Karen.

'Whether you appreciate it or not, I couldn't care less,' Richard said, his anger rising to match Philippe's. 'Your behaviour is way out of line. I know you're sleeping with Karen again. It won't be long before Julia finds out too. It's not something that can stay hidden for long.'

Philippe laughed then. A short sharp derisory sound.

'So let me get this right,' he said, his voice trembling with anger. 'I'm being lectured to by a man who got another man's wife pregnant. Not exactly entitled to the high moral ground, are you?'

But Richard was not so easily sidetracked. He was not about to enter a slanging match about his relationship with Kate.

'And what if Karen gets pregnant to you again like she did before?'

Richard thought he was delivering the ultimate bombshell. Instead, in the half light from the verandah, he saw Philippe smile.

'You thought I didn't know that, didn't you? She told me. I know she had a miscarriage. And I know why she didn't tell me when it happened. She didn't want me to have to make a choice between her and Julia.'

Richard was stunned into silence.

'I am wondering though how you knew about it? Her father perhaps. I believe you know him.'

He saw Richard nod. He knew he had guessed right.

'And if you want to know when I found out, it was yesterday.'

'No doubt when you were lying in her bed.'

Philippe looked at him. The conversation had gone on long enough.

'I'm not going to bother denying it,' he said, 'but I encourage you not to tell your sister that. We'll work this out in our own time. But there is one thing you can help me with. Or help me work out.'

'What would that be?' Richard was curious.

'Why her first husband is buying her a horse, sending a photo of it with love and kisses on it, and why she came back from her most recent trip, nervous and anxious around me, with what looked to me like fading love bites on her neck? Getting friendly with her first husband again, is she?'

There were few times in his life when Richard had been rendered utterly speechless but this was one of them. Philippe, on the other hand, saw the look of shock on Richard's face. Until that moment, until Richard had all but confirmed it with his silence, it had been mere speculation on his part as to what had taken place.

'I notice you didn't deny it. My instinct is correct then. Your sister —my wife that is—has begun sleeping with her ex-husband again. Am I right?'

'I think you've said enough about my sister,' Richard said, trying to recover the situation. 'You've drawn your own conclusions on very slim evidence and nothing I say is going to change your mind.'

'Slim evidence? Is that what you call it,' Philippe replied.

He laughed mirthlessly.

'Let me give you a piece of advice, Richard,' he said finally. 'A lie would have helped. You could have at least lied more convincingly to save your sister's reputation. So I think we're pretty even really. I'm enjoying a very warm welcome in Karen's bed while my wife seeks consolation in the arms of her ex-husband.'

Richard turned and walked away. He had come so very close to losing his temper completely he could not risk continuing the conversation. He wished now he had never spoken to Philippe. He knew then his sister's marriage was at the point of unravelling, possibly because of him. He was shocked to hear Philippe being so open about his relationship with Karen.

In the shadows of the garden, John had eavesdropped on the entire conversation. His first instinct was to defend his mother but he knew better than to create a scene. He sighed. It was all spiralling into a terrible mess from which there would be only one outcome. He wondered then what Pippa would think of her father if she knew? Should he be the one to tell her?

He pondered this thought for some time without coming to a satisfactory conclusion.

# CHAPTER 19

THE BIG HOUSE AT BERRIMA PARK had fallen eerily quiet as midnight approached, the only sounds the rustling movement of nocturnal animals across its spacious grounds.

Philippe had lain in bed alongside his wife for some time thinking about his terse exchange with Richard. He had always liked Richard but he resented his latest attempt to interfere in his private life. He wondered idly if their relationship would ever be the same again. He smiled at the bombshell Richard had expected to drop on him about Karen having become pregnant to him before he married Julia. He was pleased Karen had finally told him. It had given him the upper hand in the exchange.

And then a real bombshell had exploded unexpectedly. It had been nothing more than speculation on his part about Julia. He had hardly given it any credence. It was Richard's stunned silence that confirmed his suspicions. There was no denial. No outraged defence of his sister. Just a lame afterthought about very slim evidence.

How many times, he wondered? How many times had she been with her ex-husband? Once, twice, possibly more? And what happens next time she visits?

She'll probably be back at Prior Park before my plane has touched down in New York, he thought. Part of him wished he had never found out. Part of him wished that Richard had been clever enough to lie outright to him. To tell him the idea was preposterous. To tell him he was being ridiculous.

Which means my beautiful loving wife, probably hearing some gossip about me, has found consolation in the arms of her first husband with whom she always claimed not to be on speaking terms. A convenient lie, obviously.

She stirred alongside him and reached out to put her arm around him. He felt the warmth and softness of her body through her sheer nightdress.

*Why am I so angry with her?* He couldn't answer that question. After all she's only doing what I'm doing. Is it fair to expect more of her than I expect of myself? He knew he had neglected her. He tried to remember how many times he had made love to her recently. Once or twice at most. Did she interpret my neglect as a lack of interest in her as a woman? Had she wanted reassurance she was still attractive?

But for all his rationalisations about her behaviour, his anger remained. He turned on his side to face her. Is this what she wants? Is this what she was looking for in another man's bed? He slid his hand under her nightdress, caressing her body intimately. She was not as voluptuous as Karen but still he enjoyed the feel of her shapely body.

He felt her hands go to his chest to push him away but he pinned her down. She tried and failed to free herself from his grasp. Suddenly, he wasn't in the mood to be denied.

And then he released her so he could grab her nightdress, pulling it roughly over her head before she could protest. It ended up in a crumpled torn heap on the floor. And then he began to kiss her with an intensity fuelled by his anger. And then by his desire for her. It was as if he needed to reclaim her body for himself.

*It should not matter so much. Not if I'm going to give her up for Karen.* But he could not explain the intense uncontrollable surge of jealousy he'd felt at finding out she had been unfaithful to him.

Later, as he lay in the darkness, he felt an emptiness he couldn't explain at the prospect of leaving her. *Would Karen fill that void?* He wasn't sure. Had he reached the point where he could not turn back?

Probably. He knew Karen was expecting to become his wife. Is that what he really wanted?

Finally, he fell into a fitful sleep but not before coming to the realisation it was the closest he had ever come to taking a woman against her will.

Beside him, Julia lay wide awake, wondering what had just happened. And why? She had never seen him like that before. There had been an anger in his lovemaking. An anger towards her. As if he wanted to punish her. As if he would have relished taking her against her will had she not submitted willingly to him.

These and other thoughts robbed her of sleep for hours.

The next day, Pippa, troubled by her cousin Marianne's revelations about her mother's reconnection with her first husband, was determined to get her half-brother John alone. All it had taken was the offer of a chance for him to get behind the wheel of her new car.

As he settled into the driver's seat, she watched how he managed the manual transmission with ease, displaying the experience gained from years of driving on his father's property even before he was old enough to hold a licence. But the scattering of gravel as he accelerated down the driveway had taken him by surprise. Used to heavier vehicles, he hadn't accounted for the power of the engine in such a lightweight car.

'Wow,' he said, with a laugh, 'this baby can really move.'

As he headed out of the Berrima Park driveway onto the main road, he accelerated, going through the gears rapidly, thankful the traffic was light. He had only a vague idea of direction but at that point it didn't matter at all. He was driving for the sheer pleasure of being behind the wheel of Pippa's new sports car.

'Well, that was fun,' she said. 'I'm pleased I wasn't driving. My father would have been furious if I'd copped a ticket. How will your father react?'

'The old man will be fine. He's had worse,' John said dismissively.

They were standing alongside one another leaning against the car. He had pulled over at a local picnic spot at Pippa's suggestion. It was the first time she could remember them being together, just the two of them. Most of the time she had seen him as part of the family group at Prior Park.

For Pippa, there would never be a better opportunity to find out exactly what her half-brother knew about their parents. About their relationship.

'I've got a couple of questions to ask you,' she said warily. 'About our mother. And your father.'

John turned to look at her then. He hadn't expected such a question.

'What about our mother and my father?' he asked cautiously.

He was not going to try to second guess her. He had just days ago vowed to keep their mother's secrets safe, at least from her husband. But he hadn't counted on Pippa asking awkward questions.

'This morning, Marianne told me a convoluted story about how your father saved my mother from being thrown from her horse and then brought her back to Prior Park, everything patched up between them. He was even invited to stay for dinner.'

He said nothing. She pressed on.

'You were there at dinner no doubt. Is that what happened?'

'Pretty much,' he said, trying to play down the significance of it.

'Were you at home the next day when she apparently went to your place to thank your father for saving her?'

He was about to say *no, I wasn't at home then. I was in town.* And then it all became clear to him. Crystal clear. He had wondered why he hadn't thought of it before. He suddenly remembered when he had called in to see her the next day at Prior Park his mother had been very offhanded with her account of her visit to his father yet there had been an unusual nervousness about her.

But, later, at the wedding, his parents were on good terms, some onlookers even said *intimate terms.* He'd known from later gossip they had spent the night together but that was after the wedding. What he hadn't realised at the time was the significance of his mother visiting his father when his father was at home alone two days earlier. It had been an opportunity for a reconciliation between them in every sense of the word. He realised then she had been with him not once but twice during her visit.

He thought quickly.

'I don't remember to be honest,' he said. 'I was in and out all day.'

He was annoyed with Marianne. She should have known better than to tell Pippa about the incident with his father and everything else that had occurred. Pippa looked at him then. She knew he was being evasive.

'Do you think it unusual that my mother told us nothing of this when she got back home? She never mentioned seeing your father. She did say she'd gone to the wedding where you were groomsman, but we assumed she had gone with Alice and William.'

He shrugged, trying to downplay everything.

'And then the photo of the horse turns up in your Christmas card. That was remarkably indiscreet with the greeting on the reverse side. I'm sure my father saw it. The question is: what was your father doing buying my mother, the woman he supposedly wouldn't even speak to, an expensive horse?'

He folded his arms then and let out a deep sigh.

'Listen to me Pippa,' he said, trying to stay calm. 'I know things about our mother. About my father. And about your father. Things it would be better you never know.'

He had to say something. He could not stand by and let her speculate on their mother's behaviour while her father's went unchallenged.

She stood up straight then and started to pace around the small clearing. He could see the internal struggle raging within her, between the need to know everything and the fear of knowing everything.

'I'm not a child, John,' she said finally. 'Neither are you. I think we can face the truth about our parents.'

But he shook his head. *Does she really want to know what I know?* He was reluctant. None of it would be easy for her to hear.

'Don't force me to tell you, Pippa. Just don't make me tell you. You've speculated about our mother with my father,' he said quietly.

'But that's not the full story. We haven't mentioned your father. You have set your father on a pedestal. He won't be there after I tell you what I know, what I overheard.'

But she was determined to know. She wanted to know everything.

'What about my father?' she asked. 'Is it about his relationship with Karen Clarke?'

He nodded.

'It is.'

'Is he having an affair with her? Is he sleeping with her?'

He nodded again.

'Yes, he is.'

Just as he expected, she shook her head emphatically as if to deny such a thing was even possible.

'I don't believe it. Did you overhear some gossip? How could you possibly know?'

Why was he the one to have to tell her? Secrets had torn their family apart before. He was very much afraid they would do so again. He took a deep breath.

'If you must know, I overheard your father and Uncle Richard having a row last night after dinner. I heard every word, Pippa. Every word.'

'What was the argument about?'

'Can't you guess? Uncle Richard accused your father of sleeping with Karen Clarke, of cheating on his wife.'

He saw the shock in her eyes. He noticed tears starting to form.

'And what did he say? Surely, he denied it. He must have denied it.'

There was no part of her that could believe her father capable of being unfaithful to her mother.

'Pippa, I'm sorry, he didn't deny it. In fact, he admitted it.'

He saw anger in her eyes. And he saw the beginnings of disillusionment.

'What do you mean he admitted it? How did he admit it?'

She was almost hysterical now. He had never seen her so upset. But it seemed she would never believe what he had told her unless he repeated the actual words her father had spoken. He shook his head, wondering not for the first time, if he had been right to begin this story.

She asked again, 'how did he admit it?'

He tried again to avoid repeating her father's angry words.

'He was very annoyed, Pippa. Angry with Uncle Richard. With his interference.'

'Tell me,' she demanded. 'Tell me what he said. Otherwise, I won't believe any of this.'

'Alright,' he said finally, 'but don't say I didn't warn you. Your father's exact words to Uncle Richard were *I think we're pretty even really. I'm enjoying a very warm welcome in Karen's bed while my wife seeks consolation in the arms of her ex-husband.*'

There, he had said it. In one sentence he had torn down Pippa's belief in the father she idolized. Until that moment he had been her hero. She shook her head from side to side, disbelieving.

'You must have misheard, John.'

'I didn't mishear. I wished I'd heard none of it.'

It was as if all emotion had drained from Pippa's face. Nothing had prepared her for what she had just heard.

He stood there helpless as he watched her belief in her father's loyalty, in his honesty, in his integrity evaporate as surely as the morning mist evaporates in the rising sun.

'Why did you tell me this, John?' she said, tears flowing unchecked down her cheeks.

'Because you and I deserve to know the truth about our parents.'

'So it's true about our mother sleeping with your father again?'

He nodded.

'Oh yes, it's true. Everything I've told you is true. I wish it wasn't but there you have it.'

'Is he serious about Karen Clarke or is it just a fling do you think? Maybe he'll come to his senses.'

It was the one last shred of hope she could think to cling to. John shrugged. To him it seemed unlikely.

'I think it's more serious than you think,' he said.

There was no point now in withholding information.

'Your father and Karen Clarke were lovers before he married our mother. Karen was pregnant to him but she miscarried the child. She never told him at the time. He only found out very recently I believe.'

For Pippa, it was as if everything she had thought she had known about her father had been proven to be a lie.

'What changed him, John? I wouldn't have thought it possible six months ago. We seemed to have a happy family life.'

He knew whatever he said could only be speculation at best. Only one person could answer her question truthfully.

'Inheriting all that money perhaps? It could change a person.'

Pippa thought about that for a moment.

'Possibly. But I also remember Karen Clarke being involved in a really bad car accident. There was gossip about him seeing her again regularly in the hospital.'

She had remembered overhearing fragments of gossip.

'Do you think the thought of losing her made him realise how much she meant to him? More than perhaps our mother meant to him.'

He shrugged.

'It's possible,' he said. 'There has to have been something that prompted him to pursue her again.'

For the moment, Pippa chose to ignore his unflattering description of her father's behaviour.

'And our mother?' she asked. 'Was her reconnection with your father the cause of my father's renewed interest in Karen Clarke? Or a symptom of it?'

He understood what she was trying to say. He half smiled, remembering his father's look of triumph.

'I think my father exploited her unhappiness at being neglected by your father. You must realise he has hated your father since it all came out. So think about it. She turns up, low in spirits and then by mere chance, he comes to her aid when she needs him, when she is nearly thrown from her horse. He turns on the old Fitzroy charm and she can't resist.'

Even Pippa managed a slight smile at his description of his father. She could see in John some of the Fitzroy charm she had heard others speak of. She wondered how many hearts he'd already broken.

'What was their marriage like John when you were a child?'

She had never asked that question. Never even thought about it before but now she was curious.

'It was pretty good, I think. What does a child know? They were simply my parents. But I know my father was unfaithful to her a couple of times. But never, ever, with the intention of replacing her as his wife. He just couldn't resist the occasional pretty face.'

She wondered how he knew about his father's affairs. He had only been nine years old when his parents had separated, when the secret of her own birth had been exposed.

'You would have been too young to realise any of that, surely?' she said.

He nodded. He hadn't known at the time.

'I thought about some of the incidents later,' he explained. 'There were inconsistencies about where my father said he had been on certain occasions. As I got older, I heard some of the gossip about his past conquests and figured it out.'

But there was more he wanted to say. There would never be a better time to say it, to demonstrate that their points of view differed on one crucial aspect.

'You would not have liked it. My uncles would not have liked it. Your father would have been angry. But forgive me if I was not. For one evening, I had the pleasure of seeing my father and my mother on good terms, enjoying each other's company. Just like old times.'

She was beginning to see and understand the other part of her mother's life. The part where she had been James Fitzroy's wife and John's mother.

'I had no idea, John,' she said. 'I had no idea how the breakup of their marriage affected you.'

For the first time, she was beginning to understand the pain he had suffered in losing his mother.

'You thought you were the only abandoned child, didn't you, Pippa?' he said, challenging her to deny it. 'But you weren't. Did you ever actually understand she abandoned me for you?'

Pippa shook her head slowly from side to side. She had never thought about it in those terms. She had only ever thought in terms of herself, her mother and her father. She had never spared a thought for her half-brother.

'John, it was not my fault. I'm sorry. I had no idea. No idea you felt like that.'

He reached out then and put a brotherly arm around her.

'I know that,' he said. 'My father drove her away but as a child of nine, it was hard to understand that at the time. I grew up without a mother really.'

She saw then the sad shadow of his smile as he thought about his childhood and she saw too how his intense brown eyes spoke of a pain so deep he could not bear to acknowledge it.

For the second time in her short life, she began to feel her world was being ripped apart, all the certainties she had come to rely on dissolving before her very eyes.

'Tell me, John,' she said despairingly. 'What are we supposed to do now? What are we supposed to do, knowing all this?'

'Nothing, Pippa,' he said, shaking his head. 'We do nothing. This mess just has to play out.'

He had chosen to tell her the truth. He wondered then if he had been right to do so but it was too late now. He couldn't unsay what had been said.

What a mess it's likely to become, he thought. And Pippa and me? What do they talk about in war? Collateral damage. That's what we are, we're collateral damage.

He hugged her then and opened the door of the car for her, before sliding into the driver's seat. He hadn't wanted to be the one to shatter Pippa's illusions about her father. And about their mother. But he had been left with no option.

He worried then, in the cold light of day, if she might come to despise him for his honesty.

# Chapter 20

JULIA SAT AT HER DRESSING TABLE staring at her reflection in the mirror. She was relieved the bruising on her arms had become less obvious. She wondered idly why her daughter had seemed so preoccupied and quiet on their return journey together from Bowral. But then she had been distracted by her own thoughts too.

Why had Philippe been so angry with me, she wondered? She had never seen him like that. She wondered if someone had spoken carelessly about her most recent visit to Prior Park. But who? Certainly not John who barely spoke to him. Alice? Unlikely. Richard? Why would he say anything to Philippe? Had it been a casual remark about her meeting up with her first husband that had caused him to doubt her?

And then she began to think more deeply about Philippe's own behaviour? Was he seeing Karen Clarke as gossip suggested? She had asked herself this question many times recently.

And if I challenge him about it, what then? What if he admits he is having an affair with her?

She continued to sit at the dressing table oblivious to the darkness slowly enveloping her bedroom, her mind drifting back to happier times. She remembered the overwhelming feeling of happiness in their unexpected meeting. And then becoming a family with Pippa.

But she knew the marriage was not what it could have been. What it should have been if they had married when Pippa was born. But Pippa had been a teenager when they met again.

She had married him with so much hope and expectation. She wondered then if the shadow of Karen Clarke had always been there in the background, silently undermining their marriage. He might have been seeing her off and on for years. The thought had not occurred to her until now. And then she heard his footsteps.

'I wondered where you were,' he said. 'What are you doing sitting here in the dark like this?'

He switched on the bedside lamps and walked to the window to draw the curtains. He waited for her to speak, to say something. Anything. He was trying to gauge her mood. Is she still angry with me, he wondered? But he knew it was up to him to make the first move. It was his behaviour that had been unacceptable. He came up behind her and put his hand on her shoulder. He bent forward to kiss her.

'I'm here to apologise for my behaviour, my darling,' he said quietly. 'I'm so sorry about the other night. My behaviour was inexcusable.'

She turned to look at him. He could see tears in her eyes. And along with the tears, a mixture of hurt and disappointment, as if his actions had undermined her faith in him, as if she was about to accuse him of destroying their marriage.

'I don't understand,' she said, choosing her words carefully. 'You seemed so angry with me, Philippe. Why? What did I do to upset you?'

She waited for him to reply. He sighed. What could he say that would explain his behaviour without accusing her outright of being unfaithful to him?

'I'm sorry,' he said. 'I had a feeling that you were getting friendly with your ex-husband again. That you hadn't told me you were now on good terms with him again. That you were keeping secrets from me.'

His explanation for his behaviour was a calculated gamble. No outright accusations, just vague suspicion. Would she believe that was reason enough for his behaviour?

He knew if they were honest with each other there would be no way forward for their marriage. Divorce would be the only solution.

He wasn't yet ready to give up on their marriage. He was proud of her as his wife. He still loved her. But he wondered if she was ready to give up on him. He waited.

'That's a ridiculous reason, Philippe,' she said, shaking her head, 'being jealous of my former husband. I didn't tell you I'd seen him for that very reason. For fear you would put the wrong interpretation on it, which you obviously did.'

He smiled to himself at how readily she lied to him. But he knew he would have done the same had she asked him about Karen. He would have denied their affair.

'I'm so sorry,' he said. 'Can we put it all behind us? I love you. I will always love you. I'm sorry I hurt you. Please forgive me.'

Yet, inch by inch, he knew their marriage was beginning to erode. His trust in her could never be what it had been. And her trust in him? It was probably only a matter of time before she discovered her suspicions about him were correct. He was relieved to see her smile.

'Let's put it behind us, Philippe,' she said.

He moved closer to her. She felt his arms close around her. This time, his lovemaking was gentle, caring, considerate as if he wanted to erase the memory of his angry humiliation of her.

Afterwards, as she lay in his arms, she closed her eyes briefly, wondering what the future held for them. If she ignored the gossips, could their marriage survive? Could she go on believing he was her loyal, faithful husband?

Philippe looked at her, pleased that she had accepted his apology but shocked and ashamed of the bruising still evident on her midriff and on her upper arms where he had briefly held her down.

But, still, there was one thought he could not block from his mind.

Had she lain alongside James Fitzroy in the same contented way after their lovemaking, her body pressed up against his, his arm around her, his free hand caressing her just as he was doing now?

He understood then what jealousy felt like. Deep uncontrollable jealousy. And he knew why. It was knowing another man had been with his wife. It was knowing another man had enjoyed her body just as he had done. It was knowing she had enjoyed another man's lovemaking. Try as he might he could not banish these thoughts from his mind.

But it was the idea she would, at some future time, betray him again with her first husband that would return time and again to torment him. Yet, in the midst of these thoughts, he recognised the hypocrite he had become.

# CHAPTER 21

PHILIPPE LOOKED AT HIS WATCH. It was still early. He had already finished his breakfast and was on to his second cup of coffee. For once, he had the leisure to finish it before heading to the hospital. He barely glanced up from his newspaper as Pippa walked into the kitchen.

'Good morning,' he said, expecting her to respond with her usual cheery greeting. They had not spoken since she had arrived home with her mother late the previous day.

'Is it?' she replied. She sounded bitter.

He put his newspaper aside then.

'What's up? Is there something troubling you, Pippa?' he asked, with no inkling of what was on her mind.

She shook her head as if she did not want to even speak to him.

'No, why should there be?' she said, trying to keep her tone light.

But there was no accompanying smile. He noticed a sadness in her normally lively eyes.

'I thought you would have enjoyed being among your mother's family down at Bowral,' he said. 'You seemed to enjoy the engagement dinner and seeing your cousins and John.'

'Oh, I enjoyed that part of it,' she said, her voice rising, 'but it's the conversation John overheard between you and Uncle Richard that ruined everything for me. He heard everything. *Every single word you said.* Please explain to me why you are cheating on my mother.'

How easy it had been for John to say *do nothing and let them work it out themselves*. But how was she meant to see her father every day and know that he was deceiving her mother. And say nothing at all. To pretend she knew nothing. There was no way that was possible.

Philippe stood up suddenly and grabbed his jacket from the back of his chair.

'Pippa, I'm not going to have this conversation with you here and now. You're off until tomorrow, aren't you?'

She nodded.

'Why don't you meet me for lunch. I have some things scheduled this morning but I'll be free at one o'clock. Come to the hospital and we'll go somewhere from there. I obviously need to talk to you. But not here.'

She laughed, a bitter unhappy sound.

'Because you don't want my mother to overhear our conversation?'

He nodded.

'Yes, that's right,' he said, determined to keep control of the situation. 'And I'd appreciate you not telling her anything either. It's not your place.'

She shrugged.

'So you're going to tell her yourself, are you?'

But he wouldn't be drawn into agreeing to anything.

'Let's talk at lunch,' he said, as he turned and headed for the front door, leaving Pippa to stare after him.

There was a steely edge to his voice she hadn't noticed before. Money has changed him, she thought, and not for the better. Or was it simply that he'd been caught out.

She headed back towards her bedroom with a cup of tea. As she passed the spare room where her father spent most nights, she noticed the bed was undisturbed. And then she saw her mother emerge from her bedroom and head towards the bathroom. She peered into the bedroom from the doorway. She could see clearly there had been two people in the bed. She smiled but there was a cynical edge to her amusement.

He thinks by becoming an attentive husband again, everything

226

will be alright and she'll forget about her suspicions. And then he can go on doing exactly as he pleases with his mistress.

She shook her head. She would be interested to hear his explanation for his behaviour over lunch. Until then she had a plan for her morning.

She headed to the living room in search of the telephone directory which usually lay neglected on the bottom shelf of the bookcase. She picked it up and ran her finger down the listings of Clarke telephone numbers until she found what she was looking for. It only took a minute. There it was in black and white. Karen's address in Rose Bay.

It had taken Pippa less than twenty minutes to drive the short distance to Karen Clarke's address. She parked along the street and quickly walked back to the entrance to the apartment building. She did not want to run the risk of Karen seeing her approach.

She pressed the doorbell and listened to it echo throughout the empty stairwell. Finally, Karen opened the door, grateful for Philippe's warning phone call just minutes earlier. He hadn't been sure but he told her it was possible Pippa might pay her a visit.

'Pippa, what are you doing here? This is a surprise. Come in,' she said, her bright greeting hiding her anxiety.

Pippa waited while Karen closed the door behind them. She looked around the apartment. It wasn't especially large but it was beautifully furnished. To her right, she could see a doorway to what she assumed was the master bedroom. Karen deftly steered her towards the living room. She did not want Pippa to glance through the doorway and see the photograph of her father on the bedside table.

'Can I ask what brings you here, Pippa? I wasn't expecting you, was I?'

'No, Karen, you weren't expecting me,' she replied. 'Expecting my father maybe although probably not today. I think he's busy at the hospital and my mother's back home.'

Karen sat down on the sofa and pointed to a chair opposite inviting her visitor to sit. For a few moments, Pippa looked at her dispassionately. By every measure, she was beautiful. But it was more than mere beauty. It was her sensuous warmth that would appeal to men, Pippa decided. And other women? Other woman would simply be speechless with envy.

'Pippa,' Karen said quietly but kindly, 'you're the very last person I'm going to talk to about your father.'

'But you don't deny he's your lover, do you?'

Karen smiled and shook her head slowly from side to side.

'Pippa, please don't ask me questions like that about your father. I'm not prepared to answer them.'

Yet Pippa noticed her slight smile at the mention of his name.

'Why not? I thought you'd be delighted with your victory at getting him back. I thought you'd be happy to talk about him.'

Karen shook her head and said nothing.

'It was a shame about you miscarrying your baby,' Pippa said, her last desperate ploy to get Karen to open up to her. 'Otherwise, you might have been able to get my father to marry you instead of marrying my mother.'

She saw then a look of complete shock on Karen's face. She heard the swift intake of breath.

'How did you know about that, Pippa? Who told you?' she demanded.

'It doesn't matter how I found out, Karen. We both know it's true so I hope you're swallowing your little pill every day. By the sound of it, you'll need it to stop yourself from falling pregnant to my father again.'

And then a disquieting thought occurred to Pippa.

'Or have you flushed them down the toilet and decided you'll set a trap for him again?'

Karen got up and walked to the door. She wasn't prepared to sit and listen to any more of Pippa's bitter tirade.

'Please leave, Pippa,' she said, trying very hard not to cry. 'But just let me say one thing in my defence. I'm in love with your father. I've been in love with your father for a long time. Is that a crime?'

'No, Karen, it's not a crime. I'm sorry. I didn't mean to upset you so much. It's my father I'm upset with really. I just want you to give him up. Will you please give him up?'

She did not reply except to shake her head.

'I know you're angry with him, Pippa, but whatever happens don't let it ruin your relationship with your father. He'd be very disappointed if that happened.'

Pippa shrugged her shoulders.

'It's easy to say, Karen. You have no idea what it meant to me that he left New York to settle in Sydney to be with me. And he married my mother to give me his name. I thought he loved my mother. I expected them to go on being happy together.'

Karen reached out to her and hugged her briefly.

'Be kind to him, Pippa. He fought against this for a long time.'

But what about my mother, she wanted to say? Had he spared a thought for her?

She felt sorry for Karen in that moment and for the bitter nasty words she had spoken. She noticed tears beginning to trickle down Karen's cheeks. She saw something else too. She saw a woman who had fallen in love with a man who lacked the courage to admit his love for her when he should have. She knew then her father had made the wrong choice. He was in love with Karen. He had simply spent years denying it.

Philippe greeted his daughter with a warm embrace and then they walked together to his car. Her being angry with him did not change the way he felt about her. He was relieved to see she was slightly less angry with him than she had been earlier in the day.

'Before you say anything, I know you went to see Karen.'

He watched her reaction closely. There was going to be no point in denying anything to her. He had decided to be honest with her.

'How did you guess that's what I was going to do?'

He looked at her and smiled.

'Well, you did exactly the same in New York. Went off on your own to investigate my family. I thought there were parallels with this situation.'

He eased the big car into the traffic and headed towards Rose Bay.

She shrugged. She couldn't quite see the similarities in the situation but he was a highly intelligent man who always seemed to be one step ahead of everyone.

'Karen was upset by your visit. I'm not sure what it achieved, to be honest.'

Pippa shrugged. She wasn't sure herself now.

'I wanted to talk to her. I wanted to get her to think about ending it with you. Doesn't that make sense?'

He smiled to himself. He had never considered his daughter might be a go-between in his affair.

'And does she want to end it with me and just isn't prepared to tell me?'

He looked around at her. They were stopped at traffic lights for a few moments. Pippa shook her head.

'No,' she admitted. 'There's no sign she wants to end it with you. The question is: do you want to end it with her?'

He took a deep breath as he concentrated on the traffic that had started to move.

'No, Pippa, I don't want to end it with her. I have no plans to end my relationship with her.'

'Just like that,' she shot back at him. 'No equivocation. You're just content to go on seeing her. And what about my mother? Don't you think she deserves to know?'

He did not reply to her immediately. Instead, he concentrated on driving until he finally pulled into a parking spot.

'Let's walk,' he said, opening the door for her. 'This is my favourite place.'

They walked together in silence for some time along the harbour-side, a bevy of small boats bobbing at anchor near the shore, the summer sun glistening off the water, a cooling breeze lessening the early afternoon heat, the deep blue sky cloudless overhead. He thought the scene as near to perfection as anywhere he had ever been.

'Did you know this was the site for Australia's first international airport?' he said.

She shook her head. How could that be, she wondered?

'In the 1930s, Empire flying boats took off from here to fly to Southampton in England. They took ten days. They couldn't fly at night so there were nine overnight stops. It all ended with the war of course.'

'That's all very interesting,' she said, 'but you're avoiding the subject.'

'I am, aren't I?'

He smiled at her earnestness.

'When are you going to tell my mother about Karen?'

He turned to face her then. He wanted her to see he was sincere even though she wouldn't like his answer.

'I'm not going to tell her about Karen.'

Pippa was stunned by his answer.

'So you're just going to go on seeing Karen, or should I say, sleeping with her, whenever you can and expect that my mother is never going to find out. Everybody knows.'

'But nobody is going to tell her, are they? Unless you tell her?'

She shrugged her shoulders. He was too clever. He knew she wouldn't do that. She couldn't deliver the brutal truth to her mother. How could she ever have imagined she could do that?

'You knew I wouldn't be able to do that, didn't you?'

He nodded.

'Yes, I knew that. Because if you tell her, it means taking responsibility for what happens next.'

'And what would happen next?'

'You would force me to make a choice,' he said.

She nodded, understanding for the first time why he was reluctant to admit his affair.

'And that choice would be?'

She wondered then if he would answer her. For some time, all she could hear was the gentle lapping of the water against the harbour wall and the sound of traffic far off in the distance.

'I'm sorry, Pippa,' he said calmly, 'but that choice would be Karen.'

'So if you're sure of that now, why the delay? Why not tell my mother today?'

Once again, he did not answer her immediately. He wondered why life was so black and white to her. But perhaps I was like that too when I was her age, he thought.

'Because, Pippa, I want to be absolutely sure. I want Karen to be sure. I think I owe it to your mother to consider this step for a little longer.'

'Or, perhaps, you really don't want to make a decision at all. You just want to go on as you are, seeing Karen but remaining married to my mother? Is that how you see it working?'

He thought for a moment.

'To be honest, I don't know how I see it working. I've decided to take it a day at a time. And I think your mother has made that decision too.'

'What do you mean?'

He shook his head. She was forcing him to say things he didn't want to say.

'Pippa, you claim John told you about my conversation with your Uncle Richard. Is that right?'

She nodded.

'He heard it all. Every little detail.'

'If he heard every little detail, then you'll know about your mother. Do you think you've singled me out a bit unfairly? After all, how many times has she slept with her ex-husband? Just this most recent time when she was up there? How would I know for sure?'

Pippa was shocked into momentary silence. She hadn't expected him to fight back in this way, to sully her mother's reputation. She felt she had to say something in her mother's defence.

'She met him for the first time in years, according to John. And Marianne too. He came to her rescue when her horse nearly threw her off. And then he had dinner with them all at Prior Park.'

'And let me guess,' Philippe said. 'Her ex-husband took her to the wedding where John was groomsman. The one where she let us assume she had gone with Alice and William. And then he was so delighted by their reunion, he bought her an expensive gift. A new horse.'

He was grateful, in a way, for Pippa filling in the missing pieces.

'Pippa, I gave your mother the opportunity to tell me and she lied to me, so perhaps you can start to see things from my point of view too.'

Pippa looked at him closely. His mood had grown cynical.

'How do you feel about that?'

'Jealous. Angry. Betrayed.'

'Which is exactly the way she will feel when she finds out about Karen.'

'I know that.'

'Did you lie to her too?'

She was curious. Had her mother asked him outright if he was being unfaithful to her?

'I didn't need to,' he said. 'She never asked me.'

'So it's some sort of standoff, is it?'

'Looks like it, doesn't it?'

He put his arm around his daughter.

'I'm sorry if I sound bitter and cynical. I love your mother. I really wanted our marriage to work. Maybe it still can. Part of me is just not ready to give up on it. And that's the plain truth. But if you force my relationship with Karen into the open, then we'll be headed to the divorce court.'

'So that's it, is it? You just want me to go on ignoring what I know.'

'That's right, my dear daughter, you have to go on ignoring what you know. About me. About your mother. Besides I'm going back to New York for a few weeks very soon. Your mother isn't coming with me this time. It will give us both breathing space. And then we will all go over in the spring. As a family.'

'And pretend we're a happy family like we did last time we were all there together?'

'Yes, that's what I want. If we act like we're a happy family, then I believe we can be a happy family.'

She pulled away from him in disgust.

'Pippa, I've been honest with you. Too honest, perhaps. But I want to take time to make sure no one has any regrets. Now let's go and have some lunch.'

They had walked back the way they had come and as they

approached the carpark, he noticed a familiar car parked near his own. They stopped as Karen got out of the driver's side. She came towards them.

Despite everything, he was pleased to see her. Pippa watched as he slipped his arm around her waist and kissed her on the cheek.

'This is a surprise,' he said quietly.

'Not an unpleasant one, I hope.'

He laughed.

'No, my daughter knows all about us. My fault entirely.'

For Pippa, it was a surreal moment. With every thought, with every gesture, with every endearment, he's betraying my mother. And will go on betraying her. And my mother? Disappointed with her marriage, she seeks comfort from her ex-husband. What a mess, she thought.

'Let's all have lunch.'

She shook her head, ignoring her father's outstretched arm.

'I'm sorry but I've lost my appetite. You go and enjoy your lunch. I'll find my own way back.'

She turned then and walked away from them so they could not see the tears streaming down her face. He had told her the truth but now she wished with all her heart he had lied to her. She wished she had never pressured John to tell her what he had overheard.

But now she must live with the consequences. And live with the knowledge that one day the fairytale of their happy little family would collapse like the house of cards it was.

# CHAPTER 22

FOR SEVERAL HOURS, PIPPA drove around aimlessly as if she was a tourist taking in the highlights of Sydney's eastern suburbs. Watsons Bay. Bondi Beach. Coogee Beach. Each crowded with summer holidaymakers. Sunburnt bodies. Melting ice cream. Raucous shouts from impromptu games of cricket. But she had no appetite for seeing people enjoying themselves, especially the happy families with young children.

She sat, hunched over the steering wheel of her sports car, trying to decide how she could go home. Trying to find the courage to face her mother again. And her father. To watch them together, pretending their relationship was not teetering on a knife edge.

She started the engine again, not sure where she was heading. As she pulled out of the carpark, she headed without thinking in the direction of Woollahra, instead of choosing the more direct route back to her own home.

Without having made a conscious decision about her destination, within minutes she was walking up the driveway of Robert Clarke's house, unsure of what she was going to say, but needing to talk to someone.

She knocked on the door. She had hoped Anita would open it, rather than her father, but instead she came face to face with Robert Clarke.

'Is Anita home? I need to talk to her please, Dr Clarke.'

If Robert Clarke was surprised to find Pippa on his doorstep, he did not show it. He called out to his daughter and ushered her inside.

'Are you alright, Pippa,' he asked, alarmed at her distressed appearance. 'Why don't I make you a coffee? Or something stronger perhaps?'

She accepted the offer of a glass of wine, not because she wanted it, but to occupy him so she could speak with Anita.

'Pippa, what's up?' Anita asked, wondering why her friend was visiting unannounced.

And then Pippa burst into tears.

Anita looked across at her father as she ushered her friend towards a chair on the terrace. Father and daughter knew exactly what was coming then. They could see the anger, the dismay, the disbelief in her face. But how had she found out? And why now? Anita put her arm around her.

'Tell us what's wrong?'

Pippa looked at her then. She had hoped to speak privately with Anita but she noticed Robert Clarke hovering in the background.

'Did you know, Anita? Are my mother and I the last people to know?'

Anita saw the warning look in her father's eyes. She was careful what she said.

'What do you mean, Pippa? You're speaking in riddles.'

'I'm talking about my father and your cousin. How long has it been going on? How long has he been cheating on my mother?'

Anita shook her head.

'They're not questions you should be asking me, Pippa,' she said gently looking towards her father. 'Or my father for that matter.'

Pippa looked from one to the other.

'But you both knew about it, didn't you? I had no idea until a couple of days ago. I thought you'd be interested to know my father confirmed it to me today.'

She was met with audible gasps of shock.

'What do you mean your father confirmed it? Has something happened?'

It was Robert Clarke who posed the question. He wondered how it was possible a man would say such a thing to his daughter. He had never been in that situation but he could imagine that denial would be any man's response.

Pippa took a deep breath. Her crying had stopped.

'We were down at Bowral for a family dinner. My father had an argument with my Uncle Richard,' she explained. 'He accused my father of cheating on my mother. It was meant to be a private conversation but my half-brother John overheard it. I forced him to tell me what he had overheard. It was devastating. According to John, my father said, *I'm enjoying a very warm welcome in Karen's bed.*'

Robert Clarke shook his head from side to side. The revelation had come as no surprise to him, except for the way it had come.

'I tackled him this morning about it. He wouldn't discuss it with me at home. I met him at lunchtime. He confirmed it all. And then he took Karen to lunch. He actually invited me to have lunch with them.'

There was silence. No one could think of what to say.

'My father married my mother because of me. But it wasn't enough, as it turned out. I know he had an affair with Karen before he married my mother. It wouldn't surprise me if it's been going on all the time my parents have been married.'

Robert Clarke shook his head. He could see how disappointed and disillusioned Pippa had become. Would her relationship with her father ever recover? But what could he say?

'Has he indicated he's going to tell your mother, Pippa? Or are you going to tell your mother?'

She shook her head.

'No, as my father cleverly pointed out, no one is likely to tell her, regardless of how much they gossip about it. I have to go home now and pretend I know nothing. Pretend I don't know Karen was pregnant to him before he married my mother. Pretend that I don't know, as my mother and I were driving to Bowral together, he was with Karen.'

The three of them sat together on the terrace, sipping wine, not knowing what else to say. It was Robert Clarke who finally spoke.

'You know once this is out in the open there will be consequences. It would be a big burden to be responsible for bringing it into the open.'

Pippa nodded.

'I understand that Dr Clarke,' she said. 'It's what my father said.'

'What's he going to do?'

She shrugged.

'Nothing for the moment. That's what he says.'

He nodded. He had no experience of situations such as this but Philippe's unwillingness to confess his affair to his wife did not surprise him.

'This may be cold comfort but I'm sure he didn't have anything to do with Karen again until very recently.'

'Until he started to see her in hospital every day, I assume,' she said.

He gestured helplessly.

'It seems likely that's where it restarted.'

'Did you know she had been pregnant to him, Dr Clarke?'

He shook his head.

'No, not until very recently when my brother told me. She miscarried the baby in London. But I always assumed your father never knew about it.'

Pippa shrugged.

'Well, he knows now. My uncle tried to shock him with that piece of news but apparently Karen told my father recently.'

She was calmer now. She had needed to talk to someone. Anita and her father were the only people she could think of who would understand. She was pleased Anita's mother had been out. She trusted Anita and her father but she would not have spoken so freely in front of Patricia Clarke.

'I hope it's helped to talk to us, Pippa,' he said. 'We won't repeat any of what you've said. But it would be a shame if this affects your relationship with your father.'

She looked at him then. *How could it not?*

'I always thought he was above reproach, Dr Clarke,' she said sadly. 'He was someone I looked up to. He'd sacrificed his career in New

York to be near me. He had gone to great lengths to find me. Our relationship seemed special. His relationship with my mother seemed special. And it turns out he's just like a lot of other men, a two-timing cheating husband.'

He made one last attempt to help her get past her disappointment.

'I'm very reluctant to say this, Pippa,' he said, 'but perhaps it needs to be said. My niece Karen has always been in love with him, ever since they first met here in this house. I know he loved your mother but I think he's always been in love with Karen too. I think it would be a mistake to see this as just a tawdry affair.'

She thought about it. Perhaps he's right. But it would take her some time to come to terms with the person her father really was. And that he was not the man she had placed high on a pedestal.

'Thank you for listening to me,' she said. 'I should get home now.'

Anita closed the door behind her friend and turned to face her father.

'Damn him,' she said. 'And Karen too. As if Pippa hasn't been through enough in her life. She's at a point in her life now when everything's rosy. And then she discovers her father can't keep his hands to himself.'

Robert Clarke looked at his daughter. How much does she know? He sighed. He too felt the burden of secrets.

'As I said to Pippa, I think it's much more than an affair to him,' he said.

He had come to believe Philippe had made the wrong choice in turning his back on Karen.

'You saw that stunning diamond pendant Karen was wearing on Christmas Eve? He gave it to her. And her fashion business? It's now debt free, thanks to him. And your mother heard from Karen's mother just today that she and Bianca are going to New York at the end of the month. Is it just a coincidence that Philippe has told me he'll be away for up to four weeks from mid January seeing to matters regarding his father's estate? His wife isn't going with him.'

Anita sat down abruptly then. She began to see the depth of his involvement with her cousin.

'This is only ever going to end one way, isn't it?'

He nodded.

'Unless his wife is prepared to turn a blind eye to him keeping Karen as his mistress.'

Anita thought about this for a moment.

'If you want my opinion,' she said, 'Karen would be happy with that for a while but not forever.'

'I agree,' her father said. 'She won't be prepared to go on being the other woman indefinitely. But she won't give him up easily either. Not this time.'

Anita wondered then how much more her father knew.

'I had no idea Karen had been pregnant to him before he married Pippa's mother. That was a shock,' Anita said, thinking back over what had been said.

'It was a surprise to me too when your uncle told me only a few weeks ago.'

'But she never told Philippe until very recently. Doesn't that strike you as strange?'

He tried to avoid his daughter's direct gaze. He was not good at dissembling. One reason had occurred to him when he had heard she had told Philippe. But Anita was too clever for him. She had worked out why he was suddenly being so reluctant to answer her question.

'If the topic of pregnancy came up between them, do you think it could be because she's pregnant to him again?'

She looked at her father closely, trying to decide if he was being evasive.

'Isn't that how most women get reluctant men to the altar?' he said. 'She might decide it's a way to hasten things along, although his divorce would take time.'

Would Karen do that, she wondered? She would be at the upper limits of her child-bearing years. And with a history of miscarriage, it was more likely to happen again.

'She might miscarry for a second time.'

She watched her father's response carefully. Did he know something about Karen's condition that no one else did? Had she consulted him?

'Possibly but it could have been a one-off. It doesn't mean she won't carry the next baby to full term.'

'The next baby? That's a bit specific. Has she been to see you?'

He shook his head.

'No, it was just speculation on my part. It could be wide of the mark. I have absolutely no idea whether it's true or not.'

He poured another glass of wine for Anita and then for himself.

'Whatever happens, you'll need to help Pippa. You'll need to be there for her because there will be no way to avoid a scandal. Her father is of much more interest to the gossip columns now he's wealthy. And they'll have a field day with this. Especially if Karen is pregnant to him.'

'And Pippa's mother?' she asked. 'How will she cope?'

'I think she'll be devastated. And if Karen is pregnant to him, you can add humiliation to that too.'

Anita thought about it all for a moment.

'The only thing that will stop it being humiliating for her is if she decides herself the marriage is over. If she's ready to move on.'

Her father looked at her, unsure of what she was thinking.

'Is that likely?' he asked.

'Who knows but a few people noticed her flirting with Nicholas Gleeson at our drinks party on Christmas Eve. He was certainly being very attentive to her, having realised Karen was unavailable.'

Her father remembered then how his own brother had commented on Gleeson's interest in Julia.

'Your uncle thinks he's a pretty good chap. His first wife treated him appallingly, he told me. Said she was a bitch.'

Neither of them had heard Patricia Clarke come home. She walked quietly onto the terrace where father and daughter were sitting to hear the tail end of their conversation.

'Was that Pippa Duval's car I saw leaving our street?' she asked, without really needing a reply.

Robert got up to give his wife the customary peck on the cheek to welcome her home.

'It was,' he said, without elaboration.

'She looked pretty upset about something.'

'She was,' Robert replied, 'but we're not going to talk about it.'

She laughed derisively.

'Let me guess. The poor girl has discovered the truth about her father.'

They both nodded but said nothing.

'I don't suppose you're interested in the fact that I spotted her father down at Rose Bay a few hours ago with his arm around Karen. Bold as brass. As if he didn't care who saw them. Is that why Pippa was here? She needed someone to talk to. She does know, doesn't she?'

'She knows.'

He did not elaborate.

'And Julia?'

'Not yet,' he said.

She laughed then.

'It's always the wife who is the last to know. Why does that not surprise me. But then, from what I was told today, she may have her own secrets.'

'What do you mean, her own secrets?' Anita demanded.

She knew how much her mother loved to gossip.

'Angela Dixon was at lunch with us. We got talking. She's been talking to Kate Lester or should I say Kate Belleville, Julia's sister-in-law. Gossip is apparently swirling around up where she comes from about how friendly Julia had suddenly become with her first husband after years of not speaking. During her most recent visit apparently. I bet Pippa didn't mention that.'

'What's wrong with friendly?' Robert asked. 'He would be the father of Pippa's half-brother John. They have a child together.'

She smiled at her husband, as if to say *how naïve can you be?*

'There's friendly and there's friendly if you get my meaning,' she said relishing the fact that she could counter their news with her own gossip.

'They spent the night together after a wedding she went to with him. That's how friendly she is with him now.'

Robert Clarke was genuinely shocked. He had thought it very

unlikely that Julia Duval would be the type of woman to betray her husband, even if he was betraying her.

'And Angela confirmed all this from talking to Kate?'

Patricia smiled.

'Well, let's just say I pieced it all together and Angela didn't deny it. She's wondering if Julia and Philippe will still be together by the time Paul Belleville marries Nancy at the end of July. Which reminds me, Anita, we're going to have to get together with Nancy and the other two girls to start thinking about the bridesmaids' dresses. And Angela is going to host a pre-wedding party for Nancy.'

She looked wistfully at Anita then.

'The first of your friends to get married. Who's going to be next, I wonder?'

Anita threw back her head and laughed.

'Well, it won't be me, Mother. It won't be me.'

# CHAPTER 23

ROBERT CLARKE LOOKED UP at the sound of a sharp knock and his office door opening almost simultaneously. It was late afternoon and he was finished for the day.

Normally he would welcome a visit from Philippe but the recent revelations about his private life had eroded his respect for his colleague. He greeted him cautiously as Philippe eased himself into a visitor chair. He sensed the lack of warmth in his colleague's greeting.

'Robert,' he said, 'I think it's time we chatted about my future here. I'm struggling to do justice to my patients and manage the other parts of my life. I don't want to risk making a catastrophic mistake during an operation. I want to leave before there's any chance of that.'

He paused, waiting for a reaction. He fully expected Robert Clarke to try to talk him out of leaving so his ready agreement surprised him.

'I think you should leave too, Philippe,' he said, hardly pausing for breath. He was grateful Philippe was going to make it easy for him.

Surprised, Philippe merely nodded. He had always been valued, lauded even, as a top surgeon at the hospital. But he could see something had altered Robert Clarke's opinion of him.

'By the sound of it, you think I'm no longer the asset to the hospital I once was, Robert. Is that what you're trying to tell me?'

Robert Clarke shook his head. What else could he be but honest?

Brutally direct even.

'It's not your work that's the problem. It's the scandal that's about to break over your head that I need to distance the hospital from.'

Philippe sighed. At least he's being honest, he thought, but I'm not going to make it easy for him.

'And what scandal would that be, Robert?' he asked, his voice suddenly icy.

'Oh, come off it, Philippe. Your affair with my niece. Everyone knows about it. It's the worst kept secret in the hospital.'

He was annoyed that his private life should be so openly discussed.

'I don't see what that's got to do with anything here. It's nothing to do with my professional life.'

But Robert Clarke shook his head.

'That's where you're wrong. The board expects a certain level of personal integrity. A senior surgeon should be setting an example. A moral example if you like.'

Philippe laughed out loud at that suggestion.

'Really. That's what they expect? And they all lead exemplary lives, do they? Don't make me laugh. I've seen at least two of them in doubtful company. And your brother is hardly a paragon of virtue.'

But Robert would not be sidetracked.

'That's not the point, Philippe. You've become the very public face of this hospital in recent times. The gossip columnists are going to have a field day with this story. It's not what we want for the hospital.'

'So you're worried about a story that will last a day until something more salacious comes along? That's if it ever sees the light of day.'

Robert shrugged his shoulders. It wasn't something he really wanted to discuss but Philippe had annoyed him with his high-handed contempt for public opinion. He could not stop the anger rising in his voice.

'And tell me, Philippe, how does your wife feel about your relationship with Karen? Is she happy to turn a blind eye to it?'

It seemed improbable to him that Julia would still be ignorant of her husband's infidelity. All the signs were there, at least to everyone else in their circle.

'I haven't discussed my relationship with Karen with my wife if you must know.'

The irritation in his voice was beginning to show.

'But your daughter knows.'

'Yes, she does.'

He wondered how Robert knew about Pippa and then he realised Pippa had most probably confided in one of her best friends but he needed to know for sure.

'I guess Pippa told Anita?'

Robert nodded. It was as far as he was prepared to go in breaking Pippa's confidence.

'And what happens next, Philippe? I know Karen is besotted with you. Will she just go on being your mistress?'

Philippe was beginning to run out of patience with the personal questions. He was not used to being interrogated.

'Yes, Robert,' he said, his voice hardening, 'your niece is happy to go on being my mistress. And before you ask, I expect Julia to go on being my wife.'

Robert Clarke was shocked at the arrogance in his voice. Somewhere along the way he realised Philippe had changed. He was in no doubt that his sudden wealth had changed him.

'You sound very confident but what if your wife finds out about Karen, which surely she must?'

Philippe shrugged.

'Then I'll be left with a decision to make, depending on how Julia reacts.'

Robert shook his head slowly from side to side.

'Just like that. You think your wife will accept you being unfaithful to her when it suits you.'

He didn't enjoy Robert's moralising.

'It might shock you to know that she might accept it. There are two sides to every story, Robert. Remember that.'

'Two sides, Philippe. What do you mean by that?'

He couldn't imagine why a woman such as Julia would willingly accept her husband's continued infidelity.

'You may be interested to know it's not just me you need to lecture. I found out recently my beautiful loving wife is being unfaithful to me.'

Robert had never expected the conversation to descend into such tawdry revelations about Philippe's marriage. He was careful not to reveal he had already been told about Julia.

'I see you're struggling to believe it. Just like I struggled to believe it too. But by the time my plane lands in New York, I expect my lovely wife will probably be enjoying the amorous attentions of her former husband.'

'You seem very sure of that, Philippe. Has she admitted it to you?'

Philippe laughed, a hollow cynical sound.

'Do you know how it feels to have caught your wife lying to you about another man? Or to have her return home to you after ten days away with fading love bites on her neck?'

This was all beyond Robert Clarke's experience. He had never heard a man destroy his wife's reputation quite so contemptuously.

'You speak about your wife in a way that tells me your marriage cannot possibly survive.'

He shrugged his shoulders.

'You're probably right, Robert. But it may surprise you to know I still enjoy making love to her. It's not a loveless marriage. Far from it.'

Robert wondered then if his niece knew that but Philippe could see immediately where his thoughts were taking him.

'If you feel tempted to tell Karen, please don't.'

'Why not? I think someone needs to open her eyes to you.'

He laughed cynically.

'Do you really think so? For a start she wouldn't believe you.'

'She might.'

Philippe shook his head.

'No, she wouldn't. And she would only be upset that you tried. She's your niece so I will save you from the embarrassment of hearing the intimate details of how welcoming she is when I can get the time to see her.'

Philippe saw the look of distaste on his colleague's face. Had he gone too far? Probably. But he deserves it, Philippe thought.

'So it's just sex for you with Karen, is it? That's it. She's a very sexy woman who's available to you whenever you want her. It strokes your enormous ego.'

At some point in their conversation, the friendship between the two men began to fall apart. All the things Robert had admired about Philippe were being torn asunder.

'No, Robert, it's not just about sex, as delightful as it is to be her lover. I love her. But my problem is I still love my wife too.'

After all that he had heard from Philippe, he found this statement impossible to believe.

'Yet you speak about your wife with such contempt.'

'No, not contempt, Robert. Disappointment is the right word. But I accept I'm partly to blame for having neglected her for months. But I'm sure she'll go on being unfaithful to me. I don't think her former husband is the kind of man to take *no* for an answer. He'll want her in his bed again.'

There was nothing more Philippe could say that could shock Robert Clarke. He was seeing a bitterness in Philippe or was it jealousy? Jealousy that his wife might have discovered she preferred her first husband to him.

'It's Karen I'm concerned about,' he said, trying to remain civil. 'What if she gets pregnant to you again?'

Philippe laughed out loud. *Was nothing private between him and Karen now?*

'So all the secrets are out now, it seems.'

Robert nodded.

'They are. But you haven't answered my question.'

'She isn't pregnant. Not as far as I know unless you know something different?'

'No, I don't.'

'Then we'll cross that bridge when we get to it, if we get to it. And just so you know everything about my private life, Karen will be in New York when I'm there. I'm helping her and Bianca get into the

New York fashion scene. But I'd be grateful if you kept this information to yourself.'

He looked at Philippe closely. He was seeing a different side to the man he had known and admired for more than a decade. A man seemingly unconcerned about being unfaithful to his wife. A man apparently expecting his marriage to remain intact despite the accusations he had levelled at his wife and his own extramarital activities. A man whose wealth now gave him the means to lavish expensive gifts on his mistress. There was nothing much left to say.

'Will I draft a resignation letter for you to sign?'

'Yes, Robert, let's do that. I'll sign it tomorrow.'

'And when you are back, we'll have a farewell dinner in your honour.'

'Thanks, that would be nice,' Philippe said as he got up to leave.

And then he turned back from the doorway.

'I've been very frank with you, Robert. Too frank perhaps. I'm asking you as a friend not to repeat anything I've said.'

'I won't, Philippe, I won't repeat anything. But I do hope you find a resolution to your personal life.'

'So do I, Robert, so do I.'


Robert Clarke continued to sit in his office as the late afternoon turned to early evening. He was trying to make sense of it all.

He couldn't imagine continuing with a marriage where he knew his wife had been unfaithful to him, knowing that she would probably be so again. Nor could he imagine keeping a mistress as Philippe was quite prepared to do while expecting his marriage to continue. Yet he knew it was not an uncommon practice for wealthy men, including his brother.

But he was disappointed to see his niece cast in that role.

And then he began to contemplate the prospect of Karen being happy to continue with the arrangement. He realised everyone had always assumed she would one day want a wedding ring on her finger but he wondered, for the first time, if her relationship with Philippe suited her too. After all, she's fully immersed in her fashion business and she can do exactly as she pleases without reference to a husband.

Perhaps Philippe's marriage would continue as he predicted. Perhaps his wife would turn a blind eye to his infidelity in return for him doing the same with her. He shook his head. Those ideas felt fanciful when he examined them more closely. He was pleased there were none of these dramas in what others might regard as his very dull private life.

Philippe was surprised to find both Julia and Pippa were out when he arrived home. The house had an empty, silent feel as he began going from room to room turning on the lights before pouring himself a glass of wine.

He looked around him. For the first time, he was convinced it was time to exchange their relatively modest house for a harbourside mansion. A house with a view down the harbour was suddenly a very appealing prospect.

He was too restless to sit down. Instead, he began to pace around the living room, preoccupied with what he had said to Robert Clarke. He realised he had lost control of the conversation in a way he hadn't planned. He had said some things he shouldn't have said.

And then he thought about Pippa. In the nearly two weeks since their conversation, she had hardly spoken to him. Julia had noticed and quizzed him about whether they had argued. He had brushed it off as a petty disagreement. But he knew the big risk lay in Pippa not being able to keep her side of the bargain. He heard the front door open then. He expected the two of them to walk in, but it was Julia by herself.

'Pippa not with you?'

Julia tossed her car keys onto the hall table. The sound echoed through the quiet house.

'Didn't she tell you? She's moved out. She's sharing a flat with a friend from the hospital. I've just come from helping her settle in.'

He tried to keep his voice calm.

'That was a sudden decision.'

'It was,' she said, trying to gauge his reaction.

He poured her a glass of wine and handed it to her.

'Perhaps it will be a good thing for her,' he said evenly. 'Give her more independence.'

He looked at Julia closely. He was always good at reading her moods but not this time.

'By the way, I have some news,' he said. 'I will be signing my resignation letter from the hospital tomorrow. I can't give the work my full attention anymore.'

She shrugged. She knew it must come, sooner or later. He was getting too busy to be able to fulfil such a demanding role.

'Robert Clarke was no doubt disappointed.'

'He was expecting it, really.'

She nodded. *It saved him the embarrassment of asking you to resign,* she wanted to say.

'There'll be a farewell dinner for me when I get back.'

'Which is when?' she asked.

He had not told her specifically when he would return.

'Third week of February most likely.'

We could be casual friends the way we're exchanging this banal information, she thought. He's on edge, holding himself back. Being careful about what he says.

'When you get back, we should talk about our relationship,' she said, sipping her wine. She wanted to see his reaction.

He looked up at her then. He had been concentrating on some business papers he had just picked up. He set them aside and walked across to where she was standing.

'This is sudden,' he said. 'I thought everything was good between us.'

She shrugged her shoulders. Now that the moment had come, she couldn't bring herself to accuse him outright of what Pippa had hinted at. More than hinted at.

'I heard some rumours, Philippe. Disturbing rumours about you.'

He smiled, relieved that she seemed reluctant to be specific. Could it be because she doesn't want me to ask her the same question, he wondered?

He took her face in his hands. He kissed her gently.

251

'You shouldn't listen to rumours, my darling,' he said smoothly.

If only I could believe him, she thought. He had sensed her doubt.

'You have absolutely no reason to be concerned,' he lied. 'I'm as committed to our marriage as I ever was.'

He turned then and opened his briefcase. He handed her a small box. She opened it to discover a slim single strand diamond necklace nestled in the satin lining with small delicate earrings to match. He lifted the necklace out of the box and put it around her neck.

'It's beautiful, Philippe,' she said, delighted by the simple beauty of the necklace and the matching earrings. 'You are way too generous.'

But he shook his head.

'Being too generous is not possible when it comes to buying you gifts, my darling,' he said. 'I have not always been the most attentive husband in recent months. Nor the best husband.'

To her, his words sounded sincere but there was now the nagging doubt of the stories that would not go away. She had probed Pippa's anger towards her father. There had to be a reason for it. She had never believed it could be explained away as a petty disagreement.

*Ask him, Mother*, Pippa had said. *Ask him how friendly he is with Karen Clarke. Ask him about the diamond pendant she wears constantly.* She had seen a deep anger in her daughter that alarmed her. But she could not bring herself to mention Karen's name to Philippe, not with his departure imminent.

'We'll do something special together when I get back,' he said. 'I think we should move house too. Why don't you start looking for a property with harbour views while I'm away? In the eastern suburbs. It will keep you occupied. Or are you planning to visit your family?'

She couldn't mistake the hard edge in his voice when he asked about her plans.

'No specific plans at the moment, Philippe,' she said.

He laughed quietly then.

'I thought you'd be keen to ride the horse James gave you before Christmas.'

He had the satisfaction of seeing a flush of colour on her cheeks. He knew it had been a cruel thing to say but he couldn't help himself.

There were times when he could not get beyond the fact she had been unfaithful to him.

Perhaps Robert Clarke is right, he thought. Our marriage can't survive. And then he thought about Karen. He hadn't seen her for weeks so he was already looking forward to their reunion. The itinerary for Karen and Bianca's travel to New York was carefully hidden in his briefcase. It was his jealousy of his wife's infidelity that had clouded his thinking. But what would she feel when she knew the truth about his affair with Karen?

In quiet moments, he remembered back to the day more than a decade ago that had changed their lives forever. The day he and Julia had met in a hotel dining room. A happy accident. Serendipitous some would say. It was the day Julia realised he had not died in the war as her mother had insisted. The day she realised she would eventually get to meet the child she had given up for adoption.

Later, with the collapse of her marriage, it had seemed inevitable they should marry. Nearly ten years on, the question now was whether their marriage would survive. He clearly remembered the anguish of being caught between his desire for Karen and his desire to fulfil his promise to Julia.

He wondered if the deterioration in their relationship had its origins in his uncertainty all those years ago. Had there ever been a time when he hadn't been torn between his love for Julia so deeply rooted in their shared past and his love for Karen? He clearly remembered the pain of turning his back on Karen to marry Julia. Yet, for years, she had never been far from his thoughts. And now? He knew he could not turn his back on her again.

He remembered Pippa. Young, excited to meet him all those years ago. Hero worshipping him. Putting her entire trust in him. And now? She could hardly stand to speak to him. Had he been too honest with her? Could he have been more conciliatory?

He had sounded cold and unfeeling when he recalled their conversation. Looking back, he realised he had handled it badly as if his anger with himself had coloured every conversation since.

And Karen? She was trusting too. Giving herself to him without any commitment in return. Delighted to see him whenever he was available. Was Robert Clarke correct when he said it stroked his ego to have such a beautiful woman as his mistress?

There were times when he did not like the person he had become. He wondered if he had become the type of man he had long despised. Arrogant. Entitled. Self-centred. Had money done that to him? Had it eroded his integrity in a way he was only beginning to understand?

'You look as though your thoughts are a million miles away, Philippe,' Julia said, finally breaking the silence that had descended between them.

He looked at her and smiled.

'I think we need a fresh start,' he said.

Yet the hollow sincerity of his words echoed through his mind.

'Yes,' she agreed. 'Let's talk when you get back.'

He put his arms around her almost as if he was apologising to her. Despite everything, she found his physical closeness reassuring. She wondered then what compromises would be needed for their marriage to continue. Was it enough to continue it for Pippa's sake and have the outside world believe everything was fine?

Once she would have scoffed at the idea. Would it be better for them to start to live separate lives and remain married? She had no appetite for a third marriage. She had no appetite to return to her first husband as his wife. Yet it had surprised her how much she enjoyed being with him as a lover.

There was one role she would refuse to play. The wronged wife waiting at home for him. The woman other women would pity. She began to think about her future. Think about the things she would do just for herself. Not because she was Philippe's wife. Or Pippa's mother. Or John's mother.

And when she felt like it, she would slide the rings off her finger and become Julia Belleville again. She would be herself. Not some-one's wife. Not someone's mother. Just herself.

But what life could she fashion for her new self, cut adrift from everything that had anchored her life for the past decade? Her husband. His work. His friends. Their life together had been her life.

But the next phase of Philippe's life? She was beginning to face the fact that it would very likely be without her.

# CHAPTER 24

DAVID CLARKE STOOD ALONGSIDE his daughter Karen looking at the showroom floor of the latest dealership he had just added to his portfolio of business interests.

'Take your pick,' he said, his arm around his daughter. 'I thought you might like something different.'

'My new car is only a couple of months old,' she said.

It had recently been replaced after being written off months before in the accident that had almost claimed her life.

'I thought you might like a sports car like Pippa Duval's?'

She surveyed the range of gleaming MGs and then turned and pulled a face.

'Don't you think that would be a bit obvious, Father,' she said.

'Well, he could have got a good deal buying one for his daughter and one for you.'

She shook her head.

'I need too much space for my samples and all that stuff I carry around. A sports car would be an indulgence. It would be impractical.'

And then she began to understand why her father had gone all out for the dealership when it had come up for sale.

'You thought Philippe might set a trend for wealthy fathers indulging their daughters? Or sons perhaps?'

He laughed.

'If you'd seen the figures, you would have seen how the sales have picked up since his daughter was pictured with the car in the Sunday paper. Is she talking to him again or is she still mad with him about you?'

She shrugged.

'I don't know,' she said. 'I haven't seen him since that day at Rose Bay. But Anita told me she's moved out of her parents' house. She's pretty upset with her father. And me.'

'Well, you'll be seeing him soon. She wouldn't like that if she knew.'

She nodded. He was right. Pippa would be incandescent with rage.

'Pippa told Anita she sees his trip to New York as a chance for her father to have some thinking time alone. I hope my mother doesn't go on talking about my trip. Someone will know he's away too and put two and two together.'

He noticed then a stunning diamond on the finger of her right hand.

'Another gift?'

She nodded.

'He's very generous.'

She held out her hand so he could admire the ring.

'Wrong hand though, isn't it?'

She gave him a sly look.

'Perhaps. And perhaps when the mood takes me, I wear it on my left hand.'

'And what does he say about that? Or do you not do that when he's around?'

'Oh, no, I do it to tease him.'

He understood then how easy it was for his daughter to tease a man and get away with it.

'But he hasn't said he will leave his wife for you, has he?'

She shook her head.

'No, not yet. He feels guilty because he wasn't there to marry her when she was pregnant with Pippa. Marrying her was his way of making amends. And making amends to Pippa.'

'But he left you in the lurch, my dear girl. Don't you forget that.'

'He didn't know I was pregnant,' she said, continuing to defend him. 'But I told him about that recently.'

She saw the look of surprise on her father's face.

'What did he say?'

She shrugged.

'What you might expect. He was sorry that he had put me through all that. He'd had no idea.'

David Clarke looked at his daughter closely then. There was a new maturity about her, a new contentment but also something else, he thought. A sense of anticipation at what was to come in her life perhaps. He decided to probe a little further.

'Something tells me you haven't quite given up on having his child, am I right?'

He got no direct answer except a slight smile as she slid her arm through his.

'Let's go and have some lunch,' she said quietly. 'You don't want people here gossiping about me, do you? It's the wrong place to be having this conversation.'

They walked together through the showroom to the offices at the back. As they walked, they were greeted deferentially by the staff keen to please the new boss. The gossip about his beautiful daughter had preceded their visit but Karen was oblivious to the admiring glances of the male staff members and the envious sighs of the female staff members. She would have been alarmed to know they all knew she was Philippe Duval's mistress.

Karen stood at a large window on the first floor of the dealership waiting patiently for her father to gather his papers. She had a good view of the most secluded part of the customer car park. Her father looked up, wondering what was attracting her attention. He walked across the room to stand alongside her and then followed the direction of her gaze.

'I'd know that car anywhere,' he said, nodding in the direction of the silver Mercedes, 'but he left for New York last week, didn't he?'

She nodded.

'He did indeed.'

Father and daughter watched as Julia Duval got out of the driver's side. But it was the passenger who drew their attention. They saw him walk to the driver's side and extend his hand to her. And they both saw her look at him and smile.

Father and daughter watched transfixed as the unknown passenger bent his head towards Julia and kissed her, his arms encircling her. There was no doubt in Karen's mind nor in her father's mind they were looking at Julia with her lover.

'A very tender scene. I wish I had a camera. It might be a way to speed up Philippe's decision making about his marriage, don't you think?'

Karen was simply shocked. Philippe rarely spoke about his wife to her. She had heard snippets of gossip which amounted to little more than speculation.

'Do you think Philippe knows he's being made a fool of?' she asked, without really expecting a reply.

'Well, if he doesn't, I'm sure you'll find a subtle way to tell him.'

They had been so enthralled by the scene they had not heard Tony Macintyre, the manager of the dealership, walk up beside them.

'That's probably Mr and Mrs James Fitzroy. They have an appointment to look at an MG B for their son's twenty-first,' he said, noticing who had caught his boss's interest.

'Oh, really, you think that's Mrs James Fitzroy, do you?' Karen said with a harsh laugh. 'She was once Mrs James Fitzroy and she looks like she'd like to be Mrs James Fitzroy again but she is actually Mrs Philippe Duval. That's Julia Duval.'

He was trying desperately to make sense of the information.

'Really? You seem to know a lot about Mrs Duval and her husband,' he said before he realised the extraordinary faux pas he had just committed.

He'd been told only that morning by staff members better informed than himself that Karen was Philippe Duval's mistress. He had been assured it was gossip that had set the eastern suburbs social scene alight for months, especially with his becoming so wealthy through his American father.

'I think we'll just go quietly out the staff entrance, Tony,' David Clarke said.

He did not relish the prospect of his daughter coming face to face with Julia Duval.

'And whatever you do, don't mention my name or Karen's to them. You'll lose a sale if you do that.'

Karen laughed. It was always a question of commerce for her father. That was always foremost in his mind. But the scene had left her feeling a frisson of excitement. *So Julia is not quite as in love with Philippe as everyone imagines. Or is it simply that she isn't going to play the part of the little woman at home pretending everything is delightful with her marriage.* These thoughts would continue to occupy Karen for some time.

'That was a surprise,' she said, as she settled into the front passenger seat alongside her father.

'Indeed, it was,' he said. He too was thinking about the implications for his daughter's relationship. 'I reckon she's going to be spending the afternoon in bed with him by the way he was groping her.'

And then he remembered something else he'd been told.

'I hear Nicholas Gleeson is taking her to the law firm's Australia Day cruise on the harbour which they put on every year for their good clients. You remember he met her at Robert's house on Christmas Eve. He was pretty keen on her. Would you like to come with me? Your mother's not keen on boats. Might be fun. You might find it interesting to report on his wife's activities.'

She smiled. He could see she was weighing up the pros and cons.

'It would be fun, wouldn't it?'

He nodded approvingly.

'That's the idea. Assemble your ammunition. Go after what you want. He's not going to move on from her unless you put pressure on him.'

She laughed.

'You make it sound like a difficult business deal where I need to get the upper hand.'

'Something like that. My advice is you must use whatever leverage you have if you want to be his wife. If you don't want him to marry you, then settle for being his pampered mistress but make sure the diamonds keep coming.'

She looked across at her father then. She was amused rather than shocked. But he had surprised her.

'I thought you'd be shocked at the idea of me going on being his mistress.'

He shook his head.

'Not if it's what you want.'

'And if I was to have his child?'

'I think you'd want him to marry you then, surely?'

'Perhaps. It would take so long to get a divorce I'd be having the baby out of wedlock anyway.'

He shrugged. His daughter always had the capacity to surprise him. He had seen no sign of pregnancy.

'It's up to you but you know I'd never say *no* to a grandson. But if you're not married, he must have the name of Clarke. Not Duval. I could cope with that.'

'I'll keep that in mind,' she said, laughing, as he drove back towards the eastern suburbs and one of their favourite lunch spots.


David Clarke would not have been surprised to know his prediction for Julia's afternoon activities came close to being very accurate.

Having successfully negotiated the purchase of the same model of car Philippe had bought for Pippa, they had headed out of the city and by mid-afternoon, they were checking into the best suite at the famous landmark hotel in the Blue Mountains.

James walked to the window with its sweeping views of the Megalong Valley which stretched for miles below them. He turned back towards Julia.

'A wonderful choice,' he said as he slid his arms around her waist.

'I thought it was better to get out of the city.'

'Good idea,' he said. 'A very good idea.'

And then he looked at her closely.

'I'm sorry if I was the cause of trouble between you and Philippe. I heard he ...'

But he couldn't finish the sentence. She finished it for him.

'You heard he forced himself on me?'

He nodded.

'It's my fault he hurt you. I'm so sorry. I hope he apologised later.'

'He did.'

He waited for her to say more.

'Who told you about what happened at Bowral?' she asked. 'Was it Alice?'

He shook his head.

'I first heard about it all from John.'

'John? Really? What did he tell you?'

He realised then he should not have mentioned John's role because Julia had spoken only to Alice.

'You don't know, do you, that John overhead a heated discussion between Philippe and Richard after the dinner.'

She sat down on the bed. Everything started to make sense.

'Please tell me what John told you. Did Richard accuse him of something?'

He came and sat alongside her and put his arm around her.

'He did. Richard accused him of cheating on you.'

'Did John hear what he replied?'

'He did but I don't think I can tell you.' He shook his head. 'I don't think I should tell you.'

He noticed then the bruising on her arms had not quite faded completely.

'He did this to you, didn't he?'

She nodded.

'He got quite physical with me. Angry. He must have been pro-voked by what Richard said.'

But James shook his head.

'It wasn't what Richard said. It was what he didn't say.'

'What do you mean?'

'John told me Philippe asked Richard outright if you were getting friendly with me again. Philippe described you as being nervous and anxious around him when you came back to Sydney.'

He reached out and stroked her neck.

'Remember the telltale signs I was so careless as to leave. He'd noticed them too.'

She put her head in her hands.

'Of course, he's a doctor. He's used to looking at patients. He'd notice things others wouldn't. But how would Richard know about us?'

'I never thought about the need to be more discreet. I'm so sorry. There was a lot of gossip about us after the wedding we went to. And John told me we'd been seen afterwards. I suspect John might have told Richard.'

'And Richard was then too slow to deny it to Philippe?'

'I believe that's what happened.'

At least she now understood his anger.

'He won't do it again,' she said.

But she could see James remained unconvinced.

'He was ashamed of himself,' she said, defending him.

James said nothing. In his mind, Philippe had crossed a threshold it would be easy for him to cross again if he got angry with her.

'But you haven't told me the other part, James. Don't you think you should tell me? Don't you think I deserve to know the truth about my husband since he seems to know the truth about me?'

He heard the rising anxiety in her voice. He paused. *Was it his place to tell her?*

'It shouldn't be coming from me, but, yes, he's apparently been seeing Karen Clarke for months. To use his own words, *he's getting a very warm welcome in her bed.*'

She nodded. There was no surprise in what she had just been told. She had suspected it for months. Christmas Eve at the Clarke's house had confirmed it. She had seen the way he had looked at Karen. The way he had reacted to another man with her. The way his anger and jealousy had flared suddenly. How many times had she noticed Karen's distinct sickly sweet perfume on his clothes?

'Thanks for telling me, James,' she said, as she continued to sit alongside him. 'Pippa knows everything. Perhaps John told her. That's why her relationship with her father has completely fractured. She's moved out, you know.'

'John did tell Pippa almost everything. He felt he had to. He said there had been too many secrets in this family.'

She smiled.

'You know he's right, James. Look at how long I spent keeping quiet about Pippa.'

He nodded. It had been kept a closely guarded secret so she could secure him as a husband. But he was honest enough to know his young self would have rejected the idea of taking on another man's baby.

'You do know had things turned out differently, I could have been bringing her up as my own daughter.'

She thought about what he had said.

'Had I been more devious, you mean?'

He laughed then.

'It was what I said to Alice recently. You should have let me make love to you and then announced you were pregnant a month later. I'd have been delighted.'

She laughed too as Alice had done at the improbability of such a scheme working out.

'I did think about it briefly but I was too far along by the time I realised I was pregnant. And too much in love with Philippe. Too confused. Too naïve to carry off a devious scheme like that. And what if the baby had looked like Philippe?'

'Except that she doesn't,' he said. 'And everything was completely controlled by your mother as I recall.'

She nodded.

'I couldn't hide my condition from her. My morning sickness was exactly like she had suffered. She recognised it immediately.'

He knew what had happened in the intervening years.

264

'And then my anger ended our marriage.'

'I think you were entitled to be angry,' she said.

What could he say but agree with her? But he knew, looking back, their marriage had been blighted by the shadow of her former love and the baby she had been forced to give up.

And now? With everything open and honest between them, he knew he would have her back. But he doubted very much that would ever happen. Not as his wife. Not fully committed to a life together. But he was patient. Hopeful.

'I've been lectured repeatedly not to take advantage of you again,' he said.

She laughed quietly. He wondered idly if she preferred him as a lover over her husband. But he couldn't ask. He would never ask such a question but there was something new and uninhibited about her now. As if she had finally come to understand her own needs as a woman.

For Julia, the pleasure of being with her ex-husband had come as a surprise. It was as if, without the constraints of everyday life as his wife, she had been able to enjoy their new relationship with its shared history but now with no strings attached.

And Philippe? She knew now he had never been quite as much in love with her as she had been with him. Only part of him had been fully committed to their marriage. There had always been a part that belonged to Karen. And now Karen was winning.

# CHAPTER 25

SYDNEY HARBOUR WAS at its sparkling picturesque best for the celebration of Australia's national holiday. Blue sky overhead. Bright sunshine. The landmark Harbour Bridge silhouetted against the skyline. Boats of all sizes bobbing in the water, most going nowhere in particular, the breeze gentle, the sun warm.

Nicholas Gleeson leaned on the railing alongside Julia to get a good view of the Opera House, the construction of which was well under way, as the boat glided past at a leisurely pace.

'There's quite a crowd, Nicholas,' she said. 'I hadn't expected quite so many people.'

He smiled and handed her a fresh glass of champagne.

'It's a sought-after invitation apparently,' he said. 'I was so pleased you came.'

'I'm pleased you invited me,' she said, 'but tell me, would I be right in thinking you're hoping I avoid Karen Clarke?'

'You noticed her then?'

She shrugged.

'Quite frankly she's hard not to notice. And wearing the diamond pendant Philippe bought for her too. Did she know I'd be coming?'

She heard his quick intake of breath at what she had just said.

He was pleased she hadn't got close enough to Karen to notice the diamond ring on the wedding finger of her left hand. He knew that was a present from Philippe too.

'I don't know if she knew you were coming but I did tell her father I would assign my senior associate to take care of him and his daughter as I had another guest to escort.'

'And what did he say to that? He wouldn't be very happy at not being your top priority.'

He laughed.

'Do you really want to know?'

She nodded and waited for him to speak.

'Duval's wife, I suppose. Well, you'd better look after her. He's not doing much of a job of it.'

He tried to mimic David Clarke's deep voice which made her laugh.

Just then, the boat hit the wash from one of Sydney Harbour's stately ferries. Julia would have lost her balance had he not caught her. He didn't let her go immediately.

'Thanks,' she said. 'That took me by surprise.'

He kept his hand lightly on her waist as if he was concerned the same thing might happen again.

'What surprises me is that you seem to know about your husband and Karen Clarke now. Something's changed in the month since we first met at the Clarke's.'

She shrugged.

'Long story. He hasn't admitted anything to me but I found out via other means.'

She knew he would have been shocked to find out her first husband had been the one to finally tell her.

'And how does that make you feel?'

She shrugged.

'The way you'd expect. Angry. Disappointed. Wondering if our marriage was ever what I thought it was.'

'And the future?'

She shook her head. She wasn't prepared to speculate.

'We haven't had that discussion yet but the diamonds keep coming by the way. A sign of his guilt perhaps?'

She put her hand up to the slim circle of diamonds at her throat and then he noticed the absence of rings on her left hand. He touched her finger where her rings should have been.

'No rings. Is that meaningful?'

She smiled noncommittally.

'Sometimes I just enjoy being Julia Belleville again.'

He couldn't help himself. He had to ask the next question.

'And do you plan to go back to being Julia Belleville permanently?'

She did not answer the question because she did not know the answer but seeing Karen Clarke flaunt Philippe's expensive gift had annoyed her. Could she really go on being married to him knowing at every opportunity he would slip off to Karen's apartment for a few hours?

She turned back and leaned on the railing. Nicholas sensed a sudden shift in her mood. He put his arm around her waist and leant in closer to her.

'You know I'd like to see more of you,' he said quietly.

'And here I was thinking you were only interested in my legal affairs,' she said, teasingly.

He smiled.

'Actually, what I'm far more interested in is you, my dear Julia,' he said. 'You deserve better treatment than you're getting from your husband. Much better treatment. I want to be part of your life.'

For a few moments, he pulled her closer to him, his arm beneath the light summer jacket she was wearing. She felt the light touch of his free hand on her arm and on the side of her breast.

'Not in public, Nicholas,' she warned him.

'In private then? Later?'

'Perhaps,' she whispered. 'Dinner on Friday?'

He glanced over her shoulder then and saw the firm's managing partner give a slight shake of his head as he approached them.

'Done. I'll pick you up at seven,' he said before adding a warning. 'Watch out. We're about to be joined by the managing partner.'

'It's so good of you to join us, Mrs Duval,' he said, forcing Nicholas to let go of her. 'I'm Kenneth Wright, the managing partner.

Perhaps I can introduce you to the other senior partners apart from Nicholas.'

She smiled and allowed Kenneth Wright to guide her to a new group of people.

Looking on from the upper deck, Karen smiled and whispered to her father.

'Nicholas was getting too intimate with her for Kenneth Wright's liking. He'll get a ticking off I imagine.'

'Perhaps you should go down and console him?'

'What a good idea,' she said.

Within minutes, she was standing alongside him.

'Got sprung did you Nicholas, trying to romance the wife of the firm's most important client. Kenneth Wright didn't like what he saw, did he?'

'And *hello* to you too Karen,' he said, giving her a quick kiss on the cheek.

'So is she ready to swap her ex-husband's bed for yours?'

'What are you talking about?'

'My father and I saw her at one of his dealerships earlier in the week with her first husband James Fitzroy buying their son a sports car for his twenty-first birthday. She seemed to be on very *friendly* terms with him.'

She had emphasised the word *friendly*. But he was well aware of Karen's tendency for exaggeration.

'I'm not going to get too wound up about her being friendly with her ex-husband. Besides did you know she knows all about your affair with her husband? And she knows he bought you the diamond pendant you're wearing.'

He waited to see her reaction. She simply shrugged as if she did not care at all.

'And of course, you're off to New York in a few of days' time, courtesy of your lover. I'm sure you'll have a lovely time over there with him.'

'While you hope to have a lovely time with his wife?'

He simply smiled. He would not be drawn into Karen's games.

There was no way he was going to tell Karen he had arranged a dinner date with Julia. No way he was going to tell Karen anything at all about Julia.

A week later, Julia stood alongside Nicholas Gleeson at the water's edge. The full moon was beginning to rise. Lights twinkled across the water. Most of the pleasure craft were now moored. Only the ferries continued to move across the harbour.

'Thank you for a lovely dinner,' she said.

He reached out to her and put his arm around her waist. She knew what was coming.

'It's a pleasure, Miss Belleville,' he said.

He had noticed the rings were still missing from her left hand as they had been earlier in the week.

She laughed.

'I don't hear that name very often anymore,' she said, 'except from you.'

He pulled her towards him ever so slightly.

'But that's what I'm hoping will become your name very soon.'

She noticed his gaze move from her face to the low cut dress she had worn. She wondered if wearing such a provocative dress had been a mistake.

'And you are a very beautiful woman,' he said, as he began to caress her with the lightest of touches.

'Do you often romance married women?'

He shook his head.

'I'm not in the habit of it,' he said, 'but for you I'll make an exception.'

He bent his head to kiss her then. She knew at that point she should have pushed him away. But there was a part of her that wanted him to kiss her, part of her that wanted to enjoy his attentions.

'Shall we go to my house in Bellevue Hill?'

She hesitated. Was this a good idea?

'Can I trust you?' she asked.

But she knew what he would say.

'Yes, of course,' he replied as his hands wandered over her body. 'I won't do anything you don't want me to do.'

She laughed quietly.

'That's hardly the way to demonstrate your trustworthiness.'

'But you haven't stopped me, my darling,' he said, using the endearment for the first time. 'You've given me reason for hope.'

And her body had given him reason for hope too. He could feel the warmth of her, her anticipation of what was to come.

He guided her back to his car and opened the door. As he slid into the driver's seat, he reached across to kiss her again. Away from prying eyes his hand slipped beneath the low neckline of her dress. She knew then she had reached the point of no return with him.

Within minutes, he was showing her into one of the most fabulous houses she had ever seen in Sydney, with views stretching to the Harbour Bridge, now brightly lit against the luminescent sky.

'Beautiful house,' she said, looking around her.

He was proud of the house too.

'My mother's house. She decided she wanted to move to an apartment, so we swapped homes.'

She noticed champagne glasses on the sideboard. And then the champagne in his hands. He popped the cork expertly.

'Are we celebrating?' she asked.

He handed her a glass of champagne and then raised his glass to her.

'We are,' he said.

'And what are we celebrating?'

'Love.'

She looked up at him then.

'Is that a bit premature?'

'Not for me,' he said.

In the privacy of his home, all restraint was gone. For him. And then for her.

Finally, he put his half-finished glass down on the table. And then he took her glass from her hand.

'I want to make love to you now,' he said, as he led the way to the bedroom.

She followed him to the master bedroom. Beyond the floor to ceiling windows, she guessed the daytime view would be magnificent.

He began to undress her slowly.

'Is it too late to say no?' she said, teasing him.

'Yes, my darling, it's too late. Much too late.'

For just a moment, she wondered what she had become. Having two men as lovers in just over a week. And neither of them her husband. She had never done such a thing before. Never imagined she would. But her disillusionment with her marriage had cut deep. And now she knew Karen was going to be with Philippe in New York, the reason he hadn't asked her to go with him. It was as if he had deliberately wanted to humiliate her. He must have known I'd find out, she thought. He must have known.

But they were brief thoughts as she responded to Nicholas's lovemaking with a new and different passion, enjoying his tenderness, his reverence of her, his delight in possessing her.

And later as her blonde hair splayed over the pillow next to him, he caressed her body with the gentlest of touches, delighting in the image he had conjured of her in his bed becoming a reality. Delighting in the knowledge she had been unfaithful to her husband for him. And hoping she would go on doing so. For him, it was a sweet pure victory.

He had set out to romance her because Karen Clarke had turned him down in favour of her married lover, but that motivation was long forgotten. Forgotten because he had, in a very short time, fallen in love with her.


Nicholas Gleeson stood beside his mother Dorothy as together they farewelled Julia. She had cautiously accepted his invitation to Sunday lunch which his mother was hosting for her friends. It was one of the few times his mother came back to the house she had given over to her son.

'She's a very elegant woman, Nicholas,' she said as he closed the door and they walked back inside. Privately she thought Julia was the type of woman she could imagine as mistress of the house she still regarded as hers. She had not liked Nicholas's first wife and had said so.

He smiled.

'You are so transparent, Mother,' he said.

But it was her turn to smile.

'I saw the way you looked at her,' she said. 'Remember I know you too well.'

He shrugged. What was she trying to say? He did not want to prolong the conversation.

'You're sleeping with her, aren't you?'

She waited for his reply.

'Mother, really, you shouldn't ask me a question like that.'

She had always known when he was being evasive.

'Why not? Is it because she's married? A word of advice. If you meet her with her husband out socially, I'd be very careful. He mightn't miss the signs either.'

He laughed then.

'Really, Mother, your imagination is running riot.'

She knew he would have simply denied it if it had not been true.

'Be careful,' she warned. 'The Law Society might take a dim view of your conduct if it came to light. Are you hoping to handle her divorce too as well as her business matters?'

He was trying desperately to think of how he could change the subject.

'I don't usually handle divorce,' he said. 'Besides her husband is a client of the firm. I don't handle his matters though.'

'Her name, Belleville, puzzles me.'

It had been his suggestion for Julia to use her maiden name in their dealings and it was how he had introduced her to his mother.

He had been giving her some general advice regarding the wording of the deed of the trust fund she had inherited. Her name in all the documentation had been Julia Belleville. He had been thinking ahead. It would also separate her matters at the firm from her husband's.

'She isn't known by that name now,' he said cautiously. 'That's her maiden name.'

'So under what name might I have heard of her?'

He shook his head.

'Forgive me, Mother, but I'm not telling you.'

There was too much at stake for him now to run the risk of his mother gossiping with her bridge friends about her son's latest client. But his mother was already adding up the small, seemingly insignificant clues.

'She was wearing serious diamonds and her dress looks like it came from a New York fashion house. She mentioned people she knows from the medical fraternity.'

He shook his head.

'Not one word to your bridge ladies, Mother,' he said, pointing his finger at her as if he was lecturing her.

'Well, I'm hardly going to go to the next bridge afternoon and say *my son is sleeping with Philippe Duval's wife*, am I?'

He shook his head. He simply did not want to discuss Julia with his mother.

'Please don't mention her at all, Mother,' he said finally.

'Don't worry, I won't. She deserves you if you consider how her husband is two-timing her with that hussy Karen Clarke. One of the women I play bridge with has a daughter who lives in the same apartment block as Karen Clarke. She's seen Philippe Duval's car outside on quite a few occasions. She's seen him leave too in the early hours of the morning.'

But none of this was news to Nicholas.

'You don't sound surprised at this? Does she know?'

He demurred.

'She does. And she deserves to be treated better.'

'And he's extremely wealthy now, am I right?'

'He is. Very wealthy.'

He thought about the diamonds Philippe had bought Julia recently. He had seen the invoice and the accompanying photograph arrive at the office. And then he noticed she was wearing the set again as she had on Australia Day.

'And you say you're not going to handle her divorce? Are you sure?'

He smiled then. His mother was too clever to deceive.

'Just as I thought. You hope to be the one to deprive the good doctor of some of his fortune. Am I right?'

He laughed.

'I'm already building up a case,' he admitted.

'Well, just make sure your name doesn't get mentioned in two places. As her lawyer on your filing and as co-respondent on his petition.'

'I'll remember that advice,' he said, as he kissed his mother affectionately.

'And what advice would that be, Nicholas?'

He turned to greet his sister.

'Melinda,' he said. 'It's lovely to see you here.'

'You too, brother,' she said, as she slipped her arm through his. 'Now tell me why I'm suddenly seeing you with Mrs Philippe Duval on your arm? I didn't know she was separated from her husband.'

He was shocked into silence. He had not thought any of the guests at his mother's Sunday lunch party, including his sister, would know Julia's real identity.

'She isn't separated from her husband,' he said simply, wanting desperately to end the conversation.

'Oh, so you're her bit on the side while her husband is romancing Karen Clarke. Well done, brother. And good for her I say. He's humiliating her.'

'You seem to know a lot about it?'

He was curious. The gossip about Philippe had penetrated further than he had imagined.

'You forget, Nicholas, that I'm part of the medical profession too. Not in the same field as Philippe Duval but I've heard him speak at conferences. I've seen his wife with him at cocktail parties. And I've seen him a couple of times with Karen Clarke draped all over him.'

'So he's not as discreet as he thinks he is.'

She laughed.

'Discreet. That's not a word I would use. He may not know it but the entire medical profession is talking about him. His wealth. His wife. His daughter who won't speak to him. His mistress. And I'm just waiting for Karen Clarke to spring the final trap on him.'

'The final trap?'

'If he thinks Karen is on the Pill, he's in for a surprise. Unless he's written the prescription for her himself, my friend who's her doctor said her prescription ran out two months ago and it hasn't been renewed.'

He laughed out loud then.

'Well, I should have thought of you earlier, Melinda. I had no idea you would be the fount of knowledge you've turned out to be. But that's very personal information.'

He felt he had to caution his sister. Her medical colleague had certainly breached her patient's trust.

'Don't worry, Nicholas, I haven't repeated that piece of information to anyone. And I won't. But I thought you might have a special interest in it. My money's on Duval becoming a father before the year is out.'

'I honestly thought she might be too old to have a child.'

'Not according to her doctor. There's no reason why she won't conceive, I was told.'

'What a lot of gossips you are,' he said.

And then she cautioned him much as his mother had done.

'I would be careful being seen with her in public too much. He's wealthy. A lot of people are starting to court him because he's going to set up a foundation that will fund medical research. According to people who know him better than I do, he's become quite arrogant since he inherited all that money. He's gone from the poor boy outcast from society to being flattered by everyone who matters. He could ruin your career if he gets wind of your relationship with his wife.'

'Thanks for the warning, Melinda,' he said, with a smile. 'I think I can look after myself.'

'Really? I wonder how many people noticed you pull her into your bedroom for a few minutes. It's not the first time she's been there I take it?'

He shook his head and smiled. She laughed.

'Well, a nice change from your first wife who none of us could stand. She would certainly make a delightful second wife for you.'

He held his hands up.

'I'll pretend I didn't hear that, Melinda,' he said.

She looked then to his mother who had listened to their conversation with a growing sense of unease.

'I think this has been a big shock for our mother, Nicholas, all these sordid revelations.'

He shook his head.

'I think we've all said enough, don't you? I think my mother needs to get back to her other guests.'

She smiled.

'She does indeed.'

Melinda put her arm around her mother and together they walked away to join what remained of the lunch party.

For Nicholas, the level of gossip around Philippe and Karen was disturbing. And also reassuring. Could any marriage survive that? He very much doubted it.

# CHAPTER 26

*America*

KAREN CLARKE STOPPED BRIEFLY to admire the imposing French Renaissance-inspired building that towered above her until she was urged by her friend Bianca not to leave them standing in the cold and the snow. The remnants of the monumental blizzard New York had endured the previous week were still very much in evidence. Snow, once white and pristine but now disintegrating into grey slush, was piled high on either side of the hotel's driveway.

Behind them, the hotel porter was struggling with their bags. In front of them, the doorman waited patiently for the new arrivals and then issued his customary greeting, *welcome to the Plaza Hotel, Miss Clarke, Miss Ferrari.*

But he missed nothing. He noticed the chauffeur-driven car that had brought the two women to the hotel edge carefully out of the hotel driveway and back into the traffic. He knew because it was his business to know exactly who the car belonged to and who paid the chauffeur's wages.

Inside, the hotel clerk handed room keys to Karen and Bianca and the hotel manager welcomed them warmly. Discretion was everything in the hotel business. He knew exactly who would be paying their hotel bill. And seeing Karen, he could even begin to speculate why the newly rich Dr Philippe Duval might be doing so.

Clarence, who had observed their arrival from a comfortable chair in the foyer, walked up to introduce himself. Karen held out her hand and smiled sweetly.

'Philippe has told me how helpful you are to him, Clarence,' she said, watching him carefully.

'And this is my business partner Bianca,' she said lightly. 'We're here to try and promote our fashion range, perhaps get a department store interested. Philippe is a good friend of my uncle's. They work together in the medical field.'

Clarence smiled. One look at Karen and he knew he was hearing a carefully rehearsed story which had a certain element of truth in it.

He had thought nothing of it when his employer had asked him to make all the arrangements. He recalled Philippe's words *I'm doing a favour for my colleague Robert Clarke. I said I would help his niece try and get her fashion business established in New York. Please organise their travel. Rooms at the Plaza as a treat. Get Frederick to pick them up.*

It had seemed such an innocuous assignment. It had all seemed so casual, as if his employer did not want to be involved at all. As if it was all a bit tedious but he had made the offer and must fulfil the obligation.

But that was before Clarence laid eyes on Karen Clarke. He shook his head slightly. And then he yielded to a feeling of profound disappointment. Would Philippe Duval turn out to be just the same as the other rich men he had observed? He shook his head again. *Perhaps I'm reading too much into it.* And then he saw the diamond pendant at her throat as she removed her coat.

He noticed her face colour slightly under his gaze. Philippe had warned her, *be careful. He sees everything.* She realised then wearing the pendant had been a mistake. But she loved the feeling of it against her skin. She loved the envious glances of other women. But most of all she loved it because of the giver.

'Dr Duval hopes to join you here for dinner tonight,' Clarence said, 'unless you are too tired?'

Both women smiled. How could they be tired? Besides, they had only flown from San Francisco today after a stopover.

'Tell him we'll both look forward to seeing him,' Karen replied, with the emphasis heavily on the fact that it would be the three of them.

Clarence smiled again and took his leave. The doorman saluted him. He had already called for Clarence's car to be retrieved from valet parking. His employer's name had been unknown six months ago. Now it was a name on everyone's lips. And it was the business of the staff of New York's most famous hotel to know just who formed the inner circle of a man who, some said, now ranked high among America's wealthiest men.

'Clarence not around today?' Walter asked as he sat down opposite Philippe to discuss the progress towards setting up the charitable foundation and the opening of the Eastbury Hall grounds to the public.

He'd been delighted to see Philippe after an absence of some months. He knew the lawyers had pressured him to visit to finalise estate matters, including the sale of Cox Industries, despite his reluctance to fly to New York in the northern winter.

Philippe continued to examine the architect's plans as he answered Walter, his manner offhanded.

'He's doing something for me. A couple of friends from Sydney arrived this morning. He's helping them settle into their hotel.'

This was such an unremarkable piece of information Walter did not comment. And then a thought struck Philippe. Four at dinner was a much more comfortable number in a restaurant.

'I'm meeting them for dinner tonight. Why don't you come with me?'

'If you want me to,' Walter said, without any real enthusiasm.

'Good,' Philippe said. 'You can drive us. Give Frederick the night off rather than have him hanging around waiting for us.'

'Sure, no problem.'

Walter never needed a second invitation to get behind the wheel of his Camaro.

'Where will we be heading?'

'Plaza Hotel.'

Walter raised his eyebrows.

'And the name of these wealthy friends?'

Philippe never answered him as if the question hardly warranted a response. He had already moved on and wanted to discuss a specific detail of the plans spread out in front of him.

Walter Cox handed the valet parking attendant a very large tip and pointed to his car.

'See that car,' he said, 'it's pristine. Not a scratch. Please make sure it comes back to me that way. No one is parking next to it, do you hear?'

'Yes, sir, I'll block that other space right away,' came the quick response as the young man checked the notes in his hand.

Philippe laughed. He wondered if Walter's car was his most prized possession.

The doorman welcomed them to the hotel. Philippe hid his surprise at being greeted by name. Together they walked into the brightly lit foyer.

And then he caught sight of Karen who walked across excitedly to greet him. Before he could warn her of Walter's presence immediately behind him, she had slipped her arms around his neck. He tried to keep her at arm's length, allowing his hand to rest on her waist for a few moments as he whispered, *it's lovely to see you but you have to behave, I have someone to introduce to you.*

She giggled and kissed him on the cheek before releasing him. Bianca, sensing his discomfort, mirrored Karen's greeting although with less abandon. *She's going to get you into trouble one of these days,* she whispered.

Karen caught sight of a wide-eyed young man standing immediately behind Philippe, who turned and motioned him forward.

'Walter, come and meet my friends, Karen Clarke and Bianca Ferrari. This is Walter Cox, my nephew.'

Walter stepped forward and shook hands politely with the two of them. He stepped back then, watching as Karen turned her attention back to Philippe. She's everything a man might want, he thought. Beautiful. Alluring. Sexy. Her eyes sparkling with delight. He watched as she slipped her arm through Philippe's. It's as if she's never going to let him go, he thought.

And then Walter, like Clarence before him, registered a profound sense of disappointment. He'd known his father had kept a mistress for years until she had grown bored with him. He remembered the telltale signs. Over-compensating his mother. Expensive gifts. Being kinder to his mother when his conscience bothered him. Flattering her when she challenged him.

But in Philippe, until now, he had seen none of these things. In that moment, his heart broke for Julia. He wanted to turn and walk out. He wanted to pull Philippe aside and say *your wife does not deserve this*. And then he noticed how Philippe looked at Karen and his heart sank. She's got him completely wrapped around her little finger. And then Bianca came to stand beside him.

'I would try to look a little less shocked if I were you,' she said quietly. 'He was perhaps unwise to invite you to join us.'

Walter turned to look at Bianca, her understated elegance so different from her friend.

'So tell me I've misinterpreted what I'm seeing,' he said earnestly. He was desperate for someone to tell him he was wrong. 'Tell me there's another explanation other than that I'm looking at Philippe's mistress.'

Bianca stopped then and looked at him. She could see he was young, idealistic, possibly hero-worshipping Philippe in place of a father who had not been all that he could have been. She had heard the story of Walter's father from Philippe.

'What can I say,' she replied. 'You should trust what you can see with your own eyes. But if someone else were to ask me, I would deny it. And if someone were to ask you, you should deny it too. If not for his sake, then for his wife's sake.'

'Do you know Julia, Philippe's wife?' he asked suddenly.

'We have met once or twice but I make sure our paths don't cross. Karen mostly avoids her.'

Walter could not resist asking the next question.

'Do you think she has any idea?' He nodded towards Philippe and Karen walking several paces ahead of them.

'Until recently, I didn't think so but I'm not so sure now. I feel she must have heard the gossip about him. But he does like to keep the two parts of his life separate.'

She took his arm then and together they walked into the restaurant.

It took all of Walter's self-control to join in with the spirit of the evening. He had admired everything about Philippe. He had thought him superior to his own father, to his grandfather, by every measure. Decency. Honesty. Integrity.

And now, here he was, seated at dinner with a woman who was clearly his mistress. And I will be asked to keep this secret for him, he thought. For Walter, it was a moment of profound disappointment.

The following morning Clarence was doing what he did every morning. Drinking his first coffee of the day and reading the newspaper. It was not a time he liked to be disturbed so he was irritated by the knock on the door of his private sitting room. And then a familiar face appeared.

'This is early for you, young Walter,' he said as he consulted his watch. It had just gone eight o'clock.

Getting Walter to a meeting by nine o'clock had always been a challenge so Clarence wondered idly what was so urgent to bring him out at such an early hour but glancing at his face he knew immediately. Clarence got up and went to the sideboard to pour his young visitor a coffee.

'You look as though you need this.'

He handed the cup to Walter.

'I do, Clarence, I do. Thank you.'

'And before you ask, Dr Duval is not at home,' Clarence said in a flat even voice. 'He spent the night in town. Frederick left earlier to pick him up.'

Walter nodded.

'I know. I left him there after dinner last night. I just saw Frederick leave. I guessed where he would be going.'

Clarence, for whom discretion was a byword, said nothing more. He waited. He noticed Walter check the door. It was slightly ajar so he walked over and closed it deliberately. He turned a troubled face towards Clarence.

'You met Karen Clarke yesterday I believe,' he said, wondering just how to phrase his question or what to say.

'I did,' Clarence said, in a voice that did not invite confidences.

But Walter ignored the warning tone in Clarence's voice. He had to ignore it. He had to discuss what he had seen with someone. And Clarence was the only choice.

'I had no idea who I was meeting last night when we headed out to dinner. Philippe did not say much. And then we entered the Plaza Hotel foyer and one of the most beautiful women I've ever seen went straight up to him and put her arms around him. She did not know I was behind Philippe. She did not know who I was. I was close enough to hear him tell her *it was lovely to see her but she had to behave.* She giggled then as if she'd been caught out.'

Clarence shrugged. None of what Walter told him came as a surprise.

'Maybe she's just a friendly girl. Australians can be like that, I'm told.'

Walter rolled his eyes and laughed.

'I saw her friend Bianca's little frown of disapproval at the public display. And as we walked together into dinner, I asked Bianca about their relationship. She said to trust the evidence of my own eyes.'

'Which was?'

'Philippe couldn't take his eyes off her. And there was ...'

He paused as if searching for the appropriate description.

'There was an intimacy between them they couldn't hide. It was on full display. He clearly spent the night with her last night.'

Clarence sat quietly, his eyes closed for a few moments, debating what he should tell Walter. He wanted to restore some of the young man's faith in Philippe. He too had suffered the same profound dis- appointment until the name had finally triggered a memory.

'Sit down, Walter,' he said. 'There's more to this story than you know. But you heard some of it before, as I recall.'

After several minutes, it was Walter's turn to sit silently and contemplate what he had been told.

'I remember now Grandfather telling me something about it. So that was Karen's father who investigated Philippe and didn't like what he found. Illegitimate child. Poor single mother. All that stuff. And then Philippe went on to marry Pippa's mother very shortly after, reviving a wartime romance that perhaps might have been better never being revived except for Pippa's sake.'

Clarence nodded. But there was more.

'Your grandfather actually embellished Philippe's antecedents a little too. He didn't want to run the risk of Philippe not doing the right thing.'

'You mean not marrying Julia?'

Clarence nodded.

'That's what I believe.'

He paused, considering carefully what more he should say.

'I'm guessing but I would say the revival of his interest in this other woman has happened quite recently.'

Walter sat quietly, contemplating everything Clarence had told him.

'So what do we do now, Clarence?'

The situation was beyond Walter's experience.

'We do nothing, Walter. Absolutely nothing. And we lie for him if necessary. We do that to protect his wife. To protect his daughter. To protect his reputation. It's called discretion, Walter. We go on pretending we have no knowledge of his interest outside his marriage.'

He made the point strongly, almost lecturing the young man. He really needed to make Walter understand this was something that should pass unremarked.

'Welcome to the adult world, Walter. We don't know the whole story. We can never know what goes on inside a marriage. My advice is to leave it alone. Just ignore it. It's his private business and we have no right to interfere. And it may run its course.'

Grim-faced but thankful for the advice, Walter opened the door and was about to walk away.

'Thanks, Clarence, it helped to talk.'

Clarence, too, had felt something of the weight of the secret lifted from his shoulders.

Philippe too had begun to have some regrets about asking Walter to come to dinner. He hadn't thought how Karen might regard being in New York with him as a chance to be less cautious about their relationship. But he did not blame her.

Yet he found himself wanting to share some part of his life with her, so difficult within the narrow confines of their circle of mutual friends in Sydney. He had thought it would be easier in New York.

He had been sitting in his study for some time in preparation for a meeting with his lawyers, the papers he had been meant to read lying unread on his desk. He looked around him. Was it really only less than six months ago he had sat in this room and been told how his life was about to change?

He got up and walked to the large window with its sweeping view of the estate and shivered at the weather. Winter. Even the best gardens took on a melancholy air. Stark leafless trees. No green shoots yet. Nothing to brighten the cold dull day. He warmed his cold hands at the fireplace.

His thoughts inevitably drifted to Karen and the pleasure of being with her, of the pleasure of their reunion the previous evening. He had surprised himself at how little guilt he now felt.

And Julia? He tried not to think beyond the fact he still loved her. Because if he did, he would think about the events of the past few months. He would think of her being unfaithful to him just as he had been unfaithful to her repeatedly.

In the quiet chill of that cold February day, he began to reflect for the first time about their future together. And about Karen. A few months ago, he would have thought Julia would have been devastated if their marriage failed. And now? He was not so sure. He shook his head. He did not want his marriage to fail but was there any realistic way for it to continue? And yet he could not give up Karen.

His thoughts were interrupted by a quiet knock on the door. He turned as Clarence brought in the coffee tray. He knew no one else would knock and enter, certainly no one from the household staff. The rules were as they had been for his father, only Clarence could enter this private domain. Clarence set the tray down on the coffee table and busied himself with pouring the coffee, which he handed to Philippe.

'The lawyers may be running a bit late with the state of the roads,' he said, indicating the weather outside.

'I expected as much,' Philippe said, as he sipped his coffee.

He sensed Clarence's hesitation.

'Was there something else, Clarence?'

'Perhaps, Dr Duval,' he said.

Philippe looked at him enquiringly. He could see he had something on his mind.

'Miss Clarke,' Clarence said, and then he faltered. This was way out of line. He thought better of it and turned to go.

'What about Miss Clarke, Clarence? Was there something you wanted to say?'

'Only that perhaps you might have been better advised not to invite young Walter to last night's dinner.'

For the first time, he felt a surge of irritation at Clarence.

'Really, Clarence, and why would that be?'

'I think you know why, Dr Duval. I think you know why.'

Philippe remained silent for several moments.

'Has he said something to you, Clarence?'

Clarence nodded.

'He has.'

'And your response?'

'That your private life is none of our business, sir,' he said, returning to the earlier formality that Philippe had encouraged him to drop.

Philippe turned towards the fire, pondering what he should say.

'Did he accept that advice do you think?'

'I hope so,' Clarence said, 'but don't be surprised if he confronts you. He has set you up on a pedestal. He sees you as a better man than either his father or his grandfather. And then, last night, his eyes were opened.'

'And he realised I'm no saint. That I'm just like other men.'

Clarence shrugged and looked away. He did not want to answer that question. He had said enough.

'I know I can rely on your discretion, Clarence. I'll speak with Walter.'

'I think that might be a good idea, Dr Duval,' he said, as he opened the door to find Walter, his hand poised to knock.

Philippe saw him and motioned him to come in.

'Hi, Walter,' he said casually, 'I don't have a lot of time. I expect the lawyers to descend on me in force at any moment.'

'I thought I'd catch you before they arrive. Clarence said they're running a bit late because of the state of the roads.'

'Sure. Come in and sit down. It's warmer by the fire.'

'Clarence has just brought some coffee. Help yourself.'

He watched as Walter poured himself a cup and added copious amounts of sugar. He could see the strained expression on his face. Clarence's warning had been timely.

'Thanks for coming along to dinner last night, Walter,' Philippe said, trying to gauge his reaction. He knew he had to mention it. He knew he had to do whatever he could to rescue the situation.

Walter said nothing, merely shrugged.

'You don't look as though you enjoyed the outing.'

Walter got up then and began to pace the room, agitated, on edge.

'It's not that I didn't enjoy the outing. Karen and Bianca are great company. But I didn't enjoy seeing you with another woman. With a woman who is not your wife. With a woman who is clearly your mistress.'

There, he had said it. He couldn't at that moment meet Philippe's eyes. The words had tumbled out of him. He felt like a schoolboy spilling on one of his mates.

Philippe took a deep breath. He knew he was looking at an angry and disappointed young man. Yet Philippe was in no mood to make excuses for his own behaviour. And he had made Karen sound like a kept woman. That angered him too.

'I will say this only once, Walter. My private life is my concern. Not yours. Not Clarence's. Perhaps it was a mistake on my part to involve you last night but Karen is part of my life. An important part of my life if you must know. I would appreciate your discretion. If my wife or my daughter were to hear anything of this from you, I would be very disappointed. Do I have your word you will not mention her name?'

Walter nodded.

'Of course, I won't say anything, to anyone.'

'Thank you,' Philippe said. 'And whatever you may think of me, I would say one thing in my defence. I don't make a habit of this. I don't have other women. Only Karen. She is special to me. If I had not already been committed to marry Julia, I would have asked Karen to become my wife. But I walked away from her. But in the end, I could not stay away from her. I hope you may come to understand in years to come. Life is not always simple or cut and dried.'

Walter nodded. He was beginning to see that, for Philippe, this was no casual affair. He wondered then where it would end. And how it would end. He turned to go but Philippe stopped him.

'Stay and join the meeting with the lawyers,' he said. 'You need to be across everything. We're getting closer to the sale and then the funds will be available for the foundation.'

Walter brightened at the prospect. He had finally found something to look forward to in his future.

# Chapter 27

'SUNDAY MORNING,' CLARENCE had said quietly on being asked his advice. 'Staff don't work on Sundays. And Mrs Anderson, the housekeeper, will be at church.'

And so it was that Karen stepped across the threshold of Eastbury Hall and gazed with wonder at the grandeur of the house, just as Julia had done before her.

'It's beautiful, in an imposing way. Intimidating even,' she said as she ran her hand along the highly polished dining table and took in the commanding proportions of the room.

'It must have been spectacular to see the house full of people, guests dining at this table. The chandeliers ablaze. The women dripping with diamonds. The men in evening dress. I would have loved to have seen it.'

Philippe came up behind her and put his arms around her.

'You would have outshone them all,' he said, kissing her lightly. 'Let's go upstairs. I have something for you in my bedroom.'

She laughed.

'As if you need an excuse to get me into your bedroom.'

Moments later, he was handing her a large box.

'It's like Christmas,' she said, untying the red bow that adorned it.

'I hope you like it,' he said as she unfurled a luxurious fur coat, letting the tissue paper fall to the floor.

'Oh, Philippe, it's beautiful,' she said, as she slipped it on and studied her appearance in the full-length mirror.

'And you're beautiful too, my darling,' he said admiring her reflection.

'You're too generous to me,' she said, but he waved away her thanks.

'And I'll go on being generous,' he said. 'I enjoy buying presents for you.'

'I thought I might see Clarence?' she asked suddenly. 'Or would that be indiscreet.'

'He's around. Probably in his private sitting room.'

'He knows, doesn't he?'

Philippe nodded.

'Can he be trusted?'

He smiled.

'Don't you think it's a bit late to worry about my reputation? I can tell you it's in tatters. But, yes, I'm sure Clarence can be trusted.'

'And Walter? He looked quite bemused if that's the right word?'

She had not seen Philippe since the night of their arrival. She had been busy with meetings and outings with Bianca but she guessed he was trying belatedly to be discreet.

'Oh, I got a thorough dressing down from Walter,' he admitted with a grimace.

Despite her concern, she couldn't help but laugh. She guessed rightly that Walter had been expressing his own disappointment in Philippe.

'And what did you say to him? Will he be discreet?'

He sat down on the edge of the large bed that dominated the room. She draped the coat across a chair and sat down beside him. She looked around. It was a gloomy room, in need of redecorating. She guessed it was the room he shared with Julia when she came with him, except that Julia had yet to make any lasting impact on it.

'I told him you were special to me and that if I had not already been committed to marry Julia, I would have asked you to become my wife.'

She wondered then if he ever looked back and regretted the decision that had changed his life. And hers. Would there ever be a better time to ask him?

'Tell me honestly, Philippe, did you ever regret your decision?'

He got up and walked to the window. How should he answer that question? He had enjoyed being married to Julia, being part of Pippa's life. But Pippa was old enough now to make her own way in the world. He opted for honesty.

'Until the past few months, I hadn't regretted it,' he said. 'I'd been content knowing it had been the right thing to do. But now that you are back in my life, I'm less certain I made the right decision.'

He walked back to where she had remained sitting on the edge of the bed and put his arm around her. He did not want to give her any cause to doubt him now.

'And now? What's ahead of us, Philippe?'

But he put the question back to her.

'What do you want from our relationship, my darling? This is not only about me.'

She did not reply immediately. She had gone for so many years pretending she no longer loved him. Assuming he no longer loved her. Convincing herself their relationship was part of her past. She still did not trust his commitment to her, as if one wrong word might burst the fantasy world they inhabited.

And then he whispered the words she had once longed to hear.

'I love you,' he said. 'I can't imagine my life without you now.'

She turned and smiled at him.

'I love you too,' she said, 'but you should not say those words to me. Not until you are free to say them.'

He smiled then. In her own subtle way, she was telling him what she expected of their relationship.

And the diamond ring he had bought her? He noticed she now wore it exclusively on the wedding finger of her left hand. He reached out and stroked her hand, admiring the cold beauty of the diamond.

'Do you mind that I wear it on my left hand?'

He shook his head.

'No,' he said, 'I don't mind at all.'

And then she too reached out. She took his hand and began to remove his wedding ring. He did not resist. He understood exactly what she wanted then. She dropped the ring into the palm of his hand.

'Please don't wear it when you're with me,' she said.

He did not return the ring to his finger. Instead, he dropped it into the drawer of his bedside table.

She smiled. He could see a hint of triumph on her face.

Did she believe, through that one symbolic act, he was prepared to declare his marriage was over? That he was ready to divorce Julia?

He could not answer that question honestly. Yet at some point he knew his commitment to Julia had weakened.

Bianca Ferrari would be forever grateful for her business partner's wealthy influential lover.

The visit to New York showed every indication of being an outstanding success for the small fashion design firm. While the enthusiastic reception of their designs owed something to the freshness and cleverness of Bianca's work, it owed more, much more, to Philippe's patronage and his request to his lawyers to help open the otherwise firmly closed doors.

Unlike Clarence or Walter, Howard Davis had taken instructions from Philippe for the firm to help in whatever way they could without comment. He had not even allowed himself the luxury of a raised eyebrow. The firm was well connected to New York's business elite. He was prepared to leverage those connections in the interests of one of his most important clients.

A newly wealthy man of whom little is known might go unnoticed in New York. A newly wealthy man who had unexpectedly inherited one of the finest properties on Long Island and one of the largest privately owned industrial companies in America was inevitably a source of much interest. And so it had proved an easier task for the lawyers than they had expected as the answers came back.

*Yes, of course, if Philippe Duval has an interest in this small fashion design company, then of course we will see them. And will Dr Duval attend any of the Fashion Week events with his protégés?*

Regardless of the answer, VIP invitations began arriving the next day. Philippe had passed most of them along to Karen but she begged him to accompany her to the Vogue party.

'You'll enjoy it,' she said, as she lay in his arms. 'You need to get away from that mausoleum of a house. It's so gothic. This apartment is so much nicer.'

He laughed. She was right. He actually preferred his mid-town apartment. Perhaps I should pull down that hideous monstrosity of a house after all, he thought.

'Did you remember to bribe the concierge here?'

She was teasing him now. He had organised for a private dinner in his apartment for just the two of them, with everything happening under the eagle eye of the apartment block's concierge.

'He got a healthy tip,' he admitted.

'What did you say to him?'

'I simply asked for his discretion and I got the most alarming wink in return.'

They laughed together then.

'Well, let's hope money is the key to his silence because he looked quite …'

She couldn't think of the right word.

'Shocked,' he said. 'I told you you've singlehandedly left my reputation in tatters.'

But she wouldn't have it.

'My darling Philippe, you've managed that all by yourself,' she said, as she swung her legs out of his bed and reached for her clothes.

'And this Vogue party is when?'

'Tomorrow night, so I must get back to my hotel and get some beauty sleep.'

'Dinner jacket?'

She nodded. She would be so delighted to be the woman on his arm. It would be a first for their relationship. She noticed his wedding ring had not reappeared.

'Come to the hotel at eight and we can go from there.'

'Do you want me to bring Walter as Bianca's partner?'

'Would he come do you think?'

'He will,' Philippe said. 'I think he understands. I may have slipped off my pedestal somewhat with him but not completely. I think he'd do it to oblige me.'

'I'll let Bianca know. She'll be pleased. She liked him. She said she wished she was ten years younger.'

Philippe laughed wondering if Walter might have been thinking he wished he was ten years older.

Against expectations, it had taken Philippe some time to persuade Walter to attend the fashion event of the year as Bianca's partner.

'Are you serious?' he had said. 'You're making me complicit. I can't do it.'

Philippe was exasperated and not really in the mood to cajole him. But he tried once more.

'I am not making you complicit. I am just asking you to escort a friend of mine to a function. It's not very hard.'

Walter had paused and looked across the desk at Philippe. He had recognised the steely edge in Philippe's voice. It was the same tone he remembered hearing in his grandfather's voice many times. They both have a way of getting exactly what they want, he thought.

'Aren't you concerned about being seen with Karen?'

Philippe shook his head.

'It will be a crush. The venue will be dimly lit. The music will be blaring. No one will take the slightest notice.'

But Philippe's confidence was misplaced. He did not notice the small bubble of conversation that bounced around the room following their entrance. He did not realise it was New York society's first look at the mysterious heir to Walter William Cox's fortune, the illegitimate son of a cleaning lady. And on his arm?

The bubble of conversation exploded with surprise, as first one, and then another, murmured, you know that beautiful redhead is not his wife. *He's very good looking. Looks like he's quickly adopted the finest traditions of other rich men.*

It was Karen's possessive grip on his arm, her warning glances at the other women who dared to look at Philippe with interest and his easy intimacy with her that turned casual chatter into gossip column inches, as he was to discover to his horror two days later.

But, for Karen, nothing could spoil her triumph. Philippe had been prepared to step out of the shadows for her. To be seen with her. To show the world he loved her. Walter had seen it too. And heard the whispered conversations.

'Can his marriage to Julia survive this?' he had asked Bianca, the despair in his voice perceptible.

She had shaken her head.

'I think you know the answer to that question, Walter. I think he's kidding himself if he thinks it can. Besides did you notice he's taken off his wedding ring?'

Walter shook his head. He admitted he hadn't noticed.

She decided against drawing Walter's attention to the brilliant diamond Karen now insisted on wearing on her left hand, obviously with Philippe's approval. She's one step closer, Bianca thought, one step closer to claiming her prize. And then she smiled.

'But I owe him a debt of gratitude. He has opened doors for us that would otherwise have stayed firmly shut.'

They moved off together then towards the bar.

'Let's forget about them, Walter,' Bianca said, as she reached for another glass of champagne. 'Tell me about yourself.'

He smiled and relaxed. She was an attractive woman, very different from Karen. Not as tall, her mid length hair bouncing on her shoulders, her fine dark eyes assessing everything with an intelligence he admired.

'There's not much to tell, Bianca. Not yet anyway. Except that I've led the life of a playboy. Disappointed my parents. Watched my father die an early death from the bitterness of his relationship with his own father. And now I see my mother following the same path. She hates Philippe with a passion that will never fade.'

As she had once done when Philippe had told his story, she gestured extravagantly as only an Italian can.

'Passion. Hatred. Revenge. You forget I am Italian. These are the very foundations of Italian family life,' she said, laughing softly.

He laughed with her.

'How wonderful to hear you laugh,' he said, as he moved a little closer to her. 'You are very beautiful, you know.'

She was so used to going unnoticed alongside Karen that she blushed.

'I am not beautiful,' she said simply. 'Karen is beautiful.'

'Well, striking then,' he said, 'so I wonder why there is no wedding ring on your finger. No sparkling diamond even?'

She shrugged. How could she answer? How should she answer, except truthfully?

'Because no one has ever asked me,' she said.

He smiled and then he raised her fingers to his lips.

'Then there is something seriously wrong with the men you've been meeting,' he said gallantly. 'Seriously wrong.'

Two days later, Philippe was sitting with Clarence, going over what he had agreed with Walter regarding the opening of the grounds at Eastbury Hall to the public.

'Walter thinks we should open up on the Memorial Day weekend at the end of May,' he said, looking to Clarence to gauge his reaction.

He merely nodded.

'It seems like as good a date as any,' Clarence said.

'You don't seem to be joining in with the enthusiasm for this project you once had, Clarence. Is there something I'm missing here?'

Clarence reached for the newspaper he had carefully folded to a specific page. He handed it to Philippe.

'You might want to read this,' he said, as he handed the newspaper to Philippe, who scanned it quickly. He realised then he had been foolish.

Below the grainy picture of him with Karen clinging to his arm, the gossip columnist had aimed both barrels in his direction and fired.

*Dr Philippe Duval, on his most recent trip to New York since he was unexpectedly named the principal heir to Walter William Cox's fortune, usurping his legitimate half-brother the late Walter William Cox the third, is pictured here enjoying the social highlight of New York's famous Fashion Week.*

*Dr Duval is championing the cause of Australian fashion design house Bianca Ferrari Designs. Co-owner Karen Clarke, seen here, is clearly a very close friend of Dr Duval's whose wife Julia is believed not to have accompanied him on this trip.*

*There are whispers abroad of his plans for the Eastbury Hall estate at East Hampton, which he inherited along with the bulk of his father's estate. We think there will be a few other whispers abroad too after Dr Duval's first foray into the New York social scene.*

He looked at Clarence.

'I had no idea anyone would be the slightest bit interested in me,' he said, 'or in what I do. Or with whom.'

'I think it's the *with whom* that's the problem,' Clarence replied, bluntly. 'It's one thing to ask me and Walter to be discreet. But this will, at this moment, be a delicious topic of conversation at the breakfast tables along the length of Long Island.'

Philippe was lost for words. He simply hoped it would be forgotten when the next salacious tidbit claimed everyone's attention.

'Hopefully, people will forget about it,' he said, throwing the newspaper onto the coffee table.

'Miss Clarke is heading home today I believe.'

He nodded.

'She is, yes. And I don't propose to discuss anything further with you about Miss Clarke,' Philippe said.

Clarence nodded. He had done what he needed to do. He hoped Philippe was right, that people would forget about it when the next tidbit emerged.

*Nor do I propose to discuss anything about my devoted wife either,* he almost said.

He remembered Karen's words on their last night together. *There's something I know about your wife you might prefer I don't tell you.* But he had pressured her. And so she had told him what she had seen standing alongside her father at their car dealership.

He did not know she had held back on mentioning Nicholas Glee-son. But he knew exactly why Karen had told him. She wanted him to know his wife was capable of making a fool of him, that she wasn't as in love with him as he thought.

But there had been no surprise for him in what Karen had told him. Only an unfathomable sense of disappointment. His wedding ring remained discarded in the drawer in his bedroom. He wondered if that's where it should remain.

Across the garden, in the smaller Cox house, mother and daughter read and reread the gossip column with a growing sense of malicious delight.

'Oh, my lord!' Barbara Cox was heard to say more than once to her daughter Virginia. 'So Philippe Duval turns out to be two-timing his pretty wife and the mother of his daughter and he's indiscreet enough to be photographed with the trollop on his arm at a New York fashion event. I wonder how his wife will feel when she sees this.'

She reached for a pair of scissors and began to clip the item from the newspaper.

But Walter had heard her high-pitched squeal of delight. As soon as he saw the photograph, he grabbed the newspaper from her hands and began to read the piece, his hands shaking with anger and frus-tration at Philippe's lack of understanding of his high profile and news value for the gossip columnists.

Barbara Cox looked at her son suspiciously.

'Of course, you knew about this, didn't you? You went out the other night all done up in your tuxedo. Were you meant to be her date to cover for Duval? And he just got over-confident and allowed himself to be photographed with her?'

He shook his head.

'No, I was not Miss Clarke's date,' he said. 'I partnered Bianca Ferrari, who is a really lovely woman.'

Virginia looked at her brother. And then she remembered.

'Of course, one of my friends was at that party and asked if I knew my brother had been there. Her exact words were *he seems to have developed a liking for older women. He was romancing a very attractive Italian lady.* But she couldn't remember her name.'

'Married, is she, Walter?'

'No, Mother,' he said, 'she is not married. I don't make a habit of pursuing married women.'

'But she's older?'

'Probably about eight years. I never ask a woman her age.'

'I suppose you spent the night with her?'

At this point, his patience evaporated.

'Mother, I am not a child. Who I choose to spend the night with, and I'm not saying I did, is none of your business.'

'And your new best friend Philippe Duval? Don't you think who he spends the night with might be his wife's business, if it's not her that is?'

He looked at her then. I know that look, he thought. She's planning to use this against Philippe. But how can I stop her?

'I don't think I have an opinion on that,' he said, 'but I do have an opinion on you and Virginia spreading malicious gossip about him that's likely to reach Julia's ears next time she visits.'

His mother shrugged.

'Well, I don't think it will need Virginia and I to do anything at all. I think he's done it all by himself. I think next time she visits Julia Duval is going to find out some uncomfortable home truths about her husband. That's if she doesn't know already, of course. Maybe that's why she didn't come this time. Maybe the marriage is already on the rocks. Had you thought of that?'

He shook his head. He hadn't considered that possibility. Until now. But still he clung to the belief she was unaware of her husband's affair.

'I don't think she knows anything about it,' he said, 'and I hope it stays that way.'

'Wishful thinking, Walter,' his sister said. 'He's fair game now. It will just be a matter of time. I hope we get to see the fireworks. Your friend Pippa will be bitterly disappointed in her father, I can tell you that now. She absolutely worships him.'

He knew that too. He didn't need his sister to tell him Pippa would be devastated. He thought sadly of the small, happy family that was about to be fractured by a scandal of Philippe's own making. Because he couldn't keep his hands off another woman, a beautiful woman who was prepared to offer herself to him with no strings attached.

In the cold light of day, he realised very few men would have turned her down. He had mistakenly thought Philippe might have been one of the few.

# CHAPTER 28

*Australia*

JULIA HEARD THE FRONT DOOR open and then the bang as it closed behind Philippe but she did not rush to greet him. Instead, she turned towards their housekeeper Grace who also doubled as their cook.

'That smells good, Grace,' she said. 'I think you've excelled yourself this time.'

The woman beamed. She enjoyed working for Julia Duval. She's always polite and thankful for everything I do, she had told her husband on many occasions. It's a shame she's got a two-timing husband who thinks he can do whatever he pleases with another woman.

'Is that Dr Duval back from New York?' she asked, untying her apron. The meal was cooked, ready to be served. Her work was done for the day.

'It is, Grace,' she replied, trying to hide her nervousness. 'I expect he'll be tired after the long flight. I'd better go and see him.'

Grace watched as Julia smoothed her hair and straightened her dress.

'I'll go out the back door,' she said. 'I think I can leave this in your capable hands now, Mrs Duval. I'll see you tomorrow.'

'Thank you, Grace,' she said as she headed towards the front hall-way.

Was Philippe anxious too at seeing her, she wondered, or would he still believe his double life was a secret? He smiled as she approached and then he put his arms around her.

'You look tired,' she said. 'And not much luggage?'

'Clarence suggested I make life easy for myself and keep a full wardrobe of clothes in both places, so I left behind much of what I took with me.'

He did not say at the last minute he had remembered to replace his wedding ring on his finger. That too had almost been left behind.

'That makes sense,' she said, realising that it meant he expected to take more frequent trips to America.

'But it's a long flight,' he said, 'and I need a shower. Something smells good though.'

Half an hour later, he took the glass of wine she held out to him and sat down in his favourite chair. For the first time, he felt real physical exhaustion from the travel. He closed his eyes briefly. Perhaps the exhaustion was from the endless meetings with lawyers and his need to concentrate on everything he was being told and what he was agreeing to.

And then there had been the difficulties with Walter too. He forced himself not to think about Karen as if thinking about her while he was with his wife was itself an act of betrayal.

'I have something for you,' he said, holding out a small, exquisite box. She could just make out the Tiffany monogram elegantly inscribed on the lid.

'I hope you like it,' he said, as she opened the box to reveal a slim diamond bracelet on a platinum band.

'It's beautiful,' she said allowing him to put it on her wrist. 'Thank you.'

She bent over and kissed him on the cheek.

'Is that all I get by way of thanks,' he said laughingly.

He put his hand behind her head and kissed her passionately.

'That's better,' he said.

But it did not ease the tension of their reunion as he hoped it might. He had felt her body stiffen as he kissed her as if she was simply enduring his physical closeness. As if, for the first time, his attentions were unwelcome.

She moved away from him then towards the table as if she needed to put some physical distance between them.

'Was it a successful trip?' she asked as if everything was normal between them. 'Did you make progress with everything?'

She was waiting for the moment, the right moment, when she would pose the one question she knew he wouldn't want to hear.

'I think so,' he said. 'The sale of Cox Industries will settle, finally, at the end of March. And we will open the estate to the public at the end of May as planned. And then we can set up the foundation.'

She listened attentively as if it would all still matter to her. As if it was still part of her future.

'Clarence will be in his element,' she said remembering how keen he was on the grand public opening.

He smiled. She was right.

'Clarence is delighted with the chance to take charge of it all.'

'Anyway, our dinner is waiting,' she said pointing to the table.

He pulled out her chair at the dining table and kissed her lightly on her cheek, trying again to break through her remote politeness.

'Did you find us a new house while I was gone?'

She pointed to the coffee table.

'There are three houses I thought might suit you,' she said. 'There are brochures on the table for you to look at.'

He was pleased she had looked but he sensed a reticence about her answer.

'And what do you think of them? Would any of them suit you? Do you have a preference?'

She half smiled at him and shrugged.

'It depends. Is my opinion important? Will I still be your wife by the time you settle on a new house?'

He looked up from his meal, suddenly alarmed. Where had that come from without any warning, he wondered? It was as if her question had ignited the simmering tension between them.

'That's not a question I expected to hear on my first night back,' he said. 'Are you telling me you no longer want to remain married to me? Is there something I'm missing here?'

She looked across the table at him. How can he not know that I now know everything about his affair with Karen? How can he not realise what it means for us? For our marriage.

'It's not what I want that matters anymore, is it? It will be whatever Karen wants that will be important. You should take her with you to decide on your new house.'

He pushed his plate to one side. Suddenly, his appetite had deserted him.

'And why do you think I should do that?'

Her mocking laughter echoed in the silence between them.

'Well, I heard she spent almost two weeks with you in New York. Is that true? Isn't that a wife's role? Isn't that why you didn't ask me to go with you? Because she was going. You preferred to have her with you.'

He tried to hide his shock at what she had just said. He knew then the conversation had the potential to spiral out of control. At least out of his control.

'Karen was there for her own business interests. Not for my sake.'

For just a fraction of a second, he had been tempted to deny Karen had been in New York at the same time. But he knew that would be futile. And a lie. A lie he couldn't bring himself to utter.

And then she laughed again, the same harsh unhappy sound.

'And you expect me to believe you didn't spend most nights in her bed. Or her in yours?'

She noticed how his expression grew serious. Slightly annoyed. He ignored her questions. He knew his only hope was to challenge her too.

'I'll answer your questions if you tell me what you were doing with James Fitzroy. I heard you were seen in an intimate embrace with him at a car dealership. I assume you spent time with him while I was away. I imagine you had a good time with him.'

She got up then and walked away from the table. He followed her and grabbed her arm.

'Don't walk away from me,' he said, his anger barely controlled. 'We need to talk about this.'

She looked at his hand gripping her arm. And then at him, silently reminding him of another time when he had used his physical strength against her. He let go of her arm.

'Talk about what? Your mistress?'

He shook his head. This was all going badly. Very badly.

'We need to talk about our marriage. About us. I care about you,' he said. 'I care for you very much even if you no longer care for me.'

She marvelled at how easily he spoke the reassuring words she would once have believed without question. But now? Her eyes had been opened in the month he had been away. But still she was keen to hear his explanation. And hear whatever half-truths he was willing to utter.

'If you cared about me so much, how could you be unfaithful to me? How do you think that makes me feel? To hear everyone whisper behind their hands about my husband's mistress. And then look at me pityingly.'

His first instinct was to push back against her accusations.

'And what am I expected to feel about your adventures with your ex-husband?' he shot back at her.

She laughed quietly. *Why does it always come back to me as if it's all my fault.* That's what she wanted to say but she didn't.

'I expect you to feel the way I do,' she said, trying to keep her voice even. 'Jealous, angry, disappointed. You were ignoring me remember. Expecting me to live like a nun. Distant from me. Not sharing my bed. Hardly ever touching me let alone making love to me. As if you no longer cared for me.'

She shocked him with her candour.

'So you went looking for sex elsewhere. Was that it?'

He could match her anger with his own but he knew he risked losing control of his temper. Breathe, he reminded himself. Breathe. Slow everything down.

'Well, you were ignoring me after all. And James offered a convenient shoulder to cry on.'

He was annoyed at the casual way she mentioned his name.

'More than a shoulder to cry on, it seems. I hope you enjoyed it with him.'

'I did. Very much.'

She was taunting him now. Saying more than she intended. But she could not unsay what she had said. She was in no mood to be conciliatory.

'Did I need to hear that?'

'Yes, you did need to hear it. Because you told my brother you were *enjoying a very warm welcome in Karen's bed*. Obviously that warm welcome continues.'

He wondered how it was possible to be angry with her and yet feel desire for her at the same time. He had finally broken through her cool detachment. He noticed her cheeks were unusually flushed and strands of her blonde hair had fallen untidily across her face. He stepped closer to her and put his arms around her.

'So what happens now?' he asked. 'Where do we go from here?'

She tried to break free from his embrace but he wouldn't let her go. He's enjoying this, she thought. Enjoying having me at a disadvantage. As his anger subsided, her anger grew. She managed to get her arm free and tried to slap him across the face but he caught her wrist.

'That's not a very nice thing to do to your loving husband,' he said mockingly.

'I wouldn't attempt to do it to a loving husband,' she retorted.

'Just like I wouldn't hold a loving wife against her will,' he said, as he continued to hold her tightly in his arms.

He bent his head and kissed her. And then he let her go suddenly. She stumbled back and would have fallen had he not reached out and caught her. This time though he moved away from her as soon as she had regained her balance. He had held her close to him and felt no warmth towards him. She had suffered his kiss, not welcomed it.

'Let's talk about everything when we are both calmer,' he said.

She nodded and then she closed her eyes briefly but all she could see was Karen's triumphant face.

'Tomorrow, then,' she said. 'Let's talk tomorrow.'

He kissed her lightly on the cheek.

'Let's talk tomorrow,' he agreed. 'I'm sure everything can be sorted out between us.'

He meant his words to sound reassuring but to her it sounded like the polite opening to divorce negotiations. She could even imagine the scene. He with his lawyer, she with hers as the wreck of their marriage became exposed, bit by bit, for all to see. His infidelity. Probably hers too. Without doubt the gossip columns would get hold of the salacious details and they would have a field day. And Pippa? Would she ever get beyond her disappointment?

She smiled to herself as Nicholas's words echoed in her mind. *We're ready to act for you with your divorce any time you give the word. Your husband has humiliated you and he should pay dearly for that.*

But she was cautious. Nicholas had declared he was in love with her. She did not want to be pressured into ending her marriage only for him to have expectations of her.

Was there a compromise she could reach with Philippe? Could they just live separate lives? But what would be the point of that? She knew he would not give up Karen. And Pippa had told her Karen refused to give him up. Was she just expected to go on ignoring his infidelity while he expected her to be faithful to him?

She knew her life and his were at a crossroads. She wanted to make sure she chose the right road.

For the first time, she began to wonder if their relationship had run its course. She had to face it. He was in love with another woman. And yet he seemed reluctant to take the final step. To admit it was over for them. Was it just his last flicker of loyalty to her? To their daughter? She headed to her bedroom where she would spend yet another night alone.

It was early morning but Philippe had already been up for some time. He tapped on Julia's bedroom door. He carried a tray with her favourite Earl Grey tea already brewed. He put the small tray down on her bedside table.

She sat up and looked at him. Had he slept at all, she wondered? 'You're up early?'

'I couldn't sleep,' he said. 'And it's a beautiful day.'

He walked to the window and opened the curtains. The sunlight came streaming in. She sipped the hot tea, waiting for him to say something further.

'I have to see Robert Clarke this morning. My weeks away served as notice but he wants to clear up a few things with me and discuss my farewell dinner.'

She remained silent. She wondered if Karen would be his partner for the farewell dinner.

'The lawyers want to see me too,' he said, 'but that can wait. Why don't I come back and we'll go and have lunch together? Then we can drive past the houses you've picked out.'

This whole conversation is surreal, she thought, as if their conversation of the previous evening had never occurred.

'And our marriage? When are we going to discuss that?'

He sat down on the edge of the bed and leant over to kiss her on the cheek.

'Let's talk over lunch,' he said, 'but I want you to know one thing. I still love you. Very much.'

'But there is another woman you love more, isn't there?'

He did not reply.

She threw back the bedclothes then and headed for the bathroom, almost upsetting her half-finished cup of tea. As she stood in the shower, she let the water stream over her face and wash away the tears she did not want him to see.

But the water could not wash away the aching emptiness she felt. She had lost him once; now she was losing him again. She cried the same tears, her heart broken as she began to contemplate a future without him.

It was the first time he had been to Karen and Bianca's premises in Surry Hills, a faded suburb on the fringes of the city, its streets narrow and uninviting. He waited impatiently for the outdated lift that rattled slowly to the ground floor. It was an old building, the brickwork grimy with years of accumulated dirt and neglect. But it was a great workspace, Karen had told him.

She greeted him as he stepped out of the lift. The warmth of her welcome reassured him. There was no hint of restraint in his response. Did it matter anymore? His wife knew all about his relationship with Karen. Did it matter who saw them together?

'You look tired,' she said, concerned for him.

'A rough homecoming,' he said quietly.

She desperately wanted to ask what he meant but he shook his head slightly.

'I'll tell you later,' he whispered.

He handed her the department store contract he had brought back with him, which had been the reason for his detour on the way to meet Robert Clarke.

He greeted Bianca warmly as she joined them in the untidy room that doubled as Karen's office. It was all clearly too small for their operation now. He looked around him.

'Time for better premises, I would say.'

Karen looked at Bianca and shrugged.

'Better premises won't make us more money at this stage,' she said.

But he would have none of it.

'This building should be condemned,' he said flatly. 'Find something better and I'll pay for it.'

'I think you've been too generous already, Philippe,' Bianca said.

She knew the trip to New York had been expensive. But he shook his head. He had his arm around Karen as if she was a possession he didn't want to let go.

'It's an investment, Bianca,' he said. 'Better premises will tell your customers you are doing well.'

'Very well. We'll start looking,' she said.

She laughed quietly to herself. Didn't he realise better premises will be dismissed as just another indulgence by a wealthy man towards his mistress?

She watched as Karen walked with him to the lift. She felt sorry for his wife because she was now being betrayed, even humiliated, openly. She liked Philippe but she did not admire his treatment of his wife. She had seen, bit by bit, how his arrogance had grown.

And Karen? She had always known Karen was in love with him. And that Philippe would do anything for her. Well, almost anything. There was one last step he seemed reluctant to take. To divorce his wife. But she wondered if he was a step closer to that decision now. He was different with Karen now. More interested in her life, she thought, not just in her as a sexual partner. She took that to be a good sign.

Robert Clarke stood up and extended his hand towards Philippe. There was no obvious rancour between them now but the previously close ties of friendship had loosened considerably since their terse meeting a month before.

He had made sure Philippe's name had disappeared very quickly from the list of doctors practising at the hospital. The few personal items left in his office had been collected and boxed awaiting his return from New York. Only one or two documents required his signature to end his career as a surgeon at the hospital.

'You look relaxed,' Robert said, in some ways envying Philippe the freedom from responsibility that dogged the daily footsteps of practising doctors.

'I feel a bit tired to be honest,' he replied. 'It's a long flight back from New York.'

'And your trip to New York went well?'

'Very well. I've signed everything to settle the sale of Cox Industries. The lawyers are working on setting up the foundation for me and the monstrosity of a house I inherited is due to be open to the public at the end of May. Well, the gardens are, to be precise. The house will act as a headquarters for the foundation.'

Robert listened attentively.

'It sounds as if much of your future life will be in America, Philippe.'

'Yes, much of it will be probably.'

The next question was one that could have almost been scripted by his brother David Clarke.

'Are you thinking of returning there permanently?'

'No, not permanently. But certainly frequently. It depends a lot on Pippa.'

Robert Clarke had expected him to say his wife. Or even Karen.

'Why Pippa?'

He was curious. Did Philippe's wife or even Karen not influence his decision-making as much as everyone thought? He waited for him to explain.

'Well, if Pippa ever decides to speak to me again, I can find out if she's serious about wanting to run a branch of the foundation here in Sydney.'

'That would be a big job for a young woman, don't you think?'

'I'm sure it's possible to get a couple of people around her who know what they're doing. I've already got feelers out to see who I can poach from other foundations. Perhaps even link up with an existing foundation.'

Robert was silent for a few moments. He had heard a lot about his niece's trip to New York which Philippe had paid for. He had been pressured by his brother to find out what Philippe's ultimate intentions were. He tried again.

'I understand you've done a great deal to help my niece's fashion business. My sister-in-law was boasting of her daughter's success in New York recently. I don't think your name was mentioned though.'

He smiled to himself at Robert's not-so-subtle questions.

'I spent quite a bit of time with Karen in New York. Is that what you want to know Robert? Is that what her father wants to know?'

Robert gestured ambivalently. He wasn't a man who was normally interested in salacious gossip. But, like his brother, he cared how Karen was being treated.

'And yes, it's been a great boost to their business. I just dropped off a department store contract to her and Bianca on my way here. Is that what you wanted to know? Or did you want to know how many nights I spent with her?'

Robert Clarke shifted uncomfortably in his chair. He could see Philippe's arrogance re-emerging. He ignored the question. But he couldn't help but ask the question that had been troubling them all.

'And the large diamond on the ring finger of her left hand. Is that meaningful?'

Philippe shrugged.

'I promised her a diamond ring so she has a diamond ring. And yes, I'm happy she wears it on the wedding finger of her left hand.'

Philippe's attitude was beginning to annoy Robert Clarke.

'Are you just toying with her, Philippe? Indulging her like a spoilt child? Does she know you expect Julia to go on being your wife? At least that's what you told me before you went away.'

He was beginning to worry that Philippe was about to let her down again.

'Robert, believe me, Karen will be the first to know when I file for divorce. Or when my wife does. But that decision hasn't been made yet. I think that's a private matter, don't you?'

He looked at his watch.

'I've promised to take my wife to lunch. That's my immediate priority now so I must get going.'

Robert got up from his chair to shake Philippe's hand.

'It's good to see you again. We miss you here,' he said.

Philippe nodded. He could see Robert's comment was genuine. It had been Philippe's private life that had been the cause of friction between them, not his professional work.

'By the way, we can skip the valedictory dinner if you find it all too embarrassing, Robert,' he said as he headed out the door.

Philippe was annoyed gossip about his private life had marred his final months in medicine. He knew he had been a fine surgeon. But he worried everyone would remember him for entirely the wrong reasons.

'I think your former colleagues would consider it an omission if we failed to mark the excellent contribution you have made to this hospital over the years,' Robert said, ignoring Philippe's flippant remark. 'We hoped to hold the dinner Saturday week, if that suits you. And if it suits your wife.'

He nodded. Would Julia even want to come with him? He didn't know.

'That sounds fine, Robert,' he said. 'Whatever suits. Just let me know the details.'

He stopped to speak with one or two people he met on his way out of the hospital, each one expressing their regret he had resigned. It took him a full twenty minutes to reach the carpark. This time he was parked in a visitor park.

He looked back wistfully at the hospital that was now part of his history. He knew it had been time to move on but he felt a tinge of regret. Until recently his whole professional life had been about his work as a doctor, as a surgeon. Sometimes he yearned for the way his life had been.

And now? He was wealthy. Wealthier than most people could guess in fact. The inheritor of a fortune. Having to make decisions about unfamiliar matters.

And his future? For the first time, he realised he would need to live in New York or Long Island for probably the greater part of each year. But he would probably be doing so alone. Not because he wanted to be alone. But because he knew his marriage had almost run its course.

Deep in his heart, he knew he had treated his marriage to Julia with contempt and now he was paying the price for it. There was no way back now.

And Karen? She had a life in Sydney without him. Her work. Her friends. Her family. It would be unfair to ask her to give up everything for him, to ask her to fit her life around his.

And the closeness he had once enjoyed with his daughter? He prayed that relationship at least could be restored to what it had been.

# CHAPTER 29

THIS IS ALMOST A RERUN of the walk I took with Pippa, Philippe thought, as he and Julia ambled along the harbour front at Rose Bay. It was a warm day, with the sun high overhead. A bright heat shimmered off the surface of the water. He remembered how badly that had turned out. His daughter had barely spoken to him since.

'It's a beautiful day,' he said, hoping the sunshine would brighten her mood.

She nodded. It was a beautiful day. Entirely the wrong type of day to be discussing the future of their marriage. It should be raining and miserable, she thought, to match her mood.

'Let's sit down for a moment,' she said, pointing to a timber seat close by. She found the water calming.

He sat alongside her.

'Do you remember when we first met, Philippe?'

He smiled. How could he forget? He had not been driving the army truck but he had always felt himself responsible for the accident.

'I was worried you were badly hurt,' he said. 'And we were at fault.'

'Our lives have taken quite a torturous path since that day, if you think about it.'

She looked at him. She could see that he too had delved into his past to remember. To remember their first meeting.

For her, it was remembering the shock of finding out she was pregnant to him with no way of letting him know.

'We've shared a lot together,' he said, taking her hand in his.

'We have,' she said.

'And what of the future?'

The question hung in the air between them. He waited but she did not respond.

'We have to face the future. Our future. Do we have one?' he asked.

To her, it sounded like the same conversation they'd had the previous evening. As if he was asking her to make the decision. As if he was happy to be bound by her decision.

'Do you think it's possible for us to have a future? Don't you want to be with Karen? Isn't that what this is all about?'

He looked at her then but he did not answer her directly. He found it hard to discuss Karen openly with her.

'I'm sorry for what I've done to you. The way I've behaved,' he said.

He paused and took a deep breath. He wanted her to understand he still had feelings for her.

'I'm struggling to face the prospect of not having you in my life anymore,' he said finally.

It was the first time he had apologised. It was the first time he had admitted he was at fault, that a part of him wanted their marriage to survive.

She shrugged. It was all too late.

'Well, you should have thought of that before.'

He could see how much he had hurt her. But he wondered if she realised if he had never met Karen, he would have been perfectly content with their marriage? But how could he put that into words?

'Do we have to make a decision today?' he asked.

She shook her head.

'No, we don't. But whether it's today, next week or next month, I think we have to face the fact that our marriage is over.'

It was the first time she had said it directly. And it was the first time she noticed a flicker of sadness in his eyes.

'Perhaps you're right,' he said. 'Perhaps our marriage is over but I'm in no rush for us to start divorce proceedings unless you are?'

She shook her head and turned away from him so he could not see the tears that had gathered in her eyes. She had desperately wanted to remain composed.

'I take it that means you have no plans to revive your first marriage. I thought you might be keen to get to the divorce court to be rid of me?'

She was surprised he had made that assumption.

'No, I'm not planning to become James's wife again,' she said, 'but I might well ask you the same question. I thought you might be in a rush to make an honest woman out of Karen.'

He laughed quietly.

'Could it be that we both find being married a way to avoid new commitments?'

She shrugged. She was genuinely surprised by his comment.

'That's one possibility,' she said, 'but I think Karen will be very disappointed if you don't divorce me. Someone told me she's already flashing a diamond ring on her wedding finger. Is that true?'

He couldn't deny it, so he remained silent. He realised then how indiscreet he had been. She took his silence for confirmation.

'There's something else I have to consider,' he said. 'Now that my medical career is at an end, it's likely I will have to spend more time in America, setting up the foundation, taking charge of the Cox family investments, making sure everything else goes according to plan.'

She wondered if he had told Karen. It was the first she had heard of it.

'And why are you telling me this?'

'I wanted to give you an idea of what lies ahead for me this year. That I might not be around much, in any case.'

'No doubt Karen will be happy to go with you.'

He ignored her remark. It was as if she wanted to remind him she had already ceased to be important in his life.

'And my daughter? She's obviously spoken to you about everything. Do you think she will ever speak to me again? She won't return my calls. I take it she's still angry with me.'

How can he not know how devastated she is?

'She's angry with you, Philippe,' she said. 'She set you up on a pedestal. She hero worshipped you. And now she feels you let her down. And let me down. In time I hope she'll forgive you.'

'So will you talk to her for me?'

She sighed. Why must she act as go-between? But it was Pippa's future too. For that reason, she would do it.

'I will,' she said. 'I'll see if I can catch up with her tomorrow.'

He got up then and held his hand out towards her.

'Let's go and have some lunch,' he said, 'and then we can go and look at these houses you picked out.'

'Do you think there's any point in that?'

He shrugged.

'There may be,' he said. 'I haven't given up on us entirely. Not yet. And quite regardless, if I'm going to continue to live in Sydney, I've decided I want a house with a harbour view.'

He put his arm around her. He wanted to show his affection for her.

'If you want to separate,' he said gently, 'you can stay in our current home if you want to. I'll sign it over to you. You can sell it. You can do whatever you want with it.'

Was that the first point of agreement in their separation, she wondered?

They walked together in silence back towards the restaurant, knowing that nothing had been decided irrevocably but each of them knowing their marriage was slowly but surely unravelling.

The following day, Julia was relieved to see Pippa after days of trying unsuccessfully to contact her daughter.

'I hope you haven't been avoiding me, Pippa,' she said as she kissed her daughter on the cheek and then indicated the chair opposite her at their favourite coffee shop.

Pippa shook her head.

'No, I've been busy. I've been trying to have a life too,' she said. 'I'm trying to move on. Is he back from New York?'

She couldn't bring herself to mention her father by name.

'Yes, he's back. He got back a couple of days ago.'

'And?'

Julia shrugged. What could she tell her daughter? They had still not made any firm decision on whether to end their marriage. Or, more accurately, when to end their marriage.

'What do you want me to tell you, Pippa?'

'I don't know. That he's dumped Karen Clarke. That he's apologised to you and begged your forgiveness. Or has he asked you for a divorce?'

Her daughter's very direct questioning unsettled her. Her conversations with Philippe seemed almost too private to repeat, even to their daughter.

'We're in no rush to end our marriage officially.'

Pippa sipped the coffee that had just been put in front of her. She looked across at her mother.

'What does that mean?'

Julia shrugged.

'It means we haven't called in the lawyers yet. But he is looking to buy a new house. A harbourside house. He's offered me our current home if I want to separate from him.'

'And do you?'

She paused for a moment. How easily does a woman turn her back on a marriage? On a marriage to a man she yearned for all those years. She had idolised the idea of him as her one true love and then as a husband just as Pippa had idolised him as a father. And now? She had begun to feel a deep sense of bitterness at his behaviour. At how he had let her down.

'It seems like the only possible course of action but I'll make the decision when he's ready to move to a new house.'

Pippa was silent, digesting what her mother had said. It was as if, at some point during their conversation, she had finally transitioned from child to adult.

Her disappointment at the failure of her parents' marriage cut deeper than she ever imagined. For the first time in a long time, she wondered what her great aunt Edith Henderson would have thought. Devastated probably. Perhaps it's just as well she's no longer alive to see the disintegration of the fairytale. She could still vividly remember the excitement of their wedding day when she had been a young teenager. Her great aunt had shared so much of that early journey in her life.

'Is it true he's left the hospital?'

'Yes, he resigned before he went to New York. They're putting on a farewell dinner for him. He said Dr Clarke hoped you would come.'

'Should I come?'

It was the first sign of a possible thawing in her attitude.

'You should, Pippa. He's been a fine surgeon. Respected. He deserves to be honoured.'

'And his plans for the future?'

'You should talk to him, Pippa. He really wants to know if you are still interested in being involved in the foundation he's setting up. He's talking about spending a lot more time in America too.'

'By himself? With you? Or with Karen?'

'I think time will decide that. I will still go across for the opening of the gardens at the end of May. Quite regardless of what happens, he's offered me a seat on the Australian board of the foundation he's setting up. I would go in that capacity.'

It was the first Pippa had heard of such an offer.

'Are you going to accept the offer? When there are events on, you'll see him with Karen on his arm. How will you cope with that?'

'I'll have to get used to it, won't I?'

She could see for the first time the look of deep disappointment in her mother's eyes.

'And will you ever get used to seeing her look of absolute triumph?'

Julia shook her head sadly from side to side.

'You're not making this any easier for me, Pippa. I can't do anything about the fact your father has fallen in love with another woman. Do you plan to be angry with him forever? Even I will have to get beyond my anger at some point.'

Pippa's eyes filled with tears.

'I thought he was better than that, Mother. I thought he was an honourable man. But he's just like so many other men. He couldn't keep his hands off her.'

'But he's still your father, Pippa. And he loves you.'

She sighed deeply.

'Then I suppose I'd better see him. See what he's got in mind because I really need a change of career.'

'Then why don't you have dinner with us tomorrow night? Wherever you choose.'

She nodded.

'I will. I'll do it for you.'

She leant across and kissed her mother on the cheek. She understood for the first time how devastated her mother was at the failure of her marriage.

Even as they sat and drank coffee together, Pippa wondered where he was. Meetings with lawyers and looking at office space for the foundation, her mother had told her. But she wondered if, in the late afternoon, she would find his car outside Karen's apartment. The thought depressed her. She drained her coffee and bid her mother farewell.

'Until tomorrow night. The Italian place? Seven o'clock?'

Julia nodded.

'I look forward to it.'

As Pippa was saying good-bye to her mother, Philippe sat opposite Kenneth Wright, the managing partner of the local law firm he used.

'I was pleased to meet your wife during our Australia Day cruise, Dr Duval,' he said, conversationally. 'It was a shame you were away. It was a beautiful day on the harbour. I think our clients enjoyed it.'

Philippe looked up from the documents he had been sorting through.

'Really. That's not something my wife mentioned. I had declined the invitation for us as I recall.'

Kenneth Wright shifted in his chair. He knew then he should not have mentioned it. He was keen to move the conversation along.

'Can you fill me in on the progress with the estate settlement? And what your plans are locally?'

But Philippe was not ready to move on.

'Do you want to tell me how my wife came to be at an event your firm was holding without me to partner her? Has she been consulting someone here?'

Kenneth Wright straightened in his chair and leant forward. The question put him in an awkward position.

'I thought she might have told you. She's had some meetings with Nicholas Gleeson, getting advice about the deed of the trust fund she inherited.'

He gestured, trying to indicate how innocuous the whole thing was.

'The deed is old and no longer fit for purpose,' he explained. 'Nicholas is applying to the courts to change the trustees. It's an old firm that's been subsumed by takeovers and the original partners are all dead. Quite routine stuff really.'

But Philippe had a clear memory of Nicholas Gleeson, how he had turned his attention away from Karen to spend time chatting with Julia. In the back of his mind, he was starting to draw conclusions that came very close to the truth.

'No, she didn't tell me. Not a thing. Perhaps it slipped her mind.'

Kenneth Wright breathed an inaudible sigh of relief. He had, just the day before, cautioned Nicholas to remove the photo of himself and Julia Duval taken during the Australia Day event from his office. He remembered his words clearly. *I don't want to know what you're doing with Julia Duval out of hours but I ask for your discretion. Her husband is too important to this firm.*

'Tell me, would Nicholas Gleeson have access to information about me and my business that passes through this firm and the associated accounting firm?'

It was a question for which Kenneth Wright was totally unprepared.

'No, he shouldn't have. Why do you ask, Dr Duval?'

'Let's be frank, Kenneth. There are some expenses on my account related to a certain young woman that have come through here. I have a feeling Nicholas Gleeson has made it his business to know this information and has passed it on to my wife.'

Kenneth Wright sat very still. The accusation was serious. He knew he should have taken steps to protect the information but he had never considered it necessary.

'Do you have any proof of that, Dr Duval? It's a serious allegation.'

Philippe laughed quietly.

'My only proof is how much my wife actually knows about certain things I did my best to keep from her. That's what I pay you for. For your discretion.'

The meeting was beginning to turn sour for Kenneth Wright. But he could not afford to antagonise one of his most important clients.

'I will have a word with Nicholas, Dr Duval,' he said, 'but I am sure he would not break our rules of client confidentiality. His reputation is impeccable.'

'Except when it comes to my wife I suspect. Pillow talk perhaps?'

Just as he had done with Richard, he posed a question to Kenneth Wright that was pure speculation. He noticed the colour drain from the older man's face.

'I don't think I quite understand where you are going with this line of questioning, Dr Duval,' he said. 'I don't think there is anything but a professional relationship between Nicholas Gleeson and your wife.'

Had he said enough to deflect suspicion? He hoped so. He did not know anything for certain. It was only office gossip that had reached him.

Philippe shrugged.

'Perhaps you're right. But I should warn your colleague if I were you. My wife and I are likely to divorce. If I find he has been sleeping with my wife, I will certainly cite his name on my divorce petition. A very nice scandal that will be for your law firm.'

Kenneth Wright simply nodded. He didn't need to be told about the potential for professional misconduct. But it had been the first time his client had mentioned the possibility of divorce.

'Do you wish to consult one of our divorce specialists, Dr Duval?'

'Not yet,' Philippe replied. 'Besides my lawyers in New York have advised me to wait until the proceeds of the sale of Cox Industries are transferred to the family trusts before entering any divorce negotiations.'

Philippe was remembering his final meeting with Howard Davis before he left New York. He remembered his lawyer's words of caution. If you should divorce, you would do well to wait until the proceeds of the sale are held in your trust accounts. It had been offered as good advice but it had annoyed Philippe all the same that his private life was the subject of so much scrutiny.

'To put the bulk of your fortune out of reach in a divorce settlement, I imagine. I take it your wife's name doesn't feature in the family trust arrangements?'

To Kenneth Wright, there was nothing remarkable about the strategy. He knew every trick rich men used to hide their wealth from the wives they were about to divorce.

'No, her name doesn't feature at all. My daughter is the beneficiary of my new trust after my death. And the existing family trust will be split between my half-brother's two children and my daughter eventually.'

'And when will the transfer of funds be finalised?'

'Early April, I believe. It's the US lawyers being cautious that's all. I will offer my wife a reasonable settlement if we decide to divorce.'

He had heard enough about Philippe Duval's private life not to be surprised at the discussion of divorce.

'If I may add a note of caution here, I'm aware of your relationship with a certain lady. Does she know she is likely to be cited in any divorce proceedings? The quickest way to divorce is via admitting adultery. It's very tawdry but there it is.'

It wasn't the discussion he'd expected to have just yet.

'I haven't discussed it with her. Not yet. I don't think she'll care, to be honest.'

'But her father may care.'

Philippe shrugged his shoulders dismissively.

'And you expect me to worry about what David Clarke thinks? I don't think so. But I think it's time we stopped talking about my private life and talked about the business in hand.'

Kenneth Wright too was keen to move on to the more familiar territory of what would be required to set up a non-profit foundation in Australia as a subsidiary of the American foundation. And to make a recommendation of a commercial agent to find suitable office space to house the foundation.

After an hour of intense discussion, they had made good progress.

'I think we've done enough for today,' Philippe said.

The earlier discussion had unsettled him and he was losing concentration.

Kenneth Wright began to gather his papers together. He had a legal pad full of instructions. There was certainly enough to be going on with.

'I'll see you out, Dr Duval,' he said as he walked his client to the door of the meeting room.

As he opened the door, he was tempted to shut it quickly and delay Philippe on any pretext. But it was too late. They both spotted Karen Clarke leaving Nicholas Gleeson's office just as she saw Philippe.

Her face lit up at the sight of him.

Kenneth Wright and Nicholas Gleeson watched transfixed as Philippe put his arm around Karen and kissed her on the cheek in a very warm greeting. He did not let her go. They heard too how he greeted her.

'A happy coincidence, my darling,' he said.

She smiled at him.

'Just signing some more boring documents for my father,' she explained.

She put her arm through his and guided him to the lifts.

'I think you've set the gossips alight,' she whispered.

'Don't worry, they're already well alight,' he said as he followed her into the lift.

In the privacy of the lift, he kissed her.

'I wanted to find out if Nicholas Gleeson has been feeding information to my wife. I'll be interested to know if she hears about the little show I put on just then.'

She laughed.

'You can be very devious sometimes,' she said, as they walked out of the building hand in hand.

Upstairs, Kenneth Wright followed Nicholas back into his office.

'Well, that was eye opening,' Kenneth Wright said. 'He clearly thinks he can do what he pleases now his wife knows about his outside interest.'

Nicholas, too, had been stunned. Stunned that Philippe was now publicly betraying his wife with apparent disregard of any conventions. But he said nothing.

'By the way, why is it that our most important client thinks you are sleeping with his wife? And that you've been feeding her information about his expenses in relation to his mistress.'

He could think of no other way to describe Karen Clarke.

'That's pretty rich coming from him, don't you think? He's trying to catch his wife out while he flaunts his relationship with another woman.'

He was clever enough to avoid answering the question about Julia.

'I'm pleased David Clarke wasn't here. He would have been annoyed.'

'David Clarke will be annoyed with him until he puts a wedding ring on his daughter's finger,' Nicholas replied.

Kenneth Wright sympathised with David Clarke. It would be hard to stand by and see your daughter as the sexual plaything of a wealthy married man, which is what she undoubtedly was. Yet Kenneth Wright couldn't help but notice she was absolutely delighted to see Philippe.

'You had a long meeting with him, Kenneth. As Mrs Duval's lawyer, is there anything I need to know about? Was divorce discussed?'

Kenneth looked at his younger colleague then.

'How's this going to work, Nicholas? Me and my team representing him and you and your team representing her. Is that how you see it shaping up?'

Nicholas laughed.

'I'm already miles ahead of you there, Kenneth. He's going to have to pay for the humiliation of my client during their marriage.'

'So you've discussed this with Mrs Duval? Have you taken instructions from her?'

He shook his head.

'Not yet but I expect to do so soon. Very soon.'

'Not, I hope, while she's lying in your bed.'

He laughed.

'Whatever gave you that idea, Kenneth.'

It was as if they were already adversaries in the divorce that was guaranteed to send the gossip columnists into overdrive.

As Kenneth Wright entered his office, he turned to his secretary.

'I need to dictate a memo,' he said.

His first preliminary act to protect his client was to make sure Nicholas Gleeson and his team were excluded from seeing anything in relation to Philippe Duval's affairs.

This is going to get ugly, he thought. But then divorce always does. Always.

# CHAPTER 30

AS THE AFTERNOON LIGHT began to fade the next day, Philippe swung into the last available park in front of Karen's apartment block. He sat for a moment in the car thinking about what had occurred in the short time since his return from New York.

He had arrived home expecting what exactly? Certainly not to be greeted by a wife with full knowledge of his affair. What had she said? He remembered then. *It's not what I want that matters anymore, is it? It's what Karen wants.*

He knew he had hurt Julia deeply with his betrayal of their marriage. Nothing he said was ever going to change that now. In the course of a couple of days, everything had unravelled at a speed he hadn't expected.

Karen opened the door to him before he could even knock. Her arms went around his neck. He felt the warmth and welcome of her body against his.

'I was surprised to see you yesterday at the lawyer's,' she said, 'but I was even more surprised that you didn't keep me at arm's length.'

He laughed.

'I thought I'd give them something to talk about.'

She laughed too. She was feeling as reckless as he was.

'Can I ask what you discussed with your lawyer? Or was it just business stuff?'

She was sitting alongside him now on the sofa, his arm around her. Being with her relaxed him, especially after the difficult conversations he'd had with his wife in the past two days.

'It was mainly business stuff,' he said dismissively, 'but the question of divorce has come up if that's what you want to know.'

She put her head on one side, trying to gauge his mood.

'Because you and your wife have discussed it? Or because your wife has asked you for a divorce?'

He did not respond immediately as if he was deciding what to say to her, how to say it. In the end he opted for honesty.

'Would it surprise you to know I'm finding it hard to contemplate the end of my marriage. It's not something I ever thought would be likely to happen until recently.'

She understood instinctively how much hope and expectation had been invested in the belated fairytale end to their romance.

'Until I came back into your life?'

He nodded and held her in his arms, enjoying the warmth of her body against his.

'Yes,' he said with a smile. 'You are entirely to blame.'

He kissed the side of her neck and stroked her long luxurious hair that he so admired.

'Our separation is something that will happen over time. A gradual unwinding of our lives until there comes a day when we walk away from each other.'

She was unsure then how he saw the future for them.

'Thank you for being honest with me,' she said. 'You sound very uncertain about what's going to happen. If you decide you don't want to divorce your wife, that's up to you.'

He laughed quietly.

'My darling,' he said, 'my wife knows all about us. She knows you were in New York with me. I've told her I'm not giving you up. I doubt my wife will see our marriage as a long term prospect under those conditions.'

She relaxed then. Confident of him again.

'Does she know where you are now?'

'No, she doesn't. I don't have to account to her for every hour of the day,' he said, 'which reminds me. I wanted to tell you I'll be spending more time in New York to get all my plans bedded down this year. I'll be away quite a lot.'

'And your wife? Will she travel with you?'

'At the end of May for the opening of the gardens. After that, who knows? But I have offered her a seat on the Australian board of the foundation. I did that for Pippa's sake.'

'So you will go on seeing her even if you divorce?'

'I guess so,' he said. 'She's Pippa's mother. She won't leave my life entirely.'

'Is your daughter speaking to you again then?'

He laughed.

'We're meeting her for dinner tonight. I'll find out then. I hope so but she's very disappointed in me.'

She turned to face him.

'And me,' she said. 'Don't forget how angry she is with me too.'

She tried to imagine what his daughter would think if she could see them together now. His free hand had begun to caress her body.

'I thought you'd be heading out the door now to get to your family dinner.'

He laughed softly. He consulted his watch. If he was very late, they would certainly guess where he had been.

'When have I ever been able to walk away from you, my darling,' he said.

As he made love to her, she wondered if she was closer to being able to say to him, *you're mine and I won't share you with anyone else*, just as he had said to her. It was almost then as if he had read her thoughts.

'I'll remember this when I go back to my lonely bed tonight,' he said.

'And your wife?'

'Well, her bedroom door is firmly closed to me if that's what you want to know.'

She did not ask whether his wife had rejected him or he no longer wanted to make love to her. Either way, it did not matter. She allowed herself a small smile of triumph.

Mother and daughter, seated across from one another, menus discarded on the table, were discussing everything but the one issue that loomed over the dinner. Where was Philippe? Why was he late? But Julia knew. And Pippa knew too.

'It's a farce, Mother,' she said.

'What's a farce, my darling girl?'

Philippe slid into the seat alongside his daughter and gave her a quick kiss on the cheek.

She was about to answer him with a stinging rebuke and then she saw the slight shake of her mother's head and the silent plea to say nothing.

'Hospital rosters,' she said, thinking quickly. 'I'm surprised any junior doctor stays the course. They're completely designed to make life as miserable as possible for us.'

He sympathised even though his years as a junior doctor were long behind him.

'What's everyone having?' he asked, his tone casual and light-hearted. It had been a long time since he had dined with his wife and his daughter, just the three of them.

'I think we're both having ravioli,' Julia replied.

She had already chosen the wine in his absence.

'I'm sorry I was a bit late,' he said, casually. 'I lost track of time.'

Please don't lie to us, Pippa thought. Please don't lie about where you were. She knew he had been with Karen. She had seen his car outside her apartment block. It had only taken a short detour to check. Surely my mother knows he lost track of time because he was in Karen's bed.

With the food orders given, he turned to Pippa.

'I'm pleased you agreed to meet me,' he said. 'I want us to move forward. I know you're disappointed in me and I'm sorry for that. But I don't want to be shut out of your life.'

He waited for her to say something. Would she continue to shut him out of her life? Would she walk away and never see him again? The idea left him suddenly bereft.

'So do I just have to accept the happy family we had together is no more? Is that how it's going to be?'

He smiled at her but there was a touch of sadness in his eyes.

'I think we should remember the happy times we had together as a family,' he said. 'And be grateful for those years.'

He looked across at Julia. He realised for the first time he was beginning to see her as part of his past, not his future. For her to remain as his wife, he had to give up Karen. He had done that for her once before but he could not do it again.

'I'm sorry it's happened this way. But it's not something I can change,' he said.

She nodded. She looked across at her mother. Her composure seemed unnatural. Why doesn't she lash out at him? Call him a bastard for ruining their marriage. Yell at him. But all she saw was the deep disappointment of a woman whose dreams lay shattered around her. Who never thought there would be a time when her husband preferred another woman over her? A strained silence descended on the table for just a moment. Pippa was the first to speak.

'Your plans for the foundation? Mother said you wanted to talk to me about that?'

'I do, Pippa. I want to know if you want to be involved in setting up a local office. I'm doing it for you. If you don't want to, it will be completely American based, which means I will spend more time back in America.'

She looked at him then.

'Are you thinking of moving back there permanently?'

'It depends on what happens.'

'What happens? Meaning?'

'Pippa, do I have to spell it out? Really? Potentially I have fewer reasons to continue in Sydney now I've ended my medical career. I'm expected to have a presence on Long Island. To manage the family's investments, from which you'll benefit handsomely one day. But I have ties to Sydney that I can't turn my back on.'

She sat back as a plate of ravioli was placed in front of her. For just a moment, she had an image of her father, in his old age, alone in that massive old house, manipulating everyone around him just as his father had done.

She glanced towards him. So much about him had changed since he had inherited his father's fortune. Great wealth had, without him being aware of it, sucked him into its evil vortex. It was almost impossible to see the man he had been.

'What's the next step then,' she asked. 'How do we go about setting up the foundation here in Sydney?'

He smiled and relaxed, pleased with her response.

'The lawyers are already on it. You should come and meet with them. You should know what's going on from the beginning. And help me decide on office space.'

Through all this, Julia had remained silent and detached from the conversation. She was pleased to see something of the earlier close relationship re-emerging between father and daughter. But for herself, she knew her tears were exhausted. He was beginning to move on with his life. Pippa too would move on with her life.

How will I move on with my life? He will not be alone. Karen will always be there for him. As his mistress. Possibly as his wife. But Karen would be there in some way. Always involved in his life. Pleasing him. Flattering him.

And me? I'm nowhere, she thought. I don't belong now in the world I knew before I married him. And I'm leaving his world behind as I divorce him. I don't even know who I am anymore. How do I build a new life for myself? How do I become another person? She had no answers. Not yet. But she was determined not to play the role of the bitter divorcée, discarded by her husband for a younger, sexier woman.

She reached for her glass of wine as the conversation between father and daughter grew ever more animated and excited about the prospects for the foundation. At least I have achieved one thing, she thought. The terrible fracture in Philippe's relationship with his daughter was being slowly but surely repaired.

Nicholas Gleeson had expected Julia at least half an hour ago. He glanced at his watch again. Was she nervous about visiting him at his house? But he had suggested it because her husband was in and out of their law offices practically every day and he needed her to sign a formal letter of appointment for him to handle her divorce negotiations. He was worried she would drift into agreeing to whatever Philippe offered her.

As her lawyer, he was in no mood to let Philippe off lightly. Julia had been humiliated by him. He had long ago decided she should come out of the marriage well compensated for her husband's infidelity. Finally, he heard the intercom chime and he pressed the door release to let her in. She was full of apologies.

'I couldn't get away,' she said. 'Not without unnecessary explanation.'

He was seeing her for the first time in some weeks. She had turned down all his invitations since the Sunday lunch she had attended. And then her husband had returned making communication with her difficult. He led the way into his study. He was doing his best to focus on the business he wanted to discuss.

'This is what I need you to sign,' he said, holding out a document for her to read.

'Why the urgency, Nicholas? Is there something going on I don't know about?'

He wasn't sure but without her formal appointment he couldn't ask.

'I think you know your husband is having a lot of meetings with his legal team. I have a feeling the matter of your separation, if not your divorce, is being discussed. How are relations between you? Have you agreed anything with Philippe informally?'

She smiled at his anxious questioning.

'No, we've had a discussion. A stalemate really. I have a choice, I guess. To stay married to him in name only and let him carry on with Karen Clarke. Or to push for a separation. He's refused to give Karen up. He's looking for a new house. A house with harbour views. He's offered me our current home.'

He wanted to be clear he understood what this meant.

'Is he suggesting he move to a new house and you separate then?'

'Something like that, I think. We're not husband and wife anymore if that's what you want to know. We're two people living in the one house and trying to stay out of each other's way.'

He could see the sadness and disappointment in her eyes. It had clearly been a marriage that had started with so much hope and optimism. She took up the pen from his desk and signed the letter of appointment. He took it back from her and put it in his briefcase.

'I'll do my best for you,' he said.

'I don't want a big chunk of money from him,' she said. 'Don't make this about money, Nicholas. He wasn't a wealthy man when I married him.'

'But now he is, Julia, now he is. We'll see what he offers by way of settlement. And be prepared for this to leak out into the press. Your marriage split is going to be gossip column fodder for some time.'

She sighed. This was all becoming too real.

'I don't want our marriage to end in bitterness and spite,' she said. 'I don't want that at all.'

He nodded.

'I understand,' he said. 'I'll do what you want but I have to protect your interests.'

He could see how much Philippe's betrayal had hurt her. Did she need to know how much he was flaunting his relationship with his mistress now? And then he paused. He realised the scene he had witnessed might have been a trap for him. If Julia came to know about it, Philippe would know there could only be one source, so he said nothing.

He sensed there was something else she wanted to ask him.

'The actual grounds for divorce? How would that work?'

'I think his adultery is well established.'

'But he could cross petition, couldn't he?'

He was worried then.

'That's an unusual question. Has he suggested he will do that? Accused you of being unfaithful to him and has proof of it. I can't see how he would know about you and me. He was in New York at the time.'

He thought for a moment. He could see Philippe might do it to share the blame for the failure of their marriage. To protect Karen to some degree. He looked at Julia closely. He had the sense then she was about to tell him something he would rather have not known.

'Nicholas, this is going to be hard for you to hear but you need to know as my lawyer.'

'Go on,' he said. 'What is it you have to tell me?'

She got up and began to pace around the small room. She couldn't face him. Not directly.

'It may never come up but Philippe knows I've been unfaithful to him. With my first husband James Fitzroy.'

It was his turn to feel disappointed. Bitterly disappointed. But was that fair? He had no claim on her. She obviously still felt something for her first husband. He had thought Karen was simply exaggerating when she told him.

'I assume your marriage to your first husband collapsed when you discovered Pippa and he found out you'd had a baby before you married him.'

She nodded.

'He was angry with me. More than angry. He would hardly speak to me. He didn't speak to me for years.'

'And now? Are you planning to reconnect with him? Has he got over his anger with you? But that's a silly question, isn't it? Clearly, he has.'

He almost spat the words at her, his disappointment was so profound.

She shrugged. She did not feel she had to explain herself to him.

'Well, thanks for telling me. At least if it comes up from the other side, I won't be caught out protesting your innocence and calling it rubbish.'

His opinion of her had shifted even as she had shattered his illusions. But something told him such behaviour was out of character for her. It had taken her a lot of courage to be honest with him. He admired that.

'It's not something you've made a habit of, I imagine, cheating on your husband.'

She smiled and shook her head.

'No, I was happy with him until he started neglecting me, not sharing my bed,' she said. 'I hadn't realised until recently how Karen's shadow had hung over our marriage for years.'

He listened carefully. She was confiding in him as she had not done before.

'It's not that he was seeing her, you understand, except in passing. But he always wanted to see her. And then there came a point where he could no longer ignore her and he decided to pursue her again. She has him completely wrapped around her little finger, from what I'm told.'

He thought that was a very apt description.

As they spoke, he had calmed down. She had been badly used by the men in her life, even if her first husband was now realising his mistake and trying to romance her back into his life.

'Come and have a drink,' he said, holding out his hand to her. 'It's lovely on the terrace at this time of day.'

As he poured her a glass of wine, he smiled at her reassuringly. She put her hand on his arm.

'Thank you for your understanding, Nicholas,' she said. 'It means a lot to me that I can trust you. As my lawyer. And as my friend.'

They sat side by side, he pointing out Sydney's famous landmarks as the sun faded in the western sky, she relaxing and enjoying his company. He put his arm around her tentatively. And then she felt his lips brush the top of her head. She turned to face him.

'Is this in danger of getting out of hand?'

He put his hand underneath her chin and tilted her face towards him.

'It is, my darling,' he said.

He kissed her lovingly, admiringly. Desiring her as much as he ever had, despite her revelations of earlier. She got up then.

'I have to go,' she said suddenly.

He got up too and stood alongside her, his arms around her.

'Do you really have to go?'

'Yes, I really have to go,' she said. 'I have to protect your reputation.'

He let her go reluctantly. She was right. If her husband found out she was sleeping with him, his professional reputation would be damaged irrevocably.

He walked with her to her car which she had parked a short way up the street. He bent to kiss her as she opened the door, ready to slide in behind the wheel.

'Not here, Nicholas. Not here.'

He smiled and closed her car door. He watched her drive away, his disappointment at finding out she had another lover apart from him forgotten. He knew he was still in love with her. Even more so now.

But she had been damaged by her failed marriages. She would need to be cared for. Looked after. Protected. And above all loved. And he was sure he was the man to do it. He hoped she would eventually feel the same way.

# CHAPTER 31

PHILIPPE STOOD BEHIND HIS WIFE, admiring her reflection in the mirror. Her elegant beauty still moved him. He watched her put the finishing touches to her make up and then held out his right arm for her to fix his cufflink.

He could have chosen the gold Belleville cufflinks she had given him on their wedding day but he did not. Would he ever wear them again? Somehow, he doubted it. He had chosen instead his favourite sterling silver cufflinks with the fine etching of the American flag.

He smiled at her admiringly and told her she looked beautiful. Her eyes lit up for a few moments at his compliment.

As they headed towards the front door, he put his arm around her as if everything was normal between them, as if they hadn't spent the past week avoiding each other, saying little to each other. Outside, the warm night air was just beginning to cool after the heat of the day.

'I've ordered a car and driver to take us,' he said, pointing to the chauffeur waiting beside a gleaming black saloon.

She wanted to say how easily he had adapted to the ways of rich men but she knew such a comment could be misinterpreted. Despite the disintegration of their relationship, she wanted him to enjoy the evening. He was entitled to the celebration of his medical career.

'I imagine this is a bittersweet evening for you,' she said.

He nodded.

'It is in some ways. I had expected to go on for a few more years yet but I found I couldn't. There was too much at stake for my patients. Being a surgeon is not something you can do well if it's not the main focus of your life.'

She wondered if it was only the change in his circumstances with his inheritance that was the reason for giving up his medical career. Had his affair with Karen played a part too? He lent over then and kissed her on the cheek.

'Thank you for agreeing to come tonight. I really appreciate it.'

His fingers briefly touched the sapphire and diamond necklace she was wearing. It had been the first piece of jewellery he had bought her. It was the first time he could remember her wearing it.

'It looks lovely on you,' he said. 'You look lovely.'

He lifted her fingers to his lips. He found her presence reassuring.

*But not lovely enough for you,* she wanted to say.


Within minutes, he was handing her out of the car and together they walked arm in arm into the function room already crowded with his former colleagues, each one keen to greet him.

He spotted David Clarke across the crowd and breathed a sigh of relief his wife Deborah was by his side. As a board member of the hospital foundation, he had fully expected David Clarke to attend. He hoped to avoid him in the crush.

As Philippe's attention was claimed by his former colleagues, Patricia Clarke slipped her arm through Julia's.

'You look beautiful, Julia,' she said, casting an envious glance at her designer dress and her expensive necklace. 'It's lovely to see you here with Philippe. We haven't seen you for ages.'

Julia murmured her thanks for the compliment. What else could she say?

'Did I hear there's a move in store for you? I heard your husband has had a bid accepted for a house in Point Piper. It sounds wonderful.'

Do they have nothing else to gossip about, Julia wondered, but our private life? But why not tell the truth.

'My husband is moving next week. Paying rent on it until the sale settles at the end of March.'

It took Patricia Clarke a few moments to register what Julia was really saying.

'Are you not moving next week?'

Julia hesitated for a moment and then shook her head. She knew the news they were separating would now spread like wildfire.

'No, I'm staying in our current home. He has signed it over to me.'

'Forgive me, Julia, I shouldn't have asked. I had no idea.'

'What, no idea we were separating? Or no idea my husband has been having an affair with Robert's niece for months?'

She noticed one or two people around them had stopped talking and were listening to her conversation with Patricia. Her voice had apparently become louder.

'You look stunned, Patricia,' Julia said, wondering if she should apologise. Perhaps it had been quite the wrong time and the wrong place to say such things. Perhaps she had drunk too much wine too quickly.

'I am stunned, Julia,' she said, struggling to know what to say. 'I always thought his interest elsewhere would just be a phase. Not something that was going to be serious. Well, not so serious as to jeopardise your marriage.'

How do you sympathise with a woman whose husband has been humiliating her for months with another woman, she wondered? She had no experience to guide her, not in her own marriage at least. She breathed a sigh of relief at being spared the need for further conversation by Pippa's arrival.

Standing together mother and daughter could be sisters, Patricia thought. The same blonde hair, the same smile, the same eyes except that Julia's beauty was more refined, more polished. But Pippa had changed too in recent months. Her girlishness had all gone. In its place the promise of the same elegant beauty as her mother's.

'Pippa, it's wonderful to see you. You look lovely.'

She noted the simple diamond pendant she wore. No doubt a gift from her father. He probably bought something for his wife and daughter every time he bought something for Karen, she thought cynically. He could certainly afford it now.

'You too, Mrs Clarke,' Pippa said, responding politely. 'It's quite a turnout for my father tonight. It's very good of you and Dr Clarke to host the event.'

'My husband was very keen for your father's outstanding medical career to be recognised by the hospital. Robert was very sad to have to accept his resignation.'

They all knew her statement was only partly true. Robert Clarke had worried about the scandal he predicted was coming. The scandal all of Philippe's making. A scandal unacceptable to a hospital with its well-known religious affiliation. They all looked towards Philippe who, surrounded by a group of doctors, was deeply involved in an earnest discussion.

'He'll miss this,' Pippa said. 'I think he already misses it.'

'But I hear he's setting up a foundation to help fund medical research. Are you involved in that, Pippa? Is that where your career is headed now?'

'It is, Mrs Clarke,' she said. 'We're setting up an offshoot of the American foundation here in Sydney. The Ella Duval Foundation. I'm looking forward to the challenge of being involved, possibly heading it one day.'

'You must be proud of your daughter, Julia,' Patricia said. 'She's taking on a big challenge.'

Julia listened politely. Her daughter had begun to remind her of her own mother. A hint of steel. But maybe it's the Cox blood too, she thought. Whichever it was, she knew her daughter wouldn't be pushed around. She wanted her daughter to have much more control of her life than she had ever had.

The chatter in the room began to subside as everyone moved to their allotted tables for the dinner that was about to be served.

Patricia looked on with interest as Philippe pulled out Julia's chair. She noticed how he took her hand and raised it to his lips before he moved to his own seat alongside her. Is he just trying to maintain the façade of a happy marriage for this evening, she wondered, or was there some lingering affection for his wife?

She turned to speak to him as he sat down next to her.

'It's a very good turnout, Philippe, to honour your illustrious career,' she said.

'Illustrious? That's probably overstating it, Patricia,' he said, 'but I'll take it as a compliment.'

'And your plans now? Pippa seems excited to be involved in the foundation you're setting up.'

'Yes, I believe she is. She found she had no stomach for the daily grind of medicine but it will be useful background for her as we come to assess grant applications for research funding.'

To Patricia Clarke, it all seemed a very worthy endeavour.

'The foundation will be headquartered in Long Island, I understand? Does that mean you will spend more time in America in the future?'

He smiled to himself. He had been asked that question repeatedly, it seemed. But behind each question he knew lay the burning desire to know how it would affect his private life.

He was saved the necessity of a reply as Robert Clarke rose to his feet to deliver a speech that Philippe thought he probably didn't deserve. Not completely.

He rose then to reply as the applause died down. He had chosen his words carefully. There would be no revelations to fuel the gossip that swirled about him. It was the speech he was expected to deliver, with special thanks to Robert Clarke.

As Philippe finished his speech, Deborah Clarke whispered to her husband.

'He seems very affectionate towards his wife,' she said. 'Karen would be furious.'

Deborah Clarke had taken some time to come to the full knowledge of her daughter's involvement with Philippe. It had been her father David who had known everything from the beginning, not her mother, who could float through life ignoring anything that posed any potential difficulty to her settled way of life. David Clarke too had looked on with some dismay.

343

'Maybe he's just a good actor,' he said.

'Or maybe he's come to realise what he might be giving up,' she said as she noticed Philippe put his arm around the back of his wife's chair and lean in close to her.

Pippa too noticed how attentive her father had become. But for others in the room, there was nothing remarkable about the attention Philippe was paying his wife because they all assumed his wife did not know about his affair.

As the wine continued to flow, the hubbub of conversation and laughter grew louder until, as the evening neared the end, Philippe began to do the rounds of the tables, thanking everyone for coming.

He knew he could not avoid David Clarke, however much he wanted to. The encounter was as awkward as he expected it to be.

'You'd be pleased at the turnout, Duval,' David Clarke said.

'Very gratified,' he said simply. 'Thank you for coming.'

'It was a shame my daughter wasn't invited,' he said.

There was a stunned silence among the other guests seated at the table. Philippe couldn't help but notice the sudden interest in his reply.

'I wasn't in charge of the guest list, David,' he said. 'Your brother was.'

Everyone noticed the edginess in his voice. But there were to be no fireworks. Philippe moved on. He had fuelled enough gossip. He guessed Karen would receive a full report of the evening from her father.

Julia had witnessed but not heard the terse exchange between Philippe and David Clarke. But she did not want to upset the pleasant mood that existed between them, so she made no comment. And then it was time to go.

He pulled her chair out and drew her arm through his.

As they said their final good-byes, Robert Clarke walked with them to the door. He watched until the chauffeur-driven car was out of sight. He realised then his wife Patricia had come to stand along-side him.

'Well, that was unexpected,' she said. 'Apparently, he's moving out next week into the house he's bought in Point Piper. And she's staying in their current home. But they don't look like a couple on the brink of divorce, do they?'

Robert shook his head. He too had his doubts having seen them together for the first time in a long time.

'They don't, do they?' he said. 'Or maybe he doesn't want to acknowledge it but I'd say he's still in love with his wife. They look perfect together. They look right for each other. And he's about to throw it all away.'

But his loyalties were divided. He knew his niece had pinned everything on the rekindling of her relationship with Philippe. He wondered then if, over time, Philippe might come to regret his choices.

'You must be pleased with how the evening went,' Julia said as he closed the front door behind her.

'I am,' he said. 'It was good of Robert to organise it. It was nice to see everyone again. And even the wine was good. No doubt because of Robert.'

He looked at her then and she giggled unexpectedly.

'Too many glasses perhaps?'

'Perhaps,' she said. 'I needed to relax. I needed something to help get me through the evening. All those people sitting there gossiping about us as if we were some prime exhibits in a freak show.'

He laughed too.

'Come on, it wasn't that bad surely?'

She stumbled then, catching the heel of her shoe on the edge of the hall rug. He reached out to stop her from falling.

'So you're trying to tell me you're not drunk?'

She shook her head vigorously, several strands of her blonde hair falling over her face.

'No, I caught my heel,' she protested. 'Of course, I'm not drunk.'

He had not let her go.

'You look beautiful tonight,' he said, gently brushing the hair from her face and letting his fingers linger on her cheek. 'Very beautiful. It meant so much to me that you came with me.'

'Philippe, don't say those things to me. Don't do those things to me. Not now.'

She tried to push him away but he continued to hold her. She felt his lips brush against the side of her neck. And then he reached around to unclip the necklace which slid off into his hands. He dropped it onto the hall table. She felt his lips trace the outline of where the necklace had been.

Why is he doing this, she wondered? Why now? She felt his lips brush against hers. Lightly. Tentatively. Testing her response. And then he felt her relax in his arms and begin to respond to him. He pushed the door of her bedroom open. Within minutes, he was making love to her, his passion for her reignited. The feel of her body familiar but exciting. It was almost as if making love to his wife was now an illicit passion, something forbidden to him.

Later, as she lay in his arms, he kissed the top of her head. He felt her hand gently stroking his chest until she turned to look at him.

'Is this how you planned to say good-bye to me, is it?' she asked as she teased him with kisses and caressed his body. 'One last night of passion.'

But he didn't reply. He had no idea how he was going to leave her. No idea how he was going to turn his back on her. And yet this was the path he had chosen. Within minutes, he was making love to her again, this time slowly, sensuously, deliberately. Enjoying her as he had not done in a very long time. Wanting her with a new powerful desire that almost hurt him with its intensity.

And in her he sensed a depth of desire he hadn't known existed as if there was a part of her he had never explored. He blocked out the thought that formed briefly in his mind. Had another man awakened these feelings in her?

They lay together for a long time, their arms around each other, eventually drifting into sleep. Until the blaze of morning sunshine heralded a new day.

Philippe had showered and dressed, doing his best not to disturb Julia as he eased himself out of her bed. He sat on the back porch of their home, sipping his first cup of coffee of the day.

He closed his eyes against the bright morning light. He was trying to understand what had happened between them, what had reignited his desire for her. And Julia? She had been different too. More demanding of him.

He was so deeply immersed in his thoughts he did not hear her until she was alongside him. He hesitated for a moment and then he stood and put his arms around her. He kissed her on the lips and trailed his fingers through her still damp hair. She stepped back from him.

'What was that last night, Philippe? What is this now?'

He looked at her closely. In her expression he saw a mixture of confusion and regret. Or was it disappointment? It could even be disbelief, he thought.

'Last night was something delightful between us, my darling,' he said.

'So I was right,' she said. 'A final night of passion to prove you can still have me if you want me. Is that it?'

'Is that what you really think? Because it's not what I think.'

Somewhere in the back of her mind, a voice was reminding her to protect herself. To remember how he had flaunted his mistress. To remember how readily he had betrayed her. But there was a sincerity about him too. But the voice in her head struck back. *He's always been able to charm you. To get what he wants from you.*

'What do you think then?' she said.

She hadn't meant her voice to sound so accusing.

'I think I told you recently that I was struggling to face the prospect of not having you in my life anymore,' he said, gently stroking her bare arm, 'but I don't think you believed me.'

She shrugged. She remembered the conversation. And then she looked closely at him, trying to decide whether he was being sincere or whether he was simply trying to make their separation less painful for her.

'Even if I believe you, does it matter anymore?'

'It depends.'

'Depends on what?'

'It depends on whether our separation leads us to divorce or to reconciliation.'

It was the first time he had mentioned the possibility of reconciliation. She had always assumed their separation was simply the first step to an inevitable divorce. There would be no going back. They would move on with their lives. He with Karen. And for herself? There was no clear path for her. She didn't quite know what to say.

'I think a break from each other might help us both sort out what we really want,' he said gently. 'Let's give it a few months and see how we feel.'

He knew he wasn't yet prepared to meet her demands he give up Karen. He still didn't know whether he could. Or he wanted to.

And Julia? He knew she had been unfaithful to him again with James Fitzroy. He knew how easy it had been for her first husband to exploit her unhappiness.

Yet in the dark corners of his mind, for no reason he could fathom, the name Nicholas Gleeson kept bubbling to the front of his mind. Why, he wondered? Was he a more dangerous rival for her affections than her first husband?

He banished these thoughts from his mind and held out his hand to her.

'Do you feel like my Sunday special?'

Together they headed to the kitchen and he began the familiar Sunday ritual of making pancakes.

*Author's note*
This story has further to run.
Look out for the sequel, *Price to Pay*, published Nov 2024.